WHERE WAS BARRABAS?

Lee was halfway through keying the message on her radio when the shadows at the foot of the ravine began to flow. They flowed steadily upward toward her in an eerie silence that confused her for a moment.

Then the shadows sprouted arms, legs and heads. She saw the faintest of gleams from eyes and blackened weapons.

"Charlie," she whispered, "get down. Now." Lee crouched lower, waiting until the Spetsnaz were in the best part of the ravine and tried to count them. One was taking point, two more backed him, and a fourth held the sea end.

"Uhhh." It was a soft animal sound from C̶l̶̶ fear and helplessness boiling ov̶̶ enough to alert the Spetsn̶̶

His SMG came up, Both fired together ̶ had a clear target.

The three foremost Sp̶̶ ̶̶mselves up the ravine just as the gr̶̶ ̶̶ved and the walls of the ravine quiver̶d. Lee thought she saw one of them smeared under a shifting slab of rock, but the ravine under and around her was moving, too. She and Charlie were sliding downhill among boulders and slabs of rock in a cloud of dust, straight toward the Spetsnaz.

JACK HILD

THE BARRABAS WAR

A GOLD EAGLE BOOK FROM

W⦿RLDWIDE®

TORONTO · NEW YORK · LONDON · PARIS
AMSTERDAM · STOCKHOLM · HAMBURG
ATHENS · MILAN · TOKYO · SYDNEY

First edition October 1989

ISBN 0-373-60104-2

Special thanks and acknowledgment to
Roland Green for his contribution to this work.

THE BARRABAS WAR

CHAPTER ONE

Captain Lieutenant Semyon Ignatievich Pokrovsky knew about the drop-off. Ten meters behind him, the bed of the Aegean Sea plunged sharply, the depth increasing instantly from twenty-five meters to nearly one hundred.

Pokrovsky was known in the Soviet Spetsnaz Naval Brigade as "the Frog Prince." He was said to be at home both on land and in the water, and always in command. Most of his attention was aimed forward toward his target. The rest was directed at his comrades on either side.

He'd given the drop-off all the thought he felt it deserved. They might be able to hide the body there, if they couldn't return to Seahome with it. They might even hide the Iron Dolphin, if they had to abandon it and swim to safety.

A less experienced diver might have worried about the depth and what could happen to a man forced down there. But Pokrovsky had dived to a hundred and forty meters with the same equipment he carried now. With nitrogen flushed out of his system and helium in its place, a hundred meters was easy for him, and twenty-five was a child's wading pool.

Pokrovsky looked up. A bright day on the surface would clearly silhouette any descending diver. He still wouldn't shoot, though, until he could be sure of a hit, and if possible not until he could use the darts instead of the harpoon.

The harpoon would kill just as fast as the darts, but it left a suspicious wound. The darts, tipped with cyanide or a nerve poison derived from sea-snake venom, left no wounds. The Spetsnaz Naval Brigade owed much to the Indian Ocean Fleet's research into the toxicology of snake

venom. The poison was almost impossible to detect unles
you knew it was there in the first place.

Pokrovsky checked both the long harpoon gun and the
short-barreled, easily concealed dart thrower. He had
checked them ten minutes ago. If no target appeared, he
would check them again ten minutes from now. There was
no such thing as too many weapons checks when you were
working underwater. Survival meant keeping a constant
watch against the sea's power to destroy you and your
equipment.

The seabed sloped upward from the boulders where
Pokrovsky and his comrades lay hidden. Piles of debris
dotted the sand and rock and lurked among the weeds—
cans, crates, bits of old ships and new ones from every military conflict in this area since the Trojan War. In places it
was hard to see the bottom.

Pokrovsky knew that the political instructor back at Seahome would say the debris on the floor of the Aegean was
the product of capitalist pollution. The *zampolit* hardly ever
dived, and had obviously never dived in the Black Sea. Off
Yalta the bottom was just as big a mess.

A hand tapped Pokrovsky's arm. He turned to see one of
his comrades pointing upward. High above them a diver was
descending. From his single-tank scuba gear and ragged
trunks, he appeared to be a sponge diver.

The man looked like a perfect victim. Would he take the
bait?

Pokrovsky tapped both his comrades on the shoulder
acknowledging that he'd seen the diver. No other signals
were needed. The three men were the elite of Team
Typhoon, itself the elite of the naval brigade. They had
worked together so long and had shared danger so often that
they sometimes seemed more like brothers than a captain
lieutenant and two warrant officers.

The other two men now did their weapons checks carefully and quietly. Not a single puff of disturbed mud betrayed the waiting Spetsnaz divers to their prey.

SPYROS KOUSTAS WAS TIRED. This was his fourth dive of the day. He had barely filled a single bag with sponges, and most of them were small. A few, he suspected, were diseased.

Some men could still make a living from the Mediterranean by ferrying tourists to Crete or crewing sailboats off Euboea or waiting on tables aboard a cruise ship wandering through the islands. But if sponge diving was in your blood, you were doomed to the devil's own luck.

Koustas had heard that sponges still thrived in the Gulf of Mexico off the American coast. Would Cousin Alex find him a place there? Certainly Alex had done a lot of diving, even if he didn't talk much about where.

Spyros finned rapidly downward. Tired as he was, he knew no sponges floated on the surface. Dead fish, old tires and garbage thrown overboard from ships, but no sponges.

He would make one last dive, for the honor of the family name, then go home. Before he dived again he would talk to Cousin Alex.

Spyros did have one doubt about his cousin visiting from the United States, Alex Nanos—how did the man earn a living? He was obviously as hard and fit a diver as God made, but he also seemed to have no job. He said he was no longer in the Coast Guard. Yet he certainly had plenty of money to rent a cottage, stuff himself with squid and retsina, even cross to the tourist islands to admire the women in their bikinis.

Was Alex smuggling drugs? Then Spyros would not ask a favor of him, because to ask a favor of one doing the devil's work was to put yourself in the devil's power. Spyros Koustas had many sins on his conscience, but that one he would not have.

This vow took Spyros most of the way to the bottom. He leveled off three meters above it. The water was clear enough that he could see even a single sponge from this distance.

Back and forth he swam, not expecting to find anything but doing his best because his father and grandfather and great-grandfather had all sought the sponges. He began to think he could have swum halfway to Crete by now. Another thought was less of a joke—that he might have strayed into Turkish waters. The boat was only about two kilometers outside the limit the Turks enforced and—

"Holy Mother."

Not even in church had Spyros Koustas ever uttered such a heartfelt prayer. Below him was a patch of sponges three times as wide as he was tall, and thicker than his own body. He stopped, doubled and plunged to start stuffing them in his bag.

He'd grabbed four as large as his head, when he noticed something odd about them. They were not fixed to the bottom, as they would be in their own bed. They were just lying about, as if someone had dropped them.

Sponge pirates? It was hard to believe anyone would think a boatload of sponges worth so much, but stranger things had happened. Well, neither the pirates nor their victims were going to get these sponges. Spyros Koustas would get them, and much ouzo would they buy him!

He went on stuffing his bag, tossing aside an occasional sponge picked too long ago and already rotting. He had nearly filled the bag, when he felt a prickle of pain in his left side just above his belt.

That was an odd place for the bends to strike, but he was too experienced a diver to ignore the signs. He reached for one last sponge, but somehow his arm and hand would no longer obey him. As he struggled to master them, he found that an iron band was tightening around his chest. And had clouds covered the sun, or was he sinking deeper? Or was there some other reason everything was going dark—

Spyros Koustas never finished the thought. He rolled over like a dead fish, and his slack jaws released the mouthpiece of his scuba gear. The last air in his lungs raced toward the surface as a few bubbles. Too few for even the sharpest-eyed observer to notice.

THE THREE SOVIET DIVERS waited until Spyros Koustas drifted down onto the sponge bed and lay there. If you didn't notice the absence of air bubbles and the floating mouthpiece, you might have thought he was asleep.

Now the Spetsnaz went to work with the ease of years of practice. At a familiar task like this, they could nearly read one another's minds, and easily read one another's slightest gestures.

Pokrovsky removed the dart, checked the body for loose or missing gear and made it look as natural as possible. They didn't intend to abandon it where it might be found, but intentions counted for little in Spetsnaz work. Only thorough preparation was worth much.

The diver known as "the Rope" picked up the remaining sponges. They had served their purpose, luring the Greek to his death the way the Sirens had tried to lure Ulysses. Now they had to be removed. Left where they were, they would decay. If they were found, they might make someone suspicious.

Besides, Seahome generated a modest amount of hard currency for Spetsnaz operations through the clandestine sale of what its divers collected while going about their other business on the bottom of the Aegean Sea. The sales also left some Greek, Turkish and other merchants open to blackmail.

The last Spetsnaz diver, known as "the Golden Giant," vanished, his black-finned feet moving as fast as a ballet dancer's. He was back in ten minutes with the Iron Dolphin, the most sophisticated manned torpedo in the world. Ten meters long, it could carry four divers at fifteen knots for more than a hundred kilometers. It could run on the surface, dive to a hundred meters and steer itself or be steered by wire from a larger submarine. If it fell into enemy hands, it would blow itself up, along with anyone trying to learn its secrets.

Pokrovsky settled into the pilot's saddle of the Iron Dolphin. The others finished strapping the dead Greek and the bulging sacks of sponges in place, then took their places. A twist of the throttle fed electric power to the twin counter-rotating propellers, and the Iron Dolphin was angling downward, homeward bound.

ALEX NANOS STEPPED OUT of the low cabin of his cousin George's fishing boat. He ducked to clear the door, blinked until his eyes adjusted to the glare off the blue Aegean, then walked forward. His muscle-corded legs quickly carried him forty feet to where George was sitting, apparently contemplating the boat's ancient two-cylinder diesel.

From closer up, Nanos could see George wasn't really looking at the diesel. Not at the diesel, not at the cleaned sponges, ropes and diving gear littering the stained wooden deck, not at the rocky islands two miles off to port or the Turkish coast six miles beyond that.

Nanos had been vacationing with his Koustas cousins on the island of Ikyros for nearly a month now. He knew when something was bothering George.

"Problem, George?" Nanos asked.

"Spyros has been gone longer than I expected."

Nanos looked at his watch, a waterproof Rolex that could withstand the pressure at three hundred feet underwater. It had needed a custom stainless-steel band to fit on Nanos's massive wrist.

"He still should have twenty minutes of air."

"That might not be enough to let him swim back underwater."

"Did he take his snorkel?" Nanos asked.

Trying to keep your head out of water with the weight of a scuba set on your back could exhaust the strongest swimmer. The best thing then was to ditch your weight belt, the cheapest part of your equipment, pop a snorkel tube into your mask and swim home just below the surface.

"No."

Nanos didn't quite call Spyros a fool. You didn't call any Greek a fool in his brother's presence, even if you were a relative. Not unless that brother used the term first.

"Spyros has not been happy these past few months," George said finally. "The diving is all he has lived for. If he could not make a living that way.. ;"

You also didn't imply that a Greek might want to kill himself. Particularly when that probably wasn't true.

"Did he say which way he was going?" Nanos had dived twice that day, before what was left of his hangover had put him to sleep for a couple of hours.

"Over toward Haustim."

"Constantine and I were over there three times in the past four days. If there's a sponge we missed, it has to be too small to see."

"He spoke of going farther."

Nanos grunted to cover doubt. Farther in that direction would take a man to the Elias Trough. The head of an underwater canyon running south toward the Mediterranean, the trough was no place for a diver proud and stubborn enough to be careless.

"How about you hook the motor onto the Avon? I'll run over to the edge of where Connie and I went. Then I'll dive and start searching."

"To move the boat will be faster."

"Yeah, but what if Spyros comes back and we're not here? Besides, that way's toward Turkey. The Turks might not notice a dinghy. They'll sure as hell notice a full-size boat. No, George. Bend a nice long line onto the dinghy anchor, give me a double-tank rig and I'll have all I need."

"Except luck."

Nanos punched George in the shoulder. "Hey, that I don't need to borrow. I make my own."

"Then I will pray that you make enough to spare some for Spyros."

If Nanos had been the praying type, he'd have prayed to give Spyros enough common sense to bring him back safely.

If this wasn't Spyros's last dive, it was time to talk to the man.

Alex Nanos had turned a broken career in the Coast Guard into a prosperous career as a mercenary. Along the way, he'd acquired contacts with people who'd pay a good diver more in a year than sponges would in five. Many of the jobs were even legal. Maybe it was time to call in a few debts, for Spyros's sake.

By most people's standards, Alex Nanos and the Koustas family were only distantly related. But by Greek standards, Alex had a duty to help them if they needed help. He knew he'd neglected his relatives for a lot too long, and some of them might not have too many years left for him to make that up.

Nanos certainly didn't. A diver could predict the risks he'd face in the sea and take precautions against most of them. A mercenary faced human enemies, often as ruthless as the sea and always a hell of a lot harder to predict!

CHAPTER TWO

"Come in!" boomed Captain First Rank Isakov.

Pokrovsky pushed on the sliding door to the captain's office and felt it stick as usual. By the time he'd wrestled it open, most of his hoped-for dignity was gone.

The rest disappeared as he stepped high over the door sill and ducked low to avoid banging his head on the pipes that ran just above the door. Seahome was as large as a senior Politburo member's dacha, ninety meters long and thirty meters wide. But so much had to be crammed into that space that Pokrovsky often thought there should be a height limit for Seahome crew the way there was for tank men in the Soviet army.

Such a limit would do more than save banged heads, barked shins and dented equipment. It would eliminate both Captain Second Rank Fokin, the political instructor, and Captain Third Rank Belyusev, the KGB representative. Oh, Belyusev was on the books as an oxygen-generator specialist, and he seemed to know his business. But he'd left nobody in doubt about what his real job was, or what would happen to anyone who crossed him.

Right now Fokin and Belyusev looked as if simply having to breathe the same air as Pokrovsky annoyed them. Isakov looked even more as if he wanted to be elsewhere.

Pokrovsky's rule was, When in doubt, start with military courtesy. He remembered the story of a distant relative of his grandmother in the Purges—quite distant, or his grandmother wouldn't have been alive to tell the tale. He'd pointed out that the KGB executioner had a dirty pistol, and reminded the man that it was the duty of a defender of the Soviet Union to keep his weapons in first-class condition, even for shooting enemies of the state. It hadn't saved his life or even prolonged it, but the story went that the executioner saluted and aimed straight, and that the relative died with a grin on his face.

Pokrovsky doubted anything like that was going to happen to him, at least until they came up with a team of divers for Seahome as experienced as his own. That would be when collective-farm cows gave yogurt. Belyusev knew that, too.

"You are late, Semyon Ignatievich," Isakov said.

The clock on the fiberglass bulkhead behind the captain's desk was hidden by Belyusev's head. Pokrovsky looked at his watch. Looking down also hid his smile. It was an old trick of Isakov's to criticize Pokrovsky for some minor omission. That way he appeared to be on the side of the two political watchdogs without really having to do anything.

Isakov was not a diver, but nobody who had commanded four nuclear submarines could be a fool. Not being a fool, he knew how much Seahome and his own future depended on getting the best out of Pokrovsky and Team Typhoon.

"I beg your pardon, Comrade Captain," Pokrovsky said. "But I wanted to see that the body of the Greek diver was properly stowed before coming."

"That's not part of your duty, as I recall," Fokin said blandly. "Or don't you trust our laboratory comrades?"

"Actually, I trust the comrades in the laboratory completely," Pokrovsky said. He couldn't look down this time, so he kept his face straight. "It's the cooks I don't quite trust. I wanted the body in the deep freeze."

Fokin swallowed hard and turned slightly green, or maybe it was just a fading of the lights. Isakov's mouth twisted with the effort not to grin. Neither he nor Pokrovsky had ever known a *zampolit* with a stomach for the ugly details of the real world. They perched on their chairs, barricaded themselves behind their tracts and texts and let everybody else get their hands dirty.

"I think that requires an explanation," Belyusev said. He fumbled at his breast pocket for nonexistent cigarettes.

"At our last meeting, it was decided to carry out one final killing before we moved into phase two of Operation Claw," Pokrovsky said. "It was also suggested that the killing be carried out in such a way that it could be used as a starting point for phase two."

Pokrovsky went on with an edited version of how he and his team had chosen their tactics, then a complete account of the Greek diver's death. With long practice, Pokrovsky could roll bureaucratic jargon off his tongue as easily as he could check diving gear for faults. He had the nasty feeling this talent might bring a promotion—one he would have to accept for his own safety, but one that might take him away from day-to-day diving.

"I thought we might want to do more than make the diver disappear this time. I thought we might want the body found somewhere that would cast suspicion explicitly on the Turks."

"Which does not explain why you are risking the contamination of our food supplies!" Fokin growled.

"The body is in a sealed bag. Apart from the effect of the freezer on bacterial activity, those bacteria that aren't frozen can't get out of the bag. We won't have Greek shit mixed with your borscht, if that's what you're worried about."

"A little respect for the comrade *zampolit*, if you please," Isakov said. "But why not use a preservative solution?"

"We hardly have enough in the whole Seahome to handle a human body, at least not until our next supply drop," Pokrovsky said. He grinned. "I'd expect our comrades in the laboratory to cut my balls off with a dull dissector if I stole all their formaldehyde.

"Besides, freezing a body for a few hours leaves no traces except to a very skilled autopsy. Formaldehyde stinks so, that even a Greek or a Turk could detect it."

At a nod from Isakov, Pokrovsky sat down. The politicals might want more information, but he'd be cursed if he'd give it like a schoolboy reciting important dates in the life of Lenin.

"The next duty of my—of Seahome's divers—will be to place the body where we want it found. Or where the currents will carry it to that place. In this we await your orders."

If they had to wait while the politicals got permission in sextuplicate from Moscow, Pokrovsky was going to shove an air tank up somebody's asshole—sideways, if the body wound up useless and the divers' efforts wasted.

"I thought we wanted it found so that it appears the diver wandered into Turkish waters and was killed there," Belyusev said. "Phase two calls for provoking retaliation by the Greeks against the Turks. But does it matter who retaliates against whom?"

Pokrovsky didn't dare gape at the spectacle of a KGB man making an intelligent remark. Although when he thought back on it, he realized Belyusev wasn't the only one of that breed who seemed to know something besides beating confessions out of prisoners.

Pokrovsky resigned himself to listening to Fokin for the next ten minutes, spouting like a whale on the politically correct decision. He reminded himself that punching a *zampolit* in the teeth might cost him a trip to the gulag.

"Since the Greek government is far closer to being a socialist ally than the Turkish," Fokin concluded, "they will be more receptive of any offer of assistance the Soviet people may make. Therefore, we should as quickly as possible create a situation in which they will welcome that assistance."

Pokrovsky interpreted this to mean they should start phase two by making the Greeks angry. If the Greeks got angry enough, they would undoubtedly find some reason to blame their troubles on the Turks.

The government might try to blame them on the Americans at first. But the Americans were a long way off to the average Greek fisherman or peasant, and they really didn't seem that bad. The Turks were close at hand and the hereditary enemy.

When the Greeks decided the Turks were up to their old tricks, they would retaliate, officially or otherwise. Then the Turks—a proud race of warriors if ever there was one—would retaliate in turn. Once the cycle got nicely started, it would be as close to a perpetual-warfare machine as anybody could ask.

Meanwhile, Pokrovsky and his divers of Team Typhoon had a busy few weeks ahead of them, proving that Seahome Four was worth every kopek spent designing it, building it and smuggling it a few pieces at a time into the Aegean Sea under the noses of the NATO navies.

"I'll go get the current charts," Pokrovsky said. "Do you want to wait, or do you want me to come back after dinner?"

Isakov rose and held out his hand. "After dinner, by all means. You've worked hard, done well and deserve some rest."

Actually, Pokrovsky felt as if he'd had no more than a vigorous workout. The warm upper waters of the Aegean made few demands on a man who'd begun his diving training plunging naked into a river where chunks of ice still bobbed downstream.

"Thank you, Captain."

Belyusev rose in time to leave right on Pokrovsky's heels. The diver headed for his quarters. The KGB man caught up with him just past the miniature lock that fed specimens to the laboratories.

"The chartroom is the other way, Captain Lieutenant," said Belyusev.

"The chart I want is in my cabin," Pokrovsky replied. "In a sealed package and locked in my desk drawer," he added. In the Soviet armed forces, maps were classified documents. Having one without authorization or being careless with an authorized one were serious offenses.

"You can verify all this and my authorization, too, if you wish," Pokrovsky went on. "I wanted to memorize the whole area's currents, including weather effects." He had also wanted to let the rest of Team Typhoon memorize them, but he'd be damned if he'd tell the KGB that he'd allowed petty officers to look at maps!

"I'm quite sure everything's in order," Belyusev said.

His grin reminded Pokrovsky of a shark.

"Better order than our *zampolit*, certainly."

That was such a transparent effort to feel out Pokrovsky's political opinions that his first reaction was one of contempt. But all he did was shake his head.

"Captain Fokin does seem to run by his own clock. But I found his lecture most instructive. If his analyses help the diving teams carry out Operation Claw more effectively, I don't care how long they last."

"You consider it possible that they might not be so useful, then?"

Pokrovsky wasted no time cursing himself for walking into that one. "I think socialism has given us a more scientific understanding of politics than any other system. But I also wonder if we will ever understand politics as well as, let us say, the effects of nitrogen on divers at a certain depth. There may be two kinds of laws operating here."

"True. Failing to recognize that was one of Stalin's great errors. Good day."

The KGB man turned and walked off so abruptly that Pokrovsky spent a whole minute wondering if the man was angry. Was he testing Pokrovsky's loyalty? Or could he be trying to enlist Pokrovsky as an ally in getting rid of the *zampolit*?

Joining the KGB in a plot was somewhat like taking swimming lessons from a shark. Both might be able to teach you, but both might also decide you'd make a better victim than pupil.

In the end, Pokrovsky shrugged and headed for his cabin. It was a good thing Belyusev hadn't come with him, because now he remembered that he'd left the chart out on his bunk.

That wouldn't have mattered, if he hadn't been sharing his cabin with the chief sound officer. The man was an expert on computers and underwater sound, but a complete disaster as a housekeeper. He could easily have mislaid the chart, either in adding to the mess or in one of his rare efforts to tidy up.

Either way, Pokrovsky resigned himself to spending his dinnertime hunting for it.

FROM THE ROOF of George Koustas's house, Alex Nanos could see to the west halfway across the island of Ikyros. A ridge in the middle cut off the rest, thrusting an old ruined monastery against the darkening sky.

To the east, a well-thrown stone would have reached the sea. It would have had a long drop, for most of the houses in the village, this one included, perched on either side of the narrow, steep-sided harbor. Only the net makers and boat builders lived by the water's edge. The rest of the village's eight hundred or so people lived in three clusters of whitewashed houses, joined to the harbor by streets so steep that in places they turned into stairways.

Alex watched the sea turn from blue to purple, then darken almost to black. He watched a cruise ship steam past well out to sea, lights blazing as if the people aboard neither knew nor cared that the rest of the world was ready for sleep. He listened to the sigh of the wind in the olive trees behind the house, and the subdued sounds of mourning from inside. Finally he lifted the bottle of wine, poured the last of it into two glasses and raised his.

"To Spyros, a diver who gave himself to the sea over and over, until at last she took him."

George had started to raise his glass. Now he slammed it down on the table, hard enough to spatter both of them with wine. "You think we should do nothing about Spyros?" he shouted. "Do nothing about my brother, not even learn the way he died?"

He emptied his glass, raised the bottle to refill it, then threw the empty bottle hard against the wall. As it shattered, the wailing from downstairs rose higher.

"What kind of a Greek are you?" George went on, loud enough to drown out the wailing. "Does family blood mean nothing to you?"

Nanos pushed his chair back. In another minute George would work himself up to a fight, and that would be messy. Nanos could spread George in little pieces all over the village if he had to, which would solve exactly nothing.

"Maria!" he shouted down the stairs. "Send for Christina the wise woman. George is sick."

"You mean he's drunk!" Maria shouted back.

If she'd been doing any of the wailing, it didn't show in her voice.

"And on the very day of his brother's death. What he needs is for you to tie him in his bed, Alex. Not that old witch," she finished.

George stood so quickly he knocked over his chair. Nanos almost went into karate stance, but just in time George sat down again. A fight with his wife was a lot more frightening than one with Cousin Alex.

From what he'd seen of Maria Koustas, Nanos thought George was being sensible. She was a handsome woman, but with a tongue like an electric drill and arms like a power bender. Even if she hadn't been off-limits as family, Nanos would have thought twice before touching her.

Nanos let George sit quietly for a minute. At the end of that time, George's face sank into his hands. His shoulders began shaking with the effort a strong man puts into trying not to weep.

"George," Nanos said gently. "I don't want to make you feel any worse than you already do, but I suspect you know something about Spyros's death you aren't telling me.

swear by my mother's honor that it will go no farther. Unless it will help bring his killers to—'' Forget justice, Nanos thought. That was always a pretty shaky concept. In this land of the blood feud, it was damned silly. ''—to the fate they deserve,'' he finished. ''Then I will ask your permission to tell...some friends I have. They are very good at bringing down killers nobody else can reach.''

Another minute of silence which seemed a lot longer than that to Nanos. Finally George rubbed his eyes and shrugged.

''I suppose I feared too much the shame of not having talked before this. I apologize for what I said. You know what is due to family probably better than I.''

A faint smile flickered across George's dark, heavy face. The smile vanished as he began his story.

''Spyros is not the first man to vanish like this. He is not even the fifth. Not all of them have been men, either.''

George went on to list seven people—five men, a boy, and a woman—all of whom had vanished in the past four months. Three had been divers, one a fisherman, three a family taking their boat from one island to another by night.

''Not the wisest thing to do,'' Nanos pointed out.

''In a boat Peter built with his own hands, in waters he knew better than he knew his wife, on a calm night? And when his little girl had been sick with a fever three days running and the nearest doctor was on Kepsos? Do not insult the memory of a friend and his family!''

''Sorry. Go on.''

''What more is there to tell?''

''Where did they disappear?'' George started to look stubborn again. Nanos slapped the table with the flat of his hand. ''I swore to use nothing you tell me except to avenge Spyros and the others. Do you doubt my word now?''

''No, no...'' George muttered.

Nanos still had to drag more details out of his cousin. All the people had vanished within a ten-kilometer radius of where the Koustas's boat had been anchored that afternoon.

"That's fifteen kilometers at most from Turkish territo rial waters," Nanos said. The half of Alex Nanos tha wasn't Greek was a Slavic tossed salad. All his ancestors o both sides had fought the Turks for centuries. Even so, h still had one problem with blaming the Turks. They wer always aggressive, but usually honorable, as well. So fa this sounded like petty, vicious treachery.

"Cousin," George said slowly. "Cousin, if I have bee told the truth..." He sighed. "I have a...man I meet a times. For business I would rather not talk about. But he i a Turk. A Turk who knows these waters even better tha Peter did. A Turk, God help us, who knows that the sea i more an enemy than the Greeks."

"I've met a few like him," Nanos prompted. "Greek. too. Has your Turk had some trouble?"

"Not he, but two of his friends have disappeared. On was a diver from an archaeological camp on the island c Haustim, not far from here. Also, there was an America couple—hippies, I think you call them. They went swim ming one night and never came back."

"All in the same area?"

"We looked at a map together. He would not tell m everything, but—yes, I think so."

Nanos began to smell something a lot stronger and a l less pleasant than the fish and tar from the harbor and th olive trees in the garden. It smelled very much like som thing he ought to mention to Nile Barrabas, formerly a co onel in the United States Army Special Forces, currentl Alex Nanos's CO in the small band of elite mercs known the Soldiers of Barrabas.

Definitely a matter for Nile, preferably with one mo detail filled in....

Nanos went downstairs, pulled a bottle of Old Grandda out of his suitcase and took it upstairs. He kept it under h jacket to hide it from Maria, who was busy consoling Spy ros's sister and fiancée. Their wails had faded into sobs, an the smell of coffee filled the kitchen.

Back on the roof, he wiped the two glasses with his handkerchief and filled them with the brown whiskey. George didn't so much as ask what his glass held. He hoisted it, gulped, then coughed so long and so hard Nanos was afraid Maria would hear.

But the wailing had begun again. George coughed himself into silence, then drank more cautiously. That didn't keep him from finishing the whiskey, then holding out his glass for a refill.

"You—you go tell your friends who can help about this?"

"Yes. Now I don't say they can pull off a miracle. But they're a pretty tough crew." That was an understatement, considering all that the SOBs had survived and all the people who hadn't survived the SOBs.

The Old Granddad sank lower. Nanos was beginning to feel its effects himself. He also knew that bourbon on top of Greek wine was going to produce a historic hangover.

He still wanted that last detail before George drank himself under the table, instead of just onto it. The man's chin was sinking about an inch every minute, so there wasn't much time.

"George, I don't want to make you feel guilty, but why the hell didn't you tell somebody about this? Why the hell hasn't anybody else talked? I understand about you and the Turk, but—"

"You understand nothing!" George shouted, knocking over his glass. He grabbed the bottle and poured a refill before Nanos could stop him. "You haven't seen what the police do—don't do—when you can't pay them. We are none of us rich on Ikyros. Not even the fat priest."

"But this might not be just ordinary crime."

"No. No, it might be big crime, the kind where they bribe the police. Or the Communists, and you know Athens is screwing with them all the time. Anybody complains, maybe they wind up going the same place the others do."

"That won't happen with my friends." Not unless the
SOBs had very bad luck, indeed, and even if they did there'd
be fewer bad guys around afterward, Nanos knew.

"When I see them—" George began.

"You will. As soon as I can get back to Rhodes—"

"And screw your movie star."

"She's a starlet, not a star."

"A what?"

"A starlet," Nanos explained patiently, forcing each word
to come out clearly, "is a woman who is going to be a star.
Or thinks she is going to be a star. Or has been told she is
going to be a star. Or wants everybody to believe she is going
to be a—"

A raucous snore interrupted him. George hadn't quite
fallen under the table, but his head was resting in the spilled
whiskey and his eyes were closed.

Nanos looked at the rest of the bottle, then shook his
head. He'd need all the sobriety he had left to get George
downstairs and stuffed into bed before Maria noticed. Given
a choice between fighting opponents like those the SOBs
often faced and fighting Maria Koustas, Nanos would a
damned sight rather fight the professionals.

CHAPTER THREE

Alex Nanos watched the moonlight stroke the body of the woman in the bed beside him. Then he slipped out of bed and walked to the telephone, which stood on an age-darkened olive-wood table by the bedroom window.

Beyond the window, tiled roofs marched in ragged ranks downhill to the harbor of Rhodes. Unlike those in Ikyros's harbor, any fishing boats here had been converted for carrying tourists around among the islands. The rest of the harbor held yachts, from thirty-footers up to a diesel-powered giant nearly as big as Alex's old Coast Guard cutter. Rhodes epitomized the tourists' Greece, as much as Ikyros did the Greeks' Greece.

Nanos reached into his suitcase, which rested on a chest beside the phone, and lifted the false bottom slightly. He removed a black rectangle about the size of a pound of cheese, with a couple of deceptively ordinary-looking tools taped to it. Two minutes' work, and the black rectangle was wired to the telephone. Nanos lifted the receiver, listened for thirty seconds, nodded in satisfaction, then began to dial.

George had been partly right. Nanos had come back to Rhodes for another night or a few with Cheryl—which might even be her real name. But he'd also come because on Rhodes he could find a private telephone that would take one of Nate Beck's new portable scramblers. On that scrambled telephone he could then call a certain number in Amsterdam.

Nanos perched on the windowsill as the telephone in Amsterdam began to ring.

THE NARROW STREET wasn't a canal, but it had water in it. It was old, the drains clogged with trash, and there'd been a heavy rain that day.

The water wasn't quite deep enough to float the corpses of the two drug addicts it had drowned. It did lap gently against the bottom step of number 58, a crumbling eighteenth-century house whose better days were at least one hundred years in the past. The Dutch kept most of Amsterdam immaculate, but around the Central Station even their fastidious housekeeping failed.

The door of the apartment on the third floor looked just as warped and stained as the others. Anyone trying to break in, however, would have quickly discovered it had two locks and a steel core.

If they'd tried to break in while the apartment was occupied, they would also have discovered that the door had a silent alarm. That might well have been the last discovery of their lives. Nile Barrabas could be very short-tempered with people who tried to kill him. And Erika Dykstra, when seriously provoked, wasn't much more charitable, even if she wasn't quite as dangerous. She was merely less accurate and fast with a weapon.

Right now Barrabas was almost as short-tempered with the bedside telephone. But you couldn't shoot a telephone, not if you wanted to talk on it. Besides, the pattern of the ringing told Barrabas it was one of his SOBs calling.

Correction, one of *the* SOBs. His being their leader didn't make them his property, as one or two potentates with more money than brains had been told in plain English. The SOBs were all very much their own persons, and nobody owned them and their variety of lethal skills but they themselves.

Barrabas picked up the telephone. "56345. Go ahead."

It was Alex Nanos.

"Boss, I'm sorry to get you out of bed at this hour, but I've got a serious offer on the *Claribel*. There's still a question about financing, though. Can we put our heads together about a discreet investigation?"

Either Alex didn't trust the Nate Beck Handy Dandy Scrambler, or his phone was unsecured. He was using the code worked out to match his current cover as a yacht broker and general man-about-boats. It was a better cover in many countries than his actual off-duty profession of security consultant. "Security consultant" meant "police" or even "CIA" in a lot of places. In those same regions, "yacht broker" meant somebody who would help keep the tourists and their dollars coming in.

In that code, Alex was saying he was on the trail of a problem that might need the SOBs, but he wanted to sit down with Barrabas and discuss it in more detail than he could over the telephone.

It sounded as if Alex was playing a hunch. But there were only two kinds of mercenaries—those who played hunches, and those who were dead. Waiting until all the facts were in paid off in some professions. In the mercenary business, the pay was in body bags—assuming there was enough left of you to put in one.

"No problem. Tuesday at the downtown office. Do we need to alert the investigating staff?"

That meant a meeting at the Bussum Huis on Sarphati Straat, and was it time to call in the rest of the SOBs? They really were an investigating staff, among other things—although one look at them would have probably given the average finance-company executive a heart attack.

"I've got one or two discreet sources lined up already," Nanos replied. "If I don't have to leave until Monday, maybe I can find a couple more. If they all pan out, *then* we can shout for the cavalry."

"Damned straight. Good luck, and let me know if the owner gets any private offers."

Translation: "Shout loud and clear if any overt or covert bad guys show up."

"Thanks, boss."

Barrabas hung up and sat down on the bed, which took up more than half the bedroom. Not unreasonable, considering how much time he and Erika spent there when they were in the apartment. Erika had propped herself up on one elbow. The light over the vanity revealed her long, lithe, tanned nudity. Her breasts didn't sag, even in that awkward position and even though she hadn't been a teenager for quite a while.

But right now Barrabas wanted a little distance between himself and Erika, while he sorted out courses of action. So he moved to the only other seat in the room, the stool in front of the vanity. Unless he put a little more distance between himself and Erika, he would lie down, take those breasts firmly in hand and go on from there.

"Nile, is it another mission?"

"Maybe."

Erika sat up and slapped bare feet on the floor. "Nile, I don't mind lies about what you've done or where you've been. I understand that the less I know about some of your missions, the safer I am. Besides, turnabout is fair play. You're better off not knowing about a few of my deals."

She smiled briefly. She and her brother had a modest family business of transporting high-value, low-bulk goods. Some of the business was legal, but it was smuggled goods that had brought Erika and Barrabas together in the closing stages of the Vietnam War.

They'd had their problems—mainly Barrabas's occupation—and as to what had kept them together a good part of the time since then, Barrabas had given up trying to understand. Great sex had to be part of it, but it couldn't be the only thing.

"What I don't want to start," Erika went on, "is lies about whether you're going on a mission at all. When you walk out the door, I want to be sure you're on your way to the wars."

Barrabas's first impulse was to accuse her of jealousy. His second thought was that this would be the last thing she wanted to hear. Probably the last thing she *would* hear from him, too.

"Erika, word of honor—as much honor as I have. I really don't know if there's a mission coming up. Alex suspects something and wants to talk privately about it."

"Something in Greece?"

"Greece or Turkey or both. The Aegean Sea, anyway."

Erika could look both meditative and erotic at the same time. She did so very nicely now. Barrabas didn't always like the results of her meditations. He liked a knockdown, drag-out fight even less.

"I have some contacts in that area," Erika began. "The smugglers, you know. Nonpolitical as they come, but some of them..."

"Some of them owe you favors?"

Erika nodded. "I might end up owing them favors if I ask too much, but I think I can learn what they know without going that far. Of course, they may not know anything."

That was one of the occupational hazards of intelligence or any kind of covert operations. You had to throw an awful lot of darts in the dark, without being sure there was even a dart board at the other end of the room.

"Be careful—"

Her fine nostrils flared. "Would you tell Lee Hatton that?"

So much for not having a fight....

"Erika, I'm not concerned for your safety. Not that way. I couldn't keep you in a bottle if I wanted to, and I don't want to. If you'd let me finish, I would have said be careful about asking questions before I've talked with Alex. Asking questions might tip off the people responsible if word gets back to them."

"I see. You're not concerned about my safety. Just about tipping off your enemies."

"That won't help matters," Barrabas said. "Neither will your getting involved before the SOBs are in the field. Then somebody might decide to kill you if they thought you were the source of the trouble. If they decided you might lead them to somebody else, you might be snatched. Either way you'd be in hot water without having done any good. I'm not being overprotective. I'm just concerned about wasting good people. They don't grow on bushes."

Erika's voice was still clipped. "You're hinting I don't know much about intelligence work. I'm not sure that isn't as big an insult as being overprotected."

Barrabas hoped he didn't look or sound as edgy as he felt. Was Erika angling for a place on the team as an alternative to their breaking up?

He couldn't blame her if she was tired of sweating out each mission. Yet he couldn't add her to the team. She was almost good enough, but "almost" in this business could get you and everybody with you killed.

Damn the woman for forcing this decision on him at three o'clock in the morning!

Nile Barrabas could have led the SOBs, or a Special Forces A-Team, or even an infantry rifle battalion, at any time of the day or night. His tactical mind never slept. But making decisions about the future of his relationship with Erika Dykstra was something completely different. Right now he wasn't even sure he could avoid hurting Erika, let alone saving the relationship.

Damn— No, the first thing to do was stop damning Erika. The situation wasn't her fault.

"Erika, you haven't been in the field with the KGB or the GRU. The Soviet secret police and military intelligence aren't like any national police force or even Interpol. They've got more resources, no scruples at all and some very intelligent people working for them. Your barging in—"

"I don't barge!"

The Dutch accent was stronger, but at least she was still speaking English. Erika spoke five languages fluently, but preferred her native Dutch when she really wanted to take someone apart.

"You wouldn't mean to. But it's like a minefield. The sharpest eye and the best of intentions won't save you, if the mines are sown thickly enough. You'll still get blown up.

"Blown up, with *not a goddamn thing to show for it*!"

The silence lasted long enough for Barrabas to wonder how fast he could pack. He decided that if he left everything but one change of clothes and the modified Browning Hi-Power, he could be out the door in two minutes.

Out the door, and out of Erika Dykstra's life, which wasn't where he wanted to go, but if she'd made up her mind...

"Nile," Erika said in a small voice, "I'm sorry. I—well, this isn't the time for a fight about anything. It certainly isn't the time for a fight over my joining the team."

The way she said that, it sounded as if she considered it an open question for some future time. Well, maybe there were arguments on her side worth listening to—at that future time.

"So you'll go slow?"

"The only man I'll be talking to in the next three days is a former Bundespolizei officer who did a couple of years exchange duty with the Turks. He'll help me sort out which of my old contacts are still likely to be useful."

"I hope he's discreet."

"I can keep him quiet. He was on my payroll for a few years before he retired."

"For how much?"

Barrabas whistled at the figure Erika named. She'd paid about seventy-five thousand dollars to the West German police officer over a five-year period. But that was like Erika. One reason for her success was her generosity with people who helped her.

That thought led Barrabas to put both hands on Erika's tanned shoulders.

"Kiss and make up, Nile?" she said.

"Well, if you really want to stop with kissing—"

"That will do to start with."

She lifted his hands from her shoulders, then wrapped her arms around his lean, scarred torso. Warm, moist, incredibly mobile lips began to play up and down his skin, lingering as long on the scars as on the more sensitive areas.

The kissing went on for a long time, but they didn't stop with that, or stop at all until dawn elbowed its way down Amsterdam's narrow streets.

As it did, Barrabas took a final look at Erika—sprawled nude and fast asleep. He hoped he'd made her forget how soon he might be going back to the wars. He knew he hadn't done a bad job of making himself forget his chances of not coming back. That did no harm, here in Amsterdam, beside Erika. Just as long as he didn't forget it once he reached the field, where enemies waited to shoot at him the minute he showed up in their sights.

There was a technical term for soldiers who forgot the dangers they faced.

They were known as "casualties."

ALEX NANOS HUNG UP the phone and turned back to the bed. Cheryl was sitting up, wearing only that impish grin that looked so well on her wide mouth.

The moonlight silvered her slim body—too slim to attract him, Nanos would have said, until he saw her in a bikini. Then she told him she was forty, when he would have sworn she wasn't more than twenty-six.

Honesty and the bikini together made the right sort of chemistry. Nanos had the feeling that Cheryl was going to linger in his memory longer than most women.

"Sorry I woke you."

"Actually, I was sort of hoping to be woken up."

"But not by a business call?"

"You got it, Alex. Now how about coming over here and apologizing?"

Nanos was already on the way. One secret of his success with women was making the ones who said yes feel they had his undivided attention as long as he was with them.

Before they were done, they'd pushed the pillows and sheets off the bed and nearly gone onto the floor themselves. Finally they relaxed, pleasantly sweaty, with Cheryl's head pillowed on Alex's massive chest.

"You really have to fly out tomorrow?"

"Not until Monday. I may be right back, too. It depends on how much money our prospect has. Or at least how much he's willing to admit he has."

"I was hoping you'd be staying a little longer. I wanted you to look over a few boats for an old classmate of mine. She's an archaeologist, Dr. Adrienne Biggle. Ever heard of her?"

"Working around here, isn't she?" A small bell had begun to chime in Nanos's mind, rather like the alarm on a fishfinder.

"Over on Haustim. It's just inside Turkish territorial waters, east of Ikyros."

The alarm stopped chiming and began to ring loudly. Haustim was within the area of the mysterious disappearances. An archaeological expedition there might have seen something, and hadn't George mentioned an archaeological expedition that had lost a diver?

"She needs a boat?"

"She had one, rented locally. Her college can only grant her a starvation budget. But then her diver disappeared, a relative of the boat's owner, and the owner said he didn't want anything more to do with Adrienne. She's been stuck with diving off the island or out of dinghies for the past month."

Nanos's alarm now sounded like an alert for incoming missiles. He didn't reveal his mounting interest in the archaeologist when he said, "Well, if she's damned near broke there's only so much I can do to help her." Unless, he thought, she was willing to help him find out what had happened to her diver. In that case the SOBs might arrange for a brand-new trawler yacht for Dr. Adrienne.

"I thought you might have contacts."

"I do, I do. And stop trying to bribe me, woman. I always like what I do."

"Who said this was a bribe? Haven't you ever met an insatiable woman before?"

"I've met a lot who said they were."

"Then prepare for a new experience."

"I am up to it," he said.

"And you're as good as your word," she purred throatily as she let their bodies merge.

CHAPTER FOUR

One of the dining rooms of the Bussum Huis was aboard an old canal barge moored to a quay in the Amstel. Washed three times a day, the windows gave Nile Barrabas a good view of the river.

Looking the other way, he got an equally good view of Walker Jessup, helping himself to the restaurant's *rijstaffel*, a Dutch-Indonesian version of the smorgasbord. The Bussum Huis had one of the best of these in Amsterdam. Barrabas suspected it wouldn't be quite so good for at least a week after Walker Jessup went home.

The fat man known in covert-operations circles the world over as "the Fixer" finished loading a second plate. Either one would have fed a family of three quite comfortably. Balancing both plates and an armful of bottles of Grolsch beer, Jessup lumbered back to the table where Barrabas and Alex Nanos sat. Barrabas would have sworn that the barge listed slightly as Jessup moved.

The chair certainly creaked as Jessup's three hundred odd pounds settled into it. It creaked louder as he bit down on a piece of chili pepper in his first mouthful and snatched a bottle of Grolsch. Popping the stopper, Jessup swigged half the bottle before the fire went out and he set it down.

"Okay, Nile. I don't mind being here. I'm flush. Amsterdam's got good restaurants. Besides, there may be a mission or two for you coming up. If we can find a secure place—"

"We won't find a more secure one than here," Nanos said. "The colonel's lady friend owns half of it and all of the owner."

"One of her old people?" Jessup asked, raising shaggy graying eyebrows.

Barrabas shook his head. He knew Jessup wasn't quite sure if Erika was a security risk or not. All the checks made on her said she was clear, but Jessup didn't have that much faith in the checks.

Neither, in fact, did Barrabas. His faith was in Erika, which was kind of hard to explain to a professional spook like Walker Jessup.

"Somebody who happened to be Erika's enemy, too, decided to snatch the owner's daughter. They think he was planning a white-slave deal in the Person Gulf."

" 'Was'?"

"Erika whistled up some of her people. The daughter wound up safe and sound, and the man who'd planned the snatch wound up in the Amstel. Any friend of Erika Dykstra's is safe here, unless they set the place on fire or proposition the owner's wife."

"You mean, unless the owner's wife accepts," Nanos put in. "I've met her. If she wrestled a grizzly bear, I wouldn't bet on the grizzly."

Jessup opened another Grolsch. "Okay, I'm persuaded we can talk here. So talk."

Nanos repeated the report he'd given Barrabas, which Barrabas had then summarized over a secure telephone line to Virginia. Anyone who didn't know Jessup would have said he was bored out of his skull. But Nanos and Barrabas knew that Jessup could soak up amazing amounts of information and retain it all, even while stuffing himself with enough food for a platoon of Marines.

Finally Jessup emptied both plates and set down his fourth and last bottle of Grolsch. "Okay, Alex," he said, "you interest me. But these disappearances—who's to say what's behind them? Is it just a hunch that it's bad guys playing games? Or is it something more?"

Barrabas and Nanos looked at each other. It might weaken their position to admit they were playing a hunch.

It would weaken their position a lot more to be caught lying to Jessup. One of the unwritten Iron Laws of the American intelligence community was Thou shalt not even try to bullshit the Fixer.

"A hunch," Nanos said.

"The hunch of a trained man, on the spot, with a lot of back—"

"Yeah, I've heard the sermon before," Jessup said. "There are two kinds of mercs—the ones who play their hunches, and the dead ones. I don't suppose it's occurred to you that the same goes for my business?"

It had, but not lately. It was sometimes hard for Barrabas to remember that inside that mass of fat lay one of the most formidable minds in the history of American intelligence. Walker Jessup hadn't earned his nickname of the Fixer by eating restaurants into bankruptcy. He'd earned it by finding economical, reliable and deniable ways of doing things that everybody else said were impossible.

Besides, the fat man had saved Barrabas's life in Vietnam. For that, Barrabas owed him at least common politeness—most of the time.

"Sorry, Fixer. It's just that my ass is a little farther out on the line than yours most of the time."

"We get many more jobs like Prince Su's rubies and that too, may change."

Jessup was referring to a recent SOBs mission to snatch a fortune in Chinese rubies out of Tibet one jump ahead of the Chinese army. During that mission the SOBs had done their usual lion's share of the fighting, but there'd been enough leftover to keep Jessup throwing teak chests, firing Sterling submachine guns and unloading airplanes.

"I can't wait to see you show up at Jake Gold's for a bodybuilding course," Nanos said.

"You've got a long wait ahead of you," Jessup said. He signaled the waiter for clean plates. "You've also got a long wait before I come up with full funding for this kind of hunch."

"So what the hell did you come to Amsterdam for?" Barrabas snapped. "Besides the restaurants, that is."

"I didn't say we couldn't manage some kind of fix," Jessup said. "I didn't say there won't be *any* money. I just said no full funding right off. If you hairy-chested merc types would use your heads for something besides keeping your ears out of your armpits..."

Insults aside, Barrabas had to admit the Fixer had a point. The chain of command that ended with the SOBs used to go back to a secret committee of legislators, particularly to the totally ruthless and amoral senator who was its chairman. But the senator, after a run-in with Barrabas, was no longer central to their missions, what with a contact in NSA enlisting the aid of the SOBs much more frequently. The chain of command now vanished into the murky labyrinth of the American intelligence community, though at times the senator still surfaced and created a stir, and set off occasionally yet another mission.

But it did not matter much who set things in motion. All politicians and bureaucrats had one priority: cover your ass. That meant none of them could be trusted any more than the rest. It also meant that all of them would sooner or later need a completely deniable team of expert fighters, to carry out missions either impossible or unsafe for anybody else. This would keep the SOBs in fees and fatigues until either they died or peace broke out.

Barrabas knew which would happen first.

Unless the SOBs suddenly started not getting paid. In that case they might make their own private peace, and the covert-operations gurus could go whistle for dirty-work experts. Barrabas was willing to accept a little confusion over who signed the SOBs' checks. On the other hand, no checks at all and...

"What exactly are we supposed to do for free?" he asked.

"Nothing," Jessup replied.

"Nothing?" Nanos said.

"I didn't hear an echo when I came in," Jessup said. He paused to let the waiter deliver his clean plates and three more bottles of Grolsch.

"All I can promise for investigating this hunch is expenses. Now I won't mind you naming a figure—"

"A thousand a day. Each. Plus an equipment allowance, or another fifty thousand down," Barrabas said.

"Remind me never to try selling you a used car," Jessup muttered. He opened another bottle of Grolsch and looked into it as if the beer were the Aegean Sea. Finally he nodded. "I'd be surprised if I can't swing that. I'll hit the local merchants for the equipment—"

Barrabas shook his head. "Not Amsterdam."

"For Chrissake, Nile! If this is serious, then every day could count."

"If it's that frigging serious, then call it an official mission and give us our half mil," Nanos said. "Then we'll fish up our own stuff and do the job our own way. You want us to work cheap, you gotta help a little."

"Right," Barrabas said. "That means staying out of Amsterdam. I know Erika and I have had a few hassles here. But there's nobody here *permanently* who wants a piece of our hide. You go farting around in the arms warehouses, Fixer, and that may change. And if it does, there's only one question about what's going to happen to you."

"What's that?"

"Who gets your balls and who gets your ears. Personally, I think I'll let Erika have your balls. She can think of nastier ways of cutting them off."

Jessup waved the now-empty beer bottle at the two SOBs. "Your sense of humor kills me."

"Not yet, fat man," Nanos said. "But don't make bets for the future."

"Let's not make bets on there *being* a future, until we're a little farther into this," Jessup said. "Okay, give me your shopping list and I'll find someplace else to work. I'll also see if I can get some information if I can't wangle any money. It would be nice if we didn't find ourselves going up against Armenian terrorists.''

"I don't see that," Barrabas said. "The Armenians wouldn't be wasting Greeks unless the Soviets were bankrolling them. That's the last thing the Sovs are likely to do right now. Their own Armenians are kicking up a rumpus."

"I read the papers, too," Jessup said. "How about you let me cover my hunches if you're going to drag me into yours?"

"No sweat."

Now they had working answers to the questions who—all the SOBs; how much—expenses; how fast—asap; and with what—everything on the shopping list Barrabas was scribbling as Jessup went back for more *rijstaffel*. The only thing left was to come up with a cover story.

"How about I go back to Rhodes?" Nanos suggested.

"And to Cheryl?" Barrabas asked.

"I got a reason for cultivating that lady," Nanos said. "*Besides* the one in the *Bible*. Or is it the *Kama Sutra*? Anyway, suppose I go back and hunt her up a boat for her friend the archaeologist. Then you people show up as its crew, and we all sail off to fish up Greek pots, dead divers and Russians who are minding other people's business.

"That's going to be a damned well-crewed diving boat," Jessup said. "But I like it. Colonel, you have any problems with that?"

Barrabas shook his head. He didn't have any problems with the cover story. He also didn't have any problems with Alex Nanos coming up with it. Nanos was probably the least intelligent and least mature of the SOBs, spending all his free time chasing women, girls, female aardvarks.... He also probably knew more about boats than the rest of the SOBs put together. In that area, slow Alex was a genius.

It was the same with the rest of the SOBs. Some had more general smarts than others, but all of them had some particular area of expertise. Those areas overlapped, so when the team was together it had at least two people who could solve damned near any problem the SOBs might face.

It had been better when Nate Beck was active and Geoff Bishop was alive, because then they had a genius-grade hacker and a pilot who knew planes the way Nanos knew boats. But the SOBs could still pool their knowledge and put up one hell of a fight. The best evidence of that was that they were still alive. Barrabas intended them to stay that way.

Concentrating on his list of weapons and equipment, he hardly heard Jessup muttering about "getting through to Dr. Biggle's department head, if he's the one I'm thinking of." He only lifted his head from the notebook when the owner of the restaurant tapped on the table with an empty beer bottle.

"Mr. Barrabas? The bill, I am sorry to say."

"I thought—"

"For any friend of Fru Dykstra, mostly I do not charge. But the fat man who just left—the profits of a week went into his stomach if *someone* does not pay."

Barrabas looked at the check, then looked at it again. The astronomical total was the same both times. It was not a hallucination.

"All right, Pieter." Wearily Barrabas dug into his pocket and came out with a battered wallet. "American Express or Barclay's?"

THE BED CREAKED OMINOUSLY as Ioannes Trikoupi stepped up his pace. Adrienne Biggle locked her legs around his buttocks and her arms around his shoulders. For a wild moment she imagined she could pull him all the way into herself.

A warm tide rose in her, then turned hot. She cried out as the tide swept her away, so loud she barely heard Ioannes groan.

After that she slept, but not for long. She awoke to hear murmured words of praise in Greek. She also heard the honking of horns as Athens woke up, and she smelled coffee, exhaust fumes and sweat.

Trikoupi rolled over toward her and ran a finger delicately down between her breasts. "Ummmm," she murmured.

"Is that an American word I do not know?" he said with a grin. He had a broad face with high cheekbones and a mouth molded in a perpetual smile. He looked cheerful even when he was sad, which wasn't very often.

"It means this time Cheryl won't be able to say I wasted my vacation," Adrienne told him.

"Cheryl? Ah, your old friend from Hollywood." Then Trikoupi clapped a hand to his head in mock horror. "My God, you mean in America women compare notes on such things?"

"I suspect it's not just in America," Adrienne replied, laughing. "But, yes, Cheryl and I do compare notes, as you put it." For a moment her voice hardened. "She is very proud of how many more men she has seduced than I have."

"There are obviously many men with no taste," Trikoupi said.

"That's gallant of you, but let's be realistic. Cheryl's a lot better-looking than I am, apart from living in Hollywood, where she meets a lot more men than I do in academic circles."

She lifted Trikoupi's thick wrist until she could read his watch. "Good God! I should have been out of here half an hour ago!" She sprang out of bed naked and ran for the closet.

"Alas, to see beauty veiled," Trikoupi said as she pulled on green slacks and a faded rose top. "I suppose I could not persuade you to unveil it again?"

"Not this morning," Adrienne answered. "I don't dare miss *Circe*. There won't be another boat sailing for Haustim for a week."

"Is there such a hurry?"

"Professor Stewart is leaving tomorrow for the United States. 'Consultations,' he calls it. Probably the damned Navy wanting a piece of our action again."

"You object?"

"I don't like the military. They have their own agenda, and freedom to research isn't usually on it. That means all their money comes with strings attached. I'd rather be free to choose my own line of research, even if it means taking a boat instead of flying."

"I honor such dedication."

"Even in a woman? Sorry, that was nasty. But I've met too many Greek men who look at a professional woman like she's Medusa, going to turn them to stone."

"Well, you have certainly turned part of me that hard, many times. I would like to do something for you in return."

Adrienne picked up her hairbrush. "Settle any little hotel charges. I'll leave you the money."

Trikoupi came up behind her and put his hands on her breasts. "I can even drive you to Piraeus. But surely something more . . ."

"If you know anybody with an old boat for charter, give them my name. We can't afford much, but we don't need much, either. Cheryl's met up with a free-lance yacht broker named Alex Nanos, who may have a lead or two, but— Is something wrong, Ioannes?"

"Alex Nanos . . . She is screwing him?" Trikoupi's voice was suddenly harsh.

"Probably. Why?"

"Then she— No, wait a minute. Did she describe him?"

"A Greek hunk was what she said. That means good-looking, lots of muscles—"

"Ah, your friend is safe then. The Alex Nanos I was thinking of, he is a small man, slim, with one ear missing."

"Your work?"

"If I ever meet him again, he will be missing more than an ear."

Adrienne reached under the sheet and squeezed between Trikoupi's legs. "Like that?"

"Among other things. It is a private matter, you understand, but a serious one. Fortunately your friend is amusing herself with another Alex Nanos."

"Will you really drive me to Piraeus?"

"I will run all the way with you on my back, if nothing else will get you to *Circe* on time!"

Adrienne let his hands slide under the waistband of her slacks. "Let's see if I leave you in any shape to even get out of bed!"

Trikoupi and Adrienne not only had another good time, they even got Adrienne through the morning traffic to the Vassileos Paul Dock in Piraeus. She sprinted up the gangplank half a minute before the crew pulled it up. From the boat deck, she waved to Trikoupi, who was standing on the roof of his ancient Peugeot.

By the time *Circe*'s vintage diesels had pushed her out beyond Sounion Head, Adrienne was below, unpacking. On interisland ferries like *Circe*, cabin assignments were mostly on paper. Squatter's rights were what really counted, particularly if you were a woman traveling alone.

Once she'd laid claim to a bunk and a couple of hangers, she had time to realize she hadn't eaten breakfast. She didn't mind sex on an empty stomach, but now that the sex was over, she was definitely hungry. All the dining room had left, unfortunately, was dry croissants and overripe grapes, but the coffee was good. Adrienne gulped one cup and sipped a second as she watched the coastal traffic bob past.

More ferries, full-size cruise ships, little freighters, fishing boats, so many yachts you could practically walk to Turkey across their decks... The shape of the ships had changed since Ulysses roamed the "wine-dark sea" three thousand years ago, but the marriage of the Greeks to the water had endured.

Adrienne ordered a third cup of coffee and wondered if Trikoupi had managed to find breakfast before he went to work. Or was he still stuck in traffic between Piraeus and his agency's office?

Trikoupi was neither at breakfast, at work, nor stuck in traffic. He was on the telephone to his contact in the local Soviet intelligence network, a GRU man whose cover was accountant for the Athens Intourist Office.

"Alex Nanos, eh?" the man said. "Did she say *where* he was looking for a boat, or what size?"

"No."

"You should have—"

"Don't tell me I should have pumped her. I got as much as I could in the time we had. If I'd made her suspicious, she might not have planned on coming back."

"Who made you an authority on intelligence procedures?"

"Nobody. But God made me an authority on women. You've admitted that yourself. Are you taking it back now?"

"God had nothing to do with it, but I'll admit you're gifted that way."

"Thank you. Anything else I should look for, besides more on what Alex Nanos is doing and where?"

"Ring me back in twenty-four hours. I may have an answer then."

The GRU man hung up and made a mental note to find some way of improving Trikoupi's manners. Short of terminating him, though, he wasn't sure it could be done.

Meanwhile, the fact that Alex Nanos was at large in the eastern Mediterranean was undoubtedly of interest to Moscow. They should have that news as soon as possible.

That turned out to be longer than the GRU man or Moscow liked. By mistake, the message was put on the GRU network that ran through Sofia, the capital of Bulgaria, rather than directly to Moscow.

In Sofia the mistake got worse. The GRU maintained two offices there. One, so far undetected by even the Bulgarians, did serious work such as trying to assassinate the Pope.

The second, penetrated by every intelligence service larger than the Grand Duchy of Luxembourg's, was a sort of Devil's Island for GRU people who didn't come up to standard. Its staff knew they were watched, knew they were outcasts, and spent most of their time drinking home-brewed vodka and cheap Bulgarian wine to forget these unpleasant facts. The message about Alex Nanos went to the second office. It waited there until three different key people recovered from their hangovers, which took two more days.

Then it reached Moscow during shift-change time at the decoding center. It made no difference that the Soviet Union was the worker's paradise, or that the threat of the gulag hung over the code clerks. At the end of the shift, their minds were already out in the streets of Moscow. So two more shifts went by before the message was finally decoded.

After that, things moved a little faster. But four days had passed since Adrienne Biggle's mention of Nanos's name, four days that no amount of swearing, screaming or threatening could win back.

Walker Jessup, often a victim of similar screwups in his days with the Company, might for once have sympathized with his opposition in Moscow.

SEMYON IGNATIEVICH POKROVSKY had never heard of Walker Jessup, and wouldn't have cared for him if he had. In his experience, bureaucrats were all the same breed of trash fish.

He would have felt differently about Alex Nanos if he'd known about the man. A fellow sailor and expert diver was always worthy of respect, even while you were doing your best to kill him.

At the moment, both bureaucrats and fellow divers were a long way from Pokrovsky's mind. He was sitting in Isakov's office, listening to the Rope translate an article from a Greek newspaper.

In theory, the men in Seahome were supposed to wait for official translations of relevant documents. That meant waiting for Moscow to send a translation of a newspaper that an agent could pick up on any street corner in Istanbul or Athens.

Isakov respected Moscow's orders, but respected the value of time more. "I didn't command nuclear submarines by waiting for Moscow to tell me I could wipe my ass" was how he put it.

So Seahome's crew included somebody fluent in every language spoken between Yugoslavia and the Persian Gulf. The Rope was one of the experts in Greek, although Pokrovsky suspected that a lot of his Greek consisted of words for exotic sex acts. Now he was working through an article headlined MISSING DIVER FOUND ON TURKISH COAST. Under the headline was a large picture of the well-ripened corpse of the Greek diver.

"'Once again there is Greek blood on Turkish hands,'" the Rope translated. "'Once again it has gone unavenged. Will the government continue to claim to represent the Greek people, when it leaves them naked to the aggression of our ancient foe?'"

There was a lot more along the same lines. Pokrovsky sneaked a glance at the *zampolit*. He looked as if he couldn't wait for a chance to deliver a lecture on the political implications of the situation.

As far as Pokrovsky was concerned, the political implications stuck out like the devil's prick. The Greeks were getting stirred up. Pretty soon some of them would strike out at the Turks, whether their government did anything or not. Then the Turks would retaliate. After that, the Greek government would *have* to move.

"Good," Isakov said. "Semyon Ignatievich, how soon can you simulate a Greek attack on the Turks?"

"That depends on whether our Type 88s arrive on time, how many there are and what condition they're in," Pokrovsky said.

"You seem to rely too much on external and technical factors—" the *zampolit* began.

"The captain lieutenant knows he is responsible for the safety of Soviet divers," Belyusev put in. "I think he is doing no more than exercising his judgment in a matter where he has demonstrated his competence."

Pokrovsky nodded. He would pay for this good word from the KGB, but it might turn out to be worth its price.

He also wanted to mention something everybody seemed to have overlooked. "Even if the Type 88s arrive tomorrow, who knows what the Greeks may do on their own? We should be ready to simulate Turkish retaliation for a Greek attack, as well as the other way around."

Isakov nodded. "I think we need more Turkish newspapers, to assess their mood."

A carnivorous grin spread over Belyusev. "I think I can arrange for that, if we have some information to trade."

"What about sound data on Turkish warships?" Pokrovsky asked. They seemed to have a lot of such information, if he understood his roommate correctly.

"I suppose we can go ahead on that basis," Isakov remarked unhappily. Pokrovsky knew the captain hated the way the Soviet Union's two intelligence services bargained like a couple of old babas over a basket of onions in a private-plot market. If there'd been a God to thank, Pokrovsky would have thanked Him for being well out of that business. Isakov wasn't so lucky. He was a commander by training, but his job made him a negotiator.

If Pokrovsky was really lucky, the Type 88 midget submarines would arrive in a day or two. Then he wouldn't have to attend any of these meetings until the 88s had been checked out and prepared for operations.

CHAPTER FIVE

"Come on, you candy-ass mothers!" Claude Hayes shouted. "An old lady on crutches could go faster'n that!"

Some of the twelve black teenage boys jogging along the Harlem streets behind him grinned. Some gave him the finger. All of them ran faster.

Around the corner of an abandoned warehouse and onto 132nd Street. Now it was a straight half mile back to the Cavendish Boys' Home.

Boys' Holding Pen, rather. The place beat the streets or most of the other places the kids came from, but that was about all anybody could say for it. Still, the hundred-odd boys there were getting just a little bit of a second chance. For some of them, that might be enough. So when an old college classmate of Hayes's asked if he'd help with the physical education program, he'd volunteered.

"You don't want *any* money?" Charlie Grubbs asked.

"A cup of coffee now and then," Hayes replied. "Hey, man, I still got money coming in from the Army."

"Sure as hell can't be a disability pension," Grubbs said, looking over Hayes's lithe and limber six-feet plus.

"Who said it was?" Hayes answered, and that was the end of the discussion. Grubbs knew about Hayes's career as a black revolutionary and about his time on a Southern chain gang. He didn't know much about what happened after that, the SEALS and the African liberation movements. He didn't know a thing about the Soldiers of Barrabas, and Claude Hayes would make sure he never did.

Hayes's running shoes slapped the pavement in a steady rhythm. Past a boarded-up theater—no, one being renovated. Harlem wasn't nearly as dead as it had been fifteen, twenty years earlier. It would be nice if some of these boys could come back to life as easily.

Behind Hayes, the pounding feet got louder. He risked a look back over his shoulder. Damned if those kids weren't trying to catch up with him! They probably thought they ought to be able to run a middle-aged asshole like him into the ground without working up a good sweat.

Those boys were about to learn a lesson.

Adrenaline flowed into Hayes's system as if he'd opened a tap. A pile of litter sprawled across his path. Without breaking stride he jumped it, coming down running on the other side. Clatters and crunches told him the boys behind him hadn't done quite so well.

Hayes stepped up the pace until he was holding his distance from the fastest three boys. The rest were beginning to straggle. A couple of them looked as if they were going to be in trouble before long.

"Hey, remember the rules about helping each other!" Hayes yelled back.

Two of the leaders gave him the finger again and kept running. One of them nodded and dropped back to help the stragglers. Hayes wasn't surprised to see it was Otis Gleeson. Survivor of a broken home, gangs, drugs and detention centers, Gleeson still somehow had strength to spare for others. Give him a chance to live some way other than dog-eat-dog, and he'd take it.

Hayes slowed to a trot for the final two blocks to the home. Otis Gleeson was the last one in, helping the fattest of the stragglers with an arm around his shoulders.

"Ain't my brother, but he still ain't heavy," Gleeson called to Hayes as he climbed the steps.

Grubbs stuck his head out of the office. Hayes had seen telephone booths larger than the office, but Grubbs didn't seem to care. The home usually didn't have two spare nickels to rub together, and if it did, they were spent on the boys.

"Got a call for you while you were out," Grubbs said. He pointed to a number scribbled in red pencil on the peeling yellow wall to the right of the phone. "Said you'd call back as soon as you came in."

Hayes looked at the number and nodded. "Old service buddy. Probably wants to know if I'm available for a consultation job."

"You going to say yes if he asks?"

"Depends on how much and how long. The guy saved my ass a couple of times in Vietnam and a couple of times more after that. So I still owe him one, if he really needs it."

"Damn," Grubbs said. "Claude, you are about the best thing to come down the pike for these boys since I started working here. I sure hope to hell you can stay around."

"If I can't, I'll get back as soon as I can," Hayes said. "That's a promise."

As he dialed Nile Barrabas's New York message drop, Hayes knew he'd spoken the truth. If he came back from this job in a body bag—or not at all, the more likely fate for a merc—the Cavendish Boys' Home was shit out of luck. Otherwise Charlie Grubbs and the boys had a piece of him for as long as they needed him. Running those twelve kids through the streets of Harlem was a lot more fun than anything else he'd found to do between missions—out of bed, at least. A man couldn't keep it up all the time!

"Claude here," he said when the recorded message told him to speak. "I'm available and I'll be at the meeting."

He hung up and turned to Charlie. "I got a feeling this may be a long one. Mind if I lay some bread on you so you can hire someone to cover for me if this takes a month or so?"

"Does the bear shit in the woods? Okay, but bring your black ass back in one piece, brother. Those boys need you, and that means *I* need you."

"Gee, just what I always wanted. A hundred boys warm for my form."

It wasn't so funny when you thought about it. Had he finally found a place where he could do more good than he could wasting bad guys?

Maybe. Or maybe he was just thinking he had, because he
knew his parents would have approved of his work here a lot
more than anything else he'd done. They were dead now,
but his sister still thought the same way. Was he getting old
enough to want peace with his family, even if it meant giving up living on the edge? Living in the only place he'd ever
felt really alive?

A lot of questions, no answers, and anyway, the answers
could wait. What couldn't was packing a bag and heading
for Boston.

That was a funny place to plan a mission, but who could
tell? Maybe the Fixer was on to a Soviet plot to infiltrate the
codfish!

> "So live every day knowing you might die.
> To live that way spits in death's eye.
> Fear's the only thing that kills.
> The rest is just a clash of wills."

Tepid applause rose from Liam O'Toole's audience in the
North Beach bar. He listened to it, looked at the other poets,
guitar players and the saints only knew who else waiting
their turn on amateur night, and sighed.

An encore would not be a good idea.

He jumped down from the stage of planks set across
sawhorses. Somebody shoved a beer as tepid as the applause into his hands. He'd chugged half of it when he
found somebody else in his path.

"Hey, man. You talk like, you know, you *been* there."

O'Toole sized up the speaker as some kind of student,
bigger, softer and drunker than he was. Also not very smart
even when he was sober.

"I have."

"Nam?"

"Among other places."

"You a real live mercenary?"

"Would I be standing here hoping you'll be after gettin' out of me way if I weren't alive?"

O'Toole saw a fight shaping up, and he didn't want it. He also saw three other student types weaving through the tables toward him. He didn't know if they were coming to restrain their friend or join him in the beating.

O'Toole didn't want to find out. Not that a fight would be difficult—four yahoos like this were no more than healthy exercise to work up a decent thirst. But it would be messy and expensive and lead to hassle and no more drinking in San Francisco's North Beach bar strip. A man who liked his liquor and his women, Liam O'Toole didn't want to have any more bar strips closed against him.

He decided to use a variant of the drunken parrot technique that had turned him into an unorthodox but effective martial-arts adept. As the students closed in, O'Toole seemed to become a spinning top. Without touching them, he sailed up onto a table to their left. Then he sailed off the table, landing spring legged on the floor behind them.

They whirled around so fast that two of them collided and fell over, landing on a table at which a middle-aged woman sat alone. She jumped clear as the table went over, but her coffee and sandwich were a total loss, part landing on the floor, the rest spilling on the two students.

From the front and back of the room, the owner and his two bouncers converged on the scene. O'Toole decided to split before the owner decided he'd have to go, too. He'd done his best to avoid a fight, but some of the students might have parents with clout.

So the owner would have to look impartial, and that meant rousting O'Toole, as well. It wasn't fair, but in a long career in several armies—including the Irish Republican—Liam O'Toole had learned how much to count on fairness.

It made the gold of the leprechauns look like a Swiss bank account.

Outside, the night fog was rolling in. Or maybe the day-time fog had never left. O'Toole was lighting a cigar, when he sensed someone behind him.

"You *do* look like a man who's been there. Sound like it, too."

It was the woman who'd lost her meal. In the fog-dimmed streetlights she still appeared middle-aged, but a very trim middle age.

"Like I told those guys, I have been."

"I wondered. You sounded a lot like a man I knew in Vietnam. I was a nurse in the hospital where they sent him after his LRRP team ran into trouble. I guess you could say we were in love. At least, I was. I don't know if he ever loved anything but fighting and training his Viets to fight, too."

"Do I remind you of him?"

O'Toole wished he'd been able to think of a brighter an-swer. This wasn't a violence groupie, a Rambolina. This was somebody who knew something about living on the edge.

"Quite a lot. But there's one important difference. You're alive. Raul's dead. They still say he's MIA, but I can't see him as a prisoner. He—"

One of the bouncers stuck his head out the door. "Mr. O'Toole?"

"Hey, I'll pay for the damage—"

"Not that. Boss says there's a call for you. Something about a speaking engagement with Associated Charities."

"Can I take it in the office?"

"Sure."

The woman was looking at him. Returning her gaze, O'Toole saw that she had mahogany-colored hair and, if her slacks didn't hide too much, spectacular legs.

"Sorry, hon. I'm their adviser on veterans' affairs. They've got somebody else to advise them on veterans' marriages."

The woman smiled. "You single?"

"Two-time loser. Faults o' both sides, I always thought."

Which was why O'Toole stuck to one-night or maybe weekend stands now. Marriage wasn't for him. An indignant husband could come at you with a gun, but that wasn't half of what a divorce could do.

"Maybe I should get myself another sandwich while you're on the phone."

"Make that two, and a Bushmills on the rocks, if they have any."

The woman gave a mock salute. O'Toole hurried inside, hoping she really would wait and cursing Nile Barrabas and call forwarding.

Associated Charities was one of the cover names Barrabas used for calling the team together. It wasn't what you'd call deep cover, and O'Toole hoped the nurse wasn't job hunting.

As for call forwarding, without it Barrabas's call to O'Toole's current pad up by the Presidio wouldn't have tracked him down at the Frog Pond. O'Toole began to regret spending some of his Hollywood checks on fancy telephones. At least the checks didn't bounce, which was about all he could say for his brush with Hollywood.

He'd hoped to make connections there that would finally get his poems into print. Instead he'd been bought and paid for as a technical adviser for some spectacularly dumb action flicks. He remembered one scene where the superstar playing the hero had mowed down a whole VC company with an M-60 in each hand!

That was a physical impossibility, of course. O'Toole had told them so. The superstar didn't give a damn, and the director cared more about keeping the superstar happy than about authenticity.

O'Toole's connection with the production had ended soon after that. But somewhere in the production company was an honest man, and every so often a sizable check found its way into Liam O'Toole's mailbox.

He reached the office, picked up the telephone, and there was Nile Barrabas on the line.

"We have a meeting of the Speakers' Committee in Newton, Massachusetts, at 2100 tomorrow."

O'Toole looked at his watch. "Colonel, with all due respect, the committee doesn't need me that badly."

"With all due respect, Mr. O'Toole, I disagree. Get your ass on a plane in time, or that ass will be grass."

"Okay, boss."

What else could he say? Barrabas didn't use that tone very often unless he thought something hot was about to break for the SOBs. He was usually right, too.

Maybe the nurse would go with a half-night stand?

And maybe pigs will fly.

O'Toole went back to the table. Not a glass but a whole bottle of Bushmills sat in the middle of it, surrounded by sandwiches.

"I recognized the look on your face," the woman said. "Raul had it when he was going into the bush. I—" She gripped O'Toole's hands.

"Your place or mine?" was all he was up to saying.

"Mine," she answered. "I'm about a mile from the airport. I can drop you off on the way to work."

O'Toole felt more charitable toward both Nile Barrabas and call forwarding. In fact, he felt more charitable toward the whole world.

He was too good an Irishman to doubt omens, and this was a good one for the coming mission. He even began to hope this wouldn't be his only time with—

"My name's Liam O'Toole. What's yours?"

WILLIAM STARFOOT II, known to the SOBs as Billy Two, walked across the sacred lands of the Osage Indians.

He kept expecting Hawk Spirit to come and walk with him, but so far this morning he'd covered ten miles and he was still alone.

As he reached the top of a low hill he decided to take off his shoes. He wore only faded Levi's and running shoes, but perhaps the running shoes were offending the spirits. Part of them was canvas that had once been living plants, but the rest was a product of the white man's chemistry.

Billy felt lighter when the shoes were hanging by their laces around his neck. He moved just as fast, since the soles of his feet were leather tough, hardened by martial-arts training and barefoot walking. He loped down the hill, skirted rusting barbed wire around an abandoned shack and began climbing the opposite hill.

In the little stand of greasewood near the top of the hill, he waited for Hawk Spirit to come to him. Briefly he thought about his first such experience, then wondered how the others saw him. He knew that Lee Hatton, the team's doctor, was the least skeptical about Hawk Spirit's reality. The rest tended to believe that Hawk Spirit was the result of brain damage Billy had suffered while in KGB hands. The interrogation techniques to which he'd been subjected had included injections of sulfuric acid.

Billy didn't doubt that his mind had been affected at that time. But he didn't view the results as damage. Rather, he'd experienced an opening of closed paths; he was aware now of what had once been beyond sight and hearing.

It seemed as though Hawk Spirit picked up on his thought, for he sought Billy out with a question.

"Have you joined them in doubting me?"

"Those were not my doubts in my thoughts, Hawk Spirit. I do not doubt you. And I do not doubt my bond to them. Do you find fault with that?"

"You feel very free to ask."

"I am a free man, not a slave to anyone, not even to you, Hawk Spirit, for surely then I would be worth less to you."

Hawk Spirit was silent again, but Billy sensed he was still present.

"Hawk Spirit, my warrior brothers and sister are as fit as I to walk the sacred lands of the Osage and see that justice is done. Indeed, there is so much to be done that all the others of my own blood, each and every one together, would be too few. My warrior comrades are needed, and they are of the kind that each one of them makes up for more than the work of several more ordinary people, but they, too, have diminished in number. That makes the weight on their shoulders even greater."

"That is true. Now that one is dead and a second has betrayed—"

"Nate Beck did not betray us!" Billy saw the cattle down the valley lift their ponderous heads and move away, and knew he must have shouted out loud. He returned to his silent communications. "Hawk Spirit, I cannot demand that you cease these insults. But I will not turn my loyalty from them, and will stand up for them even despite your anger...."

"Ah, yes. You said you were no slave."

"Yes, and I will say it as often as I must, until you *listen*."

Hawk Spirit was silent again, still present but apparently having nothing further to say. If the spirit wants me again, let him call, he decided.

For himself, he had to get back to his Blazer and check in with the old shaman whose guest he was. The god's reference to the SOBs probably foretold, as it had on other occasions, that the colonel was calling the team together for an assignment.

Billy started retracing his steps. Halfway back to the ruined hut, he began to run. His bare feet seemed to skim over the dry grass.

As he approached the barbed wire, he lengthened his stride, then leaped.

An ancient Osage war cry burst from his lips as the barbed wire flashed beneath him. He did not need to look back to know he had jumped farther than his own unaided muscles could ever have done.

Hawk Spirit, I thank you.

He might have just imagined it, but Billy thought he heard Hawk Spirit give a most unspiritual chuckle in reply.

LEE HATTON LAY on her back in the Caribbean sun, her tanned arms and legs stretched out across a huge yellow towel. A green-and-yellow-striped beach robe served as a pillow. She wore only sunglasses and a liberal coating of sunblock.

Under the sunglasses, her dark eyes were closed. The distant rumble of the surf and the cries of the gulls didn't break into her heavy thoughts.

The last time she'd lain nude on this Martinique beach Geoff Bishop had been with her. Now he was dead, probably not even buried, the victim of a hidden eddy of the secret wars.

A hidden eddy that was either so silly, so ugly or so secret that even Nile Barrabas wouldn't give her any details. As time went by, Lee found she resented the lack of information almost as much as the fact of Geoff's death.

Did Nile think she would go off half-cocked on some crazy private mission of vengeance? Did his ability to think of her as a comrade and not as a woman go only so far?

No. Probably even he didn't know exactly what had happened. Geoff wasn't the first mercenary to end up in an obscure grave. He wouldn't be the last, either.

Tinnnggg.

The alarm in the electronic watch tucked under the beach robe chimed insistently. Lee looked at the sun and decided she'd been out long enough. She wanted to tone up her naturally olive complexion with a tan, not acquire a blazing sunburn!

A pair of nude beachboy types walked past as Lee sat up. Their eyes lingered on her pleasantly, but she didn't return their looks. Like most of the men at Libre Soleil, they were too young for her. The rest were with women better looking than she was.

Still, it was nice to be able to enjoy a man's look again. She could even believe that someday she might meet another man she'd let do more than look.

She pulled on the robe, wrapped the towel into a turban around her hair and walked back to her cabin. She'd just finished her shower and had started giving herself a manicure, when the telephone rang.

She recognized the pattern of the ring, and as she expected, the caller was Nile Barrabas.

"Hello, Lee. Anything on?"

"I just stepped out of the shower, if that's what you mean."

"Fine. Just let me turn on my picture phone—"

"Nile, isn't this a business call?"

"Sorry, Lee, it is, strictly business. If you can get away to Boston by tomorrow night, it would help a lot. Call the Associated Charities number when you get into Logan, and they'll take it from there."

"Anything else I need to know?"

"There's a good chance we'll be expanding our programs. Start thinking of qualified people you know."

"I'll start thinking when I get on the plane. It's too nice and warm to think down here."

"Then it's a good thing I called. The atrophy of Dr. Leona Hatton's brain would be a disaster."

"Your flattery's improving, Nile. Have you been taking lessons from Alex or Liam?"

"Just practice. Have a good trip, Lee."

The phone clicked into silence. Lee finished her manicure and started on her toenails. She hoped Nile's new charm was being directed mostly toward Erika Dykstra. The last thing Lee needed was for Nile to start thinking of her as a woman.

No, that wasn't quite right. What she meant was she didn't want him to think of her as a woman in any way that would affect the team. Nile was in fact always aware that she was a woman as well as a doctor, a soldier, a martial-arts adept, and—along with Claude Hayes—resident conscience of the SOBs.

Come to think of it, she'd been aware of Nile Barrabas as a man for some time. She knew he was a man who had been in the same places she'd been, had seen what she could do in those places and understood how and why. There was a friendship there, and for her, that meant a certain potential. She needed friendship in any meaningful relationship.

Maybe she'd just put her finger on what she needed from men in an intimate involvement. With Geoff Bishop, it had been comradeship that turned into love.

Would the same thing ever happen with another man?

CHAPTER SIX

Pokrovsky walked around the Type 88 minisub. He didn't know what he was looking for, but that didn't bother him. He had a sixth sense that spotted things wrong with any diving equipment. He didn't understand it, couldn't put it into words, but his sixth sense was almost always right, and it had saved his life and the lives of his comrades a dozen times already.

The Type 88 filled almost half the dock. The new module with the larger dock for two more Type 88s was still on its way from Novorossisk. Pokrovsky wondered what the delay was. Probably some bureaucrat so eager to get away to his dacha with his mistress for a weekend that he hadn't signed the essential papers.

Well, the Soviet armed forces had survived Stalin and Hitler. They could survive horny bureaucrats, as long as there were men like Isakov and the Rope.

Stepping wide to clear the shrouded bow propeller, Pokrovsky came face-to-face with the Rope. He started, and had to look twice to make sure he hadn't conjured the man up by thinking about him.

The Rope wore his usual preoccupied expression and the stained coveralls the *zampolit* kept trying to banish. He had a small can of black paint in one hand and was painting a name on the sub's bow.

"*Galina*," Pokrovsky read. "Anybody I know?"

"She was from Odessa, before I joined the navy," the Rope said.

"She must go back to the days of the Golden Horde, then," Pokrovsky said. "I thought you'd been in the navy forever."

"Only since the time of Peter the Great," the Rope replied. "Galina was like this little iron lady. Very good, but dangerous if you didn't handle her right."

Pokrovsky nodded. The Type 88 was probably a generation ahead of every other midget submarine in the world. With a fuel cell based on the one used in the Mir space station, it could reach thirty knots as fast as a regular nuclear submarine. If you needed to be stealthy rather than quick, it had silent batteries and a rubber coating on the carefully designed hull. Creeping along the bottom, it was almost impossible to detect even in shallow water—and it could submerge to two hundred meters. No other midget submarine in the world could get you out of danger so quickly. It could get you into danger just as quickly if you were careless.

But Pokrovsky believed trouble was something he and *Galina* would make for others. It—no, with a woman's name this sub had to be "she"—could carry torpedoes, mines or divers for infiltration or sabotage, and could stay away from the mother ship for five days.

Pokrovsky was not afraid *Galina* and her sisters wouldn't be the deadliest weapons of the Spetsnaz. He was only afraid they wouldn't find worthy targets.

"In what way was our lady's namesake dangerous?" Pokrovsky asked.

"She liked sailors. Some of them didn't like her and said so. Two of those wound up dead in back alleys. Nobody could prove anything. Or at least nobody was allowed to prove anything."

"A high-ranking friend?"

"Who knows? I just hope our low-thinking *zampolit* doesn't come around before we leave."

Pokrovsky looked at his watch. "We'll be suiting up in an hour. Can you slap some tape over the paint before then?"

"Sure. It's almost dry already."

"Good. The first time we send a diver out, he can strip off the tape. When we come back, we'll have a few Turks in our bag. I'll stuff them in the comrade *zampolit*'s mouth if he opens it.''

The Rope saluted. "Aye, aye, Your Highness." A good many people knew Pokrovsky's nickname, "the Frog Prince," but only Team Typhoon was allowed to address him as "Your Highness."

It was closer to two hours than one before the three divers were suited up. But the *zampolit*'s curiosity was having an off day. He only mouthed a few platitudes about the Type 88 representing the superiority of socialist technology over capitalist, then insisted on shaking hands with Pokrovsky and the divers.

Pokrovsky couldn't avoid the handshake, but his hand didn't feel quite clean until an hour later, when he went outside himself and stripped off the tape. Five minutes later he was back inside, and *Galina* was arrowing north toward the Turkish coast.

CAPTAIN OKUZ WATCHED the Fathometer flare up like a match, then go dark. He stuck his head through the hatch and shouted down into the bilge. "What in God's name did you do to the Fathometer?"

"Tried to fix it, Captain, as you ordered me."

"Well, you fixed something all right. It's not reading at all now."

"Let me try splicing the wires."

Ali spliced, sliced, braided and unbraided the wires of the Fathometer. He got a couple of electric shocks, which made him swear loud enough to be heard in Crete. He worked for nearly an hour, as *Bodrun*'s ancient diesel carried her steadily closer to the rock-studded coast.

Nothing happened. The Fathometer stayed as dead as Suleiman the Magnificent.

Not that it had been anywhere near as useful, even when it was alive. But Okuz needed it if he was going to run his load of cement to its destination.

Ali finally came on deck, winding a bandage around an electrical burn. He shrugged. "I could try praying. I've tried everything else."

"Ask Mehmet for his *Koran*, then. Me, I'm going to get on the radio. Maybe Mr. Karatay can send out a boat to pilot us in."

"That'll delay delivery."

"It'll delay delivery a cursed lot more if he has to fish his cement off the bottom of the sea!" Captain Okuz snarled.

Personally, he didn't much care whether Karatay built a warehouse with the cement or rammed it up his arse. The man did pay, though. Okuz needed customers who paid, to keep *Bodrun* running for a few more years. When he finally grew too old for even coastal voyages, then he could see her towed off for scrap. They'd been together too long for him to give her up as long as he could still stand on her bridge.

Okuz threw the engine room telegraph over to DEAD SLOW. The asthmatic rumble of the diesel changed to a faint purr, and the wake turned from white foam to a ripple.

The deckhand went forward to unship the anchor for lowering. Okuz unfolded a chart, checking anchorages. He'd memorized every one along this coast years ago, but he couldn't be sure Karatay wouldn't need chart references.

Half an hour later they were in the lee of the Maiden's Reef, and Okuz signaled to let go the anchor. It squealed and rattled down into the blue water as the diesel coughed to silence. *Bodrun* swung gently in twelve meters of water, two hundred meters from the rocks of the reef.

Okuz told the deckhand to start dinner and headed for the radio. As he climbed down the hatch, he took a last look at the sky. Fine and fair, just as the weather broadcasters had said. They probably wouldn't need the lee of the island, but Okuz wouldn't have managed to sail the Mediterranean and the Atlantic for fifty years if he'd taken unnecessary chances.

FIVE HUNDRED METERS farther offshore, Pokrovsky's eye was glued to a small periscope. With less than ten centimeters of the periscope exposed, there was small chance of its being seen unless someone was actually searching for it.

The coastal freighter looked to the Soviet diver as if she wouldn't notice a full-size attack submarine until it surfaced alongside her. He increased the magnification. No doubt about it. The ragged flag at the stern was Turkish.

"That ship must have been built when Kemal Ataturk was a boy," he muttered.

His orders to choose a Turkish target were too strict to ignore. But couldn't he find some excuse to let this ancient crock rust in peace and make *Galina*'s first kill something more worthy?

In a full-scale war the Type 88s would sneak into NATO anchorages and torpedo anything there, even a full-size supercarrier or a tender loaded with admirals and irreplaceable technicians. It was too much to expect that the Turks would offer anything remotely like that now.

Pokrovsky believed in good and bad luck for ships. It would not be good luck for *Galina* or the Type 88s if their first kill was this sitting pile of rust and museum-piece parts.

"I could go out and put a limpet mine on her," the fourth crewman volunteered. Known as "Thunderclap," he was a younger, blonder version of the Rope, assigned to *Galina* for her first mission because of his excellent record.

Pokrovsky wished the man's excellent record had included the ability to keep his mouth shut when his commanding officer wanted to think.

"She's anchored in ten meters of water, maybe less," the Golden Giant said. "In this clear water, they might see the diver."

"I would be careful."

"I'm sure you would. If the Turks were lucky, that wouldn't be enough. We'd lose you *and* the secret of the Type 88s."

The thought of endangering a state secret shut up Thunderclap for a while, as Pokrovsky considered the options.

Galina had four torpedoes strapped to her hull. They were modified versions of the standard forty-centimeter antisubmarine torpedo. Now they could use wire-guidance as well as acoustic homing. They had also been modified to remove any parts of unmistakably Soviet origin.

Anchored and with her engines stopped, the Turkish ship was too quiet for the torpedo to home in on her acoustic signature. Wire-guidance would be better, as long as the wire didn't snag on the bottom.

A straight shot with no homing or guidance would also work against this close, motionless target. Except that if the torpedo's depth control was off, it might ram the bottom. Pokrovsky was tempted. If the explosion startled the target into movement, the hunt would be far more exciting.

Maybe too exciting. Pokrovsky could do without facing Turkish antisubmarine forces at this stage of Operation Claw. That would be safer later, when the Greek navy was also at sea, ready to shoot at the Turks if they raised an eyebrow, let alone launched a torpedo.

Wire-guidance it would be.

"Are we going to do nothing? I did not think I was sailing with defeatists."

Pokrovsky's glare at the Rope was all that kept him from shoving Thunderclap through a bulkhead. Another glare turned the boy's face red. Pokrovsky wondered if he was an agent or just naturally tactless.

"Set torpedo two for wire-guidance. Quarter speed and keep it five meters clear of the bottom. Giant, she's all yours."

Torpedo two's screws purred to life. *Galina* jerked slightly as a half ton of weight left her. Thunderclap instantly adjusted the ballast to maintain depth.

Pokrovsky remembered that once he'd been a green boy with a fine record in training, no experience and a big mouth. Maybe Thunderclap's condition wasn't incurable, after all.

"Torpedo running normally," the Giant said.

Pokrovsky looked through the periscope again. No sign of the torpedo, no sign of alert Turks.

"Bottom rising. Bringing the fish up to ten meters," the Giant said. "Distance to target, one hundred meters."

"Full speed!" Pokrovsky said.

The whine of the twin screws speeding up came clearly through the water. The Turks would surely hear it, but it was too late now....

THE EXPLOSION was so violent that Captain Okuz didn't realize at first that it was an explosion. Deafened and half-stunned, he staggered to his feet from the corner of the bridge where he'd landed. Then he thanked God that he'd fallen. Shattered glass lay everywhere. A few shards stuck into his knees and hands, but the rest could have shredded his face if he'd been standing.

From below he heard the sound of metal straining, then rending apart with a machine-gun popping of rivets. Someone began to scream, long continuous howls of agony.

The deck was already heeling as Okuz plunged down the hatch. He landed off balance and fell, rolling nearly to Ali's feet. The mate was holding the deckhand, one arm pinned behind his back and a napkin stuffed in his mouth.

One look told Okuz who had been screaming and why. The deckhand must have been thrown against the stove, then doused with hot fat. His skin seemed to be all blisters where it wasn't charred half off.

The deck heeled farther. Okuz lurched to his feet, clawed for a handhold, then fell again. He cursed the years that had robbed him of so much strength.

"Captain, we have to get clear!"

"Mehmet—"

"The engine's off its bed. Mehmet's under it. If he wasn't dead right away, he's gone now. There's two meters of water in the engine room."

Now Okuz cursed those who'd robbed him of his ship and an old friend.

Ali cut him off. "Help me get the boy up the ladder, or we'll have to leave him to drown."

That would be dishonorable for a captain, unless he wanted to stay and go down with Mehmet, the boy and *Bodrun*.

No. Those who'd destroyed her would have no more easy victories.

Ali scrambled up the ladder. Okuz gripped the deckhand's belt and held him up, high enough for the mate to grab him. They all reached the bridge just as the port railing touched the water. As they hurried out the door, *Bodrun* lay over completely on her beam ends.

For a moment she hung there, air bubbling out of every port and ventilator and all the seams sprung by the explosion. In that moment the three men were able to scramble down the hull and push off from the weedy bottom into the water. Then *Bodrun* gave a final lurch and sank. A spreading patch of bubbles marked her resting place.

Okuz trod water, waiting for the life raft that was supposed to be released automatically. It finally popped to the surface, fully inflated.

Okuz looked at the reef two hundred meters away. It seemed more like two thousand, but with despair gone he felt stronger.

The deckhand was screaming again, as saltwater seared his burns. Ali finally had to knock him unconscious. While the mate supported the burned man, Okuz swam back and forth, collecting floating wreckage.

At last they had a crude raft that would keep the boy's head out of water. Okuz used his belt to tie the deckhand in place, then he and Ali started paddling toward the reef.

POKROVSKY KEPT the periscope down as the Turkish freighter sank. Any survivors would be too busy to look for periscopes, but why take unnecessary risks? Besides, the roar of escaping air and the scream of collapsing bulkheads was enough to tell him what was happening. At this range, the Russians didn't even need the sonar to hear the sound of a dying ship.

Pokrovsky looked around the closet-size control room. Two of the three men wore sober expressions. A ship sailed by men who lived by the sea had just been destroyed. Her destruction and their deaths served the cause of socialism. But that didn't make it something good sailors could enjoy.

Thunderclap, however, was grinning. He even threw his hands over his head and did a little dance. That ended abruptly when he banged his shins on a pipe. He resumed his seat, rubbed the bruises, saw Pokrovsky's expression and settled down.

"Propeller noises, bearing 260," the Rope said. "Coming on steadily. Sounds like a twin-screw merchant vessel with old diesels."

Pokrovsky raised the periscope cautiously and turned it. Approaching from the open sea was a small passenger ship, with a dirty white hull and a dirtier blue funnel amidships. Pokrovsky tried to make out the funnel markings, but the angle was wrong.

"We've got company," he said. "Looks like one of those little combination ferry and cruise ships. Don't know if our Turkish friends got off a distress call, or the ship just happened to be in the area."

He was lowering the periscope, when Thunderclap piped up, "What about sinking him, too? A really major incident like that would serve the interests of—"

"The only interests to be served right now are yours," Pokrovsky said in a chilly voice. "They will be served best by shutting your mouth."

Thunderclap either realized he'd gone too far, or was a good actor. "I beg your pardon, Comrade Captain. I wasn't implying you lacked zeal. Really, I wasn't."

"No, you were just implying I hadn't thought matters through. Sink a dirty little freighter that nobody but the Greeks and the Turks will care about, and they hate each other too much to cooperate on an investigation.

"But a passenger ship with a couple of hundred people aboard, maybe some of them tourists from NATO countries—that's another matter entirely. Everybody and the devil's grandmother would investigate it. If they found anything suspicious, NATO would be involved right away. We don't want that, not until the Greeks and Turks are already at one another's throats."

Pokrovsky locked the periscope and looked at the bottom profile on the sonar display. "Rope, take us right down onto the bottom. I want to be looking up at the tops of tall boulders. Then take us out of here dead slow, course 325."

That would get them into a deeper patch of water where *Galina* could cut her fuel cells and head for home at high speed. Or she could bottom and listen passively, with little chance of being detected and a good chance of detecting potential targets—or threats.

With a good sonarman like the Rope, Pokrovsky could decide which course to follow when he reached deep water and heard what was going on. Submariners were a lot like jazz musicians. They played practically everything by ear.

ADRIENNE BIGGLE WAS sleeping off lunch, when a sudden change in the beat of the engines woke her. Then the deck heeled so, she half climbed, half rolled out of bed. Overhead on the main deck she heard pounding feet and shouts in Greek about preparing a boat for lowering.

She jerked on clothes and sneakers, then ran up on deck. As she arrived, the engines slowed sharply, then went into reverse.

She sat cross-legged on a box of life preservers to listen to the conversation around her.

"Hurry up with that aft fall, you son of a pasha! We're in Turkish territorial waters, or damned near!"

"I'd be working faster if somebody whose ancestors ran on four legs hadn't forgotten to oil the davit."

"Why the devil should we worry about that sinking, anyway? Ten to one it's a Turkish ship."

"Ten to one they've seen us. If we steam off and leave them to drown—"

"They'll only get what the goat-fuckers deserve!"

"Shut up and get that boat lowered, or I'll demote you all to ballast!"

The last threat was voiced by a boatswain's mate who'd tried a pass at Adrienne. She decided to forgive him for the way his men shut up.

The reversed screws had pulled *Circe* to a complete stop. With many screeches and jerks and a few more curses, one of the lifeboats settled into the water. Another round of curses, and its engine coughed into life. It sounded like someone with terminal pneumonia, but the boat did get moving.

By now most of the passengers were on deck, staring at the lifeboat as it headed toward a low-lying island about a mile to the north. Rumors ran wild through the crowd, with everything from a sunken submarine to the start of World War III explaining their sudden stop.

Finally the captain had the sense to get on the PA system, in Greek, then accented English, then the worst French Adrienne had ever heard.

"Ladies and gentlemen, do not be alarmed. We have sighted a sinking ship near an island. We are sending a boat to search for survivors. Please stand back from the railing when the boat returns. If anyone aboard is a doctor, he should come to the officer's mess immediately. Thank you."

The captain wasn't as calm as he wanted the passengers to be, for long before the boat returned, he started the engines again. *Circe* swung in a wide circle, while the captain leaned over the wing of the bridge and swore at the saints, fate and Turks. Adrienne tried to pretend she didn't understand what she was hearing.

Circe slowed as the lifeboat returned. The three survivors looked like Turks—one battered and bloody old man, one intact and middle-aged and a youth who'd been horribly burned. Adrienne hurried aft to the gangway when the boat came alongside.

As the burned man reached the deck, he woke up and started screaming. Two sailors grabbed him, trying to keep him from rolling overboard. The middle-aged man appeared to think they were attacking his shipmate. He knocked one of the Greeks sprawling, got a headlock on the other and started wrestling him toward the side.

One of the Greek officers drew a small pistol. Adrienne took a deep breath, then let out a shriek. She knew she sounded like a hysterical woman. She also knew she wasn't entirely acting. "The Greeks are trying to save your friend," she said to the Turks in their language. "They are sailors, too."

Speaking in Turkish got her even more attention than the scream. The officer pointed his pistol at Adrienne, who loathed guns. She felt her stomach turn to lead, but she swallowed and went on addressing the rescued Turks.

"Gentlemen, I am an American archaeologist. I speak both Greek and Turkish. If I watch over your friend to make sure nothing happens to him, will you let the Greek doctor treat his burns? Otherwise he will die."

The boy might die, anyway, and he would certainly be scarred for life. But it wouldn't help him or anybody else to have a minor war aboard *Circe*.

The oldest Turk, apparently the captain, stared at Adrienne the longest and hardest. She silently cursed the Muslim attitude toward women, then sighed with relief as he nodded.

Circe's captain scrambled down the ladder from the bridge. He ordered the crew to clear out some of the spectators and push the rest back. In halting English, he said to the Turkish captain, "The lady speaks right. We have a doctor. Also, we call a Turkish helicopter. It come, fly man to hospital."

The Turkish captain looked blank. Adrienne started to translate, then saw two black dots lift over the horizon, trailing smoke. For a moment she thought they were helicopters, here already. Then she saw that the dots were moving much too fast.

With frightening speed the dots took shape—two Phantom IIs racing toward *Circe*, barely a hundred feet above the waves. The planes banked and turned slightly to whoosh past her on either side, still just above masthead height. Everyone saw the Turkish markings.

Everyone also clapped his hands over his ears to shut out the howl of the jets. Adrienne closed her eyes, as well, and coughed from the fumes. When she opened her eyes, the Phantoms were pulling up in a climbing turn. She heard one Greek wishing for a machine gun.

"Get on the radio to those devil's spawn of Turkish pilots!" the captain shrieked. "Tell them we are in Turkish waters on a lifesaving mission. Saving Turkish lives! Tell them that if they buzz us again like that and crash, we'll let the bastards drown!"

Adrienne couldn't blame the captain. She also knew he'd made a mistake. The Turkish captain's face was set in a grim mask. He might not understand English, but he certainly understood Greek.

NILE BARRABAS TURNED OFF the television, leaned back in the lounger and opened another bottle of beer. He felt confidence in his ability to project a more relaxed attitude than what he was actually experiencing.

The TV report on the sinking of the Turkish boat had lasted only a minute. After a laxative commercial, another minute had gone to footage of Turks demonstrating outside the Greek Embassy in Ankara. An orderly demonstration this time, but, then, only one Turk had died. What would happen when—not if—the Greeks retaliated for the riot and the death toll ran higher?

Whatever happened, it would be nasty. Fortunately some of the world's best preventers of nastiness, the Soldiers of Barrabas, were about to take the field. Without their usual fee—Barrabas wasn't looking forward to breaking that bit of news—but with their usual talents.

"Okay, people," he said. "This is a bit unusual, because we're taking a mission without our usual half million guaranteed. We've got expenses and a thousand dollars a day, plus all the equipment we think we'll need."

"Or at least all the Fixer pretends he can screw out of his higher-ups," Liam O'Toole grunted. "Nile, have you lost your bloody marbles?"

This was no time to play the Big Bad Colonel. The SOBs were among the most unorthodox professionals in their business, but they were professionals. That meant they didn't like to be cheated. Cheating them, in fact, was frowned on by insurance companies, as a few people had discovered.

"Both Turks and Greeks have been disappearing mysteriously in a particular area of the Aegean Sea. Alex Nanos came to me with a hunch that somebody's trying to start trouble between the Greeks and the Turks. More trouble than usual, that is," Barrabas added. "I agree with Alex. So does the Fixer—"

"But not enough to bankroll a regular mission?" Lee Hatton put in.

Barrabas heard the ice tinkling in her quiet words. "No. The Fixer's on our side. He'll be even more on our side after this incident. But higher-ups hold the purse strings, and he may not carry enough weight with them."

The joke made them all laugh, which thawed the atmosphere.

Barrabas went on. "So anybody who doesn't want to put their ass on the line this time can say no, without prejudice to future missions. If you say no, you can also leave before the briefing."

The temperature in the room dropped again. Barrabas kicked himself mentally for the insult implicit in his clumsy phrasing. First Erika, then his own people! His interpersonal skills recently hadn't been what you could call brilliant.

"Of course I'm not implying that any of you is a security risk. But if this turns into a real live mission, some of the bad guys' friends might decide to find out what you know. Why buy the farm without a chance to shoot back?"

Billy Two laughed. A grizzly bear who'd just played a practical joke might have sounded just like him. "Colonel, we are already on so goddamn many hit lists that if our enemies all showed up at once it'd be Times Square on New Year's Eve! One more or less won't make a friggin' bit of difference. I'm on."

"Same here," Claude Hayes said.

"Count me in," Liam O'Toole added.

"Lee?" Barrabas asked.

"Do I look like an idiot?" she said with a faint smile. "I know what Alex's hunches are worth. I just hope somebody else has a hunch that we're on a real mission and worth a real fee."

"Amen, sister," Hayes said.

ADRIENNE BIGGLE SLITHERED into the rubber dinghy. She could handle a yacht, swim or scuba dive with the best, but she and small boats didn't get along.

Mustafa promptly gunned the outboard motor and swung away from *Circe* as if she were on fire. The dinghy bounced like a Ping-Pong ball through the light chop. Adrienne hung on to everything she could grab, including Mustafa. She hoped she'd be able to hang on to her lunch.

"Slow down, for God's sake!" she finally cried.

"I want to get away from those Greeks," the Turk growled, opening the throttle wider.

"They're not going to shoot us!"

"Not with foreigners aboard, I suppose," he said. "But you can never tell with Greeks."

"You sound like Captain Okuz."

"You mean I sound like a Turk. You Americans eat at Greek restaurants and think you know the Greeks. We Turks live next to them and see things differently."

Adrienne recognized a man whose mind was too closed to admit any new facts. She decided to shut up before the man became totally convinced she sympathized with the Greeks. That was all the camp needed—to have work come to a complete halt or even to have a riot!

Calmer water in the lee of the island brought a calmer frame of mind. As they glided toward the landing, Adrienne took off her hat and wrung the water out of it.

"Any messages?" she asked Mustafa.

"One. From the Professor Stewart. He says he will be in America longer than he planned. There are some new sightings to run through a computer. Also, he says that he has authorized Cheryl's friend to buy a new boat for the expedition."

"Cheryl's friend?"

"Why should not the lovely Cheryl have friends? Many friends? Alas, that I am not one of them. She is such a delight—a woman of experience who looks like a dewy girl—"

Mustafa went off into rhapsodies about Cheryl, which Adrienne listened to with only half an ear. She was wondering why the message hadn't mentioned Cheryl's friend's name.

Was Stewart trying to hide something? If so, what? And from whom, besides herself? If he was getting back into bed with the Naval Research Laboratory or Naval Intelligence, this time she was going to go after his hide. If she couldn't line up faculty support, she'd see about contacting the students.

Damn the man! Couldn't he see that the Pentagon just wanted to use him and throw him away? Didn't he see that he could ruin Hayward College's chances of ever doing underwater archaeology again?

Didn't he see that he could ruin her career?

"WE'LL START MOVING OUT in the next couple of days," Barrabas concluded. "Unless Alex runs into trouble finding a boat, we'll be fully operational with our personal gear in a week, whether we're official or not. Now, any questions?"

"What about sterile gear?" Billy Two asked.

"Sterile gear" meant weapons and equipment not traceable to any particular country. In some areas this could be critical. But this mission was located where people had been shooting at one another for generations with weapons and gear from every corner of the world.

"When in doubt, don't buy American," Barrabas said. "Otherwise get the best. I don't want to bet on Jessup making his deliveries on time."

The others nodded. That would be betting their lives. They did that every mission, but not foolishly or unnecessarily.

"Any more intelligence on water conditions in the Aegean?" Claude Hayes said. He and Alex Nanos would be the team's principal divers, on a mission where the divers would undoubtedly be the point men.

"If Professor Stewart gets free in time, yes. He's down in Connecticut, feeding data to Nate Beck. Nate's doing special software for some experimental computerized minisonars."

Lee Hatton had been rubbing neat's-foot oil into the sheath of her twelve-inch combat knife. At the mention of Nate Beck the long fingers stopped, knotted briefly, then began stroking the leather again.

"These new sonars are supposed to give a fishing boat the ASW detection power of a regular destroyer. Apparently somebody higher up decided to let us field-test them."

"I see," Liam O'Toole grunted. "Just because we're deniable, doesn't mean we can't play guinea pigs."

"Liam, at your age do politicians have any surprises for you?"

"No, and it's one of the few things that're not makin' me wish I were younger. If you're going swimming with sharks, it's no bad thing to know where all their teeth are." He drained the last of his beer, then sailed the bottle precisely across the room into the wastebasket.

The SOBs sat and chatted for a few more minutes. That was long enough for Barrabas to make eye contact with Lee Hatton. Without a word, she stayed behind when the others left.

"Still problems over Nate's retirement?"

Lee shook her head. "I had some. But that was back when every time I threw the knife, the target had the face of Geoff's killer on it."

"I'll put a face on him if I can," Barrabas said. He'd made that promise to himself the day after he'd learned of Geoff Bishop's death. This was the first time he'd made it out loud to Lee.

"I know. But—I don't need that anymore. I'm past that. Just like I'm past being angry with Nate." She grinned, suddenly looking like a teenager. "You know what I'd have done if I'd had Nate as a patient?"

"What?"

"Advised him to do just what he did. He lived on the edge for as long as he wanted to. Much longer and he'd have been forcing himself. It would have just been a matter of time till he was gone, maybe taking somebody else with him. As it is, everybody's safe. Besides, Nate's the only one who's as useful on standby as in the field. We muscle types can't program minisonars."

Lee's knife flashed once as she drew it. It flashed a second time as it turned over in the air. It flashed a last time as it *thunked* into the wall above the wastebasket. A man standing there would have taken the knife in his throat.

Lee retrieved her knife and followed Barrabas out of the room.

CHAPTER SEVEN

The last crate thumped into the back of the Magirus-Deutz
ten-wheeler. Walker Jessup checked it off on his notepad,
then shoved the notepad into a pocket of his safari jacket.
It made another bulge, nicely balancing the pocket calcu-
lator and the Colt Python.

All of them together didn't make as big a bulge as Walker
Jessup's belly. Down to a comparatively svelte three
hundred twenty pounds, he still strained buttons and seams.

The Spanish Guardia Civil lieutenant turned and scanned
the street before cupping his hands to light another cigarette. When it was drawing well, he grinned. "Well, Mr.
Jessup. I will not say that you now owe the Guardia. I will
only say that my colonel thinks we are now—efen-stephen
is the English phrase?"

"About that," Jessup said, doing his own scan of the
dark street in this industrial suburb of Barcelona. He'd have
felt better if the arms shipment could have been delivered
straight dockside. Years of experience told him that any
unnecessary overland trip for your assets gave any turkey a
chance to take them out.

Jessup remembered something called Sturgeon's Law:
Ninety-two percent of everything is crap. That went for terrorists and thugs, too. A minority were professionals who
made it a kill-or-be-killed situation. A vast majority were
klutzes who could be relied on to massacre one another if
you just took ordinary precautions.

"I don't suppose Colonel Navarro's had his last bit of
help from us, debt or no debt," Jessup added. "We've had
interests in common for quite a few years. That's not going
to change, even if *glasnost* is all it's cracked up to be."

"That will happen at cocktail hour on the day of judgment," the lieutenant said. But he was smiling as he started to lash canvas across the back of the truck. The canvas, like the boxes, had stenciled on it the logo of a well-known Spanish motorcycle manufacturer.

The SOBs were looking after personal weapons and diving gear. Jessup was providing their surface firepower. Inside the crates of "motorcycle parts" were West German G-3 assault rifles, M-16s with M-203 grenade launchers, a pair of 90-mm recoilless rifles—old but still potent—and enough ammunition for all the weapons to fight a small war.

The lieutenant put the last knots in the lashing, and the driver started the engine.

Jessup pulled out a French five-franc piece. "Toss for who rides in back?"

"Señor Jessup, to add you to the weight already on the rear wheels—do I look like a fool?" The lieutenant shifted his H&K MP-5 around and started to climb into the back.

As the Spaniard's feet left the filthy stones of the back street, Jessup heard a sound like a sharp cough. From an alley near the corner something leaped, trailing flame.

The lieutenant cursed. The driver put the truck in gear. The lieutenant would have cursed again, but the LAW round struck him first. His arms, head and chest flew into the truck. His legs thumped to the street. His stomach and hips sprayed in all directions.

Jessup leaped up as he saw the truck about to back over him. If he'd been five pounds heavier he'd never have made it. As it was, the rear bumper knocked him to his knees.

That was a stroke of luck. The lieutenant's MP-5 lay under the truck, apparently intact. Jessup snatched it out as he drew his Python with the other hand. He fired two shots from the Python. Then he pointed the MP-5 in the general direction of the alley and let fly.

The burst didn't keep one alley rat from launching a second LAW, but it spoiled his aim. The rocket flew high, exploding against the canopy frame. Charred canvas showered Jessup. The canopy started smoldering.

The driver jumped out, cradling his own SMG. Jessup grabbed the man by the belt and the collar and shoved him back into his seat. "Drive, you idiot!"

The man glared at Jessup and started to draw a knife. Jessup remembered too late that Spaniards were touchy about being manhandled.

Then a third LAW round blew the rear bumper nearly off its brackets. Hot bits punctured the truck's gas tank. Gas gushed out, catching fire as it flowed over more hot fragments.

In three seconds the street under the rear of the truck was knee-deep in gasoline flames. This time Jessup didn't try to keep the driver from jumping out. He was too busy running for his life. He and the driver found a doorway just in time. The flames torched up and reached the gas tank. It exploded. A moment later, so did the ammunition.

Even in the doorway the blast knocked Jessup flat. He stayed down, among the garbage and dog turds, while pieces of the truck and the SOBs' arsenal rained down for blocks around. So did pieces of roofing, odd bricks, chunks of glass, stray cats and everything else the blast had knocked loose.

Jessup lifted his chin out of the garbage and saw one of the hit squad lying in the mouth of the alley. Some of his essential parts were missing, including his head. An unfired LAW lay beside him.

Brrrpppp!

Jessup jumped as the driver let off a burst. He didn't risk laying hands on the man again. Instead he worked his MP-5 out from under his belly and dug a chunk of debris out of the barrel. He was ready to join the party, as soon as a target showed up.

None did. What showed up was what looked like a motorized battalion of Guardia Civil, army and Barcelona police. They swarmed up and down the street, poked into every alley, tripped over bits of the truck and shouted at one another. Jessup's ears were still ringing from the blast. He really wished the Spaniards would make less noise!

Somewhere around the year 2011, the point men of the battalion noticed Jessup and the driver. They pulled them roughly to their feet and disarmed them. Jessup hoped the garbage all over him would discourage a search.

What prevented a search was the arrival of Colonel Navarro. He rolled up, driving his own jeep as usual, then bounded out almost before the vehicle stopped. He ran up to Jessup and embraced him, garbage and all.

"God and the saints be praised! You have escaped! Did Lieutenant—?"

Jessup jerked his head at the smoking crater in the street. "The first LAW hit him."

"I feared as much. He would not have saved himself by running. The traditions of the Guardia were sacred to him, and he upheld them to the end."

Jessup didn't give a damn about the traditions of the Guardia being upheld. What he'd wanted to see upheld was the safety of the SOBs' shipment.

Now the whole job had to be done over again. Jessup had the feeling it wouldn't be too smart to work through Colonel Navarro again. Sure, Jessup's ears were still ringing, but the man's words had the flavor of a prepared speech.

"Who were they?" Jessup asked to be polite.

"Since Franco's death, Spain draws terrorists the way rotting meat draws flies," the colonel said. "If I had to make a guess, I'd say they were probably Basques."

That made some sense there in Barcelona. But it would have made more sense for the Basques to try hijacking the weapons. Mercenaries weren't the only ones who stayed alive by acting on hunches. Walker Jessup's hunch was that he'd just been lied to. Which meant that he had more problems than replacing the weapons.

First he had to get himself out of Spain. Nine chances out of ten, Colonel Navarro would "request" him to stay

around for the investigation. Even when Jessup had officially been with the Company, that kind of request was hard
to ignore. Now that he was free-lance, ignoring it could land
him in a Spanish jail. Spanish jails were not noted for the
abundance of their comforts or the excellence of their cui-
sine.

Scratch getting himself out of Spain for a few days at
least. The best he could manage was a message to Nile, suggesting that he go ahead and see about replacing the arsenal himself.

Replacing the arsenal and keeping a *very* close eye on the
fancy electronics coming out, because replacing them would
take a miracle!

ALEX NANOS STUDIED the sixty-foot trawler yacht lying
moored stern to the pier in the harbor of Rhodes.

She reminded him a little of Cheryl. Middle-aged but not
looking it, and probably able to perform very well.

He flipped through the printout the yacht broker had sent
him. He liked its not being a fancy colored brochure. The
broker wasn't trying to disguise a sow's ear as a silk purse.

"You can see the excellence of her lines and the care taken
in keeping her up," the salesman began. "With only the
smallest amount of—"

Absentmindedly Nanos picked the salesman up by the
back of his sweater and held him over the edge of the pier.
"Mister," he said mildly. "I'm trying to concentrate."

The salesman, about two-thirds Nanos's size, decided to
let his customer concentrate.

When Nanos had seen as much as he could from the pier,
he jumped down onto the deck. Below, he rummaged
around for nearly an hour. A few tools came out of his
backpack for tests that would have made the salesman turn
white if he'd seen them.

At the end of his inspection, Nanos found the salesman
displaying a frustrated look and the beginnings of a sunburn.

"I think we can make a deal," he said. "I like the big auxiliary diesel and the extra generator. We're going to be loading a lot on the electrical system once we start diving, so the more power the better. When was she last sailed?"

"Two days before we put her on the market."

"And how long ago was that?"

The salesman looked at the boat, looked at Nanos, appeared to consider lying but was smart enough to choose the truth. "Five months."

"How fast can she be hauled out and scraped?"

Memories of being dangled over the water produced the truth. "Five days."

"I'll take her as is if we can adjust the price to reflect—"

"The price is already as low as we can go!"

"Friend, didn't anyone ever teach you not to interrupt a paying customer? Your minimum price might be right for a Sixth Fleet destroyer, but for this middle-aged lady..."

The dickering went on long enough for the salesman's sunburn to become noticeably redder. Finally he threw up his hands. "All right. Cash or banker's draft, though, if you want to take possession in a hurry."

"No problem. We're hitting up the college's emergency fund for that."

The money would actually come from the NSA through Associated Charities, from there go to Hayward College's bursar and from there to a Swiss bank. The whole trip shouldn't take more than twenty-four hours, Nanos had been told.

He hoped it was true. He was getting a prickly feeling that the unknown enemy would use any gift of time from the bureaucrats. With some enemies you'd be in a wheelchair before they made up their minds to act. But Nanos didn't think any of those people were behind the trouble in the Aegean.

"I'll see about arranging a crew," the salesman said. "How many will you need?"

"I already have a crew lined up."

"Where are they meeting you? If it's not here, you'll surely need—"

"I don't need you pimping for the local unemployed boat bums," Nanos said. He shifted the backpack to a more comfortable position. This made the muscles of his arms and chest ripple impressively.

The salesman gave a jerky nod and reached into a battered fiberglass briefcase. "Will you sign the letter of intent?"

Nanos scribbled his signature with an almost-dry Bic ballpoint. The salesman folded the letter carefully, as if he expected it to explode. Then he backed away down the pier, as if he expected Nanos to strong-arm him again.

Nanos watched him go without regret, then scrambled aboard the boat again. He wanted to make sure he could single-hand her out of Rhodes. It wouldn't be easy, but it would be a damned sight safer than taking that clown's offer of crew.

The local people might not be Communists or drug smugglers, but they'd damned sure see things they shouldn't, and talk about them afterward.

As an afterthought, he decided to name the boat *Claribel*. He'd been using that name in his cover story; it couldn't hurt to carry it on to the end.

"WE HAVE INFORMATION the Turks are planning retaliation for the sinking of *Bodrun*," Captain Isakov said.

"Excellent. A vindication of the strategic insight of our Marxist-Leninist—" the *zampolit* began.

"With all respect, Comrade, I think we need to hear more about this Turkish retaliation and apply our own strategic insight." Belyusev gave his sharklike smile. "I am sure you will make a major contribution to it in good time."

Pokrovsky restrained himself from hugging the KGB man. The briefing continued.

The Turks were apparently planning some sort of informal retaliation against the Greeks in the form of a raid on

Ikyros. All the Turks would be private citizens, but they might be armed and equipped by the Turkish navy. They might even have units of the Turkish navy ready to cover their retreat if the Greeks responded in force.

"Clearly *maskirovka* is not a monopoly of the Soviet Union," Isakov concluded. "The question is, how are we to turn such a modest Turkish effort into something that might start a war?"

Ikyros was close enough that Pokrovsky could think of half a dozen plans in thirty seconds. The problem was choosing the best one. He considered the options, giving the *zampolit*'s droning only enough attention to not look anti-Party. When he'd made up his mind, the lecture was still going on.

Pokrovsky considered the source of their intelligence, which was remarkably prompt and remarkably precise, like the last few pieces they'd received. The GRU certainly had its agents sown thickly across Turkey to have achieved such results. The Soviet navy was running up a considerable debt to the GRU.

How to pay that debt?

Pokrovsky decided it wouldn't be a bad idea to consult discreetly with Belyusev. Any good KGB man would gladly work with the navy to keep the GRU from increasing its influence in foreign operations. Belyusev would ask a price, of course, and not a small one. But Pokrovsky knew it would be worth paying if it helped keep Team Typhoon safer.

CHAPTER EIGHT

"All back full," Alex Nanos called.

"All back full," Nile Barrabas repeated, throwing *Claribel*'s diesel into reverse. Alex made a delicate adjustment of the wheel, looked quickly at the approaching cliff and shouted, "Let go, both anchors."

On the forecastle, Lee Hatton kicked both the port and starboard anchors overboard, then leaped aside as the anchor lines lashed about like drunken snakes. She wore deck shoes, a baseball cap and a bikini—the perfect picture of a female boat bum.

Barrabas concluded that if the bikini hadn't already been invented, it would need to be to do justice to Lee's elegant proportions. The fact that beneath those graceful curves were superbly conditioned muscles and sinew didn't spoil the effect.

He also decided that he and Lee had better pretend to be lovers. That way the Turks on the island might keep their distance from her. If they thought she was available, things might get nasty.

The combined effect of dropped anchors and reversed diesel brought the yacht to a stop fifty feet from the cliffs of Haustim. A ladder trailed down the cliff to a floating pier anchored to the rocks by a spiderweb of cables. Beside the ladder was a winch and cable for hauling up supplies.

"You know, in theory this island should be duck soup to defend," Billy Two said from the rear of the pilothouse. "The whole coast is like this or worse. Anybody comes here, he's going to have to turn from a sailor into a mountain climber."

"Like you said, friend, in theory," Nanos replied. "There's a couple or three ravines no good for supplies, where a man could sneak up without anybody spotting him until he was on top. Maybe not even then. Colonel, are we getting an antipersonnel radar by any chance?"

"Not that I know of," Barrabas said. "Anyway, what's all this defensive thinking? The last time I looked at our TO & E, we were supposed to be on the hunt."

"Another pretty theory," Billy Two said. "Maybe we should try something new in practice, like letting the bad guys come to us for a change. If they get word we're here, you can be damned sure they will!"

"We'll see," Barrabas said, more politely than he felt. The SOBs were doing a fair amount of griping and complaining this time.

Barrabas knew why, and also why he had to let them blow off steam. It was *because* they were professionals. They didn't like laying their asses on the line this way for no more than expenses and promises. They weren't even going to pretend to like it. If they had, Barrabas would have been a lot more worried than he was by the occasional grumble and grouse.

"When?" Nanos asked.

"After we get through the introductions. It looks like our reception committee just showed up."

He pointed at the ladder, where two bearded men, one of them blond, and a tanned woman in white slacks and shirt were scrambling to the pier. From the pictures Professor Stewart had provided, Barrabas recognized Dr. Biggle and two of her assistants.

"All hands on deck," he shouted down the companionway to the cabin. Claude Hayes scrambled up into the pilothouse, his dark skin even darker with dirt, grease and a five-days' growth of beard.

"How's the electrical system?" Barrabas asked.

"I think Admiral Dewey used it to light his cabin at Manila Bay," Hayes said, scraping a fingerful of greasy insu-

lation off his neck. "But it works. For now," he added
ominously.

On the pier, Dr. Biggle was waving them to come alongside. Finally she gave up, and she and the two men stepped
into the inflatable boat tied to the pier and rowed out. She
had a face like a fury when she finally scrambled on board.
By then all the SOBs were gathered on deck. "Are you seriously planning to anchor off?" she sputtered. "When we
have a perfectly good pier—"

"Dr. Biggle, ma'am," Nanos said, taking off his battered yachting cap, "that pier's not perfectly good or even
good at all if a southwest blow gets up."

"At this time of year?" exclaimed one of the assistants.
He looked and sounded like a Turk. "How long have you
been sailing the Aegean?"

"Long enough not to trust it more'n any other body of
water," Nanos said, shrugging. "We tie up alongside, we
don't have any maneuvering room. We can't just slip the
anchors and get underway. You don't have much in the way
of fenders, either. That pier of yours pokes a hole in this old
lady's side—how much money you got for salvage fees?"

"Hey, you can't talk—" began the other assistant, obviously an American.

"Now just a minute—" Lee Hatton interrupted, pretending to come to the rescue of her captain.

"I was talking to—" The assistant tried to go on.

"Well, why don't you talk to me?" Lee cut in.

Barrabas could have sworn she wiggled her hips, but
couldn't believe she'd do anything that crude.

Whatever she'd done, it got the man's attention. He
forced a smile and said, "It seems there's a real argument
over who's boss here."

"No, there isn't," Dr. Biggle shot back in a voice that
could have frozen the water between the yacht and the pier.
"I am. Charlie, Mustafa—knock it off."

"Why don't you come aft and talk to me?" Lee said to Charlie. "I don't feel like listening to the rest of this argument."

She led Charlie off, followed by the envious stares of the rest of the SOBs. All of them, starting with Nile Barrabas, wished their cover roles would let them get out of range of Dr. Biggle's temper as easily.

Unfortunately they had to settle this argument right now, and preferably in their favor. With *Claribel* tied up to the pier, any turkey looking for booze, parts to sell on the black market, a place to light up some hashish or intelligence for his Soviet masters could wander on board at will. It would be a miracle if sooner or later someone didn't stumble on the weapons and equipment hidden below.

They would hide the heavy weapons and electronic equipment. The diving gear wasn't suspicious and it would stay in plain sight. After they were delivered, the minisonars would be placed on "supply" or "survey" runs.

In fact, the SOBs had done their usual thorough job of planning for every contingency—except this one. They were caught flatfooted, and their only usable weapon was Alex Nanos's nimble tongue and charm for women.

Barrabas decided there was something to be said for being back in the jungle of Nam. At least there more of your problems could be shot and fewer had to be talked at.

Nanos scratched his head and looked vaguely around the cove. At least, he appeared to be looking vaguely. Barrabas knew he was actually memorizing every important distance and every possible angle of fire in sight.

Nanos scratched his head again.

"Do you have lice, Captain Nanos?"

"Sorry, Dr. Biggle. I've just been thinking. How much work are you going to be wanting us to do on land?"

"Not much, unless we have to cut the digging crews because of the money we've spent on this boat!"

"Okay. Tell you what. We keep two people on the boat at all times, and we'll tie up nice as you please. It'd help, too, if you could keep your people off the boat unless they've got business aboard."

"What are you planning, orgies and drug parties?"

Dr. Biggle surveyed the remaining SOBs with polite distaste. In their efforts to look like a pickup crew of boat bums, they'd all chosen the sleaziest clothes they could find, and all except Lee had grown beards. Nanos's was undoubtedly the finest, Billy Two's was barely visible, but they all looked scruffy.

"Nothing of the kind, ma'am. And we aren't planning to pick up anybody who falls down a hatch when we're working in the engine room, either. We will if we have to, but we'd rather not have to."

Biggle's look slowly changed from something that wasn't quite a glare to something that was almost a smile.

"I suppose it's really my fault. I can't blame you if weirdos were all you could hire for what I gave you."

It looked like the famous Nanos charm was beginning to work. Barrabas sneaked a look at the forecastle, where Lee and Charlie were sitting on a locker. So far Charlie was keeping his hands to himself. Barrabas hoped this would continue. Turkish hospitals might not be up to repairing the kind of damage Lee Hatton could do to somebody who got too fresh. Not to mention Dr. Biggle probably throwing them off the island when the bill for Charlie's surgery arrived.

"Most of my people aren't as weird as they look. Oh, Linda's a goddess worshipper—"

"Really? Did you know we found signs of a temple to Diana on the island?"

"Virgin priestesses and all?"

"Well, if you wanted to keep priestesses virgin, wouldn't this island be a good place for it?"

"Unless pirates came by."

Barrabas shot Nanos a warning look not to encourage that line of speculation. Still, Dr. Biggle did seem to be thawing nicely.

"Well, like I said, Linda's a goddess worshipper. Joe—" he pointed at Billy Two "—talks to ghosts. Jimmy—" he gestured at Liam O'Toole "—used to sell fertilizer. Mack—" he nodded at Claude Hayes "—used to run a sportsfisherman until somebody stole it to run cocaine. He tried to steal it back, and got into an argument with the thief. When it was over, both the boat and the thief were on the bottom of the Gulf of Mexico."

"And him?" Biggle pointed at Barrabas.

"Hank's a Nam veteran. Tripped a booby trap one fine day near Plei Mei, which is how come he's got all those scars."

"Vietnam?" The distaste was back in the archaeologist's voice.

"Not my idea, Professor," Barrabas said, using his last trace of Western drawl. "Not my idea at all. But the draft board said, 'We want you,' and what the...heck was I supposed to do then?"

"A good many people knew what they had to do," Dr. Biggle said. "Some of them went to jail for doing it."

"Yeah, but I don't suppose many of them got killed or crippled," Barrabas said.

Dr. Biggle looked like a Greek fury for about two seconds, then she managed to smile. "I don't suppose we'll agree on that. Just as long as you remember there aren't any booby traps here and you don't shoot up the camp thinking you're Rambo."

She turned back to Nanos. "Captain Nanos, dinner is at seven o'clock tonight. You and your crew are invited. We'll even break out a bottle in your honor."

She looked around the pilothouse. "I'm sorry I snapped at you. It's been something of a strain these past few weeks, with no boat and the politicians and soldiers making fools of themselves as usual. See you."

Barrabas waited until the three archaeologists were back on land, climbing the ladder up the cliff, before he sat down in the helmsman's seat and glared at Nanos.

"Mr. Nanos. The next time one of your stories get me told that I should have been a draft dodger..."

"Expect something lingering, with boiling oil?" Lee put in.

"Boiling crankcase drippings," Barrabas finished. "Otherwise, damned good job. Now let's start shifting those weapons around. I want to make sure that with two people on board, there's always going to be one between the weapons and any snoopy archaeologists. Without being obvious," he added. "Remember, Dr. Biggle's no dummy."

"No old witch, either," Nanos said. He looked at the top of the cliff, where the two assistants were helping their boss up the last rungs of the ladder. "Fills out those pants real nice."

"I thought you were into young chicks only," Billy Two muttered.

"Do I look like a man of no taste..." Nanos began.

Lee lifted one of Nanos's massive hands to her lips and licked it experimentally. "Garlic, onions, olive oil, some wretched wine—"

"Retsina is the national drink of the Greeks!" Nanos declaimed in an exaggerated accent. "Hey, really. I don't mind the older ones at all."

"When the younger ones aren't available, at least," Billy amended.

"Alex, how about you stay out of Dr. Biggle's pants for the time being?" Barrabas said. "If you can't do that, at least have your fun—"

"Without being obvious," the rest of the SOBs chorused.

COLONEL NAVARRO SHRUGGED. "I fear we can offer you no satisfaction in the matter of identifying your assailants. The Basque underground remains suspect. Unfortunately so do several other groups. We are following as many...ah...what is the English word?"

"Leads?" Walker Jessup supplied.

"Ah, yes, leads. We are following as many as our resources permit. But it may be a long pursuit, with only partial success in the end. We must work under the eyes of the world media, including those that have been bought by the Communists. It is not as it was in the days of the *Generalissimo*, may God rest his soul."

Jessup sipped the red wine and spooned up some more of the restaurant's special *olla podrida*. For something that was made of anything the cook had left over and was in a mood to throw into the pot, the *olla podrida* was delicious. What's more, there was a lot of it. More than enough, Jessup suspected, to get him through all the tortuous formalities of negotiating a new arms shipment with Colonel Navarro.

"Yes. Franco fought the Communists in a way equaled by few," Jessup said politely. "I would like to see the murderers brought to justice," he went on. "What help I can give will be given. In return, I hope it will be possible for me to obtain more weapons and send them to their destination as soon as possible."

"Ah, now in that matter I can give you an immediate and firm answer," the colonel said, beaming, as Jessup spooned up more stew. "It will be impossible."

Jessup stopped with his spoon in midair and nearly choked on his wine. "Impossible?"

The colonel's smile now looked painted on.

"Yes. Quite impossible."

"Why the—" Jessup broke off to swallow the wine and then the spoonful of stew. During the interval he remembered the manners so important in dealing with the Spaniards. "Is it permitted to ask why?"

"I can even tell you. As you are no doubt aware, the legality of the first shipment would not bear close examination. A close examination is what this entire affair is about to receive. Until the investigation is over, we must all keep our hands . . . squeaky clean.

"Also, Mr. Jessup, I do not think we would be doing your or our common cause a service by making you a target again. Whoever was behind the first attempt is unlikely to pursue you outside of Spain.''

Bullshit! Jessup thought, but didn't say aloud. He merely drew on all his experience in dealing with high-ranking liars to keep a smile on his face. Years of dealing with the senator, he realized, were turning out to have their uses.

"I appreciate your concern for my safety and understand your reluctance to run further risks," Jessup said. He was damned if he'd say he considered the debt paid. As sure as Texas was dusty, he was going to be back with his hand out again after this was over.

"I am glad we have reached such an agreement so swiftly," the colonel said. "Now we can savor Ramon's cooking without the ugly intrusion of politics or war."

Jessup had his doubts about that. In fact, losing his Spanish connection had damned near made him lose his appetite!

This rare affliction, however, didn't last long. Jessup ate his way steadily through three servings of *olla podrida* and managed a double portion of flan and a liqueur. But when the taxi finally carried him away from the restaurant, he was sweating from more than the hot Barcelona sun and his stomach was churning from more than digesting a heavy meal.

Not for the first time, he understood perfectly what made people take machine guns and shoot up crowds. If somebody had even hinted there was an open season on the Spanish army, Jessup would have showed up with a big enough arsenal to impress even the SOBs.

As it was, the open season was more likely to be on him if he didn't haul ass out of Spain. The Spaniards were embarrassed, and like most military bureaucrats they didn't like that. They also had terrorists running around loose, on whom any unexplained deaths could always be blamed.

It was just too likely that the Spaniards would find a way out of their embarrassment that would severely cut Walker Jessup's life expectancy. Not that anybody but the SOBs would lose anything if Jessup was zapped, but they were out on a limb mostly because of him. He owed it to them to stay alive long enough to try a few other people who owed him favors. He also owed it to his stomach to stay alive long enough for at least a few more years of good dinners.

CHAPTER NINE

Abdul lay in the bilge, holding his rifle clear of any part of the fishing boat. The boat was clean, or so they had told him when he boarded. Lying down, he discovered that he'd been told other than the truth.

He did not mind the filth himself, but there was his rifle to think about. No one who had learned marksmanship under the Mad Goat would ever forget the importance of a clean rifle—or the beatings given those fools who did forget. Also, Abdul was on an honorable mission, to teach those unweaned Greeks the folly of killing Turks. If his weapon failed him, he would not be able to play his part.

He might even be the cause of another Turk's death, a thought too horrible to contemplate. Instead Abdul contemplated the other seven men lying or sitting in the boat so that they could not be seen from over the side.

A man was at the wheel and another in the bow. They were dressed like the poorest fishermen and carried no weapons. But the man in the bow, who called himself Torgut, was the one who had arranged everything these past few days.

"Our main target is the boats of Ikyros," he'd said at the final meeting the night before. "The more of them we sink, the better. It will be hard for the Greek government to justify killing more Turks as revenge for a few old boats. But the islanders will have their lessons. They will not be their Communist government's pawns anymore."

"A bloodless fight?"

That was Ismail, always the loudest in calling for blood. To be sure, he had lost his brother on Cyprus in 1974, so he had reasons.

"Only Greek blood," Torgut said. "And only if they shoot."

"Oh, I am sure I will hear a Greek bullet passing my ear very quickly," Ismail said.

"If I don't hear the same bullet, you may hear mine," Torgut said. "We are fighting Turkey's battle, not our own."

Abdul thought the two would be the same soon enough, unless the Greeks were such great cowards they did not deserve the name of men. Surely, though, Torgut was telling the truth for tonight. This was a war, not a blood feud.

In the shadows aft, a cigarette glowed as Ismail lit up. The sun no longer blazed down into the boat. Soon it would be twilight, then darkness. Out of that darkness, the men the Greeks had held in contempt would strike.

HIGH ON THE ANATOLIAN plateau, twilight was closer and the air was colder. The man sitting just inside the door of the poppy farmer's hut shivered and reached painfully for a sweater.

So many simple movements were painful now to the man named Karl Heiss. It had begun in Vietnam, when he'd used American soldiers in his drug dealing and made an enemy of Nile Barrabas. It had grown worse each time afterward that his path crossed Barrabas's.

Would Barrabas ever give up his quest for vengeance? Probably not. It was kill or be killed for him and for Heiss. There were times when it seemed to Heiss that it might be simpler to die than to go on fighting a man who appeared to be as unkillable as a river or a mountain.

Thanks to Nile Barrabas, Karl Heiss's world always seemed twilight and cold now. He always seemed to be waiting in strange, remote, filthy places for men he had to trust to tell him what they wanted him to know.

A twice-repeated, triple knock sounded on the back door. Heiss raised his Browning Hi-Power. "Come in, Major."

Major Sinas stalked in, wearing his usual look of a prowling leopard. He'd polished his paratrooper's wings since the last time Heiss had seen him. Otherwise his shiny boots, starched fatigues and hungry face with its luxuriant mustache were much the same.

"I pounded on the front door until I was tempted to shoot the lock off," the major snapped. "Are you going deaf?"

It wasn't impossible, Heiss knew. He also knew it was impossible to get a polite greeting from Major Sinas.

"I'd have taken you for an enemy, and you know what happens to my enemies," Heiss replied.

"Some of them, anyway," Sinas said. "I could name a few who are better off than you are."

"It would be a short list, but we don't have time even for that. Has the boat sailed?"

"Two o'clock this morning. Nine good men. One of them is ours."

"One!" Heiss snarled. "If he's killed before he can run wild—"

"Then I'll send down another. *After* you send me the money for that opium. If you were as slow paying some drug lord in Harlem as you have been paying me—"

"I don't deal with the riffraff," Heiss said. "Those I do deal with know better than to hustle me. Do I have to teach you the same lesson?"

The major appeared to realize Heiss had his Browning drawn, while his own Walther was still holstered.

"It might be a lesson that would make it hard for us to work together again," Sinas said. "But you seem to forget that *I* owe a few people some of the money you owe me. I will be no good to you if their patience runs out before your money arrives."

"I'll do my best," Heiss said. "But we're probably quarreling over nothing. Anybody you send will surely kill some Greeks before they kill him. Once that happens—" he shrugged "—it is in God's hands."

Major Sinas murmured a Muslim prayer and sat down. After a moment Heiss decided it was safe to holster his Browning and try to relieve cramped leg muscles.

Heiss and Sinas weren't natural allies, but, then, Heiss had no such thing. People as thoroughly outlawed as he was weren't common even in the shadow world where crime and intelligence operations met.

Still, the two men had found a common cause. Heiss needed a reliable supply of opium close to Europe. The major needed someone to market the supply he controlled.

It didn't hurt that Heiss could also help the major with his other ambition—starting a war between Greece and Turkey. Without such a war, the major would never be promoted again. He would be stuck in Turkish Army Intelligence until he retired, still a major.

Frankly, Heiss didn't blame the major's superiors. He wouldn't have promoted a man with manners like that, either. But those manners had put the major in Heiss's hands. For that, they were worth enduring.

Of course, Heiss had no interest in causing a Greek-Turkish war. It was more than likely to ruin his opium trade. He might make back some of what he lost by selling secrets to both sides, but that was risky business even for him. The Greeks and the Turks didn't have to worry about reporters investigating unexplained deaths.

The best he could do was use his contacts with Soviet Intelligence people to sabotage the major's efforts. That should be good enough, for as long as Heiss needed the major.

THE FEW LIGHTS on the waterfront of Ikyros were enough to silhouette the Turkish boat. Focusing his waterproof binoculars, Pokrovsky saw it slow until it was almost dead in the water.

"There they are," he said into his radio. "Right on time. I am going to buy whoever gave us the intelligence a bottle of anything he drinks."

With his fabulous night vision, the Golden Giant saw the same thing without the binoculars. He reached underwater and tugged a release. A waterproof cylinder containing a Dragunov sniper rifle with a laser sight bobbed to the surface.

The Giant pulled another release, and carbon dioxide hissed into the container until he could rest the rifle on it. The water was just rough enough to make it hard to pick out man, container and weapon at more than fifty meters.

"Come on," Pokrovsky breathed at the Turks. "You've come all this way. Are you going to piss your pants and turn back now?"

A dim red light glowed beside Pokrovsky as the Giant activated the laser sight. Bobbing in the sea, even an expert sniper with a Dragunov needed all the help he could get to hit anything more than a hundred meters away.

The laser sight provided most of that help. The rest came from the old hatred of Turk for Greek. All the Russian had to do was hit a Turk or a Greek, it didn't matter which. The other side could be trusted to do the rest.

The fishing boat's engine suddenly opened wide, and white foam sprang up at its bow. Pokrovsky cursed as it turned toward the harbor, away from his men.

Beside him, the Giant grinned. "Ha, Semyon Ignatievich. Take your own advice. If they hit a Greek, I won't need to shoot. If they don't—well, what goes in has to come out, as they told me when I got dysentery in Vladivostok."

ABDUL DUCKED as the boom of a fishing boat swept low over his head. As if the boom had been a human opponent, he put three bullets into the winch at the base of the mast. He wished he had a grenade, but Torgut had said those would be used only on the way out. Otherwise the fires might illuminate the Turks for Greek marksmen.

Abdul had his doubts. If the Greeks were cowards, they weren't going to shoot back whether they could see or not.

If they were men, they were going to shoot into the darkness as soon as they reached the harbor.

The boat was halfway into the narrow harbor before Abdul saw figures hurrying down the stairs on the cliff. Ismail saw them, too, and recognized one as a woman in her nightgown. He raised his rifle and was aiming at her, when Torgut struck up the weapon.

"God curse you! Are you a woman yourself?" Ismail roared.

"Ask your sister if I am a man," Torgut snapped. "I am also the one who gives orders, and you are the one who obeys. Or the first one to die tonight." He had his Colt automatic out and the muzzle almost touching Ismail's belt buckle.

Ismail looked at the Colt and the man holding it, then lowered his rifle.

"God sends wisdom even to fools," Torgut said. He held out a case of grenades to Ismail. "Take three and pass them on. It's time to light our way out of here."

Ismail flung all three grenades into something that must originally have been a big ship's lifeboat. A fireball of burning gasoline enveloped the whole boat, lit up the harbor and nearly splattered the Turks. The man at the helm of the fishing boat swore volubly and opened the throttle.

As the boat roared down the harbor, the other Turks flung their grenades. Some threw wide and only churned up water. Others threw too far. Abdul saw one grenade blow in the front door of a café. Roof tiles showered down on a man hiding beside the building, but from the way he jumped up and shook his fists he couldn't have been hurt.

Greek boats didn't get off so lightly, in spite of the misdirected grenades. Abdul threw five grenades, saw four of them explode in Greek boats and counted seven boats burning or sinking. At least one more had a full gas tank, which exploded. The burning gasoline didn't reach the Turks, but it spattered the pier, making some Greeks try to run up a vertical cliff.

The boat's load of fresh-caught squid did reach the Turks. Pieces of smoking squid, some as long as a man's arm, rained down on them.

Ismail mimed gnawing on one.

Torgut pushed him down. "Hang on, you fool, if you want to live long enough to eat anything!" He pointed ahead.

Some Greeks with both quick wits and a fast boat were already under way, trying to cut the Turks off at the harbor mouth. The Turks' diesel roared louder and their boat lifted at the bow. Abdul leaned over one side, Torgut over the other, pumping bullets into the Greek boat's waterline.

The Greeks had no weapons except their vessel, but they stuck to it until the last moment. Then they scrambled to the stern and leaped overboard as the Turkish boat rode over their craft's bow. For a moment the Greek boat stood vertically, scraping alongside the Turks', its propeller still whizzing futilely in the air. Then it was gone, and the Turks had a clear path to the open sea.

"Good work, brothers," Torgut said. "It won't be the last lesson we teach these thickheaded fishermen—they'll need more than one. But it's a good start."

The echo of the diesel off the cliffs faded as the fishing boat headed out to sea.

THE TURKISH BOAT was moving fast, but it was on a straight course. It was also silhouetted against the fires its crew had left behind. A much worse shot than the Golden Giant could have hit it.

Three bullets struck the hull before someone shouted. Then a man stood up in the bow, raising a lamp in one hand and a pistol in the other. He was an irresistible target.

The heavy bullet flung the man backward on top of his comrades. They stood, shrieking curses and threats, and lashed the water around the boat with bullets.

Pokrovsky and the Giant ducked under. They didn't have much respect for Turkish marksmanship, but with that many bullets to spare the Turks didn't need marksmanship.

Besides, their work was done. Pokrovsky knew that as he listened to the boat's propeller slow, then speed up as it turned back toward Ikyros.

"OH, CHRIST HELP US!" someone screamed from down in the harbor. "They're coming back!"

George Koustas cursed everybody, starting with the Turks, his neighbors and his cousin Alex Nanos. If the Turks weren't here, there would be no fight. If his neighbors were running away, they wouldn't ask him to join the fight. If Alex hadn't given him that cursed little radio, he wouldn't have to stay on his roof and use it, making his neighbors think he was a coward.

The radio came on. The red lights on its face looked so much like a devil's mask that Koustas made the sign against the evil eye. Then he started tapping out the code Alex had given him to memorize. For someone who had served four years in the Greek navy, it was an easy task.

He hoped it would be as easy to explain to his neighbors and friends why he was not down at the harbor with them, fighting the ancient enemy.

"THIS FOR TORGUT!" Ismail screamed. His rifle cracked twice. A Greek on the quay threw up his hands and fell into the stern of a sinking boat. A woman ran out of a house, shrieking. She bent over the man, then fell on top of him. Even through his own sweat and fear and battle rage, Abdul saw her head explode as a bullet tore through it.

Abdul threw a grenade at Greek men running out of an alley with shotguns leveled. Some of them threw themselves to the ground before the grenade exploded. Two remained standing, to be shredded into bloody bits. But one of them let off his shotgun before he died. A Turk standing ready to throw his own grenade howled in agony. He clasped his arms across his belly, as if he could hold spilling guts inside torn flesh, then gave a little cry like a dying kitten and toppled over the side of the boat.

The Turks now headed for the mouth of the harbor again. They'd avenged Torgut as well as they could with the weapons they had.

"We won't be coming here again!" Ismail screamed, firing a burst into a boat not sinking fast enough. "There aren't enough men left with the courage to fight dogs, let alone Turks!"

Abdul wondered. Ahead he saw not one but two boats trying to block the mouth of the harbor. He put a burst into one's waterline and saw the men jump overboard. As he aimed for the other's engine, his magazine clicked empty. He searched his pouch for more and found only one.

As he loaded it, a grenade sailed into the Greek boat. Planks and gear and pieces of Greeks flew into the air. A flying arm smacked Abdul in the face. He almost vomited. He couldn't reach down to pick the thing up and throw it over the side. It was still rolling back and forth in the bilge as the fishing boat reached the open sea.

Abdul sat down to clean his rifle and let the sea breeze dry the sweat on him. He hoped his brothers weren't as short of ammunition as he was. It would be a long time before the fishermen of Ikyros dared leave their harbor. He was not so sure about other Greeks, though, who might even now be on their way to comb the seas around the island.

CHAPTER TEN

"Move it, damn you!" Alex Nanos shouted. "Get the lead out or you can all swim back to Rhodes!"

Barrabas tried not to laugh. With their usual precise teamwork the SOBs were working to get *Claribel*'s tender ready to go. Nanos was shouting to keep up their cover as a motley crew of boat bums who needed his Captain Bligh act to keep them at work. If he treated them like boat bums, chances were that Dr. Biggle would go on seeing them that way. Maybe even long enough for the SOBs to get their job well started.

The tender's cover thumped on the deck. Barrabas swung himself over the railing and dropped into the stern of the twenty-foot speedboat. Lee Hatton followed, then Billy Two, then Alex Nanos. Each of them was carrying a heavy canvas bag that clinked and rattled.

As Nanos started the engines, Dr. Biggle appeared on top of the cliff. She cupped her hands and shouted down to the SOBs. "What are you doing with the tender at this time of night?"

"A Mayday," Nanos shouted back. "A Greek fishing boat in trouble over toward Ikyros. The report was kind of garbled, but it sounds like it might be something like the trouble you saw."

"Terrorists? Why not leave them to the military?"

"The military might be too busy chasing them to pick up survivors," Nanos pointed out. "We're close enough that we might be able to help search. Don't worry. We're leaving Mack and Jimmy. They can handle the boat if we have to stay. If there's still shooting going on, we'll haul—come back, right straight off."

"But—"

"Doctor, they can really ream you—take your license, if you don't join a rescue operation when you're this close. I'm too old to be a hero, but I'm too young to go on the beach."

If Dr. Biggle replied, she was drowned out by the roar of the tender's engines. Alex didn't open the throttles more than a quarter of the way. The tender was still making fifteen knots as it passed the headland and out of sight of *Claribel*.

Alex opened the throttles wider, set the concealed autopilot and started undoing his bag. The first thing to come out was a radio, a twin of the one he'd given George Koustas. Turning it on, he listened for a minute, then shook his head.

"George is off the air. Lots of traffic, coded or garbled or both, but no George."

"Didn't he even give a description of the attacking boat?" Lee asked.

"No. He said he had to go down and join the fight."

Lee muttered something about Greeks with more macho than sense.

Nanos glared at her. "Lee, if a gang came in off the street and started cutting up people in that free clinic in New York, wouldn't you go down and start stomping them?"

Lee shook her head. "Sorry, Alex. You're right. I didn't think of it that way."

"We'd all better start thinking," Barrabas said. He didn't want to take sides, but Lee's lack of tact bothered him. They were all showing the strain of being so far out on a limb without official status, but Lee was usually the last to say the wrong word.

"Yeah," Billy Two said. "Thinking about how to find a boat we won't recognize when we find it, in about a hundred square miles of sea, and not get shot up by the Greeks because they think we shot up Ikyros."

His tone changed. "If Hawk Spirit has anything to tell me about this, I will hear it soon. If he remains silent—"

"We do it the hard way," Nanos finished.

"Or any way we can get it," Barrabas added. "Alex, leave the radio on. Let's set up so that if we do find these friends we can do something besides spit at them."

It sounded like a request; the others knew it was an order. They started unpacking their canvas bags. An Uzi came into view, along with Browning Hi-Powers with 20-round magazines and customized shoulder stocks. Bulletproof vests followed, along with Lee's big knife in its handmade leather sheath.

Right now, they were armed more like a police SWAT team than like soldiers. Barrabas didn't hope it would be enough—hoping was a waste of energy in combat. He simply knew that tonight it would be all they had.

Barrabas did spend two seconds thinking of committing mayhem on Walker Jessup and on whoever had killed Geoff Bishop.

If the SOBs had had official status now, they could be heading for Ikyros in a helicopter. Same thing with Geoff along, official status or not. He'd had a talent for scrounging up aircraft in the oddest places, as well as for flying them. As it was, they were heading for Ikyros in a boat that might not get them there in time or get them out of trouble, if that was the way it went.

Not that *Claribel*'s tender was any ordinary boat. She had twin engines tuned and supercharged to deliver about twice their normal horsepower. She had lockers for guns and ammunition, sockets for machine-gun mounts, through-hull fittings for electronics and Kevlar armor protecting oversize gas tanks. None of these details was obvious to the untrained observer, but all of them added up to a lean, mean fighting boat.

Nanos clearly couldn't have been happier if he'd been in bed with Miss America. Barrabas would still have preferred a helicopter.

He decided that if any of the SOBs got killed tonight because they hadn't gone by air, he would have some people's hides. If he was one of the KIA—well, he hoped there was a next life, because he intended to spend at least part of it haunting those bastards!

"MACHINIST KOUSTAS?" the spruce Greek navy lieutenant said as the helicopter's rotors slowed enough to let him be heard.

"Yes, sir. I don't remember—"

"Lieutenant Pappas. Do you remember Lieutenant Kipnis?"

"Yes, sir."

"He gave me your name as a reliable witness. That's why I asked for you to be here when I landed. To save time. Can you describe the boat?"

"You would have to check some of these details with others who saw it closer than I did," Koustas said. "But I think it was about fifteen meters long, three meters wide, with a dark hull—green, I think, but it was too dark most of the time to be sure it wasn't blue—"

He went on, trying to answer all the lieutenant's questions without guessing. He'd seen quite a lot of the boat, but mostly while lying under a bench on the quay, keeping his head down while Turkish bullets and Greek shotgun blasts tore the air over him. By the time he'd reached the quay, most of the men who'd survived were doing the same, and he had fired his shotgun a few times.

He still hoped to find a way of getting the boat's description to Cousin Alex. Koustas didn't know who Alex's friends might be, but he suspected they could do more with the knowledge than this trim and tailored mainland-born lieutenant.

By the time Koustas had told Pappas everything he could remember, half a dozen other survivors of the battle in the harbor had joined him. The lieutenant listened to each one describe the boat, then jotted down his own estimate on a notepad and handed the sheet to the helicopter pilot.

"Get this out on the radio right now."

"Code, sir?"

"Christ, no! Plain language. With those mother-raping Turks sailing around, everybody's in danger. Everybody has to be warned."

"Aye, aye, sir."

In the shadows at the edge of the field, George Koustas breathed a prayer of thanks and took back his harsh thoughts about mainland-born lieutenants. If Cousin Alex was half as smart as he seemed, he would be listening when the description went out—Cousin Alex and, please God, his friends.

"HEY, PEOPLE!" Nanos shouted over the roar of the engines. "I'm getting a clear message on a Greek navy frequency. Sounds like an airborne set. It's a description of the boat that shot up Ikyros."

Billy Two let out a war whoop. Barrabas grinned.

Lee Hatton politely deflated them. "We know what we're looking for, but still not where to look."

"Give me that chart, Alex."

The SOBs braced themselves as their boat tore along at twenty-five knots, and bent over the chart. This was one of those situations when Nile Barrabas stopped being the CO and became just one more contributor to a common pool of ideas. When that pool yielded a conclusion, then he would give an order as CO and it would be obeyed. Until then, ideas were needed, not rank.

Five minutes later, Barrabas pointed at a location about twenty miles west of Ikyros. "That's not the most direct route to Turkish waters. It's the one that keeps them farthest from land until they get home."

"Wouldn't they want to stay close to land, in case they had to swim for it?" Billy asked.

Alex spit into the foaming wake. "Turks hoping for safety on a Greek island after they've just shot up a village of women and kids? These guys are bad, but they aren't friggin' crazy!"

"True, brother," Billy Two said. "I think I lack the guidance of Hawk Spirit here. The hawk of the Osage was the prairie hawk not the fish hawk, so he may not speak as readily when I am upon the water."

It was impossible to tell if Billy was joking or not. After a moment, Barrabas decided he didn't really want to know.

"Okay, Alex. Set a course for that position and slow down as much as you can. We're making a big wake, and I suspect anybody in the air tonight's going to be trigger happy. Lee, check all the weapons. Billy, open the flag locker and get a few flags ready to hoist."

"Any in particular? The Thai flag's real pretty, and the Peruvian's a—"

"French, British, Greek, Turkish, and no smart remarks."

"Yes, oh, great Colonel."

Had Alex really wangled a Thai flag? Barrabas decided this was something else he really didn't want to know.

ABDUL HOPED his son would be told his father had died fighting Greek soldiers, even if it was not true. It might be the truth, of course. Certainly they'd heard enough on the radio and seen enough lights in the sky to know the hunt was on.

He also hoped his death would not make trouble for his brother. Mustafa worked on the island of Haustim, making good pay helping the American archaeologists dig up temples and find old ships. He would need to keep that job if his own family and Abdul's were not both to go hungry.

Perhaps it would be better, after all, if no one knew what happened to Abdul. Mustafa had said that the woman archaeologist did not like soldiers, which was to be expected in a woman, and did not hate Greeks, which was common among Americans. Abdul thought she was foolish, but that did not mean she would make no trouble for Mustafa. More trouble was made in the world by fools than by everyone else put together.

A distant light in the sky now seemed to be getting brighter. Had the Greeks found them at last? Abdul snapped off his safety and chambered a round.

Ismail gave an order, for once not shouting. It was passed along to Abdul:

"Do not fire until the helicopter is in range. They will have to come close to be sure we are the ones they seek. Close enough for us to take them with us. It is not only Greek fishermen who will be reminded tonight that Turks are warriors!"

Abdul prayed that this might be so, so earnestly that he didn't hear the roar of powerful marine engines approaching out of the darkness.

BARRABAS FINISHED his study of the battered fishing boat through the infrared Starlite scope. Either it was the right boat, or there were two like it in this area tonight.

No time to ask questions, either. Not with that helicopter circling, getting closer by the minute. Barrabas didn't need the radio intercepts to know it was a Greek navy helicopter, loaded for bear or Turks.

"Okay, Alex. Do your stuff."

Nanos grinned. He loved the spotlight even more than Liam O'Toole, and was a lot less fussy about how he got it. He also came through just as often.

Nanos signaled to Lee Hatton. At the stern of the tender, a Turkish flag suddenly spread on the breeze. The engines roared, the bow lifted and the wake rose higher than the flagstaff.

They raced toward the fishing boat, their weapons on display. They all wore battered and baggy fatigues and camouflage cream on their faces.

They swept around the Turkish boat in a wide arc, slowing as they finished the circle. By that time all the Turks on board were staring at them as if they were a sea monster.

Very likely the last thing the Turks had expected to see tonight was fellow Turks. They were probably surprised, delighted and hoping that the boat before them was just the vanguard of a rescue party.

Barrabas used the Starlite on the helicopter. Definitely Greek navy, with a rocket or machine-gun pod on one side. It was going to be a race between getting the Turks under control and getting shot up along with them by the helicopter!

Nanos shouted something in Turkish. The apparent leader of the Turks shouted back what sounded like a number. Nanos hand-signaled Barrabas that all the Turks were in sight.

The helicopter was hovering now. In another minute it would be heading in, the pilot arming his weapons.

Nanos signaled Lee, and all four SOBs raised their weapons.

ABDUL WONDERED what the men in the boat, with only pistols and a submachine gun, could hope to do against a helicopter. But at least the two boatloads would keep each other company in their last fight.

Then the Turkish flag vanished from the boat's stern. In its place—Abdul's mouth fell open—rippled a Greek flag!

"Treachery!" Ismail screamed. He clawed for the Colt he'd taken from the dead Torgut.

The submachine gun and one of the pistols fired brief bursts. Ismail flew across the boat, parts of his face and his chest missing.

These Greeks had the cunning of the devil, Abdul thought, to sneak up like this! Or maybe they weren't Greeks, but creatures of the devil himself!

The thickset man at the boat's helm was speaking again. "Throw your weapons over the side. Every last one of them. Now!" The big man with the Uzi and the long dark hair fired a burst over the Turks' heads.

Abdul would have fired back, accepting death as the price of defiance, if one thought hadn't popped into his mind. The Greeks had given up their best chance to slaughter the whole boatload. Maybe, just maybe, disarming would make a difference.

Moving slowly, keeping his hands in plain sight, Abdul bent over the railing. His hands opened and his G-3 splashed into the Aegean.

"One of you is almost smart enough to be a dog, if not a Greek," the thickset man shouted. "How about the others?"

A volley of splashes sounded as the rest of the boat's arsenal went over the side.

"Better than I'd thought. Now you all jump overboard."

"I can't swim!" someone shouted.

The fear in the man's voice made Abdul cringe. To show oneself that weak before Greeks was cause for shame. But the hope of living when you'd thought yourself doomed could do strange things, he knew.

"Find a friend who can and hang on to him," the Greek said, almost politely. "But do it fast. Anybody who's in the boat by the time I count ten won't leave it alive!"

The Greek only had to count to seven before the last Turk was in the water. Another burst from the submachine gun backed up an order to swim away from the boat.

Abdul swam as if sharks were nipping at his heels. He would have swum faster if he could, because whoever those Greeks were, they were clearly more dangerous than sharks.

He only hoped they would also be merciful enough to shoot him and his brothers rather than let them drown.

BACKING SLOWLY, Nanos brought the tender alongside the empty Turkish boat. Lee and Billy Two jumped aboard. Billy carried a plastic can of gasoline.

After a quick search of the boat, Billy upended the can and poured about a quart of gas into the bilges. Then he struck a match, tossed it down and leaped back aboard the tender as flames shot halfway up the mast.

Billy had just sat down, when the Greek navy helicopter started closing. A nose searchlight darted across the water to steady on the two boats. Barrabas mentally crossed his fingers. If the helicopter's crew didn't see the Greek flag, or if they felt like shooting first and asking questions afterward...

The searchlight went off. On the radio, somebody asked a question in Greek. Nanos replied. Two more exchanges and the helicopter climbed away. Before it was out of sight, the gasoline had burned out, and the smoking Turkish boat drifted empty on the calm sea.

Nanos cupped his hands and shouted into the darkness. Shouts in Turkish replied. To Barrabas, the voices sounded half frightened, half surprised.

"I told them the boat was theirs, to get home if they could," Nanos said. "I didn't care if they motored, sailed, rowed or got up on the stern and farted themselves along, but I didn't want anything more to do with them in this world or the next, and if I ever met them in either it would be tough shit for them."

Stiff-legged with anger, Nanos stalked to the helmsman's seat and sat down. The engine roared to life so abruptly that Barrabas nearly went sprawling.

The Turkish boat was long out of sight before Barrabas saw Nanos relax his white-knuckled grip on the wheel. The colonel held his tongue. What Alex had to say would be worth hearing, but he'd say it in his own good time.

They were halfway back to the island before Nanos turned around and spoke just loud enough to be heard over the roar of the engines.

"You know, Colonel, I was really hoping for a while that those dumb-ass mothers would give me an excuse to shoot them all. Then I was hoping they'd all drown."

Lee put a hand on Nanos's massive arm. He didn't jerk it away. "I know, Alex. It's—a classmate of mine once had to do a six-hour brain operation to save the life of somebody who'd beaten his wife and daughter to death before shooting himself. My friend spent six hours fighting the temptation to let his scalpel slip."

Nanos turned around and planted a brotherly kiss on Lee's sweaty forehead. "Thanks, honey. It didn't last that long for me, thank God. I told myself that sure, these goons had shot up women and kids. But maybe if they got home, those would be the only women and kids to get shot up this time around."

"If the Turks have the brains to find the bathroom when they want to pee, they'll string the whole gang up," Billy Two added. "If they don't—think the Greek army is looking for a few good mercs?"

"Mr. Starfoot," Barrabas said, "sometimes your sense of humor gets just a little out of hand."

They covered the rest of the way back to Ikyros in silence.

"MR.— What *is* your last name, anyway?" Dr. Biggle asked Claude Hayes. "I dislike calling blacks by their first name. It seems patronizing and racist."

Hayes silently prayed for patience. Right now he'd rather be patronized than quizzed. His being black wasn't exactly a secret; he wore it all over him. A lot of other things about him were less visible, and he wanted them to stay that way.

"Last name's Griffin, if you insist."

"I don't insist, but—is that your real name, by the way?"

"Dr. Biggle, you're asking a lot of questions of a man who hasn't had his morning coffee yet. How about I brew some for both of us? Then if you're still curious..."

Hayes retreated down the companionway toward the galley before the archaeologist could reply. Not that he hadn't expected the lady to be curious about where the tender and four of *Claribel*'s crew had gone last night, and not that he didn't have answers. But he wanted to warn the colonel that Biggle was on the prowl already.

Barrabas came awake in a flash as usual, his Browning snaking out from under the sheet and pointing at Hayes.

"Hey, Colonel. Just me."

"And I just got to sleep. Excuse, Mr. Hayes?"

Hayes told him.

Barrabas said something impolite about Dr. Biggle's ancestors, habits and future. Then he sat up and shook his head. "Sorry, Claude. It's too early in the morning for me to be a gentleman. Can you handle the lady?"

"Sure, if you'll buy me a drink afterward to wash the taste out of my mouth."

"I thought that sort of thing was Alex's style."

"Colonel, you know what I mean. She's got the idea that I'm broke and on the run—enough to be grateful for any little handout. I smell a deal. I spill the beans—she gets me a nice little job at Hayward College."

"So string her along. If that's the worst she can do—"

"Colonel, forgive me for saying it, but you ain't never been black. You don't know how it feels from where I sit. I'd like to throw the bitch overboard!"

"Mr. Hayes," Barrabas said, "resist the temptation. Otherwise the splash will wake the rest of the SOBs, and we will then throw you overboard. Which will blow our cover and lead to the failure of our mission. So lie nicely to Dr. Biggle. That's an order."

"Yes, sir."

POKROVSKY STOOD at attention in front of Isakov's desk. It took all his remaining strength. He had none left for listening to Political Instructor Fokin's recital of what they had learned from radio interceptions.

At least Isakov had the decency to look uncomfortable about letting the *zampolit* do the debriefing. Fokin must have been making more threats than usual.

Time for Pokrovsky to consider a little *glasnost* of his own with Belyusev, if Fokin was about to run wild.

"The death toll has been estimated at fifteen, with twenty or more wounded, including women and children. Nine boats and three houses were totally destroyed and many more damaged. The Turks have made a fine start at weaving the ropes for their own nooses."

This was true, even if Fokin said so.

"The Turkish terrorists have not been found. In fact, we have heard several comments suggesting that they have vanished from the face of the Aegean."

Belyusev laughed. "That's the Greeks hiding their own stupidity. The Greek navy couldn't find a whale in a swimming pool!"

Pokrovsky decided that if the KGB officer thought that, maybe he wouldn't make such a good ally, after all. Contempt for your opponent was always foolish, and this instance was more foolish than most. The Greek navy might not have the latest Western electronics and weapons, but it had something almost as formidable—men who lived by and on the sea and knew the Aegean the way they knew their wives' bodies.

He did not like this business of the Turks simply vanishing. He wanted to know what had happened to them, or at least that it was a real mystery of the sea and not a case of somebody helping them vanish.

The sea had real mysteries, he knew. It also had plenty of false mysteries, created by human stupidity—or human ingenuity.

"Semyon Ignatievich," Isakov said. "Please take the Golden Giant our thanks. I cannot promise the Order of the Red Banner, but I will certainly do my best."

"I thank you, Comrade Captain. I will tell him when he wakes up."

"When you wake up will be soon enough. Go and get some sleep. If the sound officer disturbs you, I'll put him to work in the galley until you wake up!"

Pokrovsky threw Isakov a shaky salute and lurched toward the door.

CHAPTER ELEVEN

Walker Jessup was careful to avoid being tailed when he left Spain. Personally, he thought that Spanish Intelligence would have trouble following an old lady in a wheelchair through a shopping mall. Still, even fools could get lucky. Also, even bad intelligence agencies could accidentally hire good people, and Jessup knew that he was a fairly recognizable figure.

Not to mention that the Spaniards might not be the only people on his tail, and some of the others *were* good.

So from Barcelona Jessup flew to Marseilles. From Marseilles he flew to Palermo in Sicily. There he read in the newspapers that the Turks had raided the Greek island of Ikyros in retaliation for unspecified Greek terrorist acts. The Turks had disappeared after the raid. The Greeks were demanding compensation and the punishment of the culprits or they would hold the Turkish government responsible. The Turkish government had repudiated any Turkish citizen who would commit such an atrocious act, "however provoked." They said compensation could be negotiated and that the criminals would be punished as soon as they could be found, which might be sooner if the Greek government would cooperate. The Greek government said that punishing Turkish terrorists was Turkish business.

All this added up to no war right away. Jessup heaved a sigh of relief that nearly blew the paper away when he finished reading. The SOBs might not have anything to do with the disappearance of the Turks, but they were in place and ready to go to work before the Greeks and the Turks were ready to go to war.

What remained to be done presented problems, but at least they were problems Jessup had a chance of solving. He caught the next plane out of Palermo on his way to solving the first of those problems.

Palermo to Rome. Rome to Bern. Bern to Athens. Athens to Alexandria. Alexandria to Smyrna. Smyrna to a town in Anatolia, far off the tourist routes but close to a major Turkish complex of airfields and army bases.

By the time Jessup staggered out of the last plane, he was forty-six hours out of Barcelona. He hadn't slept more than three of those hours. He'd eaten four times, but what they served at airports he didn't call food. He preferred to call it another four-letter word.

At least he could be sure of two things. One was that he'd spent about three thousand dollars of his own money on airfares. The sooner this mission got official status, the better for him, too. He was now more than ever on the same side as the SOBs. The other was that he'd certainly lost anyone tailing him. Maybe they'd failed to make him at some airport. Just as likely, they'd died of starvation trying to live on airport food.

Jessup laughed at the thought of KGB agents being arrested for cannibalism. Then he checked into a local hotel that the Company kept under surveillance, if not safe. Stripping to his underwear, he lay down and was asleep before he'd really stretched out.

It was one of the few times in his life that he was too tired to eat.

COLONEL JOEL RAWSON nodded.

"Can't see why we shouldn't give you all the stuff you want. Some of it may be old, of course. Now that we've started giving the Turks new stuff, they're looking to get rid of some of the old. I figure it might as well go to you as to the Turks on Cyprus. We *know* what side you're— Hey, Fixer, you all right?"

Rawson was pulling a bottle of Jack Daniels out of his desk drawer when Jessup shook his head.

"No. Just a little groggy. I slept around the clock last night. Maybe that's too much of a good thing."

What really bugged Jessup was that after forty-six hours of running all over the Mediterranean, he was getting his replacement arsenal in about forty-six seconds. Maybe a little longer, allowing for crating and delivery, but almost for the asking!

It wasn't logical, and knowing Joel Rawson, Jessup figured there had to be a catch in it somewhere. If the United States Army had a man who deserved the same nickname as Walker Jessup, it was Rawson.

In fact, he was Colonel Rawson instead of Major General Rawson only because he liked to pull his fixes on everybody, including superior officers with short tempers and long memories. Not that he'd ever done it to somebody who hadn't asked for it, as far as Walker Jessup knew, but when somebody with three stars got terminally pissed at you, you couldn't expect him to promote you.

"Then have an eye-opener."

"Don't mind if I do."

The whiskey was warm and Rawson was out of ice, but the drink soothed Jessup, anyway. It also reminded him he'd better scrape up a meal pretty soon, even if it was worse than airport food. You didn't drink on an empty stomach, not while striking a bargain with Joel Rawson.

"I don't have much trouble with that," Jessup said. "Only question is, how old is old? I know some places in Turkey where they still have Mausers that were used at Gallipoli. That old, we don't need."

"That old and the Turks sell them to collectors, not arms dealers," Rawson said. "How about G-3s, Thompson SMGs, some Belgian Blindicide rocket launchers?"

"What caliber?"

"Eighty-two or 100-millimeter, take your pick."

"One hundred."

The larger rocket launchers packed a bigger punch, and the SOBs would probably be using them from boats.

"No sweat. Uzis?"

"Of course. What about C-4 and plastic explosives?"

"Plenty, but the Turks will want a few favors for letting go of that. They need something to make up for the risk of Armenian terrorists getting hold of it."

"The only Armenian terrorist I know keeps a restaurant in Radford, Virginia. He makes people drop dead when they get the bill."

"Oh, I believe you, but the Turks are paranoid. Since the Armenians really are out to get them—"

"Okay. I wondered when we'd get to the deal. You come up with the C-4, I'll come up with something to smooth the Turks' ruffled feathers."

Liam O'Toole could make the explosives into charges with a variety of exotic fuses. Alex Nanos and Claude Hayes could place the fused charges anywhere from the top of a mountain to the bottom of the Aegean. But they needed the explosives to start with. If Rawson asked for something Jessup couldn't deliver...

"You've kept up your Company connections, Fixer. So I suppose I don't need to ask you if you've heard of Karl Heiss."

This time Jessup didn't freeze, as he had momentarily with Colonel Navarro. He didn't have anything in his hands. His stomach broke the silence with an appalling rumble.

"How about I call for some lunch, real American-type steaks?" Rawson said. "I figure we can make a deal before the cook sobers up and finds the refrigerator."

"You're on."

Rawson guessed right. The cook took his time, until Jessup was about ready to cut off a slice of Rawson's leather sofa and start gnawing it. But at least the deal was childishly simple.

"Heiss is supposed to be dead, of course," Rawson said. "But they never found his body, which I'm sure you know.

Thing is, we've got a description of somebody hanging out here in Turkey that matches what Heiss would look like now. A few years older and a lot more banged up, but alive.''

"What's he doing in Turkey? Opium?''

"Give the man a cigar. The Turks are making a really good try at suppressing opium growing. It's costing them some money to the poppy farmers. It's costing us a good deal more money to buy the higher-ups out of the business. But most of them are being reasonably honest about it.''

"Meaning if Uncle Sugar keeps on paying, they stay out of the opium business?'' Jessup asked.

"It's better than in Colombia or Burma, you gotta admit that.''

Jessup was willing to admit that much. The Turks mostly didn't play the game of accepting one bribe to suppress the drug trade and another to let it go on.

"I suppose Heiss is playing footsie with the ones who won't stay bought?''

"I don't suppose. I know. Or at least Turks I trust to know their ass from a hole in the ground have told me so. He's been particularly gung ho, going after men in Turkish Intelligence.''

Jessup held out his glass for a refill. Even thinking about what Heiss was probably up to left a bad taste in his mouth. Jack Daniels wouldn't wash it out as thoroughly as would wasting Heiss so that he *stayed* wasted, but it would help.

" 'I can see clearly now,' '' Jessup sang.

Rawson put his hands over his ears. "Another condition of the deal is no more singing.''

"My voice is inimitable.''

"Thank God. No, maybe if it could be imitated, we could use it to jam Russian military communications. We wouldn't have to block the signals. We'd just drive all the operators out of their gourds.''

"You're about as great a comedian as I am a singer,'' Jessup said. "Anyway, I suppose Heiss is cutting one of his usual deals. Intelligence from the Turks in return for distributing their opium. Help in distributing the opium from the Soviets, in return for the intelligence. And a nice slice of both pies for Mr. Heiss.''

''That's about it. And the Turks would like some non-Turks to clean out Heiss. Apparently they think he's less likely to be tipped off that way.''

Jessup also suspected that Heiss was blackmailing a few allegedly respectable Turkish officials. The man had the world's finest private collection of documents on criminal acts committed by government officials.

''Well, I'm not a Turk. But I haven't been doing a lot of fieldwork lately.''

''Somehow that doesn't surprise me,'' Rawson said, pouring out refills unasked. ''But if you've kept up any sort of contact with Nile Barrabas, and he's got any kind of resources...''

Rawson, Jessup decided, was practicing understatement. If there was one man in the world Nile Barrabas wanted dead, it was Karl Heiss. In Vietnam the renegade CIA drug dealer had murdered some of Barrabas's men to cover his tracks. Give Nile Barrabas a choice between a billion dollars and ten minutes alone with Karl Heiss, and you'd get the fastest decision in military history in favor of Heiss. Barrabas felt he owed it to his murdered men to settle their score personally.

''I won't have any problems contacting Barrabas,'' Jessup said. ''I won't even have any problems persuading him to go after Heiss. The only thing is, he's on a priority mission. It may not last more than a few days if the Turks and the Greeks can kiss and make up. If this crap in the Aegean goes on, though—''

''You want me to pull strings in Ankara?''

''If you've got any to pull,'' Jessup said.

''I do. If the Greeks don't fart around with any retaliation, maybe I can even pull them. Quite a few of the drug dealers also want a war between Greece and Turkey to improve their chances for promotion. I won't say the others love Greeks, but they know what their chances of facing both Greece and Russia together are. They also know what *glasnost* would be worth if the Russian generals ever thought they had a free ride into the eastern Mediterranean.''

Jessup nodded. ''You do your best, and I promise Nile Barrabas will do his. That's pretty damned good, in case you've forgotten. Better than your friggin' cook, anyway.'' Jessup held up one thick wrist and pointed to his watch. ''Did he have to raise the steak from a calf?''

At that moment the door opened and a Turk with a large tray tottered in. The smell rising from the tray set Jessup's stomach rumbling again, while his mouth imitated Niagara Falls. The Turk set down the tray and lifted a tarnished brass lid with a flourish.

Jessup stared at the steaks on the platter. ''Jesus Christ! Joel, the next time tell him just to shove the whole cow in the oven, then cut off pieces until I tell him to stop!''

''HEY, ADRIENNE! Good to hear you,'' Ioannes Trikoupi said.

''Over this awful connection?'' Adrienne shouted, hoping to be heard better than she could hear the Greek.

''Your voice would give beauty to Morse code,'' Trikoupi said. ''How are things on the island?''

''We're pretty sure of where to start looking for that Minoan ship we've suspected since last year. We're not at all sure how long it will take to find it, even if the politicians don't start a war.''

''It won't be the Greek politicians who send soldiers to murder women and children!'' Trikoupi snapped.

''Ioannes, I didn't mean it to sound like that. You know what I think of *all* soldiers.''

''Yes, and it is just like a woman. But I honor you for the strength of your convictions, even though I cannot share them.''

Either Trikoupi hesitated or the connection faded for a moment. Then he was back.

"I gather your Alex Nanos came up with a decent boat. How is he working out?"

"He's a lot more charming than the Alex Nanos you know, I must say. But he must have scraped the bottom of the boat-bum barrel for a crew. There's a huge guy who looks like an American Indian, a black guy who probably ran drugs once, a bimbo who looks like she dropped out of every college that let her in in the past ten years—"

"Blond or dark haired?"

"Dark haired. You know her?"

"I know of a couple like her in boat-bum circles. Just make sure you keep an eye on your cameras and things like that."

"Hmm. Maybe that's why she's trying to make every American male on the crew."

"Has she succeeded?"

"I think they're all afraid of her boyfriend. I don't know why he puts up with it, but if he did get mad—well, he's six feet something and moves like he's got muscles. He's got a lot of scars from Vietnam, he says, and the weirdest head of snow-white hair."

"How old is he?"

"Somebody else you know?"

"No. If he's an old man, I won't fight him, but if he's a fair match for me, I may just fly out. Then that—bimbo—will learn that teasing a Greek is not the same thing as teasing an American!"

"I'm almost tempted to send you a ticket. This guy's not more than forty, if that. But I'd never get any work out of the rest of the crew if you worked him over. Save up your energy for the next time I come to Athens."

"You mean your Mr. Nanos isn't quite *that* charming?"

Adrienne licked her lips. "He's vinegar, Ioannes. You're wine. Does that answer your question?"

"Yes, although it does not answer what I am to do about the desire that fills me!"

"Ioannes, this probably isn't a private line. Besides, they haven't yet worked the bugs out of sex by telephone. Goodbye, my dear friend."

"Until we meet again, Adrienne."

The connection broke. Adrienne put down the receiver and swiveled her chair to look out at the Aegean, which was turning purple in the twilight. She hadn't told Ioannes the complete truth about Alex Nanos, but she'd told him what he'd wanted to hear.

She wasn't Cheryl, who carefully picked only men who didn't mind her moving on. Nanos was interested, *and* he was interesting.

If only he didn't come packaged with that bunch of weirdos!

"NILE, the shit is about to hit the fan."

Lee Hatton spoke in a clinical tone, as if she were describing a fracture or a case of the flu. Nevertheless Barrabas tightened his hand a bit around her waist.

They were sitting on a rock overlooking the ravine on the south side of the island. On the eastern horizon, the sun was climbing through a fringe of clouds into a sky already turning blue. The islands in the distance were changing from gray blobs to their natural browns, yellows and greens. Sails and an occasional funnel shone on the calm sea.

Down in the ravine, Liam O'Toole and Claude Hayes were pretending to play archaeologist. Their "dig" was actually a cover for placing explosive charges and trip wires. Anybody coming up the ravine in a hurry would probably bring it down on top of him. Like many explosives experts, Liam was a good amateur geologist, who could find the weak point in a chunk of rock with nothing but his eyes and a small hammer.

If the charge and the falling rocks didn't wipe out the visitors, the bang would still echo all over the island. Before the survivors could get very far toward the camp, a reception committee would be ready to see they didn't complain of Hayward College's hospitality—or anything else.

"So, who's throwing it this time? The soldier's friend, Dr. Biggle?"

"However did you guess? You're so smart!" Lee looked up at Barrabas with an exaggerated girlish awe so that from a distance she probably would look like a sappy-minded bimbo worshiping her boyfriend. She continued the act by resting her head on his shoulder.

To Barrabas, it didn't feel quite like Erika's head, and not just because Lee's hair was shorter.

But it didn't feel unnatural, either.

"Charlie was after me again to go skinny-dipping with him."

"Better be careful with that. The Turks might start thinking you're available, and they're not wimps like Charlie."

"To hell with the Turks," Lee said dispassionately. "I hope I have better taste in men than to go for Charlie."

"Anyway, he was on your case about skinny-dipping?"

"He said he'd heard Dr. Biggle talking long-distance. He recognized the tone she uses with a Greek lover she's got in Athens. Apparently the Nanos charm is working as usual, and so is my boat-bum bimbo act. She's got Claude down as a poor oppressed black, or an ex-criminal, or maybe both. But she gave a detailed description of you to warn this Greek off from trying to get in my pants."

"Shit," Barrabas said, matching Lee's clinical tone. "Did Charlie have a name for the Greek?"

"He's only heard Biggle call him Ioannes," Lee said. "I suppose I could get him to find out if I promised a little more."

"Then you might have to go through with it, and the Turks would really hit the ceiling."

"I don't think there's a ceiling on the whole island, except in the tents. But I get the idea."

Barrabas was glad she hadn't asked if he was jealous. His honest answer would have been "probably not." But even the "probably" could have made trouble they didn't need.

Not now, certainly, with the mission about to get even hairier before there was any chance of its getting official. Maybe Biggle's Athenian playmate was a good reliable anti-Communist, and discreet to boot, but Barrabas wouldn't bet much on either, never mind the privacy of the phone link.

He certainly wouldn't bet the safety of the SOBs.

That recognizable description of Nile Barrabas was probably on its way to at least one pair of ears bought and paid for by Moscow. When the mouth attached to those ears got to a phone, jealous Turks were going to be a very minor problem.

"Lee, give me a convincing goodbye and hike back to the boat. Brief Alex and Billy. I'm going down to brief Liam and Claude."

"Should I say anything to Charlie if I meet him?"

"No. Wait a minute. Does he know anything about the inventory control system? We may need to steal some more explosives."

"Antipersonnel depth charges, maybe? Should I ask Alex if any of the boat's gear can be modified to detect divers?"

Barrabas looked at Lee with newfound appreciation for her versatility. Lee couldn't press twice her weight like Alex or command a battalion like Barrabas, but there probably wasn't a job in the SOBs she couldn't take a shot at. She was one hell of a lady. "Right on both counts," he replied.

"Okay, but with my act, asking about heavy matters like inventories would be out of character. I think we'd just better sneak in and pick up the stuff, then hope something happens to take Dr. B's mind off where it went."

"Fine. Just check that they haven't tightened up on the security, and we can move tonight. The bad guys aren't going to be coming that fast unless they've got telepathy."

Lee nodded and strode off toward the camp. She considerably improved the landscape, in sandals, straw hat, halter top and white slacks loose enough for unarmed combat, the leader of the SOBs thought.

Barrabas hurried the opposite way, down the ravine toward the two SOBs stringing the last trip wire. The Russians didn't have telepathy, but the SOBs didn't have much to fight with. They were in a race to see who showed up first—the Russians or Walker Jessup with the replacements for the weapons blown up in Spain.

IOANNES TRIKOUPI took two hours to reach his contact at Intourist. He spent a three-hour lunch telling the man about his discovery, what with boasting and wine.

The GRU agent memorized everything, went back to the office, put the information into the appropriate channels, then said he was coming down with something and went home to sleep off the wine.

The hangover kept him awake half the night, so he didn't reach the office until late the next morning. By the time he arrived, an acknowledgment was waiting for him. He knew that so fast an acknowledgment was high praise, indeed. He went back to work, happier from the praise he'd received than from that putrid Greek wine he'd drunk.

The GRU man's world grew even brighter the next day, when orders followed the acknowledgment. Agent 675, his pet bore, Trikoupi, was to be terminated! He was to choose a method that would advance Operation Claw.

The GRU man now realized you didn't have to believe in God to have prayers answered. For what else were these orders from Moscow? At last he was going to be done with that boasting, boring, drunken son of a bitch!

CHAPTER TWELVE

Walker Jessup went "Eeeny, meeny, miny, mo."

On "mo," he pointed at one of a stack of crated Energa rounds for a 100-millimeter Blindicide antitank rocket launcher. The two Turks beside him nodded and started opening the crate.

Jessup stepped back to give them room and also because he didn't trust that venerable ammunition. Most of it was probably old enough to vote. Most of it would probably still work, too. But Jessup wanted a random test before he accepted delivery.

"Fixer, you really think we need this test?" Rawson asked him.

"No. I think we can afford to blow Nile Barrabas and his people to bits with a faulty round."

Rawson sighed. "Ask a stupid question..."

"Yeah, and the fifth one. I know time's a-wastin'. I also know this may be all Nile and his people get to fight off a Spetsnaz raid. You want him alive to waste Heiss, or don't you?"

"Fixer, by the time I retire, I may learn it's not smart to argue with you."

"When are you pulling the pin, by the way? You must have thirty in, or pretty close to it."

"There's Jimbo to get through college," Rawson said. Jimbo was Rawson's youngest child and only son; his two daughters were already grown, and one of them was married. "Us old spooks don't have the kind of connections that make defense contractors hire us at twice our Army pay," Rawson added.

That didn't sound like fishing for a handout, but Jessup decided to make a friendly offer, anyway. "Between my friends at the Company and at NSA, I just might be able to get in a word for you."

"If we've all got our asses in the same number of pieces after this is over, I won't say no." Rawson took Jessup's arm. "Better move to the right. The back blast on these Belgian mothers is unbelievable."

Jessup shifted as the larger Turk hoisted the launcher onto his shoulder. The other hefted the bottle-shaped 100-mm rocket and held it by the tail.

"Fire in the hole!" Rawson shouted.

In the next moment, the whole world seemed to turn to fire. The two Turks and the launcher vanished in a ball of smoke, flame, dust and flying debris. A red-hot baseball bat smashed Jessup across the right temple. A giant bee stung him in the calf—several giant bees. His balance and his leg gave way together, and he toppled into the dust.

He must have blacked out for a minute or two. The next thing he saw was Rawson cutting open the leg of his trousers with a Randall combat knife. Jessup looked at the bloody patches on the hairy skin and said something rude.

Then he remembered the Turks. "Hey, Joel. How about the other—"

"Graves registration, except we don't have any around here." Rawson jerked a thumb at the bodies—or pieces of bodies—lying where the Turks had been. Already the voracious Middle Eastern flies were gathering on the mangled flesh and the patches of blood.

"What the fuck happened?"

"What you were afraid of, I guess. I take back what I said about you being too fussy. I'm sorry, Walker. Damned if the Turks didn't say this was the newest stuff they could spare. I guess I should have tried a little harder."

"Well, there's nothing left to shoot the other rounds out of, so I guess it doesn't matter," Jessup said. He put his hand to his temple and felt a scalp wound, probably bloody but certainly not deep. He was going to look awful and not feel too good for a while, but they could go on with getting the rest of the load on its way to the SOBs.

Unless that explosion wasn't an accident. If there had been any kind of a leak anywhere along the line, that round could have been rigged to explode when fired.

It might have been two or three of the SOBs scattered in pieces on the dusty ground, not a couple of Turks—who weren't expendable, either, to their families and friends.

By the time Jessup finished that thought, Rawson had finished bandaging the fat man's legs. With a little help and a lot of pain, sweat and swearing, Jessup found he could stand and even walk.

"Joel, you got an alternate route for getting the stuff out of here?"

"You're thinking Heiss might be onto us?"

"Great minds wobble and weave down the same gutter. Yeah, he or some of his friends might be snooping around. Just in case they've learned something..."

Rawson appeared to consult the sky, then the distant hills with their olive orchards, then the Turkish corpses. Finally he frowned. "If you can be security for the rest of the stuff—"

"How long?"

"Until about 2200."

That was five hours after Jessup and the weapons were supposed to be on a truck headed for the coast. In a little fishing village, they were supposed to transfer to a boat and be delivered to Haustim by dawn tomorrow.

"Maybe, if it's something worth waiting for."

"How about a helicopter?"

"Civilian or military? I want to keep our cover as long as we can."

"There's a whole bunch of little companies hallucinating about oil off the Turkish coast. Most of them have five employees, one desk and an old helicopter."

"As long as it flies. Can you pick up a few more crates of grenades while you're at it?"

"Nervous in the service, Fixer?"

"Damned straight. Our friend Heiss can't do much to C-4 or 7.62-mm NATO rounds. Grenades he could rig the way he might have rigged that Blindicide round."

"Umm. You got a point."

"Yeah, and when I comb my hair right you can hardly see it."

Now that the blood had dried, Jessup felt that nothing short of a hedge clipper would do much for his hair. It looked as if Rawson had used the last field dressing on his legs, and his scalp would just have to take its chances.

He could wing it, he guessed, if he didn't have a concussion and if the wound didn't start bleeding again. He was damned sure he was going to try, if only to warn Nile personally about who might be playing what kind of games. Then Nile would have Billy Two, who was a damned good armorer, go over everything in the pile that might go bang at the wrong time. No reason to tell Rawson that, of course. He might slack off on wangling those new grenades.

No reason not to see about getting the SOBs made official, either. Somebody was messing around, trying to start a war in the Aegean. Maybe it wasn't the Russians. Maybe all they had around here was seven old babushkas armed with knitting needles and a samovar. But somebody was playing for keeps, and that meant the SOBs ought to be backed up so they could do the same.

THE DECK under Lee Hatton's feet slammed upward against her sandals. She kept a firm grip on the gunwale and managed to stay standing to see a thirty-foot circle of sea turn to foam. As the foam subsided, dead fish bobbed to the surface, some intact, most blown open and trailing guts.

"I told you my fuses work as well underwater as on land, Alex, my boyo," Liam O'Toole said. "But you were after doubtin' me word, so much that I was tempted to make the charge about twice as big.''

''Good thing you didn't,'' Nanos said. ''We could really blow our cover, blowing this tender.'' He started the engines. ''Let's head back, in case somebody was listening down there.'' He jerked a thumb at the glistening Aegean as he opened the throttles.

''Got a date with the fair Adrienne?'' O'Toole asked.

''Ask no questions and you'll not be told to fuck off,'' Nanos replied. He put the helm over and pointed the tender's bow at the island.

Automatically Lee picked up the binoculars and began scanning the cliffs for anything suspicious. A flurry of movement that made her hold her breath turned out to be seabirds taking wing. Otherwise the gray cliffs were as sullen and forbidding as ever.

Those cliffs wouldn't protect the camp and the SOBs the way they'd protected the virginity of the old priestesses. Turning from diver into rock climber in the blink of an eye was something Spetsnaz troopers could do easily.

They made the SOBs' problem just barely manageable. The six mercs were probably the best in the world, but six people could be in only so many places at once. When they had to defend civilians, as well...

Life would be easier when Walker Jessup showed up with his new shipment and, please God, with official status for this whole fly-bitten mission! Until that happened, Lee would settle for Charlie getting off her tail about that skinny-dipping party.

Maybe she could arrange to lead him down one of the mined ravines and *not* warn him about the trip wires. That pleasant dream kept Lee smiling most of the way back to the island.

WALKER JESSUP SHIFTED position again to take the weight off his battered leg. At least the sun was almost down. The flies were no longer swarming over the dried blood on his scalp. Between the heat, the pain, the loss of blood and the flies he'd come close to losing consciousness a couple of times.

But it was 1930 now, and Rawson was supposed to be on the way back. In another two and a half hours, the oil-company helicopter was supposed to swoop down like a comic-book superhero and let Walker Jessup get off his swollen feet.

Things were looking up, ever so slightly.

Walker Jessup, too, looked up, suddenly enough to wrench his neck as a pair of Turkish F-16s swept overhead. They were losing altitude and burning fuel, probably heading for the airbase just over the ridge to the west.

A cloud of dust sprouted on that ridge as the Phantoms disappeared. Jessup unslung his Uzi. He kept it unslung and aimed even after the dust cloud turned into a Berliet light truck with Rawson riding shotgun and a bearded Turk at the wheel.

"Brought him along for extra muscle," Rawson said. "He still owes me and a couple of SAS people for getting him out of slavery in Abu Dhabi. Not that he wasn't guilty of knocking up the police chief's daughter, but it was her idea, too. So after a few words with the police chief it seemed the reasonable thing to do."

Jessup revised the letter of recommendation he'd been mentally composing for Rawson. Neither the Company nor the NSA could afford men who went off like missiles with faulty guidance systems. They started off by getting into the newspapers and went on from there. Take Karl Heiss, who'd never been mentioned in any of the newspapers that normally drooled over embarrassing the CIA—

The flap of rotor blades interrupted his thoughts. "Looks like your friends with the chopper are early," Jessup said, pointing east. An Agusta-Bell helicopter was skimming just above the vineyard walls, zigzagging toward them.

Rawson took one look at the helicopter and dived for the back of the truck. He reappeared with an M-60 machine gun. "No friends of mine." He fed in a belt and snapped off the safety. Then he said something in Turkish to the driver and waved at Jessup to get clear.

Jessup didn't need telling twice. Among other things, if the bad guys in the helicopter started shooting and hit a crate of grenades—well, the flies who had dined on pieces of Turk could breakfast on pieces of American.

The helicopter suddenly shot up a hundred feet. Peering into the shadows of the vineyard, Jessup saw two men scrambling to their feet. He looked for cover. With his Uzi he couldn't do much about the chopper, but if the ground party closed in—

The M-60 *blrrruppped*. The belt danced madly. The Turk's hands danced almost as madly as he fed it in. The helicopter's windshield turned cloudy, then vanished under the bullets. The bullets ate their way back toward the engine.

Two hundred feet up, the helicopter lost all power. Somebody in the cockpit was still alive enough to try autorotating. The helicopter lurched, wobbled and looked about ready to stabilize itself.

Rawson let off another burst. This one hit the fuel tanks. Orange flame bloomed in the air, and the helicopter reached the ground in burning pieces.

One of those pieces was alive. It staggered out of the smoke, flames streaming from head, arms and torso. A third burst from the M-60 knocked it down, a fourth ended its writhing.

Rawson heaved Jessup to his feet, then picked up the M-60. Slinging it, he scrambled to the roof of the truck.

"Only high ground around here," he reported. "You and the Turk load the rest of the stuff. Maybe our friends are still showing up, but we can't wait for them. We're back to the original plan."

"What about the guys on the ground?"

"If you move your ass and our assets, I can keep their heads down until the truck's loaded. Then they can't catch us on foot."

They could radio ahead to friends with wheels or even roadblocks, of course. But one worry at a time. Jessup slung his Uzi and grabbed one end of a case of 9-mm pistol ammunition. He surprised himself by being able to lift it. Adrenaline, he decided, could do amazing things.

Now if it could only make all the ammunition safe, transport it to Nile Barrabas and persuade Jessup's superiors that this mission ought to go official about last week at the latest.

POKROVSKY LOOKED UP from Fokin's report summarizing the Greek response and saw the political instructor grinning.

It was an unusual expression for the *zampolit*, but for once the bastard was entitled. He'd used ten words in his analysis for every two he really needed, but, curse him, he was right!

The Greeks weren't going to ignore the Turkish raid on Ikyros indefinitely, but they might hold off on retaliation for a while to see if the Turks really meant what they'd said about apologies, compensation and punishment. If they held off too long, the danger of war would fade. Long enough, and somebody with less hatred and more resources might investigate some of the incidents. Somebody like the Americans. They could follow a trail leading straight to Seahome.

That put it squarely up to the Spetsnaz of Seahome to do their best imitation of Greek retaliation. It was no longer just a case of carrying out Operation Claw. It was more like self-defense.

Which meant there was only one possible target for the "Greek retaliation," as far as Pokrovsky was concerned. "How firm is our intelligence on that American covert action team on Haustim?" he asked.

Fokin frowned. "We know they're Americans. That they are a covert action team is only a probability. Also, even if they are legitimate targets, there are other Americans on the island who are not."

This time it was Belyusev who grinned. Catching his political colleague advising caution was a rare occurrence.

"All the more reason for raiding that island. Comrade *Zampolit*, you really haven't thought the political aspects through. If the Greeks kill Americans along with the Turks, American sympathies are *not* going to be with the Greeks.

"If the Turks think they have American support, then they will forget about compensation and the rest of that shit. They may even decide to retaliate. If they don't, the Greeks will as soon as they realize they aren't going to be paid off. Then all we have to do is throw a stick or two on the fire every so often, until the pot boils over."

Captain Isakov nodded. "It's risky, but I approve, on one condition. In case the Americans are a covert-action team, we must send all our men." He addressed Pokrovsky directly. "I realize you prefer to use only the Typhoons, but Team Cyclone needs seasoning, too. You and the Typhoons aren't immortal. What happens if your luck runs out before you've taught the new men all you know?"

That would take more years than Pokrovsky suspected he had left before retirement. Isakov was right, though. The Cyclones would be much the better for going on a couple of raids under his leadership before they set out on one of their own.

There was something else that Pokrovsky did not plan to mention outside the ranks of the Spetsnaz teams. The Americans might well be the Soldiers of Barrabas, to whom the men of Spetsnaz owed a blood debt. It was army teams Barrabas had fought and slaughtered before, but did that matter? There was no law that said the naval brigade could not avenge army comrades.

"Very well," Pokrovsky said. "I will draw up a plan for using twelve men. I warn you that we risk expending a good deal of irreplaceable equipment."

"A risk we can accept," Isakov said. "We must keep up the momentum of Operation Claw. This is a decision at the highest level. It is being supported by a shipment of equipment. Everything we asked for, if not more." He handed a printed list to Pokrovsky.

The Spetsnaz officer was not easily surprised, but knew that the highest levels must indeed have intervened to produce such generosity. Would there be room on the *N. V. Glubov* for all of it? The extra silencing aboard her took up a great deal of room, even though she no longer carried a full crew or load of torpedoes.

"If all this is on the way, we can certainly afford to expend equipment," Pokrovsky said. "Not men, though. They are not so easily replaced." He fixed the *zampolit* and the KGB officer with his hardest stare, daring them to disagree.

THE SEA BREEZE DIED as the truck rolled down to the shore. The cove now reeked of sewage, dead fish, seaweed, crude oil and Turkish tobacco.

Walker Jessup decided to do something about the latter smell. He maneuvered himself to his feet, out of the bed of the truck and upwind of the Turkish driver and his reeking cigarettes.

He wished the man wouldn't smoke at all this close to ammunition, but when he'd asked him not to, he'd gotten a blank stare. Either the man didn't understand English, or he took orders only from Rawson.

Jessup felt as if he'd been dead for a week. He wondered how he smelled. He suspected that his sweat and dust-caked clothes would armor him against grenade fragments and maybe small-caliber bullets.

Here they were, ammunition and all, where they were supposed to be to rendezvous with the boat that would take them to Haustim. In fact, it was half an hour late.

The cove was empty except for a half-rotten sailboat that looked old enough to have been cast up onto the beach after the Battle of Lepanto.

Footsteps grated on the shingle, and Rawson came loping up, a G-3 over his shoulder and his favorite Browning Hi-Power Mark II in a shoulder holster. Grinning, he looked as if the past twelve hours had been a wonderful adventure.

Walker Jessup decided there was one thing to be said for retirement when the time came—he wouldn't have to deal with suicidal maniacs who could go through this sort of shit and come out grinning!

"All clear all around," Rawson said. He spoke to the Turk and pointed at the old fishing boat.

Jessup's stomach fluttered. He tried to force a smile, then he tried to force out words. His face stayed frozen, and his words came out a croak.

"Leg kicking up, Fixer?"

"No, no, it's—look, Joel. Is *that* our boat?"

"Damned straight. Who'd ever suspect something like that to be carrying hot cargo?"

This time Jessup's stomach heaved. He might have thrown up his last meal if there'd been any of it left. Instead his stomach gave one final flip, then seemed to sink down to his ankles.

"I suppose nobody would," he said, trying not to scream. "And that's because we're fucking well going to *sink* before anybody suspects us of carrying anything!" Jessup thought he'd managed not to scream, until he heard the echoes from the cliffs.

The Turk was lighting another cigarette and obviously trying not to laugh. Rawson wasn't even trying. He was leaning on the right front fender of the truck, one hand pressed against his side.

"Seriously," Rawson said after he'd managed to restrain his amusement and had caught his breath. "Are you okay to stand guard? The Turk and I can do the rest of the heavy lifting."

"Oh, I can be as crazy as the next guy," Jessup replied. He struck a Rambo pose with the Uzi, which sent pain shooting all the way up his leg and into his thigh, stomach, and back teeth.

"Good," Rawson said. "By the way, I checked out that old tub. She needs paint, but she's dry and solid and she can haul more than we're going to be loading into her. The rigging's been tightened and the sails are all patched—"

"Sails?" Again Jessup heard echoes.

"Nobody can hear a sailboat, Fixer. So even if they start looking for us, they can't use electronics—"

"Joel, listen. This is the Mediterranean Sea. You know, where they invented the galley because the wind isn't very reliable."

"I know. She's got four sweeps, too. Of course, there's only three of us, but that means one of us can rest while the other two..."

It occurred to Walker Jessup that shortly after inventing the galley, the Mediterranean people had also invented the galley slave.

He had to sit down. In another minute he was going to start laughing, and wouldn't stop until he fell over. If he was sitting, he wouldn't have so far to fall.

Jessup wondered if Rawson would ever sit down with Barrabas over a few beers and tell him about this trip. Briefly he considered shooting Rawson to make sure that didn't happen. Then he realized that wasn't practical. There was only one thing to do. Tell Nile himself—first. He couldn't look any more of a fool than he did now.

No, there was a second thing to do. Never, ever, under any circumstances in all the years from now until the end of time, no matter what was at stake, launch an unofficial mission for the Soldiers of Barrabas.

CHAPTER THIRTEEN

Ioannes Trikoupi looked up at the sound of footsteps crunching on the gravel path to the sea. A big man stood there, dressed like a Peloponnesian farmer but with a luxuriant dark beard and an air of self-confidence, almost arrogance. The man jerked his head toward the sea.

"Time to go."

"When do we get paid?" one of Trikoupi's companions asked.

"No more pay until the job is done," the bearded man replied.

"I am too poor to do it that way," the first man said, standing up. "I—"

The bearded man rested a hand on his pocket. "Are you a man or a woman?" he asked. He spoke as if he didn't care if the other man was insulted or not.

Trikoupi tried to look at both the bearded man and the one who wanted to return home. The silence dragged on.

"If he wants to go, I'll pay you back what he has been given," Trikoupi said. At least this would end the stalemate, which was beginning to make him nervous.

"Be quiet," the bearded man said. "This is between Kyril and me, and Kyril's honor, if he has any."

Kyril looked ready to spring at the bearded man. The bearded man kept his hand close to his pocket. What was in there? A gun, a knife? Trikoupi hoped he wouldn't find out. That would be a bad beginning to this blow for the honor of Greece, and unjust treatment for a man who had at least come this far.

Trikoupi looked at the other men. They seemed not to care what happened, as long as it didn't happen to them.

Most of them looked like men who didn't even own their farms, who worked for others when they worked at all instead of begging or stealing.

This wasn't the company he'd expected to be keeping when he'd answered the telephone two days earlier. Were honor and manhood really asleep among Greeks, at least among those who had something to lose? Well, there was one Greek who would show he hadn't forgotten the heritage of those who'd fought for freedom against the Turks.

Finally Kyril grunted and sat down again.

"Good," the bearded man said, smiling. "But don't get too comfortable. Our boat will be ready in ten minutes, maybe less. When I tell you, come quietly. No talking, no holding back, and don't fall down the cliff, or I'll let you drown."

Trikoupi believed that last threat.

ALEX NANOS and Adrienne Biggle sat side by side in the lee of a boulder on the ridge they'd christened Summit. As far as anyone could tell, it was the highest place on Haustim. Except for the two ravines leading up from the sea, the rest of the island was as flat as a Ping-Pong table.

In the shelter of the boulder, they were out of the wind, and could see anyone approaching without being seen. A stand of wild thyme on the other side of the boulder perfumed the air.

For Nanos, who had gourmet standards for outdoor sex, it was a perfect trysting place. He suspected Dr. Biggle would come around to his opinion soon enough, but he wasn't going to hurry.

Summit was also the high ground that the SOBs would try to hold if they couldn't hold anything else. What would happen to the camp in that case was something Nanos tried not to think about.

"I really wish you people would relax a bit," Biggle said. "Hank's still fighting the Vietnam War. Classic posttraumatic stress disorder."

Nanos wondered what Barrabas or Lee Hatton would say about that diagnosis. He also wondered whose comments would be less printable.

"Remember the old joke, 'Just because you're paranoid doesn't mean there's nobody after you.'"

Biggle sighed. "That doesn't mean you people have to behave like a bunch of undercover agents."

Nanos shrugged to cover instant total alertness.

Biggle went on. "That Mack. I wouldn't be surprised if the DEA is blackmailing him into working for them. That's why I offered to hire him. I'm sure the college could get his record cleared."

For which, no doubt, Claude Hayes would be expected to be grateful to Old Missus Biggle for the rest of his time at the college. Claude was about ready to welcome a Spetsnaz raid, before he ran out of patience with the archaeologist.

"Well, I haven't noticed him snooping around. And if any of your people are doing drugs, well, they're not doing them around any of us."

That wasn't quite true. Charlie had a matchboxful of grass in his tent, more than enough to get him a couple of years in a Turkish prison. Lee had spotted it several days ago. The SOBs were keeping the knowledge in reserve, in case they had to blackmail the archaeologists into cooperation or Charlie into keeping his hands off Lee.

"Besides, Adrienne," Nanos added, "if this Greek-Turkish brawl does get out of hand, a few people who've been shot at might help. I suspect most of your Turks will be called up. Then all you'll have left to evacuate you is the boat bums."

"We wouldn't need to evacuate," Biggle said firmly. "This is a known archaeological site, of no military importance. World opinion would be outraged if the Greeks attacked us."

Nanos thought that in the real world people rarely counted on others to act according to what world opinion dictated, but Adrienne was clearly a woman with her mind made up. No ugly facts were going to be allowed to break down the door of her beautiful theory of peace and brotherhood.

He put an arm around her waist and drew her head down onto his shoulder. She let it rest there for a moment, then sat up.

"Don't want to play with the help, Dr. Biggle?" Nanos sounded much more hurt than he felt.

"Oh—damn. Captain Nanos…Alex, you are attractive, and I don't believe in class distinctions. But…well, we'd have to be very discreet. Not being available helps when you're dealing with Turks."

"I know."

"You do? Then maybe we can work something out. Meanwhile, can you tell that floozy Linda the facts of life around Turks? She's asking for trouble."

Trouble for any Turks who got out of line, certainly. Probably for Charlie, too. Lee Hatton, Alex Nanos knew very well, did believe in class distinctions. She distinguished men who had class from those who didn't. Charlie fell into the second category, and he was going to fall into something else, like the Aegean Sea, if he wasn't careful.

"Let's not worry about Linda, Adrienne." Nanos looked at his watch, then at the surrounding countryside. In the moonlight, he memorized a few more ranges, then put his arm around the professor's waist again.

"Do you see anybody coming?"

"No."

"Do we have to be back to camp right away?"

"No."

Nanos tipped up her face and kissed her on lips that started tight, almost cold, then slowly opened, and after that warmed up quickly.

TRIKOUPI STARED at the boats waiting for the men at the foot of the cliff. If the bearded man hadn't been right behind him, he would have cursed out loud.

The boats were two inflatable dinghies, made of dark rubber with fiberglass duckboards to reinforce their bottoms. Neither had an engine.

The bearded man smiled again. "Any of you know how to row?" he whispered.

Trikoupi and two or three others nodded.

"Good. The rest of you may have time to learn if the wind's against us. If not, we should be where we want to go in half an hour."

"Are we going to row all the way to Turkey?" one of the men was bold enough to ask.

"No. But if you ask any more questions, you may have the chance to swim."

Silence fell again. Everyone seemed to know that the next one who defied the bearded man would be made into an example. Nobody wanted to find out what that meant, but the bearded man had to be armed. Even with his bare hands he looked able to break any of the others in two.

Trikoupi assumed they were rowing out to rendezvous with a fast boat too noisy to operate close to shore. His only concern was when they were going to be armed. He hadn't held a gun since he'd finished his army service, and he wondered if some of his new comrades had ever done that much!

POKROVSKY STEPPED AWAY from the map of Haustim. None of the eleven other men crammed into the room needed to get up or even turn his head to see it. There was barely room to breathe.

It would have been easier to brief his own team and Team Cyclone separately, but he had a different goal to accomplish—to make the two teams work together as one.

"Looks like a piece of shit someone stepped in," one of the Cyclones said.

"Somewhat," Pokrovsky said. "But unfortunately it's not as soft. Also, except for these two ravines, it's almost sheer cliff all around. The ravines will certainly be defended if there are covert-action people on the island. We'll assume that there are and plan accordingly. Now, comrades, what does this suggest to you?''

Asking for suggestions in the average Soviet military unit was almost anti-Soviet activity. Not in Spetsnaz, though.

A hand went up among Pokrovsky's Typhoons. "Three teams. One for each ravine, carrying the heavy weapons if we're taking any—"

"We are."

"I thought so. One team climbing up the cliff between the ravines. Then they can move fast to the central ridge and observe hostile movements on the whole island."

"What if one of the ravine teams gets in trouble?" Pokrovsky asked.

"Well, I suppose the cliff climbers could also move to reinforce that team, take whoever's facing them in the rear...."

"I hope you don't do any supposing when the shooting starts!" grumbled the first Cyclone.

"You know what he means," another Cyclone said.

Pokrovsky smiled with satisfaction. Supporting a member of the other team, against one's own teammates if necessary, was what he wanted to see.

The list of equipment had both teams cheering, but one Cyclone was skeptical. "Is all this ironmongery sanitary enough? We're supposed to be Greeks, after all."

"There is a *maskirovka* planned to keep anybody from being suspicious," Pokrovsky replied. "I have no details. Also remember that this is the eastern Mediterranean. Shooting at your neighbor is an outdoor sport. What could be more logical than desperate Greeks, disowned by their government, making deals with, let us say, Arab terrorists for Soviet arms?"

"If that's logic, give me vodka," somebody muttered, which got more cheering.

Pokrovsky raised the harpoon he used as a pointer and began filling in details. "Each assault squad will consist of four men, two from each team. The senior Typhoon will be in command. The senior Cyclone will be the deputy. This reflects the greater experience of Team Typhoon in local conditions.''

A couple of the Cyclones started to mutter, but a glare from their leader silenced them. If Operation Claw succeeded, there would be glory enough for everybody. If it failed, there would be enough bullets. That thought took the smile off his face for a moment.

"Since close coordination will be critical, each team will have a radio. To preserve our cover, each team will have one of the fluent Greek speakers assigned. If the Greek speaker becomes a casualty, communicate in code.''

"I'm not your grandmother, but I know how to suck eggs," the Cyclone leader said. "What about any boats at the moorings? Those satellite shots show at least one big one.''

"One big trawler yacht, slow as a buoy and as formidable as a New Year's party hat," Pokrovsky said. "The boats are strictly a target of opportunity. Dead people will do more damage than sunk boats, as the Turks taught us.''

That got more laughter, which faded as someone asked, "What about American civilians? Particularly women?''

"If there are any genuine American civilians on that island, they're in the shit," Pokrovsky said. "We won't do anything to them that a bunch of untrained Greeks wouldn't do. We won't cry if they get hurt, either.

"In fact, it will help if they do. The United States will think the Greeks have refused the Turks' offer to negotiate. Unofficially they'll be anti-Greek for a while. That could encourage the Turks to retaliate, without our having to lift a finger or fire a single bullet.''

SOMETHING BLACK lifted on the crest of a wave ahead. Trikoupi tried to identify it and missed his stroke. The man at the other oar cursed him softly. Heavy hands came down on both their shoulders, and the bearded man, whose name was Nikolas, whispered one word:

"Row!"

The two rafts crept across the moon-silvered water. Trikoupi began to regret that he'd given up leading hiking tours. He would have been in better shape if he hadn't. But he'd be damned if these scrapings of the Peloponnesos would think that the only Athenian to join them was a weakling!

Incredibly, the black shape turned into an airplane squatting on the water. A medium-size flying boat, in fact. Trikoupi recognized an American-built Grumman Albatross, modernized with turboprop engines.

Ironic, that an American-built plane would carry Greeks to avenge their countrymen against the Americans' Turkish pimps. Such irony had once made great poems and plays. Now all that Greece could do was assemble a handful of bandits to uphold its honor.

Trikoupi was so gloomy at the thought of Greece's decline that he nearly rammed the raft into the flying boat. The same heavy hand gripped his shoulder again. This time the whisper went on longer.

"Do you know which end of the rifle to point at the enemy? If you shoot yourself, it won't be much of a loss, except for the bullet that we might otherwise shoot at the Turks."

"I'll be careful."

"Or dead. Don't expect any other choices."

The hand lifted. Trikoupi scrambled into the flying boat. It had light metal bucket seats with canvas straps. He couldn't help noticing olive-drab bags under each seat, which didn't look like parachutes. He wanted to poke one with his foot to find out if it held ammunition. Thoughts of the bearded man made him sit down, instead.

The engines started and wound up to an earsplitting whine. Water thrummed against the hull as the flying boat raced across the sea. Trikoupi didn't move until the thrumming died away.

Craning his neck, he saw the moonlit Aegean dropping away below the plane. Trikoupi suddenly felt as if all his life before now had been an animal's existence. Tonight he began to live as a man.

CHAPTER FOURTEEN

Nile Barrabas braced his feet against a boulder and his back against the cliff. Billy Two handed him the Starlite scope.

The old Turkish fishing boat took shape in the darkness. A weary Turk seemed to be leaning on the wheel more than manning it. An encouragingly large tarpaulined pile squatted amidships. Beside the pile squatted something else large. Something large and human. In fact—

Barrabas didn't realize he'd cursed out loud until he heard safeties snapping off all around him.

"Cool it, people. No trouble—I think."

"Not sure, Colonel?" asked O'Toole.

"Well, have you ever known Walker Jessup to show up without *something* being wrong?"

This time Barrabas heard hollow groans all around him.

IN THE FISHING BOAT, Walker Jessup was straddling the gunwale. A wave lifted the vessel, then dropped it onto something solid. The jolt slammed up into Jessup's groin. He decided that a soaking was preferable to castration and went over the side.

The boat must have struck a projecting rock, because he dropped into water only chin deep. Then a wave submerged him completely. He spit out water and slogged toward the shore.

By the time he was waist-deep, four SOBs were in sight— Nile, Alex and Billy Two in the water, with Liam on dry land, keeping watch up the ravine. The first three quickly formed a human chain, and box after box passed along the chain to pile up on the beach.

Jessup watched the unloading from a perch on a weed-slick boulder. After he got his breath back, he fished out a sealed plastic envelope containing the inventory, made sure it was still sealed and went back to watching.

As far as he was concerned, he would gladly spend the rest of this mission watching other people work. He was resigned to a voyage back to the mainland on that seagoing garbage scow, but that was it. Professor Stewart and the Navy were handling delivery of the Nate Beck Specials, and the decision about making the SOBs official was out of his hands. For now he could sit back and relax.

He might even be able to sit down to a couple of decent meals. Even one would make a difference. Even a *snack* of real food might help, considering what he'd been eating on that fishing boat! Compared to that, McDonald's was a gourmet's paradise. And Rawson had scarfed the stuff down as if it were prime steak!

"Feeling hungry, Fixer?"

"How'd you guess, Nile?"

"Nothing else has you talking to yourself like that."

"I've found something, believe me. You should have warned me about Rawson!"

"Low-capacity communications will do that to you every time. What's your beef against him? Sorry, I didn't mean to mention food."

Jessup found himself spilling a complete account of everything that had happened to him from the firefight in Barcelona to landfall on Haustim. Every so often Barrabas would ask a question, usually about Rawson.

Jessup noticed the questions got quieter and quieter as the story rolled along. By the time he was finished, he detected a familiar iron note in Barrabas's voice.

"Nile, you smell something about Rawson? And don't play any goddamn games about how'd I guess. If we've got more trouble—"

"We do, but how bad it is, I don't know. From what you've said, Rawson may be working with Heiss."

"I just got through telling you he wants you people to go after Heiss once you're through—"

"Have you never heard of thieves falling out?"

"Goddamn it, Nile! Either shut up or give it to me straight. I've been jerked around by every asshole in uniform from Spain to here, and I don't need you doing it, too."

"Keep your voice down, Fixer," Barrabas said, in a different tone. The iron was back in his voice, and something else—the tone of a CO with a complex tactical problem.

"Okay," Barrabas said. "I'll give this to you fast, because we can't afford to make Rawson suspicious if you're going back on his boat. Not if you want to get off at the other end."

That got Jessup's undivided attention. Barrabas went on. "Rawson's real fond of his kids, but he's also fond of other people's teenage daughters. I remember one time, he got some sergeant's kid knocked up. She was fifteen. They'd have run his ass up the flagpole and left it to rot there if he hadn't already been playing footsie with the Company. The order came down—leave him alone, because we need him.

"Rawson was always a better spook than he was a soldier. Given a chance to have all the fun of being a Company man and all the fun of being a soldier, he was one happy boy. Not to mention that the Company would cover up for him anytime he got into the wrong pair of pants."

"So that's how he got all those generals mad at him? Not standing up to them, but lying down with their daughters?"

"Got it."

"Nile, I'm not calling you a liar, but how come *this* old Company boy never heard about Rawson?"

"Fixer, what would have happened to Rawson back where either of us came from?"

"He'd have been in jail, if he'd lived to get there."

"Right. Maybe some of the other Company boys didn't like keeping a pet like Rawson. Enough not to talk about him, anyway."

"Hey, Fixer!" came a shout from the boat. "Finished that inventory yet? I don't want to be too close to this island come daylight."

"Five more minutes, Colonel," Jessup shouted back.

"Keep it down," O'Toole muttered. "I thought I saw something moving up at the head of the ravine."

"You and Billy investigate it," Barrabas ordered.

The two men drew Browning Hi-Powers and stalked into the darkness as silently as cats, in spite of the steep, rubble-strewn slope.

"Okay, Nile," Jessup said, "explain me this. If Rawson's working with Heiss, how come he went to so much trouble to get this stuff to you?"

"I can't prove it, but...was Rawson either laughing or smiling most of the time?"

"*All* the time. I thought he was one crazy mother. Are you saying—"

"That's the way he is when he's putting on an act and making a fool of somebody. Fixer, you've been had. You couldn't have been had more thoroughly if that rigged Blindicide round had taken you out.

"I figure he's going to take one of two lines with Heiss. Either he's going to claim mistaken identity and apologize, or he's going to hope he's weakened Heiss enough to move in on him. Move in on him, and take over his drugs, his intelligence contacts, the whole enchilada."

"Shit."

"About nine feet deep and rising, by my estimate. Fixer, how long would it take before you were missed if you 'fell overboard' on the way back to the mainland? Long enough for Rawson to cover his tail?"

Jessup nodded. "I was being real careful to keep a low profile for this unofficial mission."

"Well, Fixer, now you know why we weren't too happy about unofficial status. Welcome to the ass-on-the-line club."

"You can't imagine how underwhelmed I am," Jessup said. He couldn't have moved a foot unless his life had depended on it, but his thoughts were sprinting ahead. The issues were much too important for Nile to be playing games with him. The colonel's suspicions might not be justified, but they were honest.

If they were justified, Walker Jessup might be in trouble he couldn't fix if he got back aboard Joel Rawson's boat. Boats were awfully good places for "accidents" to happen, especially to fat, clumsy, overaged free-lance intelligence types.

But the alternative was staying on the island, eating whatever the SOBs could scrounge up for him, because he'd have to hide out to avoid blowing their cover.

His stomach rumbled. His mouth watered. Then a sick feeling settled in his stomach and his mouth went dry at the thought of an "accident." And now that he thought it over, the timing of those little firefights with Heiss's men was almost *too* perfect....

If he stayed on the island and Colonel Rawson was offended, he could always be placated later. If Walker Jessup was drowned, on the other hand, there wasn't a whole lot anybody could do. Even the SOBs had problems bringing people back from the dead.

"Okay, Nile. I'll hang in here. I've put in the request for official status. I don't have to do anything more on the mainland for a few days. We'd better warn Stewart and the Navy, though. They may want to change arrangements for the delivery of the electronic gear."

Barrabas glared. "You didn't tell Rawson about *those*, I hope."

Jessup lurched to his feet and shook his fist under Barrabas's bristly chin. "Colonel Barrabas. On this mission I have been harassed, frustrated, starved, inconvenienced, cramped and shot at. I have not yet been insulted. Now will you for Christ's sake apologize for that?''

Barrabas winced. "Fixer, I'm sorry, believe it or not. We haven't exactly been having a Roman orgy here—"

"Not even Alex?"

"Not even Alex. And there's a creep of a graduate assistant with the hots for Lee, who may have to be cooled off a bit. Besides, ever since you mentioned that rigged round, I've been wondering what other surprises the great babysitter molester has cooked up."

"Yeah, I can get a little worried about that myself. How about we put Billy and Liam O'Toole on it?"

"Oh what?" said two voices in the darkness.

"You find anybody up on the ridge?" Barrabas asked.

"Not now, and no sign they ever were. I don't think any of the Americans could have come without leaving traces."

"What about the Turks?" Jessup asked.

"With all due respect, milord Fixer," O'Toole said, "who's after puttin' you in the chain of command?"

"The Fixer's taking a little vacation on scenic Haustim," Barrabas explained. He quickly summarized the situation.

"Welcome to Club Dead," Billy said when the colonel was finished. "Where are we going to keep him so as not to blow our cover?"

"Oh, I've picked out a few nice dry caves for reserve ammunition," O'Toole said cheerfully. "Assuming there's any of it and any of me left after I disarm all of Rawson's wee tricks. With a sleeping bag and a bucket and some food, any of them will be just like home for the Fixer."

"Yeah, if my home was the city dump," Jessup grumbled. It was time to imitate Cortés and burn his boats behind him. He refused to think about the cave. Instead, he pictured himself floundering in the Aegean, slowly sinking, while Rawson and the Turk laughed—if Rawson didn't shoot the Turk first to avoid having a witness.

Jessup took a deep breath and cupped his hands. "Hey, Rawson. Head on back without me. Turns out the next part of my job's here on the island."

"Goddamn it, Fixer—"

"Sorry, Colonel. No can do. You'll still get that reference."

Something that sounded like agreement floated out of the darkness. The boat's sail swung to the wind, and the oars splashed into the water. Jessup waited until he saw the Turk going forward to haul up the anchor before he turned his back on the sea.

"'Reference'?" Barrabas asked as they scrambled up the ravine.

Jessup was too busy catching his breath for a moment to reply. Then he explained.

Barrabas started to laugh. For a moment Jessup thought the leader of the SOBs had lost it. Then he realized it was kind of funny—giving a man who'd been doing Company dirty work for years a reference for a Company position.

Jessup laughed, too. And the easy understanding made him feel that he really belonged with the SOBs when you got right down to it.

THE LAST EMPTY CARTRIDGE rattled on the dusty ground. The powder smell blew away on the breeze, leaving only the scent of the sea and the straggling olive orchard that hid the training range.

Trikoupi shouldered his 7.62-mm FAL and stepped aside for the next man on the range. As he passed Nikolas, the bearded man slapped him on the shoulder as he growled, "Good shooting." It was a friendly slap.

The blow still almost drove Trikoupi to his knees—a reminder, if any was needed, that Nikolas was friendly. Everybody was sure he'd had something to do with Kyril's "stumbling" and falling to his death from the cliff the night before last.

Now Nikolas was screaming at one of the farm laborers with what Trikoupi recognized as a strong Macedonian accent. The laborer was probably the worst shot of the eight men; if he went into action with his FAL he was likely to cause more casualties than the Turks.

Trikoupi wondered again if such abuse was fit for free Greeks risking their lives for their country's honor.

He also wondered if they were getting adequate training along with the abuse. No doubt time was short, or they would have found a better place for training than this wretched little spur of rock with barely any shade and water. They had rifles, regular Greek army issue, but shouldn't they have more than rifles? Grenades, rocket launchers, explosive charges—the Turks seemed to have used all of these. Wouldn't the Greek reply seem feeble without them, and wouldn't a feeble reply merely encourage the Turks and their American masters in their arrogance?

Greeks might die because of this. Trikoupi decided to put the question to Nikolas, even if that was courting Kyril's fate!

"One RPG-7, eight rounds, waterproofed."

The Cyclone team diver, who was the mission's armorer, repeated Pokrovsky's words. Then he went over the rocket launcher and the packaged rounds. He seemed to have eyes in his fingers from the way he touched each one.

That was the way Pokrovsky liked to see a man getting ready for a mission. He took it for granted that his Typhoons did it. It was a pleasant surprise to see it in the Cyclones, as well.

Anybody on Haustim who thought he was safe was about two days from the last and worst surprise of his life.

"One ASG-17, with five magazines."

This was the first test for the waterproofed Spetsnaz version of the 30-mm grenade launcher. Pokrovsky had debated between it and an RPK-74 as the other heavy weapon for the operation. The LMG was combat-tested, but it couldn't do as much damage as fast as a stream of grenades from the ASG.

Also, if the American covert-operations people somehow escaped the grenade shower, they'd be handicapped by having to deal with mangled, screaming, panic-ridden civilians. Against Spetsnaz, Pokrovsky expected that handicap to be fatal, even if the covert-action team really was by some chance the SOBs.

For a moment his hands trembled at the thought of being the one to avenge the dead army teams the SOBs had left in their wake the past few years. Fortunately the trembling passed before the armorer noticed it.

Steadily the arsenal passed before Pokrovsky. The RPG, the ASG, three radios, four satchel charges. An AKR, silenced PSM automatic and four grenades for each man. Each man was checking out his own diving gear now and would be carrying his own knife, except for those like Pokrovsky and the Rope, who would be carrying two.

Pokrovsky laughed.

"Yes, Comrade Captain Lieutenant?"

"I was just thinking. One day, perhaps, we of the Spetsnaz should get some good out of *glasnost*. What we do will be in *Red Star*, and everyone will sing our praises the way they do of the American Special Forces."

The armorer looked at Pokrovsky as if he wasn't sure if his commander was joking.

MAJOR SINAS BROUGHT the inflatable alongside the boat. Rawson's Turkish crewman helped him up the side, then went forward to pick up his gear.

Rawson looked at Sinas, who nodded and drew his Browning. Two shots into the crewman's back, and he collapsed into the bilges. His blood turned the bilge water red as Rawson set the fuse on the block of C-4. It would go off in an hour, long after Rawson and Sinas were safely ashore. If anyone found the sunken boat and the Turk's body, they would probably chalk it up to the Greek retaliation.

They paddled ashore in silence, and Rawson didn't begin the story of his adventures until they'd reached their safe house. Sinas frowned when he heard Jessup had remained on the island.

"Jessup didn't mention the kind of business that kept him on the island?" the major asked.

His tone showed suspicion. The same suspicion, in fact, that Rawson had been wrestling with all the way back from the island.

A frustrating wrestling match, too, because there wasn't a goddamn thing he could do if Jessup was going to get smart. Rawson would have to figure out some other way of leading the SOBs into a trap, one that didn't involve using an irresistible bait like Karl Heiss.

Maybe that was just as well, too. Nile Barrabas was one mean mother, and the rest of his people were almost as hard to kill. Play bait for that kind of people and sometimes you got eaten.

Not that Heiss wasn't going to have to go sooner or later. But Rawson didn't want Heiss to go until the colonel had made himself Heiss's only possible successor. He wanted Heiss's people to come to him and offer him Heiss's position, not try to avenge their boss.

"You expect an old spook like Jessup to give anything away?" Rawson replied.

"Jessup is a ghost?"

Rawson suggested there were rabid dogs and diseased pigs among Sinas's ancestors. The major wished that God had made it impossible for infidels to learn Turkish. "Let's leave God out of it," Rawson finished. "He's probably got enough on His plate."

Which might be Nile Barrabas's situation pretty soon, come to think of it. If the Russians could stay sober two days running, they'd be setting up a "Greek" raid on that island PDQ. A dozen Spetsnaz might be a handful even for the SOBs, and Walker Jessup would be a fat, helpless target.

Just maybe Jessup had done everybody except himself a favor by staying on the island, after all.

"You seem pleased," Sinas said.

"I am." He explained.

The major was smiling by the time Rawson finished. "Now I understand your pleasure. Is it too soon to drink to our coming victory, courtesy of our Soviet friends?"

Any time was too soon to drink raki, Rawson thought. In his opinion it was the most god-awful panther piss ever distilled. But you couldn't get decent bourbon in Turkey, so drink what you could get, and thank God Turkey wasn't one of those uptight Muslim countries where you couldn't drink at all!

CHAPTER FIFTEEN

Walker Jessup grunted. It was the kind of grunt a caveman might have made when he'd learned that the tribe across the river had hunted out all the mammoths. How was he going to feed his family through the winter?

Jessup certainly felt like a caveman. The cave that hid him and the SOBs' weapons did a great job of that. Otherwise it was a bit short of comforts.

The Fixer looked longingly at the radio. He was tempted to report a suspicious sighting just to get some company out here. He'd have preferred Lee Hatton or Liam O'Toole, but he'd take Nile even at the price of another lecture about Rawson.

Hell, he'd even take Alex Nanos. "Captain" Nanos was getting a little bigheaded, "giving orders" to the rest of the SOBs. He wouldn't have won any prizes for being nice to Jessup at the best of times. Now he was damned near impossible.

Jessup walked to the mouth of the cave and looked out. The last of twilight was fading, the stars were coming out in a cloudless sky and the evening coolness was flowing into the cave. He walked back and sat down on a case of Army MREs.

In his opinion, Meals Ready to Eat made pretty good chairs, ballast, fishing sinkers—anything but food. Not to mention that Rawson might have slipped a little cyanide into the freeze-dried peaches. He'd certainly done enough sabotage to the ammunition to convince Jessup that Nile was probably right about Rawson.

O'Toole and Billy Two were planning some fun with the sabotaged ammunition. Fun for them, at least. Somehow

Jessup doubted it was going to be fun for anybody who tried to use one of the messed-up grenades.

Jessup noticed a spot on his Uzi and pulled out a cleaning kit. Nobody who'd ever been an infantryman ever lost a chance to clean his weapon, and Walker Jessup had been a pretty good infantryman many years and a hundred and fifty pounds ago.

With a working gun, he might even bag a few sea gulls and roast them over driftwood for fresh meat!

THE LIGHTS around the external lock hatch on the Type 88 faded into the dark water. Pokrovsky led his divers slowly toward the surface. He was happy to see that the two Cyclone men were as cautious as the Typhoons. Starting from fifty meters down, a hasty ascent risked the bends. That would cripple the mission just as surely as a whole Special Forces company.

The motion of the waves reached them as they approached the surface. One of the divers trusted too much to his depth gauge and not enough to his instincts. His head vanished as it broke the surface. Pokrovsky reached up and grabbed the man's left flipper.

Instead of simply submerging, the man arched his body in a full dive. Pokrovsky didn't know how much more of him had been visible above the water. Probably too much, if there was anyone around to see him.

He hoped the Cyclone leader would speak to the man when they returned to Seahome. The man had made his mistake out of inexperience, but such a mistake could wipe out a team and a mission.

The four divers of the Gamma Ravine team now spread out into a line twenty meters long. Pokrovsky's fins settled into a steady rhythm as he beat his way toward the shore. The divers slipped through the water like a school of sharks, swimming down the track of their prey.

"WATCH OUT for that loose stone, Charlie," Lee Hatton said.

"That one?" The archaeologist pointed at a rock the size of a Thanksgiving turkey, lying half-buried in the side of the ravine.

"No, the one just in front of it."

"Hey, come on, Linda. I'm no kid, as you may have a chance to find out." His leer was unmistakable. "You don't need to hold my hand to keep me from tripping over my own feet."

Briefly Lee Hatton considered taking Charlie at his word. That would be one way of getting out of peeling off her clothes in front of him. But just being a jerk didn't mean he deserved a broken ankle. It would also be kind of a hassle getting him back to camp without calling for help, if he couldn't walk.

Not to mention that the rock she'd pointed out wasn't the only one rigged to one of Liam O'Toole's trip-wired charges. If the ravine blew, all the fractures might not be Charlie's.

By good luck or good management, they covered the rest of the ravine to the sea's edge without trouble. The water chuckled and sighed on the rocks, and the sea breeze blew softly from the south. For once it didn't smell of oil slicks or dead fish. In better company, stripping and diving in might have been something Lee suggested herself.

Charlie started unzipping his jeans, then stopped. "Want some help, Linda?"

"I'm a big girl."

"So I've noticed."

Lee deliberately turned her back and gripped the bottom of her tank top, ready to pull it over her head. Then she stopped, both hands filled with sleazy blue synthetic fabric.

Out on the dark waves, something had broken the surface for a moment. It had come and gone so fast that Lee couldn't swear it had even been there, let alone what it had been.

But if it had been anything, it was a man's head, then a man's body diving. A man wearing a scuba outfit.

Lee turned back to see that Charlie had peeled to the buff. "Hey, come on," he whined. "Don't get uptight on me now."

"Who's getting uptight?" Lee said, making up her mind. Deliberately she pulled the tank top over her head, tossed it away and bent over her shoulder bag bare to the waist.

Charlie's eyes bugged out very nicely. They stayed that way while Lee explored her bag. One compartment held her knife, a second the Browning Hi-Power, a third what she was looking for—a miniature radio.

"I just need to ditch my contacts," she said. "You wouldn't want me to be half-blind, would you?" As she spoke, she unzipped her jeans. By the time she finished speaking, she was pushing them down over her hips.

Charlie looked as if swimming wasn't quite what he had on his mind. It occurred to Lee that maybe being half-blind wasn't a bad idea for any woman who really got close to Charlie. He might fill out in a few years, but right now he wouldn't win any Mr. Universe titles or even any Mr. Next Door contests.

Lee kept her bikini panties on while she keyed in Nile Barrabas's call sign. That, she figured, should keep Charlie thinking about when they'd be coming off. Then she keyed in her message.

"Nile. Lee here. I'm at the mouth of Ravine Blue. I've sighted what looks like a diver offshore."

Silence for a moment, then, "We don't have anybody out there. Pull back up the ravine, observe and report. I'll get somebody out to you right away."

"Okay. I'll have to be a little careful, though. I'm not alone."

"Charlie?"

"Got it in one."

"Any sign he's suspicious?"

"Nile, we were going swimming. He's got other things on his mind."

"Lee, I don't care whether your ass is covered or not. Get it moving up that ravine, or I'm going to land on it the next time I see you."

"Yes, sir."

She turned back to Charlie.

"I thought I saw somebody swimming out there, Charlie. I couldn't recognize him, but he had a scuba outfit on."

"Maybe we should invite him to—"

"Charlie, I haven't mentioned this before, but I think Dr. Biggle's right about some of Captain Nanos's friends being CIA. If we swim out and find one of them doing something he doesn't want us seeing..."

"Shit." Charlie sagged like a punctured balloon. "Damn. I was looking forward to this. But it would be too damned easy for us to 'drown.'"

"Yeah. So let's pick up our stuff and get back up the ravine. Far enough so they can't see us, but we can see anybody in the water."

That would also be just above the last of the explosive charges. Trip wires weren't the only means of setting them off. If the enemy wasn't cooperative, the charges could be detonated by radio command.

Charlie grinned as he realized Lee hadn't mentioned putting their clothes back on. Lee took her cue, pulling on her sandals but otherwise just throwing her clothes into her bag.

She felt Charlie's eyes on her as she led the way up the ravine, but she was more aware of the dark, gently heaving sea offshore, and what it might be hiding.

THE OUTBOARD MOTOR coughed and sputtered into silence. Ioannes Trikoupi barely heard it. All he heard was a name echoing inside his head.

Haustim. They were going to attack Haustim.

The island where Adrienne had her camp. Where Nikolas and his masters *knew* she had her camp, because the bearded man had mentioned it in the briefing!

"Our target is the Turkish workers at the archaeological camp. There are more than twenty of them, with no weapons. All are men, so we will not shame the name of Greeks by slaughtering women and children."

"What about the American archaeologists?" Trikoupi heard himself asking.

"How do you know there are Americans?" Nikolas asked.

Trikoupi swallowed, certain he was about to die but not caring. "I have—I know one of their leaders. A woman."

"How is she in bed?" Nikolas asked, and the other peasants laughed coarsely.

"I will not shame her by talking of such things," Trikoupi said. He was sure he would die too soon to save the honor of Greece, but at least he could save his own.

He hadn't died then. Instead Nikolas had shrugged. "If she stays out of the way of the bullets, none of them will hit her. If she comes running out to help her Turkish slaves, well, she must take her chances. I won't ask you to shoot her in cold blood. Is that enough?"

"Yes." Trikoupi knew that was as much as he would get and more than he had expected. He still suspected there was a hook somewhere in the bait.

For two days, the training had kept his mind off the danger to Adrienne. Danger, he now realized, that he might have brought on her. Greece had to be socialist; it could not be free any other way. But did a woman who had shared his bed have to be discarded in the process like an orange peel?

He didn't find an answer then and he didn't have one now, an hour at most from the island. An hour if Nikolas could start the motor again, three hours if they had to sail the rest of the way in these breezes. If they had to row, only God knew if they could reach Haustim at all tonight—

A faint splash made Trikoupi turn. Off to port, something rose slowly from the sea. Something so dark it was barely visible, though its metallic sheen was discernible.

Trikoupi's mouth went dry. The Turks had detected them and had sent a submarine—

But Nikolas was standing up, hailing the submarine, and somebody in the conning tower was waving back. Yet it was too small a conning tower for a regular submarine.

Nikolas stepped to the bow of the boat. "Comrades, you are about to serve your country. Our socialist friends in the submarine will see to that."

In one fluid motion he drew what he'd carried in his pocket all these days—a small automatic pistol. It cracked three times, and Trikoupi felt as if he'd been punched hard in the chest. When he looked down and saw his shirt turning red, he realized what had happened. A scream began in his throat, but died for lack of air as blood filled his lungs.

Trikoupi fell backward as Nikolas balanced himself on the gunwale, ready to jump overboard and swim to the submarine. Somehow Trikoupi landed so that he could see the submarine's machine gun riddle Nikolas, then lower its aim to riddle the boat.

He barely felt the impact of the machine-gun bullets, and never felt the pain from them. His last thoughts were almost pleasant—he'd seen Nikolas die and he wouldn't see Adrienne suffer.

BARRABAS REFUSED to run, much as he wanted to. Sooner or later the Turks in the camp would learn that something was wrong, but he didn't want a panic right off.

He also didn't want them tripping all over each other to help the SOBs unless the camp itself was attacked. Enthusiastic amateurs joining in a nighttime firefight were likely to get shot long before they could be helpful.

As he reached the tent where the trail bikes were kept at night, he saw Billy Two approaching from the other side of the camp. The huge Osage wore only jeans and sneakers, and carried a shoulder bag that Barrabas knew held an Ingram M-10.

"I don't know whether I heard Hawk Spirit or only a soldier's hunch," Billy said. "But I thought I was going to be needed."

"I hope both Hawk Spirit and your hunch are wrong," Barrabas said. "But I won't bet a can of light beer on it. Lee's holding the head of Ravine Blue. Alex is falling back on the cave, where he can command the head of Ravine Green. Liam and Claude have the boat. Let's go."

Turkish heads popped out of tents all over the camp as the SOBs' trail bikes roared to life. Turkish mouths opened to shout questions and curses as the two bikes roared past, then started coughing as dust rose in clouds.

The two mercs rolled past Dr. Biggle's tent, cut hard left and swung out onto the trail inland. Biggle's tent showed no sign of life, and Barrabas remembered that Alex had a date with her tonight. He hoped that whatever was about to happen wouldn't catch the two of them with their pants down!

THE ROPE ROLLED OVER and looked back until he was sure that the last of his squad was over the lip of the cliff. He had to look twice to find each one.

Blackened faces, black clothing and black weapons and gear added up to near invisibility at night. The diving gear now bobbed under inflatable black rubber buoys at the foot of the cliff. Ahead lay a brisk walk across country to seize the high ground of the island and hold the approaches to the camp.

The Rope was finishing his weapons check when he heard a familiar sound. It seemed so out of place there that he didn't recognize it at first. It was a small motorcycle moving across their front. No, two small motorcycles.

"Two fools out to break their necks," muttered the senior Cyclone. "Maybe we can save them the trouble if they get any closer."

If the riders were caught on the move, they'd be easy targets. Driving a motorcycle took both hands and both eyes at night on this kind of terrain. But if the riders were American covert-action men, and they had enough warning to find cover—

The Americans would be alert. The other Operation Claw teams were silent, meaning no alarm had been triggered. Even surprised American elite troops could be dangerous, as long as they lived. The Rope decided to search the area between the cliff and the high ground on the way to his squad's assigned position.

Using his hands as much as his voice, and map and flashlight hardly at all, the Rope gave his orders. The four Spetsnaz spread out and began their swift cross-country wolf-lope. In an hour they could cover ten kilometers and examine every meter of the distance.

The night, the presence of good comrades on either side and having begun the strike against the enemy combined to fill the Rope with pleasure. No woman could have given him half as much pleasure, unless she herself was a hunter.

The Rope doubted that such a woman existed, but if she did, he hoped he would one day meet her, no matter what side she was on!

ADRIENNE BIGGLE STOOD with her hands on her hips. She was glaring at Alex Nanos, and not just with her face. Nanos would have sworn a woman couldn't glare with her bare breasts, but that was before he'd met Adrienne.

"Alex, you aren't going to leave me hanging without *some* explanation. If a woman did that—"

"I know what I'd call her. But for Christ's sake, Adrienne! If it's just Hank having a nightmare or beating up on Linda, do you want everybody in the camp to know it?"

Biggle kicked at her bra, lying in the dust. It flew up and hit Nanos in the face. The hook nearly took out an eye. He wondered if bra kicking might become a new and effective combat technique.

By the time Nanos's eye had stopped watering, Adrienne had her blouse back on and was stuffing it into her jeans. She sat down to pull on her boots, and kicked Nanos when he tried to help. He jumped back, rubbing his shins.

She straddled her trail bike and started the motor, then turned to shout over her shoulder. "You can do as you please for your boat-bum friends. I won't ask questions. Just you don't ask me for anything anymore!"

She revved the motor and was off in a spray of dust and gravel.

Walker Jessup stuck his head out of the cave. He was so obviously trying not to grin that Nanos felt like kicking the grin off his face.

"What's the matter, Captain Nanos? Romance gone sour?"

"Not half as sour as you'll be if you open your goddamn mouth!"

Before Nanos could start another fight, he heard more trail-bike motors. Barrabas and Billy Two rode up, dismounted without a word, scrambled down into the cave and started passing up the weapons. Nanos and Jessup stood guard, carefully not even looking at each other.

When an assortment of G-3s, M-79 grenade launchers, ammunition and medical supplies was stacked outside the cave, Nanos finally turned to Jessup. "Sorry I bit your head off, Fixer. Thing is, it's going to be a little embarrassing around Dr. Adrienne for a while. She doesn't have much use for Hank, and she thinks I stood her up to help with a problem he shouldn't have in the first place."

"Lord bless and keep the ladies—far away from us at a time like this," Jessup said solemnly, imitating a well-known TV evangelist. "Oh, well, maybe this is a real alert. Then she'll see that we're worth having around."

Nile Barrabas straightened up from listening to his radio. "Fixer, you may just get that wish. That was Liam on the boat. He's picked up what sounds like an underwater explosion, about ten klicks west of the island. He's also heard what might be Soviet minisubs, a hell of a lot closer.

"I've ordered him to get under way but stay close inshore. Claude's suiting up. Fixer, you hold the fort here. Report if any of the caches transmit a signal."

The sabotaged weapons and ammunition were distributed over the island in several small caches. Since Spetsnaz doctrine and training encouraged the use of captured weapons, this was like leaving candy out for small kids.

"More like poisoned candy, for a street gang that's really got you pissed off," Liam O'Toole put it. "Those fulminate of mercury rounds will blow off somebody's head, and those instant-fused grenades could take out a whole squad."

If any of the caches were disturbed, miniature radios would send out an alert to the waiting SOBs. Waiting for the enemy to come to you was a good second best; knowing where to go hunting them was the real thing.

"Alex, you go reinforce Lee," Barrabas continued. "No side trips after Dr. Biggle, please. If she's headed straight back to camp, she shouldn't be in any danger."

"What the hell do you think I am, Colonel?" Nanos muttered.

"Hawk Spirit has told me you would not like a truthful answer to that question," Billy Two chimed in. "So I shall not give it."

"Fine," Barrabas said. "You and I, with or without Hawk Spirit, will be the mobile reserve. Right now, that means staying here between the camp and the ravines. Got the Starlite on the LMG?"

"Everything's locked and loaded, Colonel."

"Good. We're open for business. Now all we need is customers."

SEVERAL THINGS ANNOYED Lee Hatton. One was her near nudity, which was beginning to seem carrying a good idea too far. Her bare skin was certainly distracting Charlie, but the goose bumps on it were beginning to distract her. Left alone, she could have used yoga to cope with the chill, but Charlie's presence would keep her from the necessary mental concentration. Yoga would also take her attention off the job of watching the ravine to spot people who might be coming up it.

Those people were taking their time. Without the reported sounds of an underwater explosion and a Soviet minisub, she would have wondered if she was seeing things. She hoped it took more than Charlie's unwanted attentions to make her imagine she'd seen a scuba diver.

Their present perch was an awkward compromise. They could watch the end of the ravine without being easy to spot. They could also be caught in the blast, if anyone climbing triggered a charge and the ravine walls funneled it the way they might. Lee recalled one of Liam O'Toole's standard warnings: "There's no safe distance from an explosion in a confined space."

She saw that Charlie was looking at the sky for once, fished out her radio and started to key it in for her regular report. She would also ask for permission to move farther inland. If she didn't get it, she'd see about persuading Charlie to keep watch to the rear. She was prepared to sacrifice quite a bit to get a second pair of even amateur eyes on the job.

She was halfway through the keying, when the shadows at the foot of the ravine began to flow. They flowed steadily upward toward her in an eerie silence that confused her for a moment.

Then the shadows sprouted arms, legs and heads. She saw the faintest gleam from eyes and blackened weapons.

"Charlie," she whispered. "Get down. Now."

He turned, looking ready to argue. His look changed to surprise, then fear, as he saw the woman he wanted change into the warrior. Lee was crouched like a panther ready to spring, the radio in one hand and her Browning in the other.

Charlie got down.

Lee crouched lower, waiting until the Spetsnaz were in the best part of the ravine, trying to count them. One was taking point, two more backed him and kept a lookout for trouble from above, and a fourth held the sea end.

She wasn't going to be able to get all four with the charges unless the cat-footed bastards suddenly got clumsy. Pity about that, but at least the middle two were nicely set up. Another five yards, and the blast and falling rocks would scour them out like muck from a sewer.

"Guhhhhh."

It was a soft animal sound from Charlie, fear and helplessness boiling over. It was loud enough to alert the Spetsnaz point man.

His SMG came up. So did Lee's Browning. Both fired together. Both missed because neither had a clear target. Lee's thumb stabbed the button for a command detonation.

The three foremost Spetsnaz flung themselves forward up the ravine as the ground heaved and the walls of the ravine quivered. Lee thought she saw one enemy smeared to jam under a slab of rock.

She wasn't sure, because the ravine under and around her was moving, too. She and Charlie were sliding downhill among boulders and slabs of rock in a cloud of dust, straight toward the Spetsnaz. At least, Lee knew the Spetsnaz had to be there. But she couldn't see them, and hoped the dust would keep them from seeing her.

CHAPTER SIXTEEN

Adrienne Biggle knew she ought to slow down. In spite of her anger at Alex's dereliction, she was riding in the dark and the ground was rough. If she took a spill or blew a tire, she'd have to walk back to camp.

If she took a bad enough spill, she might even break something. Then it would be daylight before they picked her up, and that would be just the beginning of her trouble. Nobody else could run the expedition—except Professor Stewart, and he was in the pocket of the military. If Nanos or Hank got to Stewart, she hated to think what he would let them do.

She downshifted and swung to the right. Here the ground sloped upward toward the cliffs on the south side of Haustim. Some of the gullies looked as if they might once have been artificial, dug out to channel rainwater toward a central catch basin for the temple.

She'd wanted to investigate those gullies years ago, but there had only been two ways to get the money—let Stewart suck some out of the Pentagon, or eliminate the underwater investigations.

Maybe she should have cut out the underwater part of the work. If they hadn't needed a boat, they wouldn't have had the problem of Alex Nanos and his friends. Alex she could stand—memories of his body against hers warmed the cool night—but his friends...!

The bike sprayed gravel and bounced viciously as it climbed the slope. Adrienne started to downshift again as she passed a scraggly stand of myrtle. Then the ground leveled out. She saw it stretching ahead to the cliff's edge.

She also saw four black-clad figures stalking toward her, guns in their hands.

Surprise turned to fear. Fear flashed into panic, swamping her judgment and reflexes. She jerked the bike around in an impossibly tight turn. It went over, and only slow speed saved her from breaking a leg.

As it was, the gravel shredded her pants and blouse and gouged her skin. She lurched to her feet, wrestled the bike upright, then jumped back on as dust clouded up around her. The men were shooting at her. She couldn't hear anything, but she knew about silencers from mystery novels. With a *wssssh*, both tires sagged airless. The gas tank spurted foul-smelling Turkish gasoline, but didn't catch fire.

Adrenaline poured into her legs, giving them extra strength and blanking out the pain. She turned and ran.

Behind her, two of the four black-clad figures slung their silenced submachine guns and ran after her.

TO LEE HATTON, the slide down the ravine seemed to last forever. She was sure it wouldn't stop until she, Charlie, the rocks and any Spetsnaz troopers in the way all slid into the sea and sank.

She'd just thought of some choice phrases she'd like to use to Liam O'Toole, when the slide came to an end. A few rocks rolled on past her, over the Spetsnaz hit by the falling slab. He was probably dead, certainly out of the fight.

Two other Spetsnaz were somehow alive and fighting fit. Lee decided that the devil looks after his own and started to draw down on them with her Browning.

She promptly discovered two things. One was that the Browning's trigger had taken a hit from a large rock. The gun was only usable as a club. The other was that her panties were snagged on another, even larger rock. It took only a second to wriggle out of them, but that was too long and the wriggle was too noisy.

The two Spetsnaz turned toward her, SMGs probing the dusty darkness. Lee gripped a stone and threw it, hoping the noise would divert them. One looked away, but the other's eyes suddenly widened. Lee grabbed a second stone, knowing this would be a last gesture but determined to make it a good one.

"Stop that!" Charlie shouted, from up the ravine. "We're—"

He broke off in a coughing fit, but by then the Spetsnaz who'd spotted Lee had turned and fired a burst up the ravine. Bullets spanged and whined; Charlie screamed.

Lee caught the shooter from behind, chopped him across the throat, broke his spine, as well, then whirled. The dead man made a fine shield as his comrade turned and fired.

Shooting a comrade paralyzed the last Spetsnaz for a moment, which was all Lee needed. She dropped, rolled, ignoring the damage sharp rocks did to her skin, then popped up close enough to plant both feet in the man's groin.

He doubled over with a strangled scream, dropping his SMG. Overwhelmed by his pain, he didn't see the blow that crushed his larynx, or feel his neck snap. He was dead before Lee picked up his SMG and fired a burst into the back of his head.

Lee straightened and realized she was naked, her skin bruised and battered. She was also half-deaf. Those faint cries from up the ravine must be Charlie's screams of agony.

Doctor and warrior fought in her mind before sanity returned. She could be both. She could join Charlie, do what she could for him and still watch the ravine.

She took long enough to study the seaward end of the ravine for signs of the last Spetsnaz but saw no trace of him. Then she stripped the first-aid kit off her second victim's belt. Carrying it and the captured SMG, a blackened AKR with a silencer, she started scrambling up the tumbled rocks, not worrying about making noise.

Charlie's screams were fading, but they were loud enough to cover any small sounds she made.

THE ROPE SAW the two Cyclone men standing over the woman as he caught up with them. The senior man had a scratch on his cheek and his comrade was favoring one leg. The woman looked unharmed, apart from a cut lip.

"What the devil are you—" the Rope began.

"I was just thinking, Comrade Rope," the senior Cyclone interrupted. "What would Greek raiders do to a Turkish woman?"

"She isn't Turkish," the Rope snapped. "She's probably the American archaeologist. She is not our target."

"Would the Greeks know she was American? Or care if they knew?" The Cyclone nodded to his comrade. "Orphan?"

Before the Rope could move, the Orphan had raised his AKR. The other Cyclone was unbuttoning his pants.

While the Orphan kept the Rope and the other Typhoon covered, the other Cyclone knelt on one of the woman's arms, slapped her face when she tried to claw him with the other hand and stuffed a field dressing in her mouth. She arched her body and tried to spit the dressing out. The Cyclone slapped her again, harder.

The Rope kept his hands in sight and his face blank, but behind the blank face his mind raced. The woman was doomed, and if that meant trouble for him and the Typhoons, that was just bad luck. He realized that he now knew why the senior Cyclone had the nickname of the Monkey. He only wished he'd guessed or asked sooner!

At least the woman would distract the Cyclones, which would help him to regain control over them. The Rope only wished there were some way to send their heads back to Russia as a warning!

Behind his back, the Rope signaled the Yak Driver, the other Typhoon, to pretend to support the Cyclones until the Rope gave him another signal. The man yawned wide to signify agreement.

"What's the matter?" the Orphan said with a chuckle. "Seen so many women another one bores you? Or are you—"

"Enough, Orphan."

The Monkey, it seemed, wasn't a complete fool, even though he was now deep inside the woman.

ALEX PICKED UP Adrienne Biggle's trail five minutes before the turnoff to Ravine Blue. Orders were orders, and Nile Barrabas's orders something more besides. But it was going to weigh more heavily on his conscience than the G-3 on his back if he didn't at least swing back toward the camp to take a look. If he saw Adrienne had reached the open ground to the west, where nobody could hide easily...

No point in riding along fat, dumb and happy, though. He turned his bike into one of the old water channels and slowed down until he could barely stay upright. If any bad guys were around, he'd be hidden.

He'd still need help. But he could hold on by himself long enough to delay the bad guys and give the alarm. Then Adrienne would be somebody else's problem!

ADRIENNE BIGGLE HAD KNOWN it was possible to be too tired to sleep. Now she knew one could be too frightened to be panicky.

She'd reached that state somewhere around the time the second soldier, or whatever he was, ripped off the last of her clothes and knocked her around before landing on her. All the fear and most of the pain faded then, leaving her mind working as coldly as if she'd been trying to date a column or match up the pieces of a pot.

The men were disagreeing about what to do with her. She recognized Russian though she didn't understand it, and in the dark it was hard to read faces, but tones of voice were hard to mistake, and the meaning of a raised submachine gun was obvious.

She was dealing with mutiny. That was certain. The enemy leader was going to do something about that mutiny as soon as he could. That was likely. Could she help him? Not without risking her life, because all four Russians had guns and the will to use them.

The cold voice in her mind said that didn't matter, as long as she took the Russians with her.

She had only one regret—that she couldn't apologize to Alex Nanos and his friends. Whoever and whatever they were, they'd been more right than wrong.

The first Russian was kneeling beside her again. She gave a convincing moan of despair, and felt sick to her stomach at his grin.

"CHARLIE? Charlie, it's me, Lee."

"Lee?"

She could barely hear him, and bloody bubbles formed on his lips when he spoke. "Lee's my real name," she told him.

"You're...CIA?"

"Among other things. One of them is being a doctor. Now relax. You've been shot up a bit by some Russian commandos. I'll try to make you comfortable."

She knew she was talking to the wind. A fully equipped operating theater at the head of the ravine couldn't have pulled Charlie through. Still, she let her doctor's reflexes take over and guide her hands, slapping dressings over the bullet wounds until they were used up, then tearing up as much clothing as she could. The improvised bandages were hopelessly unsanitary, of course, but it wouldn't make any difference to Charlie....

By the time she was finished, Charlie had been quiet for so long she thought he'd died. But, miraculously, his eyes opened as she straightened up. She rubbed her aching back and flexed her arms, which seemed to have lost all feeling.

"Hey...you look good. Lin...Lee. Did I...hassle you too much? You know..."

He had. But she'd also played the tease—in a good cause, but she'd still teased. And what had happened to him was a lot worse than he deserved just for coming on too strong.

She bent down and kissed him. He reached up and curled cold fingers around one breast. Then his hand opened, his arm fell back and his breathing stopped.

Lee used the last bit of available clothing to cover Charlie's face, then started down the ravine to search it. First, to find any surviving Spetsnaz and to keep him or them alive for interrogation. Then to salvage her radio so she could report in, because Nile must be sweating over the explosion. She didn't really want to talk to anyone for a while, but she was a professional, doctor and warrior both, and got on with the job.

THE ROPE KNELT beside the woman. He went through the motions of undoing his pants, while shifting slowly to the left. By the time he'd finished he was leaning over her, hiding her face from the two Cyclones.

For a moment the look in her eyes stopped him. The trapped animal was gone. Something as quick and cold as a computer lurked there now. What the Cyclones had done to the archaeologist's body hadn't affected her mind.

The faint purr of a motorbike floated over the rise.

The Rope had given his AKR to the Yak Driver when he started his charade with the woman. He still had his knife. Now he drew it, slashed the woman's gag and jerked the field dressing out of her mouth.

Then he tossed the knife, caught it by the blade and threw it straight at the Orphan. It took the man as he turned. His harness deflected the point from spine into kidney, but the knife did enough damage. The Orphan lurched in a half-circle, staring, as the Yak Driver tossed the Rope's AKR to him.

The Monkey instantly saw that this made the Rope the prime target. This sound judgment didn't save him. The woman let out a scream like fifty sirens, and the Monkey stopped as if he'd stepped into a bear trap. He fired his AKR by pure reflex, shooting up a lot of gravel but leaving the Rope untouched.

The Rope stitched him from groin to chin with a dozen 5.45-mm slugs. He fell. The Orphan was still staggering about, but the woman rolled to the right and he fell over her.

The motorbike still buzzed in the distance. Now the fast *blrrrpppp* of an assault rifle joined it. The rider must have dropped off a gunner, the Rope thought. And he was good enough to send three bursts tearing over the Spetsnaz, both the living and the dead. The Orphan joined the dead, as the Rope jerked his knife free, then planted it between the Cyclone's ribs.

The Yak Driver collapsed with a sucking chest wound and half his face gone. The Rope burrowed into the sand as if he wanted to dig his way back to the sea like a mole. Then he rolled over until his mouth was clear of the ground, spit gravel and called out in Greek, "Americans! Your woman is safe. She will stay safe, if I can reach the cliff."

He drew his silenced pistol and shot the Yak Driver behind the left ear, ending his agony. The man deserved at least to die by the hand of a friend.

The woman was looking at him, sheer surprise wiping out the cold calculation.

The Rope managed a grin. "Can you stand?"

"I . . ." She rolled over and flexed her legs. The Rope backed out of range of any possible kicks. Finally she nodded.

He pulled her to her feet and gave her his arm. "You are not what I expected of an archaeologist," he said in Greek. "Are you one of the Soldiers of Barrabas?"

"The who?"

The Rope turned all his attention to his own position. If the Americans wanted the woman—whatever she was—back alive, he had a chance of reaching Seahome again.

What would happen then, only the devil's grandmother knew, and it wasn't wise to ask her questions you might not want answered.

LEE REACHED THE BOTTOM of the ravine without finding her radio. She went to ground behind a pile of loose rock and studied the sea. It was even calmer than before, with no sign that it held anything except pollution and fish.

Close to the water now, she felt chilly again in her bare skin, but she kept watch until she was sure both the sea and the little strip of beach were clear. Then she backed away from the sea, feeling her way over the uncertain footing until she reached the two Spetsnaz she'd killed.

She would rather have had a working radio than clothes, but the Spetsnaz radio was as dead as its owner. Lee had to settle for the clothes of the man she'd killed with her bare hands. Then she collected all the ammunition she could find and returned to her observation post by Charlie's body.

Even at night, a few insects were out and about, to whine and buzz and finally settle on Charlie's wounds. She tried to shoo them away at first, but finally realized the futile attempts were wearing her out. They shouldn't be, but she'd never poured so much adrenaline into a single fight.

"Sorry, Charlie," she said, resting one hand lightly on his battered cheek and holding the AKR with the other. Then she pulled on the dead Russian's socks—his shoes were about four sizes too large—and settled down to watch and wait.

ALEX NANOS'S FIRST IMPULSE when he saw Adrienne standing at the edge of the cliff was to run to her and jerk her back. He'd never seen anybody who looked so ready to jump.

Closer up, he realized he'd been mistaken. She was sore, exhausted, angry at the whole world, but not broken.

"Here." He handed her his canteen.

"Th-thanks."

Instead of drinking from it, she uncorked it and poured the contents over herself. The water only made tracks in the dust and blood, but Nanos could tell it made her feel better.

He didn't want to leave her, but there was just a chance the Russian might still be in sight. He scanned the sea through the Starlite scope, picking up half a dozen heat pulses. One looked solid enough to be worth a burst, and it faded after he fired, but it could just have been a live diver getting his head down.

When he turned back to Adrienne, she'd slumped into a tangle of limbs and dusty hair. Every few seconds a shudder ran through her.

Nanos took off his shirt. He was about to pull her up and wrap it around her, when he remembered that the last thing she'd want was to be touched.

So he held it out. She took it, put it on, then gripped his hands to pull herself to her feet. She swayed a bit, but her voice was steady.

"Alex, I haven't been too bright. I guess there are . . . soldiers and soldiers. Even Russians . . ."

Then she leaned against him. "You see, Alex? I can tell you and those—animals—apart."

"Fine," Nanos said. "But why don't we sort things out a little farther from the cliff?"

"Great idea" came a familiar voice. Nile Barrabas's head popped up from behind a patch of myrtle. "While we're doing that, suppose Mr. Nanos tells me why he's so far from the position he was ordered to take."

Nanos had his cover story ready, but he never got it out. Instead Adrienne turned around and hitched up her borrowed shirt, displaying her bruised and gouged back. "Mr. Nanos arrived in time to save me from a great deal worse than this at the hands of some Russian commandos. I want your word of honor that nothing will happen to him, or I will not cooperate further."

For the first time in his association with Nile Barrabas, Alex saw the colonel completely at a loss for words.

POKROVSKY HOPED he wasn't making a splash as he slipped into the water. Hoping was all he could do, because he was nearly deaf from the blast. If his ears were so badly affected that he couldn't dive, the cyanide capsule in his belt might be needed.

The rest of his squad was gone, and the ASG-17 buried under the rocks. The Americans' scout hadn't detected him. His black clothing and his training in lying still had been enough.

He wondered if the explosion had affected his sight as well as his hearing. He would have sworn that the American scout was a naked woman, rather good-looking, too, with an AKR in her hands. The Americans might have captured an AKR, but a woman, and naked?

Pokrovsky swam away from the island until he was five hundred meters from shore. By then his hearing was returning. He could make out the faint bubble of his breathing apparatus, and even the creaking of his gear as his muscles strained it.

When he'd swum a thousand meters, he checked his compass, then headed toward the rendezvous with the Beta Ravine squad. Gamma was gone, and there was no contact with Delta.

To a man not trained as Spetsnaz, or even to a less determined man than Pokrovsky, this would stink of failure, defeat, even disaster. But Pokrovsky believed defeat and failure existed only if you believed in them, like an African believing in a witch doctor's spells.

If you believed that victory was still possible, as long as one Spetsnaz was alive to strike the enemy, defeat was just a word, with no power over you.

CHAPTER SEVENTEEN

The Blue Spider, leader of the Delta Ravine squad, was worried and was trying not to show it. He thought he had plenty to be worried about, but no need to load any of it on his men.

Even if the worst had happened to the other squads, he still had four men and an RPG with enough ammunition to blow a big hole in American covert-action ranks. All he had to do was find the Americans. While he was hunting them, maybe he could find out what had happened to the other Spetsnaz. Dead men could be avenged; men pinned down could still be freed.

The steady advance across the island soothed the Blue Spider, so that he was almost surprised when a machine gun opened fire from the high ground. He and his men were as quick as ever to seek concealment.

He studied the machine gun's site with his infrared viewer. It had an excellent field of fire and outranged the RPG. The AKRs might as well have been slingshots.

The road to the high ground was barred. He might find a way to deal with the machine gun, but it would take time—time that would be a gift to the Americans, for bringing up reinforcements. The Blue Spider knew how open he was to the rear and the left.

He could still reach the camp and protect himself on the way. His squad would cut right, toward the cliffs, and skirt them. If he found the boats, they were targets of opportunity, and he would have the opportunity. Also a boat-killing weapon.

The Blue Spider signaled his men, and they crept to the right until they could stand up and run without drawing fire.

IN THE STARLITE, Walker Jessup watched the heat pulses of the Spetsnaz draw out of machine-gun range. He looked up to see Billy Two getting to his feet. He still wore only Levi's, but he'd added a sniper-scoped G-3 and a knife at his belt.

"Hold the fort, Fixer. If those bastards aren't after the boats now, they will be soon. Get on the horn to Claude and Liam, describe the situation and leave the rest to them."

Jessup's mocking salute wound up aimed at the Osage's retreating back. Then all at once the Indian warrior vanished into the darkness, as if Hawk Spirit had picked him up to fling him across the island.

The problem was, Billy was right. Even if Jessup had the authority to give orders to the SOBs in a combat situation, he didn't know how Claude and Liam were set up to receive unwanted visitors. The SOBs had been pretty damned closemouthed about everything Jessup didn't need to know.

It would serve Barrabas's pet mercs right if this got some of them in hot water tonight, he thought for a moment, then realized, no, it wouldn't. The kind of hot water Spetsnaz poured out could scald you to death. No SOBs, no mission. No mission, no fix and no fee for the Fixer. Not to mention, likely enough, a war between Greece and Turkey, if you were concerned about that kind of thing.

Jessup shifted his bulk to a position that was only uncomfortable instead of painful, and put his eye back to the Starlite.

LIAM O'TOOLE SCANNED the instrument panel in *Claribel*'s pilothouse. The improvised listening gear was performing at full capacity. That wasn't much, but it would pick up any diver or minisub close enough to be dangerous.

Claude Hayes climbed up the ladder, wearing his wet suit and carrying his fins and scuba gear. His knife was already sheathed on his belt and his harpoon gun slung across his chest. Black-skinned and wearing black rubber, he looked like part of the darkness.

"They're on the way, says the Fixer," O'Toole said. "Billy's going to hang in on their flank, try to take out the RPG man."

"Far as I'm concerned, he can take out the whole bunch," Hayes said. "We can be gentlemen of leisure."

"Fat chance," O'Toole replied. "The great white father wants a prisoner. You snagging one of their divers is the best chance. Maybe our last."

"Always loadin' the work on the field hands," Hayes grumbled. He strapped on his air tank and weight belt. "I think I'll just pop down under the tender and wait. Wanna bet they'll think of using it for a getaway car?"

"Claude, as long as we're not official, I'm not a gamblin' man." He looked Hayes over. "There's a Browning in the tender. Need anything else?"

Hayes shook his head, slipped on his fins and slip-slapped his way to the railing. A moment later he was gone, with hardly the faintest splash to mark where he'd entered the water.

THE BLUE SPIDER STUDIED the scene below. The big trawler yacht lay apparently empty at its mooring. A low-slung, fast-looking motorboat swung gently at the end of a fifty-meter line.

Temptation struck the Spetsnaz leader. That boat would take them back to their diving gear and torpedoes a lot faster than they could walk. If necessary, it could take them all the way back to Seahome.

He tapped a Cyclone on the shoulder. "Flea, go down the cliff and take that motorboat. Your starting it up will be our signal to hit the yacht."

The Flea nodded, uncoiled his belt line and tied it to an outcrop of rock and an exposed root. Then he vanished over the edge of the cliff.

"I'll take the sentry post," the leader told the RPG team. "Wait for the Flea, unless the yacht gets under way. Then fire at will. Aim your first shot at the pilothouse."

The two men nodded. One was a Typhoon, the other a Cyclone, but they had worked themselves into the kind of team that seemed to have been born with an RPG in their hands. What Captain Lieutenant Pokrovsky didn't know about leadership, nobody all the way up to the Politburo knew!

The Flea reached the water without any sign he'd been spotted. He slipped off the rope and into the water with less noise than a seal diving. He pulled on his fins and as swiftly as a seal headed for the motorboat.

Ten meters away, he cautiously lifted his head out of the water. The boat was still empty, rocking gently in the easy swell. He dived again and swam toward the line at the bow.

He'd just drawn his knife to cut it, when he sensed underwater movement behind him. He whirled, shifting his grip on the knife from slash to thrust.

He was too late. A shape that seemed to be darkness in the form of a man was on him and all over him. The knife was still in his hand, but suddenly his arm dangled useless, elbow shattered as quickly as a breath.

The pain struck as the Flea knew what he had to do. He allowed himself one final thought—pride in his foresight. Then his jaws clamped down hard, the cyanide capsule ruptured, and he passed beyond both pain and thinking.

CLAUDE HAYES HEAVED the Spetsnaz diver's body into the tender and looked at it in disgust. If a man was packing a cyanide capsule in his mouth there wasn't much you could do, but he should at least have thought of the possibility.

"Mack here," he said into the microphone. "I gave our visitor a proper reception. He didn't take to our hospitality, though."

"Not at all?"

"He'll never be back."

O'Toole started to say something rude, but an orange flash of flame from the top of the cliff interrupted them both.

THE BLUE SPIDER had been worried for at least two minutes when the RPG gunner called softly, "Comrade. Look, on the motorboat."

The Spider took the binoculars. A large figure with an air tank on his back was hauling a smaller figure into the boat. The smaller one was fair haired and wore only black fatigues and swim fins.

"Flea," the Blue Spider breathed. The man had swum into a trap. If he was dead, he was fortunate. If he was alive, he had to be killed.

"Fire at will," the Blue Spider snapped. "First target, the motorboat."

The loader popped in a round and slapped the gunner on the shoulder. The back blast dazzled the Blue Spider and kicked gravel and dust into his face. He didn't see the second round being loaded.

Then he neither saw nor heard nor felt anything, as a 7.62-mm round from Billy Two's G-3 drilled his brain. It was one of ten rounds, all fired on semiautomatic but so fast that they sounded like a burst.

Two of the three Spetsnaz dropped where they were. The third, the RPG loader, thrashed his way to the edge of the cliff, then rolled over. He plunged straight down to an outcrop ten meters below, bounced off and hit the water sprawling. It didn't matter; he was already dead and the weight of the remaining six rounds took him down swiftly.

Claude Hayes entered the water about the same time, just before the gasoline tank on the motorboat exploded. He stayed under to avoid the burning gasoline, then popped hastily to the surface as an underwater explosion hammered his ears.

He thrashed to the boarding ladder and scrambled up to *Claribel*'s deck, dripping water and curses.

"Sorry, Claude," O'Toole said. "Just a wee depth charge or two to discourage any of the Russian lads from lingering behind."

"You dump one of those charges on top of me again, Liam, and I'll shove the next one up your ass and command-detonate it!" Hayes's ears were still ringing like all the firehouse bells in creation together, and his chest and stomach ached.

O'Toole wasn't listening. He had binoculars fixed on the top of the cliff, where a tall bare-chested figure was signaling with hands and a rifle.

"Billy says he dropped all three of the Russians up yonder. He also says we're to get under way at once and proceed to Ravine Blue. Nobody's heard from Lee Hatton in a bit too long for the colonel's peace of mind."

Hayes started flipping switches without even taking off his scuba gear. He felt sure, somehow, that Lee was okay, but just the idea that she might not be was hard on *his* peace of mind, too.

"Claude, for the love of all the saints!" O'Toole growled. "Will you watch where you're dripping on the upholstery!"

POKROVSKY WAS FLOATING AWAY on more than the waves of the Aegean. He'd dived and his ears weren't hurting. He could hear his own breathing and the bubble and hiss of his closed-cycle breathing gear. He could hear the occasional distant rumble of an explosion, as the Americans dropped explosive charges. All of that was good.

Nothing else was hurting, either. He wasn't so sure that was good. He should be able to feel the strain in his leg muscles as he kicked his way toward the rendezvous, but he couldn't.

He forced himself to keep swimming. It was incredibly tempting to let himself float down to the bottom. He didn't know how deep the bottom was here. Even if it was shallow, he knew he might not want to move again.

Pokrovsky was so absorbed in forcing one kick after another that he nearly ran into the Iron Dolphin. It was angling in toward him from the right. Incredibly, the Rope was at the controls, with a crewman from the Type 88 behind him.

Pokrovsky frowned. This was too solid to be a hallucination. But if it was real, then the Iron Dolphin had to be making too much noise.

He hand-signaled to the Rope. "Noise?"

The reply came: "The Americans are making too much noise of their own. Besides, they think they got us all."

Pokrovsky wanted to ask how many the Americans had killed, but his hands wouldn't obey him. He felt the Rope gripping him and the crewman strapping him into one of the vacant seats. He vaguely felt the rush of water past him as the Rope pushed the Iron Dolphin to full speed.

WALKER JESSUP didn't understand Turkish, but he could recognize fear. He also really didn't blame the camp workers. They knew even less than he did about what was going on, and the SOBs weren't exactly keeping him well-informed!

Also, the Turks weren't armed, and Jessup had both the machine gun and his personal weapons. It was surprising how much it helped to have a belt or two of 7.62 mm to hold up your side of the argument.

Jessup left a round chambered but snapped on the LMG's safety. Then he stood. He looked like a whale broaching the surface. The Turkish workers stepped back.

The Fixer looked at the dark, mustached faces in front of him, trying to find Mustafa. No luck.

"Do any of you speak English?" He added one of the few Turkish phrases he'd memorized, the words for "I do not speak Turkish."

"I know the English best here, I think," said a short man with the longest mustache in the bunch. "What you say to us?"

"I am asking you to be calm. Return to the camp, and—"

The translation got that far, then all the Turks including the translator started shouting.

"They say no go back to camp with no weapons. If Greeks come, we like children with no weapons. Better yet, we get weapons, go help fight Greeks." The translator grinned, obviously planning to write another glorious page in Turkey's history of bashing Greeks.

Over my dead body will you get weapons, was what Jessup didn't say. He didn't even think it more than once, after he realized that might be just the way the Turks got them if he didn't calm things down.

"Please. Captain Nanos and his friends are a match for any Greeks. They need no help. If you need protection, stay here and I—"

The Turks' reaction to the idea of needing protection was less than polite. One of them pointed at Jessup's belly and said something that needed no translation.

Jessup would be damned if he'd hand out the SOBs' weapons to Turks who might be trigger-happy or even on the wrong side. He'd also be damned if he'd die in defense of them.

"Okay," he said. "The weapons are not mine to give out. I must ask Captain Nanos—"

"Then ask him," the translator said. Nile Barrabas himself couldn't have made it more plainly an order.

"Will you give your word of honor not to take the weapons until he gives permission?"

"Yes." The other Turks nodded.

"Okay."

Jessup carefully moved the radio to where he could use it and still reach the machine gun. He had the radio on his lap, when a trail bike came puttering up the hill. It barely made the slope because it was carrying two riders: Nile Barrabas and Dr. Biggle. Biggle was wearing Alex Nanos's shirt and a pair of black shorts and looked considerably the worse for wear.

"Hello, Colonel," Jessup said. "Our Turkish friends want to go hunting Greeks, or at least to protect the camp."

Biggle started to say something, but a look from Barrabas silenced her. The colonel propped the bike against a rock and faced the Turks.

"If we need help, you will have the chance to uphold the honor of Turkey. But first I must learn if there are any Greeks left to fight."

He sprang down into Jessup's foxhole. "The radio, Fixer."

Jessup handed it over. Barrabas's face and tone discouraged argument. The colonel pulled on the earphones, then whispered, "As far as I know, there were three Spetsnaz teams and we accounted for them all. But Lee Hatton's still missing. String the Turks along while I try to raise her."

Jessup groaned at the thought of more speeches, but had at least one consolation. For once, Nile Barrabas didn't know what was going on, either!

CHAPTER EIGHTEEN

"Damn it, Alex! This bullshit about Greeks raiding Haustim is going to get more people killed!"

Adrienne Biggle sat up on the cot in her tent. Her ragged red bathrobe fell open. Alex Nanos knew she wasn't being provocative. Adrienne had blown her cool too thoroughly to care what she wasn't wearing.

"It won't be bullshit as far as the people who'd do the killing are concerned," he said patiently. "The Turks will simply write the whole thing off as the kind of screwup they expect of Greeks. The Greeks will think that some of their people went off on a half-assed raid. The ones who make decisions will know you don't do that with Turks. You go ready for a fight, or you don't go at all."

"For a Greek, you're praising the Turks a hell of a lot!" she said, absentmindedly closing her bathrobe.

"I'm only half Greek, Adrienne. The other half's miscellaneous Slav—"

"They've fought the Turks for centuries, too."

"Yeah, and they know the Turks aren't pansies or pushovers. Adrienne, I am remarkably uninterested in what happens to people who think war's a game. No, that's not quite true. I like to see them get killed before they have kids. That way, if their dumbness is hereditary, it doesn't get passed on."

"You son of a bitch!"

"No, Soldier of Barrabas."

"What?"

"That Vietnam vet, Hank, is really an ex-Special Forces light colonel by the name of Nile Barrabas. He's been my boss in a whole bunch of situations like this."

"You're a mercenary!"

"You can call us names all you want, Adrienne, but we've had a lot worse than names shot at us. Most recently two nights ago."

Dr. Biggle stopped as if she'd been slapped. Then she shook her head. "All right. I guess I kind of asked for that. I don't resent being deceived so much that I'd rather be dead. Believe it or not, I'm not that stupid."

"I never thought you were," Nanos said gently. "Just a bit shook from your first time with your ass on the line. Not as shook as I was the first time I found mine there, either."

Adrienne sat up, again letting the robe fall open to reveal the bruises from her encounter with the Spetsnaz. Lee Hatton, who had examined Adrienne soon after she and the rest of the SOBs were reunited, had said none of the cuts would leave any permanent scars.

The archaeologist grinned as she saw where Nanos's eyes rested. "Is that a recruiting speech?"

"Christ, no! Adrienne, you might make a better merc than I'd make an archaeology professor, but that's not saying much. Let's each stick to what we know.

"Look. If we blew the whistle on the Sovs right now, everybody would think it was a lie. We don't have any hard evidence that the media would buy, for one thing. So the Greeks and Turks would think it was a cover-up and they both would suspect the Americans of playing footsie with the other side.

"The people on both sides who want a war could go right on playing games. Sooner or later there'd be a real Greek retaliation, killing real Turks. Then the Russians would be right back in the ball game. If by some miracle there wasn't another raid, they could go deep—literally, I think. They could wait out both sides, then pick a time to strike again.

"On the other hand, if they think they've got us fooled they may get careless. Then they'll be easier to catch off balance. This kind of fighting is a lot more like the martial arts than like a conventional battle. You don't butt against your opponent's strong point. You wait until he shows a weakness, *then* exploit it. Follow me?''

"Alex, I follow you, but what I'd really like is for you to drop the lecture and..." Adrienne let the robe drop from her shoulders and kicked away the blankets so she could peel it off the rest of the way.

"Adrienne, are you sure...after what they did—"

"I'm sure. It'll help me forget. Let's do something we're both good at, if I may be a bit immodest."

"Adrienne, you can be as immodest as you damned well please," Nanos said, pulling off his T-shirt.

"WHEN WILL I BE FIT for duty?" Pokrovsky asked.

Isakov shrugged. "Dr. Uspensky must have told you—"

"He told me four days, which has to be a lie. If it was the truth, you wouldn't have come here with that long face. I feel quite well, but I shall be very sick indeed if I think I am being lied to. The people who lie will be even sicker."

"Threatening a superior officer is a court-martial offense," Isakov said wearily.

"Oh, court martial the devil's aunt and be done with it! Either that, or tell me the truth."

"The truth is really what the doctor said. You should be fit for duty in four days. You can probably visit the teams tomorrow, if you relax today."

Perhaps Isakov was telling the truth, Pokrovsky thought. But something in the captain's voice and face told him there was more.... "All right. But tell me what the other bad news is. I want to break it to the team as soon as possible."

"Teams," Isakov corrected.

Pokrovsky shook his head. "We've got five Cyclones and four Typhoons left fit for duty. I'm going to combine them into a single Seahome Team. Provisional, of course, and with your permission."

"You have my permission," Isakov said slowly. "But it may require permission at a higher level, too."

"And shit smells. Tell me something I haven't known since I joined the Young Pioneers."

"Semyon Ignatievich, you are really determined—"

"I am really determined to go on and carry out Operation Claw with Seahome's own resources as long as that's remotely possible. Is that an objective you quarrel with, Comrade Captain?"

The silence seemed to last forever, broken only by the faint whirr of the air conditioning and distant footsteps in a passageway two or three modules over. Pokrovsky had the feeling that everybody in Seahome was listening for Isakov's response.

"No," Isakov said finally. "But alternate methods are being made available. I hope you have not forgotten that Operation Claw was decided at the Politburo level."

"I haven't forgotten how many of the dacha-mongers put their fingers in any sailor's pie. What have they done this time?"

"The *N. V. Glubov* is arriving within a few days."

"If that's bad news, I'm curious about the good news."

The *N. V. Glubov* was the quietest submarine in the Soviet navy. Converted from the second of the so-called *Papa*-class cruise-missile submarines, she'd lost her missiles and their guidance systems. She still had her torpedoes, sonar, twin screws and high speed.

Everything had been silenced that was even suspected of making a noise, thanks to rubber tiles on her hull, padded mountings for her machinery and retractable shrouds for her propellers. She had tested most of the silencing for the new *Akula*-class attack submarines. Now that the *Akula*s were going to sea, *Glubov* was a laboratory with no experiments to be done.

Hurrying her out to join Operation Claw made sense. She would be hard to detect, even in shallow water, and if detected, she'd be able to run from most antisubmarine weapons in the Turkish and Greek navies. If the American Sixth Fleet intervened, it might be a different matter, but

Operation Claw reckoned on Greece and Turkey being at each other's throats before the Americans knew anything was wrong.

That might not be quite so safe an assumption anymore, but still, one Special Forces company wasn't the Sixth Fleet. The Aegean Sea was still full of vulnerable targets for the Seahome Team. With *Glubov*'s firepower backing them up...

"Is there more, Captain? Are we getting reinforcements? Not that our nine men can't finish the work, but—"

"Reinforcements are on the way aboard *Glubov*. Twelve men from Team Hurricane."

"Those unweaned—"

"They will be based aboard *Glubov* and operate under the direct control of her captain and the GRU."

Furious, Pokrovsky sat bolt upright, forgetting the low overhead of his bunk. He banged his tender scalp against a pipe. Head swimming, he lay down again, rubbing his temples.

"If you do that again, Comrade, you will be off duty for eight days, not four."

"Damn the doctor. Damn you, and damn Team Hurricane, and damn the chief of the GRU," Pokrovsky said. He had the sense not to raise his voice.

"Personally, I agree with you, and I will give you everything Seahome has, to help your team. But it's obvious our superiors think some part of Operation Claw can't be trusted to Seahome."

"Haven't those fools ever heard of coordination?"

"They have. They've also heard that you're screwing our resident Chekist. They're afraid the KGB will claim a share of any further successes from Seahome."

"So to prevent that, they'll risk having no successes at all?"

Isakov said nothing. They both knew the answer to that question too well. After a while, Pokrovsky shook his head. This triggered pain and made him wince, but he ignored it.

"Very well. *Glubov* and her Hurricanes can sail to glory or to hell. I—no, I want them to succeed if we can't. But if we don't succeed . . ."

Isakov didn't ask him to finish, and after a minute or two he unpacked some books and left. Pokrovsky picked one up, a translation of an American novel about a mutiny aboard a Soviet submarine, then put it down.

His first job was going to be restoring the morale of Team Seahome.

No, his first job was going to be restoring his own!

NOW THAT MOST OF the spare weapons had been handed out to Turks the SOBs hoped were trustworthy, the cave had room for the whole team plus Walker Jessup. The Fixer was sitting on an ammunition box by the entrance, waiting for everybody's undivided attention. He reminded Barrabas of a canary so big and fat he knows no cat can handle him.

"Okay, people," Jessup said, "some good news. In fact, quite a lot of good news. First, we're official."

"What mean 'we,' Fixer?" Billy Two deadpanned.

"This mission, which really does include me."

"Probably couldn't afford the airfreight home," Alex Nanos said. "But, you mean this is official as in we get paid?"

"One megabuck apiece," Jessup said. Barrabas kept a straight face at the figure, but nobody else except Lee Hatton did.

"Somebody had the logic to figure that this mission's going to be about twice as hairy as the average, so it's worth twice as much," Jessup went on. "That may not set a precedent, of course."

"Screw the precedents," Liam O'Toole said. "What about the Nate Beck Specials?"

"On their way, along with Stewart and a couple of Navy techs. ETA, four or five days. Orders are that you should have a new motorboat and preferably a new yacht by then."

Barrabas looked at Nanos. The Greek shook his head. "New boat, maybe. But I hope they're shipping out some inflatables. New yacht—no way, not without going way off the island and leaving a trail a drunk KGB man could follow in his sleep."

"What about disguising the one we've got?" Claude Hayes put in. "You know—new paint, change the shape of the funnel and deckhouse with plywood, stuff like that. The German commerce raiders made it work in both World Wars, if I recall."

"Makes sense to me. As long as it keeps the nervous nellies off all our tails, I'll go for it," Jessup said. "Our story about Greeks is going over, particularly since they found those bodies."

Alex Nanos's hands closed on an empty ammunition can, crumpling it flat. Barrabas knew he'd spent much of the past two nights consoling Adrienne Biggle. She felt guilty over Ioannes Trikoupi's death, even though she knew that he'd foolishly stuck his neck out once too often.

"The Greeks are embarrassed. The Turks have their balls back. Both sides are publicly saying nothing, privately trying to find out what the hell really happened. I figure we have a couple of weeks before any real Greeks or Turks make any moves. Maybe we'll be that lucky with the Russians, too, but let's not bet on it."

"No argument there, Fixer," Barrabas said. "Of course, this means we'll still be shorthanded. Watching the Turks and doing the boat over are a lot of work. If we had some help with the security of the cave—"

"Colonel Barrabas, you would cheat at poker with your own mother," Jessup said. "You have the morals of a rattlesnake, the ethics of a horned toad and the charm of a Gila monster."

"Anything else?"

"No, except that I'll hang around. What else is there for me to do? My harem's turned frigid, my mansion has termites, my oil wells have run dry...."

This time all the SOBs laughed except Lee Hatton, and even she managed a smile.

It was going too far to say that Walker Jessup had bloated himself to three hundred and more pounds just as a disguise. Barrabas remembered the *rijstaffel* pig-out and a dozen similar meals.

It wasn't going too far to say that Walker Jessup hid some real loyalties inside that flab. One of those loyalties was to the men who did the killing and the dying for him and his faceless superiors. He might never admit it, he might hate the effort, but he would come through when he had to.

"How LONG IS IT going to take for our friends to get their heads out of their asses and move again?" Colonel Rawson snarled.

He thought he probably sounded drunk, but he didn't care. Major Sinas owed him a couple of answers. If the major didn't come up with them, he was going to find out that Rawson was much meaner sober than drunk.

"I don't know. And frankly, I wouldn't tell you if I did."

"I get the feeling you don't trust me."

"I trust you about as far as I could push the Golden Horn Bridge," the major snapped. "We can't do anything in Turkey. What excuse do we have, when the 'Greeks' were slaughtered without harming a Turkish hair?

"The Greeks are even worse off. The whole country's going to be combed for the fools who disgraced their country by an illegal raid that didn't even succeed! While that search is going on—"

"Okay, okay. I'm not stupid. But the friends I was referring to are neither Greek nor Turkish. They're—"

"Not your concern," Sinas said. He stepped back and dropped his right hand close to his holstered Browning. Rawson noticed for the first time that the flap was unbuttoned.

In a quick-draw contest, the major just might win. Rawson had survived both his profession and his vices by not taking foolish chances. He sat down and put his hands on the table in front of him.

"Colonel Rawson, our mutual friend is quite prepared to welcome your cooperation. It may even be rewarded. But he won't tolerate compromising some of his other connections. Those other connections would also be hostile, and might take action whatever our friend said."

Translation: Heiss would control all dealings with the Russians. If Rawson got too snoopy, he was going to be terminated—possibly by the Russians themselves.

"This isn't my idea of how to keep the pot boiling," Rawson said, more mildly than he felt.

"It isn't my idea, either," the major said. Without turning his back on Rawson, he pulled a bottle out of a cabinet beside the table.

Rawson gaped. It was real bourbon.

"I have been a poor host several times," Sinas said. "I could not help seeing you gag on raki, and I do not mind whiskey, so..."

When it came time to take over Heiss's network, Rawson decided, Major Sinas would be shot clean and quick, not disposed of slowly. Before that time, he'd be watched more carefully than the SOBs. They didn't know where Rawson was, and they were really interested in Heiss.

The major was still loyal to Heiss, as much as he was loyal to anybody. He also knew exactly where to find Rawson, if he decided Rawson was more of a menace than an asset.

The bourbon was about the worst Rawson had ever tasted, but as it went down he realized he'd hardly ever needed a drink quite so badly.

THE MOONLIGHT SOFTENED the jagged rocks at the head of the ravine, but it made the fine bones of Lee Hatton's face look harsher. Had she lost weight, too? Barrabas wasn't going to ask, as long as she was combat-ready.

In fact, he wasn't going to say a thing until she spoke. And if she said, "Get lost, Colonel..."

"Hello, Nile," she said, without turning her head. "Looking for some company?"

"The last woman to use that line on me was a hooker in Amsterdam."

Which made him think of Erika, and that was *not* what he ought to be thinking about when one of his people was hurting. Or doing a damned good imitation of it, anyway.

"I thought they all said, 'Hello, handsome. Want a date?'"

"I promise you dinner anywhere you want in New York, when this is over. Just the two of us."

"My farewell dinner?"

Barrabas jumped as if the rock he was sitting on had turned red-hot. "What makes you think that?"

"You've had ants in your pants over my mood ever since the raid. Nile, you wouldn't send me home without a good reason. But you've been doing a pretty good imitation of a man who thinks he's got that reason!"

There was no mistaking her tone or the expression on her face now. Barrabas had never seen her so angry.

Of course, she'd also never had such a good reason. She thought she'd been insulted in just about the most humiliating fashion possible—"Go home, little girl, you've muffed your chance to play with the big boys."

Barrabas would have laughed, except that he'd already insulted Lee badly enough. She didn't find the situation at all funny. Come to think of it, he didn't, either.

"Lee," he said.

She heard something in his voice that he didn't hear himself. Some of the anger left her face.

"Lee, you've been doing a pretty good imitation, too. You look like someone who wants to pull the plug, but doesn't know how to break the news. You're pushing yourself to finish the mission, whether you want to or not. I won't say we can spare you, but we'd all rather have you leave alive than stay on and—"

Lee Hatton did laugh. Not the harsh laughter Barrabas would have expected, but her usual hearty chuckle, this time filled with relief. She put a hand on his shoulder and squeezed, as if she hadn't been sure he was real.

"Nile, it looks like we were each thinking the worst of the other. Apologies?"

"Damned straight." Barrabas rested a hand lightly on Lee's shoulder, then moved to another rock that let him stretch out his legs.

"I was kind of thinking you might be on your way out," he said. "That scared me a little, and I'll tell you why, if you promise never to tell anybody. Not the President, not the Fixer, not God, and especially not the rest of the team."

"My word on it."

"Okay. We've had three people in the Soldiers who've helped remind the rest of us about the world we're defending. Three people who didn't *need* to live out on the edge of danger, because they could live somewhere else.

"Geoff Bishop was one. Claude Hayes is the second. You're the third. Each of you has been worth just a little bit more to the team because of what you are. We lost Geoff. I wasn't happy about the idea of losing you."

"That sounds like the understatement of the year," Lee said softly.

"You know us hairy-chested mercs. We hate to admit there's anything we can't solve with a 3-round burst." Barrabas grinned. "But your quitting might have been one of them."

Lee returned his grin. "I'm not quitting. Not on this mission, and not anytime soon. I think. But—well, this seems to be true confessions night. I'll tell you what really happened at Ravine Blue. I haven't been holding back anything that would endanger the mission, but . . ."

Her voice trailed off and she sat silently, like the statue of a warrior goddess in faded jeans and a tank top, one elegant leg crossed over the other and her hands resting on her knee. Then, without looking Barrabas in the face, she told him everything that had happened to Charlie.

"I can see what you've been carrying around," Barrabas said when she'd finished. "You feel we've contributed to his death by using him, not being up-front with him. But the truth would have spoiled a lot of things, including our good relations with Dr. Biggle. At any rate, he was in danger quite aside from our involvement."

"Yes. Charlie's parents won't even have the consolation of knowing their son died a hero. But—I knew what I was doing and why. I just didn't know it would be so hard."

"Lee, it's the first time for you. I've had to bullshit next of kin about what happened to somebody under my command—I've lost count of how often. The first couple of times somebody gets blown away because he was too high on cheap grass to tell his rifle from his big toe, you worry about what to tell his folks. After that, you get a tough hide."

"I'm not sure I want to have this happen that often. But if it does, this physician will do her damnedest to heal herself. If she can't, you'll be the first to know."

Barrabas nodded. There wasn't anything more to say, at least not out loud. Echoing in his mind was the question of why he always seemed to be on the same wavelength as Lee, but not Erika.

CHAPTER NINETEEN

Professor Ian Stewart shouted something in Turkish at the workers handling the big fiberglass crate. They instantly stopped heaving it around and started carrying it as if it held crystal.

"What did you say?" Barrabas asked.

"I said that if they dropped the crate I would have their pubic hairs eaten by diseased sows."

The professor appeared like a man quite able to carry out such a threat. Short and stocky, like a smaller edition of Alex Nanos, he looked younger than his fifty-five years. He also looked like a man who, by all the odds, ought to have been dead several times over.

In fact, the professor had survived a plane crash that ended his Navy career, a car crash that killed his wife and daughter, two cases of the bends and a shark attack. He'd wound up looking, to Nile Barrabas, quite a lot like Karl Heiss—if Heiss had been an honest man.

The crate settled onto the bed of the light pickup lifted in by helicopter two days earlier. Billy Two was going to fit a machine-gun mount on the cab as soon as he finished working on the yacht.

From the foot of the cliff, an outboard motor growled. A big, dark blue inflatable shot into view, carrying Billy, O'Toole and another load of supplies for the yacht. Disguising the yacht was keeping everybody busy except Barrabas.

"Want to ride into camp with me?" Stewart asked as the Turks finished lashing the crates in place.

"Thanks, but I think I need the walk."

"I want to talk with you alone, Colonel."

"You can't tell me anything I won't pass on to the team and the Fixer."

"Jessup? What's that Company clown—"

"That Company clown has nearly got his ass in a sling for us a few times. Now either you remember that he has every clearance you do and a few more besides, or I may forget we need you to run these electronics. I'm damned sure the Navy can send somebody else."

"Go on. Make my day. Cry on the Company's shoulder."

Barrabas decided that he did have a few new jobs. The first one was to keep himself from punching the professor. The second was to keep Stewart from taking charge of everything and everyone in sight.

"Professor, either Jessup and the team are cleared for everything, or I bring the team back and we take the electronics. I don't care who you're working for back in the States. Out here, we all have our asses on the line. If you don't learn that pretty damned fast, yours is going to be the first ass to be shipped home."

"You couldn't do that!"

"How much do you want to bet? All the people who are going to be killed if the Greeks and Turks start serious shooting? Professor, we're mercs. Professional killers, you people call us, except a few like the Fixer, who know better. Well, we've got a few names for people who get us killed because they want to play bureaucratic games."

Stewart said nothing, and Barrabas turned and walked toward the truck. As he pulled the driver's door open, he added, "Professor, I can deliver this stuff where you want it, or I can take it to our dump. Hop in?"

Stewart's silence went on long enough for Barrabas to start sweating. But he couldn't let Stewart pick and choose who was cleared for what. He also couldn't expect much cooperation if he publicly humiliated the professor by hijacking the electronics.

At last Stewart shrugged and walked up to the truck. "Let's go, Colonel. I know the potholes better than you do, I think."

"BOTTOM AT 600 meters. Our depth, 350 meters." The sonar operator looked at his screen again and added, "Shoaling rapidly."

The helmsman of the *N. V. Glubov* glanced at his captain. Captain First Rank Abakumov nodded.

"Steady as you go. Pass the word to all hands for silent operation."

Abakumov smiled as he heard even the faint buzz of conversation in nearby compartments die. Then ventilators followed. He knelt and took off his shoes, setting them down beside the periscope well.

"You, too, Comrade Captain Lieutenant," he told the leader of the twelve Spetsnaz divers from Team Hurricane.

"Why?"

It ought to have been enough for the man called "the Thorn" that he was under Abakumov's orders. Unfortunately the Thorn was as temperamental as a ballerina, every bit as indispensable and not nearly as good-looking. His thick belly wasn't fat, but his sallow complexion and bald head gave him the look of someone who stole babies in fairy tales. Abakumov thought he must have got his nickname from his temper, not his appearance.

"Practice, first of all," Abakumov said. "Besides, who knows who might be out there, listening?"

"You've said no Americans are tailing us."

"We haven't detected any," Abakumov corrected. Since the latest American sonars were considerably superior to anything the *Glubov* carried, this was an important difference.

"Are you saying we should be afraid of the Greeks and the Turks?" the Thorn asked. He sounded both incredulous and suspicious.

"Lower your voice, please," the captain said. He reminded himself for the twentieth time that *Glubov* was operating under orders at the Politburo level. Anything that interfered with the mission would also be dealt with at that level. A firing squad wasn't impossible. A ruined career was virtually certain. He also reminded himself for the twentieth time that *Glubov*'s success could give him his admiral's star, when he wasn't much past forty! He might even go on to become commander in chief in his fifties, maybe serve as long as Gorshkov, see the Soviet navy finally dominate the seas of the world....

"All right," the Thorn whispered. "*Are* you afraid of the Greeks and Turks?"

"Not at all," Abakumov said. "But if they can't detect us, they also can't detect an American submarine lying on the bottom in our path. If the Americans wanted to risk violating territorial waters to investigate recent incidents..."

"I understand." The Spetsnaz leader's tone didn't say that he approved.

Abakumov tapped him on the back. "Besides, we'll soon enter shoal water, and that could happen very suddenly, the way the bottom's running. Would you rather we slowed down now and crept into our area of operations like a jellyfish?"

The Thorn looked genuinely horror-struck. He was probably as eager to start running missions out of reach of Abakumov as the captain was to have his ship to himself.

"If we're that close, I'll go warn my people," the Thorn said.

With a frown on his narrow face, Abakumov watched the Thorn leave the control room. Could he persuade the Thorn to respect Greeks and Turks operating in their home waters, without being accused of defeatism? Or would he have to hold his peace and let the Thorn and his Hurricanes sail on, maybe to disaster?

Abakumov decided that if he did make admiral by enduring the Thorn, it would be a well-earned promotion.

"I'M NOT GOING TO apologize for trying to keep Jessup out of the picture," Stewart said as the truck rattled up from the cove. "We'll get more cooperation from the Navy if the Company keeps its fingers out of this pie."

"The Navy will get more cooperation from us if Jessup knows everything we do," Barrabas said. "That's a take-it-or-leave-it proposition."

"Colonel, how about I tell you what's going to be available—"

"If we sell out the Fixer?"

"You don't negotiate—"

"Damned right I don't negotiate about a few things. One of them is my need-to-know list."

The professor rubbed dust out of his eyes. "I'm beginning to think that SOBs should stand for 'Stubborn, Obdurate Bastards.'"

"We've been doing this kind of work for a while, Professor. We know what's needed to get it done. I'm not sure you and the Navy do."

"What about letting me tell you, no strings attached? Then maybe you'll at least stop thinking the Navy's sitting around playing with itself!"

Barrabas recognized a man pushed to the limit. Too much was riding on this mission to blow it by fighting with the professor—if it wasn't necessary.

"Okay, Professor. I'll shut up and listen for a change."

"Gee, thanks."

What the Navy was going to produce was two, maybe three seasoned sonar operators to use the Nate Beck Specials. "Beck's given them hands-on instruction with his software, and says they'll do just fine."

From the ex-SOB and computer wizard, that was high praise, indeed. Beck was quite sure nobody knew as much about computers as he did, and he wasn't too far wrong.

"They'll be flying in aboard a Navy helicopter once the epidemic breaks out in a couple of days."

Barrabas nearly ran the truck into a boulder. "Epidemic?"

"Nobody told you?"

"Nobody told any of us anything, including Jessup."

"That should tell you—"

"Professor, if you say that should tell me Jessup's supposed to be kept in the dark, you can swim home!"

"I was going to say, that should tell you how fast things are moving. I just got word myself, about four hours before I flew out here. An epidemic's going to break out on this island, some unknown but virulent strain of flu. The U.S. Navy will fly in doctors from the Sixth Fleet carrier *Kitty Hawk*, whose CO used to be my wing man. They'll 'treat' everybody, and arrange for Medevac by the Turkish Air Force. The Turkish Air Force will fly out all the 'sick' workers, and fly in a platoon or so of paratroopers to maintain 'quarantine.'"

That meant an end to the security problem posed by the workers. Barrabas hoped the Turkish troops would be handpicked. Otherwise they'd just be exchanging one security problem for another.

"So far not too bad. Then what?"

"Then you go on with your mission, laying out the miniature sonars and monitoring them. We think the Russians are operating from either a bottomed nuclear submarine or a permanent base near the edge of the continental shelf. Once we've got a reasonable fix on the base... Do I need to tell your divers what to do about it?"

Barrabas ignored the question. Alex and Claude might need a little help if they had to take out a base housing a dozen or two Spetsnaz divers. They didn't need amateur advice.

Finally Stewart continued. "That's what's been firmed up so far. What's left is possibilities." The professor took a deep breath. "I'll promise one thing. As far as I'm concerned, Jessup is cleared to know when the CNO takes a leak! I won't even mention our little head-butting contest. But if the Company leaks any of what they learn, it won't be just our tails in a crack!''

"Jessup's been known to keep even his old Company buddies in the dark when the mission requires it," Barrabas reassured him.

"Fine, I guess. Thing is, we may be able to lay on some air support, if you need it. Admiral Hoare, the deputy CNO for Air, was my squadron CO aboard *Enterprise*. His son is flying an F-14 with VF-96 off *Kitty Hawk*."

"So the whole thing can stay among old buddies, is that the idea?"

"Give the colonel a cigar. If we arrange for anything through channels, the Greeks and the Turks are bound to hear it. Somebody will think it's a courtesy to our distinguished allies to tell them, or leak it to the media to prove how much we're doing to help, or—hell, I don't have to spell it out for you!"

Barrabas nodded. The U.S. Navy might think it sat a little closer to higher authority than the other services, but this time at least it was earning its share of the defense budget. Air cover might make a big difference, and not against the Russians, either.

The Russians were operating underwater. If the crisis heated up again, Greeks and Turks might be flying all over the place. Then the SOBs would need air cover to protect them from their friends!

The long talk and the dusty road were making Barrabas thirsty. He pulled onto the shoulder, opened his canteen and drank generously.

Off to the south, a fat trawler yacht was ambling along. Barrabas cranked down the window, raised his binoculars and focused. Squinting against the sunlight blazing from the sea, he made out a bilious green hull, a vaguely pink superstructure with two windows, a long funnel with seats on either side and probably bikini-clad girls sunbathing on them.

The yacht turned slowly, bringing its port side into view. Being towed alongside was the inflatable boat Billy and Liam had taken out. A tall figure was standing in the boat, handing up tools and gear.

"I'll be damned!"

"No doubt, since you're Army—" Professor Stewart began.

Barrabas laughed. "I just recognized a few of our friends," he said. "Want to take a look?"

He handed the binoculars to the professor and drank more water. If he hadn't been able to recognize the yacht at this distance, Nanos's idea of disguising it was going to work fine. It wouldn't fool someone close up, but anybody looking at a satellite photograph, from a cockpit or through a periscope was going to have a problem.

And speaking of other people's problems...

"What's going to happen to the Turkish workers?"

"They'll be screened for loyalty, and held in prison until the crisis is over."

Barrabas hoped Dr. Biggle wouldn't learn that. Turkish jails were hellholes, pure and simple. He wasn't too happy himself, about sending men there whose only crime was having seen too much. But they'd be alive when they came out probably, and that was more than a lot of Greeks and Turks would be if this mission failed because somebody talked too much!

THE GOLDEN GIANT swam up from the underwater cave and hand-signaled to Pokrovsky. Pokrovsky nodded. The Giant turned and finned back down out of sight.

The next exercise was simulating the rescue of a teammate with the bends. Spetsnaz doctrine was to kill disabled team members, but Pokrovsky was bending the rule here. If a disabled man could still dive and the mission had been accomplished, he would be brought out.

Two divers swam down into the cave after the Giant. One of them, a Typhoon, went so fast Pokrovsky signaled him to slow down. Otherwise they might have a real case of the bends on their hands!

Pokrovsky wondered what Belyusev thought of this stretching of doctrine. If he was thinking of anything else but the *N. V. Glubov*, that is.

Pokrovsky almost felt sorry for the KGB man. He didn't have anyone to lead and train, or indeed much of anything to do except sit and worry. Maybe it was because Belyusev had talked too much that the GRU was sending *Glubov* to control Operation Claw. If so, he was getting paid back a lot faster than his worst enemy would have wished.

If Seahome still snatched its share of Operation Claw back from *Glubov* and her windy Hurricanes, it would be Pokrovsky's men who did it. The KGB man would get no credit—*Zampolit* Fokin would certainly see to that—and all Isakov and Pokrovsky would have to do was sit back and let the *zampolit* write his reports.

The Giant floated up out of the cave. Behind him came the two divers, with the ''bends victim'' slung between them. They'd dropped his weight belt and other heavy gear and hooked their buoy lines to his shoulder harness. They were moving slowly, with delicate fin strokes, as if their comrade had turned to glass and a sudden move might shatter him.

Pokrovsky looked at his watch. One minute ten seconds to execute the rescue. Only mermaids could have done better.

CHAPTER TWENTY

Nile Barrabas took a last look over the sea toward the Turkish coast. Even in the sunset afterglow he counted a dozen sails and a couple of small powerboats.

After a week of waiting for somebody to drop the other shoe, the Aegean was returning to normal. Cruise ships were announcing departures, charter yachts were sailing by the squadron and hotels on even the most remote island were hanging up No Vacancy signs.

It would be nice to think that the Russians' defeat on Haustim had scared them off. Nile Barrabas knew better. The Russians might fall back for a while to regroup and make new plans. Then they would come on again.

"Hey, Colonel," Alex Nanos called from the tent door. "Rafe's got a profile on our Sub X."

The miniaturized sonars had gone down four days ago. Almost immediately they'd started picking up the sound of an unidentified submarine. It was moving cautiously, staying in international waters and not surfacing, which made it a nuclear boat.

Beyond that, it was a mystery even to Master Chief Sonarman Rafael Mages, who'd been listening to Russian submarines since before the Vietnam War. He was old enough for retirement, too old for sea service, but he was another of Stewart's connections made available to the SOBs.

They'd called it Sub X and shouted for data on known Soviet subs for comparison. The data was flown in on one of the *Kitty Hawk*'s "medical" flights, along with two more sonarmen.

Barrabas ducked to enter the tent and stayed bent over to study the sheets of computer paper spread out on the folding table. Mages looked as proud as a doctor who'd just successfully delivered triplets.

"Here, Colonel. You see that if you factor in water conditions and shrouds on the propellers..."

He went on into a stream of technicalities that reminded Barrabas of Nate Beck. Nate had also liked to waste other people's time, explaining arcane bits of computer knowledge.

"Hey, Chief," Barrabas said finally. "Assume I'm just a dumb-ass grunt who doesn't know anything about sonar except what he's seen in war movies. Start with how you go ping and go on from there. Slowly, so I can follow."

"Aye, aye—I mean, yes sir," Mages said. He stroked his mustache and flicked some crumbs off the paper. "First of all, we don't go ping anymore. Not very much, anyway. That's called active sonar, and it tells the other guy you're onto him.

"What we're mostly using is passive sonar, listening to the noise the other guy's putting into the water. Screw noises— no pun intended—his reactor's cooling system, somebody dropping a pot in the kitchen—they all add up."

Mages went on to explain how each type of submarine had a fairly distinctive sonar profile. A twin-screw submarine sounded a lot different from a single-screw one, and a good sonar could even tell the difference between a submarine with a five-bladed propeller and one with six blades.

"Now we didn't have anything in the books to match Sub X," Mages said. "So I started looking for the closest thing to it. I figured we had a nuke here—she doesn't come up even to snorkel. I figured we might have something brandnew, an experimental prototype, in which case we were up shit creek. But somehow I couldn't see Ivan sneaking an experimental boat into NATO's backyard."

"Not unless she was designed for that mission," Barrabas pointed out.

"Yeah, but there are a lot of places with more sea room and fewer navies where they could try her out first. Whatever we've got here, this is her first run outside Soviet home waters. So scratch a prototype. That leaves us with a modified version of an existing sub. I went down all the different types...."

Mages took ten minutes to describe his research. This time Barrabas kept his mouth shut. Mages was an artist talking about his art, and anyone who'd known Nate Beck knew the type. He was also telling the SOBs a lot they hadn't known about Russian submarines. Which could be pretty damned useful, if the Russians were throwing an A-sub into the pot and the SOBs wanted to stay in the game.

"We tried each one with a hypothetical set of modifications. Several sets, as a matter of fact. We couldn't have done that without your good buddy's software, by the way. He can make a micro sit up and imitate a Cray 5. Any time he wants to ship out—"

"Nate's decided he's really a civilian at heart," Nanos said. "Not that it's a crime, but—suppose you found your main sonar turned into a supersize stereo rig playing sixties rock?"

Mages winced. Barrabas winced, too, at the thought of Nate Beck turned loose on the electronics of a modern submarine. There was such a thing as too much temptation.

"Anyway, he did good, saved us a lot of runs and time. We ran the whole friggin' Soviet sub fleet, and came up with this."

With the air of a stage magician, Mages put a second graph on the table beside the one for Sub X.

"This is a cruise-missile boat, what they call a *Papa* class. It was the first Soviet cruise-missile boat to be able to launch her birds submerged. She's got twin screws, torps and plenty of legs. Thirty-five knots at least.

"Now there's supposed to be only one of them, and she's in the Pacific Fleet. But we set up a *Papa* with everything silenced that can be silenced—power plant, auxiliary machinery, galley, the whole nine yards. Then we added things like shrouds on the props and rubber tiles on the hull. See what we got?''

Barrabas saw. Even to his unnautical eye, the two graphs looked damned similar.

"So we have ourselves a modified Papa boat running around loose," Claude Hayes said. "But where's the connection with what's happening in the Aegean?"

"This *Papa* could be the base. She could also be working with the base. Thing is, we've picked up her signature real close to a Type 88 minisub's five times now. Maybe she's running the Type 88s herself, or maybe the base is sending them out to rendezvous. They don't pay me to make that kind of guess."

"Thanks, Chief." Barrabas looked at Professor Stewart. "Well?"

"They do pay *me* to make that kind of guess," Stewart said. "When I've got the data. Right now...well, at least we know how to get it."

"Well, then tell us and we'll all know," Lee Hatton said.

She was smiling and she'd chosen her words carefully, but Barrabas could hear the veiled impatience. The physician did seem to be healing herself, but she still had a shorter fuse than usual.

"We start collecting acoustic signatures," Stewart said. "Anyplace *Papa*-X and a Type 88 show up together, we plot it. Where we plot the most, we start looking for Russians."

Nanos and Hayes looked at each other, then started singing:

> "The divers went down the Aegean,
> The divers went down the Aegean.
> The divers went down the Aegean,
> To sink what they could see."

Liam O'Toole ostentatiously put his hands over his ears. "What's the matter, friend O'Toole?" Nanos asked. "Afraid of us setting up in the poetry business?"

O'Toole shook his head. "I've been afraid of many things in my time, lads, but you as poets will never be one of them! Not in all the time before the Day of Judgment, which God may call sooner than He'd planned if He has to listen to much more of your singing."

The SOBs wouldn't need that much time. Enough to find, fix and destroy the Russians playing games in the Aegean was all they needed. If they didn't get it, then the Day of Judgment might indeed come sooner than expected, for quite a lot of people.

CHERYL LOOKED OUT the porthole at the main village of the Island of Tilos. The thrum of *Circe*'s engines had faded to a distant mutter. From forward came a splash as the anchor went down. A moment later the engines died, and the little grove of lemon trees on the shore no longer seemed to be moving past the porthole.

Cheryl stood up, stretched as much as the tiny cabin would allow and listened to the rattle of machinery and babble of Greek overhead. The tender was being made ready to take people ashore for a night on the town—or rather, on the village. She'd signed up to go, but did she really want to? No, not when that handsome young German art teacher was remaining aboard. He was her target for tonight, and that meant staying available.

Briefly she remembered her last night with Alex Nanos. They had had even more fun than usual. Cheryl hoped Adrienne appreciated her good luck in being set up with Alex.

What a blessed change he'd been after Hollywood! Yes, Hollywood was full of males, but with all the weirdos, homosexuals, crooks and the rare faithful husband, it was a little short of *men*.

Cheryl opened the closet and tried to decide which dress to wear. The low-cut watermelon-pink would save time getting the message across, but the burgundy lace was cleaner. More subtle, too.

"THE SHIP'S ANCHORED, Comrade Captain," *Glubov*'s sonarman said.

Abakumov put on the spare earphones, listened and nodded. "*Circe*, I believe?" he said.

The sonarman beamed, flattered that his captain had taken the time to learn the acoustic profiles of some of their potential targets.

The Thorn only grunted. Sometimes he grunted so often that Abakumov wondered if he was really human. Maybe there was a secret laboratory, somewhere outside Pskov, for turning apes into Spetsnaz officers.... And maybe there was also a ten-year term in the gulag for people who made jokes like that. The captain had turned his attention back to the Thorn, when he realized the man had actually started speaking in Russian.

"Unless there are some compelling arguments against it, we have our target," he finished. He nodded to the diver who served as his messenger and bodyguard. "Alert both squads."

"Yes, Comrade Captain Lieutenant." The man left the room.

"Are you going to use the Type 88s or the Iron Dolphins?" Abakumov asked.

"The Dolphins. We're close enough for either, but the Dolphins are quieter. Though we really don't need to worry about sound. With the tenders taking the tourists ashore for their orgies, any noise we make will be covered. When they return from their decadent pleasures, they'll be too drunk or too drugged to hear a bomb exploding!"

Abakumov ignored the rhetoric, which he knew was intended for the ear of the political instructor. He wouldn't mind listening to it for hours, though, if it kept the Thorn from changing his mind. If the Thorn continued to prefer the riding torpedoes to the midget submarines, maybe

Abakumov would be able to dump the Type 88s at Sea-home!

The captain knew that Type 88s were one of the finest achievements of Soviet naval architecture. He also knew that they were already a nuisance and might someday be a men-ace to *Glubov*. For one thing, they needed extra mainte-nance from the crew of a submarine with a dozen experimental systems already on board. His men did their best, but they still had only two hands and one head apiece.

What was worse, the Type 88s made the carefully si-lenced *N. V. Glubov* noisier. They didn't quite fit in the old mounts for the cruise-missile launchers, so part of them stuck out into the water flowing past their mother ship. That water made noise as it flowed over them, noise that an ef-ficient sonar operator might pick up someday when it would be dangerous to *Glubov*.

With the Type 88s off-loaded at Seahome, *Glubov* would once again be the world's quietest submarine. Abakumov would even have listened attentively to his political instruc-tor for the rest of the mission, in order to be free of the Type 88s.

Political instructors made a lot of unnecessary noise, but not the kind a hostile sonar operator could pick up!

AT FIRST, Barrabas thought Walker Jessup was practicing with one of the newly delivered antitank rockets. From closer up, he saw that the Fixer was using a tripod-mounted Starlite to study something out at sea.

Taking Jessup's place at the scope, Barrabas made out a slowly moving pattern of lights that suddenly formed a pic-ture in his mind.

"Navy helicopter?"

"Marine, actually. A CH-53 Sea Stallion off one of those Marine flattops, the *Saipan*. Flying from *Saipan* to *Kitty Hawk*, or maybe the other way around. Anyway, she'll fly back in the morning."

"What's the navy got in its alleged mind?"

"If the Russians make more trouble—well, a lot of American tourists will have to be evacuated in a hurry. Navy and Marine helicopters will be standing ready. Who's to know if on the way they pick up a few people from an island that isn't on the flight plan? Or lower a dipping sonar, listening for 'made in USSR' subs?"

"The Navy seems to have it all figured out."

"The Navy only looks dumb. When they're after something they really want, like peace in the Med and maybe a Type 88 thrown in—I'm glad they're on our side."

"And if the Russians pack up and go home?"

Jessup laughed. "Then you people get your quarter-mil kill fee and go home, too. If that isn't enough, maybe you can all write articles for the travel magazines."

"That won't break my heart."

"Thinking of pulling the plug, Nile?"

"What, and leave the Great Fixer without a meal ticket? Men have been tickled to death by groupies for less."

THE TEAM HURRICANE diver swam up from the bottom, flipping over at the last moment to avoid hitting *Circe*'s hull. Only his rubber fins struck the barnacle-encrusted steel.

He swam aft just below the keel, until he reached the bulge where the port propeller shaft ran through the hull. Then he signaled by tugging on the line that linked him to his comrade.

The second diver appeared quickly, since the bottom was only fifteen meters down. He was towing the float with the two limpet mines attached. The diver drew his knife and cautiously scraped barnacles from the propeller-shaft housing. Then he let the first limpet mine settle into place, until its magnet caught with a faint *clunk*.

The two Spetsnaz paused to listen for any sign of alarm. They heard nothing except an occasional distant shout or scream, and once the high-pitched whine of the tender's motor.

The second shaft housing was nearly ten centimeters deep in barnacles. The diver thought rude things about Greek shipkeeping as he scraped them away. The Greeks might be ready to be taught socialism, but it looked as if what they really needed to learn was ship maintenance!

Enough bare steel finally appeared to seat the second limpet mine. The divers listened again, then dived down and away from *Circe*. Ten minutes later, they were aboard their Iron Dolphin and creeping away from *Circe* toward the bottomed *N. V. Glubov*, ten kilometers away.

They could afford to creep. When the limpet mines went off, they would crack the seals on both propeller shafts. This would flood *Circe*'s engine room, wiping out all power for the pumps, the radio, the lights, the lifeboat davits....

The ship would sink, but she would sink slowly. This close to shore even a poor swimmer could probably thrash his way to safety. A wholesale slaughter of tourists, many of whom might be Americans or other NATO citizens, wasn't necessary. When *Circe* settled to the bottom, they would have done their work.

CHERYL KISSED Nauheim three times before he kissed her back. Even then, his kiss was so clumsy that Cheryl thought of an old joke: "Hell is where the British are the cooks, the Italians are the government, the French are the police and the Germans are the lovers." She didn't wonder how the Germans got their reputation, if Nauheim was any sample.

Well, it wouldn't be fair to turn the man off now, and Cheryl believed in fair play even for the worst turkey. She started unbuttoning Nauheim's shirt—

The deck quivered underfoot. Cheryl started, jerking a button loose. "Oh, I'm sorry."

They both knelt to search for the button, bumping foreheads on the way down. Nauheim promptly put both arms around her and kissed her in a way that promised much more than she'd been expecting.

Before Cheryl could respond, the deck seemed to leap up and slap both of them with tons of steel. Cheryl found herself lying half on the deck, half on her bunk, her cheek and one arm hurting fiercely and the taste of blood in her mouth.

She stared as orange flame stormed past the porthole. Then she screamed as the cabin door blew inward and more flame engulfed Nauheim. She couldn't see what had happened to him before he vanished in the flames.

Then she couldn't see anything at all as the flames swallowed her. Over their roar she could hear her own screams, then nothing at all.

Some of the people below decks were like Cheryl. They died in the explosion and stopped screaming quickly, when the flames went down their throats.

Others lived long enough to drown. Some of them had been burned, too. However, some were unlucky enough to be unhurt, but trapped in their cabins until the water covered them.

The Spetsnaz diver had been right about *Circe's* neglected maintenance. The second limpet mine had sent a flash into a fuel tank that hadn't been drained or cleaned for months. It was still full of volatile fumes, which promptly exploded with the force of several torpedo warheads.

This explosion touched off the fuel in neighboring tanks. Flames surged through *Circe's* engine room and crew quarters, cremating everyone there at his station. Inboard and outboard, the flames next leaped upward to the passenger cabins.

Meanwhile, the force of the explosion had ruptured *Circe's* hull in a dozen places and snapped her keel. The fire in the engine room died as the Aegean Sea surged in to douse it.

The water pouring in raised the air pressure in the passenger cabins. Bulkheads bulged, doors blew out and windows shattered, catapulting screaming people with flaming clothing into the sea.

To the watchers on shore, *Circe* seemed to be spouting flame from every hatch and porthole, even her funnel. Then one by one the flames began to go out as she settled into the water.

Before she could vanish completely, she broke in two. The heavily flooded stern section sank at once, but the bow remained afloat for a few minutes. As the flames died, the boat even provided a refuge for the handful of people who'd been topside and managed to leap clear in time.

Two-thirds of *Circe*'s passengers were ashore, and about a quarter of her crew. That included a good many crew members who weren't supposed to be there, but as they watched their ship sink they knew they'd never be punished for it.

Ninety-four people went down with *Circe*, and most of the thirty people fished out of the water were badly burned.

The Spetsnaz divers surfaced their Iron Dolphin as soon as they heard the second explosion. In fact, they had to surface, because the pressure wave jammed their mount's depth controls and painfully squeezed their chests and eardrums.

While his assistant tinkered with the Dolphin, the chief diver risked a look back at *Circe*. She was the biggest fire he'd seen since the day the main ammunition dump for the Northern Fleet caught fire.

He'd never forgotten that holocaust. He suspected that he'd never be allowed to forget *Circe*, either, particularly if he'd broiled a few dozen NATO citizens. Or had he maybe put the limpets on a warship?

That wasn't too likely, but any story was better than none if the KGB came sniffing around. Certainly ships weren't easy to identify from underwater by night, and everyone knew that. Well, maybe not everyone, but maybe enough people to keep him out of an interrogation cell....

Or maybe he should imply that *Circe* had been carrying military supplies? Yes, that was even better. His superiors and the KGB could reasonably expect him to blow up the right ship. They couldn't expect him to know that she was carrying ammunition for Greek garrisons—or even better, for Greek terrorists preparing another raid on the Turks....

"I think I've got it working again," the second diver said. "Are you fit to dive?"

"A damned sight fitter than those Greeks. I think we hit a bigger target than we knew. From the way she went up, she must have been carrying secret military supplies."

"Comrade—"

"You don't think the Greeks would run supplies to their raiders in recognizable navy ships, do you?"

"Well, now that you put it that way..."

"I do. I also ask you to think about the comforts of the Lubyanka. Think about them long and carefully, then tell me if you don't believe *Circe* was carrying ammunition."

The other man's silence was a relief. So was the fading pain in his own ears and the easy handling of the Iron Dolphin as it carried them back toward *Glubov*.

"CHRIST!" Rafael Mages said.

Lee Hatton looked up from her manual on the Armbrust. "What—" she began, then saw him signal for silence. She waited until the silence seemed to fill the tent like the smoke from a fire.

"Underwater explosion. A ways off, but a biggie. I think—" He broke off to listen again. "Yeah, breaking-up noises."

"What?"

"The sound a ship makes when she's sinking." Mages hesitated. He'd started off uncertain how to treat Lee Hatton, and he still wasn't quite sure. One of the junior sonarmen had tried a clumsy pass, and Nanos held him over the edge of a cliff until he admitted that she was an officer and a lady.

"Sounds like we'd better alert the team." Lee sat down at the radio and started tapping out the codes.

In five minutes, motorbikes and the light truck were speeding up the road. As Jessup lumbered to the tent, a jeep rattled up in a cloud of dust and dropped off the Turkish paratroop commander.

By then all three sonarmen were on their sets, with Lee manning the radio. She ran across the frequencies, ignoring weather reports, gossip between Greek island ferries and a program of medical advice for the impotent.

Finally she reached the maritime emergency frequencies. Horror exploded out of the earphones, but she didn't flinch as she turned on the loudspeaker so everybody could hear.

Alex Nanos translated, his olive skin a couple of shades lighter than usual. "Somebody blew up the cruise ship *Circe* at anchor off Tiros. Her fuel tanks went up and practically everybody aboard was burned or drowned."

"It was not Turks," the paratroop commander said. His face was even paler than Nanos's. "It could not have been. This is murder. It dishonors—"

"Not official Turks, maybe," Nanos returned. The corded muscles on his neck stood out as he struggled with his temper. "But Turkish fanatics are capable of murder, you know. Or you ought to."

The paratrooper thrust his high-nosed face toward Nanos. "Take that back, you Greek—"

Nobody saw Barrabas draw, but he suddenly had his Browning in his hand. "Just hold it, everybody. Alex, there isn't a chance in a thousand the Turks had anybody within ten miles of the ship. Start thinking with your brain and not your ancestors. You've said a lot of times that the Turks may be nasty, but they're not dumb. Tell me something dumber than this."

Barrabas's tone seemed to accomplish more than the drawn pistol.

The Turkish officer laughed harshly. "Thank you, Colonel Barrabas. I would not quarrel with that description of my people. If we start fighting among ourselves—"

Nanos held up a hand to silence him. Someone on the radio was speaking—no, shrieking—in Greek. He tried to translate as the Greek raved on, but finally gave up.

When he cut the radio off, his voice was very low. "That was a Greek navy observer. He was calling the Turks murderers and—a lot of other things. He ended by saying, 'God Himself must know it now. There will be war.'"

"Let us pray that the man is not a prophet," the Turkish officer said, almost in a whisper.

CHAPTER TWENTY-ONE

Lieutenant Eugene Hoare held his F-14 Tomcat on a steady course and speed. Flying straight and level, at 20,000 feet and 350 knots, his thirty-million-dollar fighter was a sitting target if anybody really got around to launching a missile.

At least the nervous people down there were more likely to launch at a maneuvering target. A plane flying along as if it didn't have a care in the world might look less suspicious.

Nobody was likely to get close enough to see the camera pod under Hoare's left wing. They were even less likely to get close enough to see the radar screen in the back seat. Radar Intercept Officer Wally Simms was quietly following Greek and Turkish aircraft and U.S. Navy and Marine helicopters evacuating civilians from the potential war zone. What the Tomcat's own powerful radar didn't pick up could be homed in on by the EC-2 Hawkeye AEW plane, circling over *Kitty Hawk* eighty miles out to sea.

Everything that reached the Tomcat, Wally Simms would then interpret. Simms was almost too large for naval aviation, coal-black and calm enough to make yoga adepts look fidgety. He forgave his pilot for being the son of an admiral as long as he did his job, which was bringing the Tomcat close enough to its targets for his radar and missiles to make the kill.

Thanks to their skills and their plane, they were learning a lot about what was going on in the Aegean. Almost certainly more than either Greeks or Turks wanted anyone else to know.

"Surface target, bearing 040, 22 miles," Simms said.

Hoare made a slow, shallow turn so that the Tomcat's long-range TV camera could pick out the target. Beyond a cluster of islands that were barely more than yellow-brown rocks, he saw a Greek frigate steaming north at high speed.

"*Themistokles*-class frigate, with a bone in her teeth," Hoare said into the in-flight recorder. "No sign of damage, weapons trained fore and aft."

The frigate was the same as all the other ships he'd seen, and most of the planes. Both the Greeks and the Turks were mobilizing, and they had so much afloat and aloft in the Aegean you practically needed stoplights and traffic cops to get through it.

Everybody expected the shooting to start soon, but they'd been expecting that for nearly a week now. So far, the only people who'd joined *Circe*'s dead were a couple of Turks who'd bailed out of a Phantom too low for their chutes to open.

Another twenty-degree turn, and the Tomcat was back on course. Hoare was beginning to look forward to getting back to the *Hawk* before lunch. He'd been up since 0400, and somehow he could never eat a decent breakfast when he had to launch before dawn.

Besides, he knew it really didn't matter how much he learned about the Greeks and the Turks. When they started shooting, everybody would know. What he wondered, though, was what the Russians were doing. The bastards had to have a finger in this pie somehow, but where had they stuck it in?

Hoare hoped somebody was trying to find out. He sure as hell wasn't going to do so with an F-14, unless the Russians were dumb enough to intervene openly.

For a moment he dreamed of getting a *Kiev*-class carrier in his sights, approaching her at wavetop height, then popping up to dump frag clusters on her missile launchers, sweep her decks with his 20-mm Gatling so that the parked aircraft turned into balls of flame....

Nice dream, but all the *Kiev*s were accounted for, a long way from the Aegean. A bunch of chicken *Kiev*s, that was what they were....

GEORGE KOUSTAS sat with his back to the magazine of the forward antisubmarine launcher aboard the Greek frigate *Perikles*. He was writing a letter, in spite of the vibration of the frigate's machinery as she steamed north at twenty-five knots.

A shadow fell over the paper. Koustas looked up. The petty officer known as "the Snake" was standing over him, hands on hips.

"Off duty, Koustas?"

"Unless the chief engineer needs me, yes."

The Snake frowned. He was obviously considering whether his chief, the first lieutenant, would protect him against the chief engineer if he dragged Koustas back on duty.

He apparently decided the first lieutenant wasn't quite equal to the job. "Writing a letter?" he said. His Cretan accent was thick, even when he was calm. When the Snake was angry, he was almost impossible to understand. This was one of the few virtues of his frequent rages, which had otherwise given him an evil reputation aboard *Perikles*.

Koustas nodded. "To my wife."

"What, she's missing you already? You must not have given her a proper farewell. Although most Ikyrans would probably have trouble with that, not being proper men."

Koustas wondered if the chief engineer would be able to save him if he threw the Snake overboard in broad daylight, and decided he wouldn't. By night, though, or in battle, if the Turks started shooting...that would be at least one good thing to come out of the war.

Koustas merely answered coolly, "Anybody can be surprised, as we were on Ikyros, even chief petty officers, and even by Turks. The secret is not to let it happen again, by fighting among ourselves before we've beaten the Turks."

The Snake knew when he'd met resistance too great to overcome. He stalked aft.

Koustas watched him go, praying that he'd stalk right down to the stern, trip over the dipping sonar winch and fall overboard into the propellers. Instead the Snake disappeared unharmed, and Koustas returned to his letter.

He'd already written to Maria twice, and mailed both letters when *Perikles* had stopped at Thira. Now he was writing to his Cousin Alex. His large hands did better with a wrench or a fishing net than with a pencil, but slowly the words took shape on the paper.

—cannot find the men who ruined Ikyros and sank *Circe*, then you have not paid a blood-debt honorably. If that debt goes unpaid, I will no longer call you cousin or any kind of kin.

> Yours in Christ,
> George Koustas

Harsh words, and perhaps put down too soon. Alex seemed confident that his friends would be able to do something, and he was no fool. If he said they were good, they were.

But were they good enough? Or would the Greeks stand alone against barbarians, as they had done since the wars of Athens against the Persians?

Koustas thought with sorrow of what Maria would endure as a widow, and realized that he had an answer to his problem. He would write another letter to her, and mail it when *Perikles* joined the Second Antisubmarine Flotilla at Rhodes. With that letter would go the one to Alex, to be sent to him only if Koustas died in the war Alex had not been able to prevent.

Koustas smiled. It might ease Maria's grief a little to pay Alex back for that drinking bout the night he had drawn all Koustas's secrets out of him and begun this whole—

"All hands to battle stations! All hands to battle stations!"

The alarm was howling and a voice was bellowing over it.

"Submarine contact! All hands to battle stations!"

Koustas's pencil flew from his hand and over the side as he ran for the engine-room hatch. He popped down it, stuffing the letter in the breast pocket of his dungarees. As his feet hit the floor plates, he felt them thrumming like a drum as *Perikles* worked up to full speed.

LIEUTENANT PAPPAS WISHED that *Perikles* would slow down, or better yet clear the area entirely. The contact was elusive, coming and going at random intervals, and almost unidentifiable when it came. Calling it a submarine had been a victory of optimism over caution.

The sonarman turned from the console. "If that's a propeller, it's nothing I've ever heard before. Sounds like it's slowing, though."

Exactly what a submarine would do if it thought it was being hunted. And any submarine in the area certainly would think that, considering the amount of noise *Perikles* was making.

For the next ten minutes Pappas tried to look three places at once: over his pilot's shoulder, at the sonar plot and to the rear. As if *Perikles* wasn't enough, there was that damned American Tomcat prowling around. Safe enough if he stayed up at cruising altitude, but suppose he got curious and decided to come down? He couldn't do a thing about detecting the submarine, zipping along at 400 knots, but he could easily fly right up the Lynx's ass!

Fixed-wing pilots were all like that. They regarded helicopters as an upper-class dowager regarded beggars—something not to be tolerated in a well-run neighborhood.

At the end of the ten minutes, the sonarman took off his headphones. "Lost them on the passive, sir. Want to try a ping?"

"If we want to go that way, let's leave it to *Perikles*." The frigate's sonar was much more powerful than the helicopter's.

Or had the unidentified submarine touched down on the bottom to lie doggo? Pappas looked at the chart. This far south, the bottom was too far down for anything but a titanium-hulled Alfa or Mike. Both were a devil of a lot noisier than whatever this was.

He tapped the copilot on the shoulder. "Signal to *Perikles*. Contact lost. Probable submarine, but no positive identification. Request permission to refuel."

If the submarine had gone deep and slow, *Perikles* could take over the hunt while the Lynx refueled. Then the helicopter would be ready to pursue, if the submarine tried a high-speed evasion.

The refueling would also give Pappas a chance to hand the recording of the contact over to the communications officer. Pappas didn't know where his father was sending intelligence on unidentified submarines, and knew better than to ask.

But if it was the Americans, as he suspected, then he heartily approved. He and many other Greek naval officers wanted the Americans' help against the Turks. They would not have it if they treated the Americans as lepers, the way the leftist politicians in Athens wanted!

FOUR HUNDRED METERS below the surface, *N. V. Glubov* crept along at seven knots. Captain Abakumov stood by the main sonar display, listening to the Greek frigate tearing about on the surface.

"How long are we going to be crawling along here?" the *zampolit* muttered.

"Nervous?" Abakumov couldn't resist asking. He wasn't going to tell the man how close *Glubov* was to her depth limit.

"I'm just concerned about our arrival at Seahome."

"So am I. We don't want to arrive with half the navies in the Mediterranean trailing us."

That was why he'd insisted on taking *Glubov* far to the south, into deep water where she could maneuver freely if necessary. It wasn't the most direct route, but threading their way through the islands and the shallows where the anti-submarine forces of both sides swarmed would have been foolish. If they hadn't been detected and attacked, they would have to spend half their time lying on the bottom until the hunters went away.

This far south they might encounter the Americans, who had to stay out of the Aegean during the crisis. But the Americans weren't communicating with either side.

At this point the Greek frigate started up her active sonar. The pings were way off target, the thermal layer at one hundred meters adding its own share to the confusion. Once the probing sound beam brushed *Glubov* lightly, but the rubber tiles worked well. Aboard the frigate, they'd have trouble recognizing that they'd made a contact, let alone what it was.

It seemed like hours, but it was actually only another twenty minutes before the frigate stopped pinging and moved off on a steady course.

"Probably landing her helicopter," Abakumov announced. "Ahead one-third on both engines." At one-third power, *Glubov* could reach fifteen knots and still keep her propellers shrouded.

"Well done, Comrade Captain," the *zampolit* said. He'd clearly recovered enough to be patronizing.

Abakumov said nothing. He needed the man's goodwill, and he did owe him something for agreeing to the swing south. The political officer also didn't need to know how big a part sheer luck played in these cat-and-mouse games. Submarines had been betrayed by someone dropping a wrench, and saved by a school of dolphins parading by.

ALEX NANOS WAS SITTING on his bunk when Adrienne Biggle entered the cabin. He wore only shorts, and his massive hands were spread on his knees. He was pale.

"Alex?"

No answer.

"Alex. It's Adrienne. You know something?"

"Yeah. That I'd like to be left alone."

"Alex, *Circe* isn't your fault. Okay, maybe if we had blown the whistle the Russians would have backed off. But you were right, too. They might just have tried something else, and killed even more people."

A little color came back into the heavy face—not handsome, Adrienne thought, but hard to forget if you'd ever seen it as close up as she had.

"God, a pacifist admitting a soldier's right? What next?"

His tone was sarcastic, and at first it hurt. Then she saw a smile creeping on to his face.

"Ex-pacifist now, I guess. And somebody who'd known Cheryl longer than you had."

They both held a mental picture of what it must have been like, dying in the flames and the water belowdecks aboard *Circe*. Both hoped it had been quick; both knew it probably hadn't been.

Adrienne held out her hands, and Nanos squeezed both of them in one of his. "I guess—oh, I know it's nothing new, innocent people getting wasted in this kind of shit," he said. "But before now, we've always been on the way to doing something about the ones who wasted them. This time all we can do is sit around on our cans and wait for a bunch of friggin' Navy sonar hackers to tell us X marks the spot, maybe, they hope, they think...."

Adrienne let Nanos pull her down onto his lap. "We don't have to sit while we're waiting?"

"Lie down on the job?" He slipped one hand from his knee to hers.

"If it's a job for you, Captain Nanos, you've aged a lot since last week."

He lifted the other hand and stroked her cheek. "Shall we see how much?"

The sheer relief they both felt made the kiss one of the best in Adrienne's life.

ON THE DECK OUTSIDE, Lee Hatton listened to the happy noises inside, then padded away barefoot with a sigh of relief.

No physicians, Alex and Adrienne were healing themselves the best way they could. Sometimes Lee wished she had such an uncomplicated way out—find a congenial man, grab hold of him and not let go until they were both too tired to worry about anything!

Once there had been the congenial man, but Geoff Bishop was dead. In an age that could replace livers, hearts, eyes, kidneys and limbs, finding a new man was just as hard as ever.

Lee accepted that. What she resented was the situation Alex had so accurately described. They were in another race, like the one between the Spetsnaz and Walker Jessup's weapons delivery, with higher stakes. This time it was a deadlier race, to locate the Soviet base before the Soviets' next move.

THE BLURRED PHOTOGRAPH on the table showed something vaguely conical, afloat in what might have been over-aged borscht. Actually it was the sea fifty kilometers northwest of Seahome, the evening before.

"It looks more like a sonobuoy than anything else, I admit," Isakov said finally. "Why didn't your diver get closer?"

"Standing orders," Pokrovsky replied. "Anything that might be recording acoustic signatures, we go silent and stay clear. Besides, that's close to the area where the Greeks have half their navy waltzing around. If that thing had picked up our Type 88, even the Greeks might have made trouble."

"It's much too small for any known type of sonobuoy," the sound officer said.

"Well, if it is too small for a sonobuoy, then it can hardly be one," Fokin said. "Socialist science defines the limits of what is possible. What *we* cannot do is certainly beyond the powers of the capitalist navies."

Pokrovsky carefully counted the pipes overhead, then counted them again. The *zampolit* was getting more outrageous every day. Perhaps the prospect of having a second political instructor to help him order everyone around was affecting his brain.

Pokrovsky wondered what he would have done about the cones, if he'd been in command. *Glubov* had a bigger acoustic signature than the Type 88s or the Iron Dolphins, but she also had more capabilities, apart from her Team Hurricane gang. A search for more of these mysterious cones might reveal what they were; but it might also interrupt training, wear out equipment and divers and increase the risk of accidents or enemy discovery.

In the end Pokrovsky decided that his decision to retire before he reached captain second rank was probably a wise one.

Halfway back to their cabin, the sound officer told Pokrovsky, "There is one way these could be sonobuoys."

"How?"

"Even the best Western electronics can't make something that size very sensitive, but if everything recorded was analyzed by a very sophisticated computer, the analysts might have usable results."

"How large a computer?" Pokrovsky asked.

"Bigger than any aboard American warships."

Relief flooded Pokrovsky. The Americans doubtless had plenty of such computers, but if the sonobuoys' recorded data had to be sent to Germany or even the United States, it would take time to return the results to the Mediterranean. Add more time to act on the conclusions, and the Americans would be seriously handicapped.

Even weighed down by political instructors, Operation Claw could move faster than that!

"TAKE A LOOK, Colonel."

Rafael Mages laid out a map of the Aegean and a graph of acoustic signatures. The graph was computer-generated, thanks to Nate Beck's software.

"Looks like about eighteen contacts in or around here," Barrabas said, pointing at a spot in the southern Aegean. "That's the Type 88s?"

"Yeah. Now if you add in Sub X..." Mages produced a transparent overlay. The line of contacts crept steadily toward where Barrabas had pointed.

"Looks like Sub X is heading toward the cluster of Type 88 contacts."

"Right. She'll be there inside twenty-four hours, even if she's heading all around Robin Hood's barn."

"Looks like the Russians are probably using a permanent base as well as Sub X."

"I'd bet my ass on it, Colonel," Mages said.

Barrabas fixed him with a frosty look. "Good thing you said that, Chief. Because you're about to do just that."

THE MESSAGE from Major Sinas's man on Haustim had long since become ashes, but its contents were burned into Sinas's mind.

The SOBs were preparing to move out. The informant couldn't say where, and probably couldn't find out without compromising himself. He would doubtless be able to take advantage of the weaker security after the SOBs left, particularly if any of the garrison went with them....

"By then there will be no targets left, you unweaned pig-fucker!" Sinas screamed at the wide Anatolian sky.

The sky did not answer. Neither did the hut behind him. If the people inside heard him, they gave no sign. He had too good a hold over them for them even to think of questioning him. Twenty years in Turkey's worst prison was a thought to daunt even the toughest peasants.

His going alone against Haustim was an even more daunting thought. But he could never pull together a team before the SOBs moved out. Certainly not without Colonel Rawson learning of it—and insisting on going along. Then they would have to share any credit earned. Sinas didn't want that. Rawson was too far along toward supplanting him with Karl Heiss as it was.

So Sinas had to go alone to Haustim or not at all. But perhaps a single man would have the advantage of surprise. Any Americans who'd fought off Spetsnaz would not be expecting a lone Turk. But they would learn that Turks did not need numbers to be dangerous, only skill. And Sinas knew he had that.

Nor would he be entirely alone. His informant would be with him. Either that, or dead. Worse, knowing before he died that his family would soon join him in death.

The major climbed into his jeep and started the engine. As he put it in gear, he began reviewing what he would need. Inflatable boat, wet suit with fins, snorkel, camouflage coverall and face cream, weapons. Would an M-16 be powerful enough? he wondered.

By the time he was rolling down the road to the sea, Major Sinas was feeling much better. Not being a fool, he didn't expect going up against American covert-action experts to be easy. But he had convinced himself that he could do them some damage and live to receive Karl Heiss's gratitude.

"GATHER ROUND, people," Nile Barrabas said.

The other SOBs, Professor Stewart, Walker Jessup and the Turkish CO crowded around the map-loaded table.

"Okay. The best island for operating in the critical area is Perkostri. It has water, but it's uninhabited." Barrabas pointed his Gerber at Perkostri on the map.

"That's right up close to the edge of the area. Even in it," Stewart said.

"Exactly what we want, Professor," Alex Nanos said. "We're going to swim in, or at most use the inflatables. The closer, the better."

Jessup nodded. "As soon as the SOBs leave Haustim, I drop the word into a few Greek ears that a gang of international terrorists seeking to exploit the crisis has landed on Perkostri. I describe their boat. Shortly after everyone's safe onshore, the Greek navy undoubtedly comes and blows the bejesus out of the boat. Then it's the Turks' turn. Captain?"

The Turk grinned. "We will learn that some of the terrorists escaped. So we will land a helicopter-load of troops on the island to hunt them down. In that helicopter will also be Chief Mages, his assistants and their sonar gear and computers. We shall come in with much shooting and shouting, so that everyone who sees or hears will think we are truly attacking terrorists."

Stewart was trying to glare and grin at the same time. "Worked it out all very nicely behind my back, didn't you?"

"Chief Mages volunteered," Barrabas said. "I figured you wouldn't hold him back. Otherwise, your job's pretty much done when we embark. The Navy's not going to pull the plug on us this late, or a couple of admirals are going to find themselves seeing Portsmouth Naval Prison from the inside."

That was more than half bluff. The Fixer had connections scattered through all three services, but they might not be enough to keep the professor from cutting off their naval support if he really got pissed.

What Barrabas relied on more than Professor Stewart was the U.S. Navy's reluctance to stand by and see NATO's southern flank fall apart. If they had a chance to do something effective without steaming into Greek or Turkish waters, it would be done.

Stewart's face was now blank, and his voice was neutral. "Actually, I think the Navy's committed itself. I just got word that they've put *Theodore Roosevelt* on station along with *Hawk*. That makes two full-size flattops, with about a hundred fifty birds between them. Think you'll need more?''

Barrabas ignored the sarcasm. He knew that half of what was bothering the professor was being out of the action now that it was starting. Barrabas sympathized. He himself felt years younger now; the knowledge that they were about to strike back washed away frustration, leaving only the hard core of the warrior.

"Questions, anyone?"

"What about backup gear in the helicopters?" Claude Hayes asked. "Just in case our Greek friends shoot so fast we can't get the stuff off the boat?"

"I've been working on that, Claude," Billy Two said. "We've rigged watertight containers for a complete set of charges, diving gear, weapons, the works. They can be towed just underwater, maybe a hundred meters behind *Claribel*. If the Greeks show up for the party before we're ready, we slip the lines and go over the side."

"Good work," Barrabas said. This was the first he'd heard of the containers, but he wasn't surprised. The SOBs weren't the kind to tell their commanding officer every time they blew their noses. He was supposed to assume they knew how to fight a cold!

"We'll still want a backup set on the choppers," Barrabas said. "Although I don't know if they can lift the backup *and* the Fixer, too. Maybe we should order in another Sea Stallion from the..."

Everybody laughed, including Jessup. The laughter ended abruptly when Lee Hatton asked, "Is the island Greek or Turkish?"

"Claimed by both, as I understand," Jessup said. "But it's a hell of a long way from anyplace vital. Neither side's going to get riled over the other wasting a few terrorists on it."

"You hope," Lee Hatton said, raising a hand with fingers crossed.

"We hope," Barrabas said. "We're reckoning that at this point both sides are mad at each other, but also ready to find somebody else to blame. They're too scared of what all-out war might mean."

"If you had said we were frightened of the Greeks, I would have refused to move my men," the captain put in. "But you spoke the truth. We all fear what war might mean for other civilians, women, children. I think even Greek soldiers think this way."

Barrabas nodded approvingly. The Turk was a professional, and in the same mold as the SOBs—a man who went to war so that others might live in peace.

The point of the Gerber tapped Perkostri on the map again. "How soon can you get us there, Alex?"

Nanos looked at the map, then at the roof of the tent, then at his CO. "Forty-eight hours."

"Claude, how soon can you make the hit, once you've got a firm location?"

"Using the propulsion units—eight hours."

"Allowing twenty-four hours to get that firm location..." Barrabas looked at his watch. "It is now H minus eighty hours."

POKROVSKY DIDN'T KNOW it was H minus seventy-three hours for the SOBs when he and his Team Seahome assembled in the minisub hangar, which seemed almost spacious with one Type 88 out on patrol.

"Comrades, *N. V. Glubov* will be arriving in less than two days. With her are twelve divers of Team Hurricane."

The Seahomers looked as if they wanted to spit on the floor. One ex-Typhoon actually did so.

Pokrovsky frowned. "We will maintain perfect discipline toward the new team at all times. The story of Team Seahome may be short. It will certainly tell of men who maintained the highest traditions of the Spetsnaz Naval Brigade, at base and in battle alike."

Pokrovsky didn't ask for cheers, but he got them. The "*Urras*" were so loud he knew everyone in Seahome must be hearing them.

He didn't care. Team Seahome felt like a weapon fitted to his hand. Now all that was needed was a suitable opponent. It was annoying to have to wait until *Glubov* and her Hurricanes arrived, to seek that target, but the delay would not save the enemy when Team Seahome struck!

H MINUS FIFTY-TWO HOURS.

Alex Nanos was beginning to wonder about his ETA for Perkostri. He hadn't doubted it when the storm first blew up, even though a storm this early in the summer was rare. Bad weather would foul up satellite surveillance and keep the planes of both sides on the ground.

Sonar conditions would also be lousy, and that could be bad if the storm went on. But things should have calmed down by the time Mages needed to put his gear in the water, and meanwhile nobody was going to get an acoustic signature on the yacht.

All of which didn't console him for being in the water one hundred yards behind *Claribel*, riding one of the towed cargo pods as if it were a bucking bronco.

Billy Two had rigged a couple of crude telltales on each container. Half an hour ago, one of them had signaled that the container holding the explosives, fuses and spare batteries for the propulsion units was breaking loose from its towline.

"Billy, take the helm. Dead slow, rig out the sea anchor and have somebody ready to hoist the steadying sail.

"Aye, aye, friend."

Billy Two's parody of a salute nearly poked Lee Hatton in the eye. The old yacht had a vicious snap roll in heavy seas, and Nanos was worried about the strain on her seams.

From the side of a wave twenty feet away, Claude Hayes's dark head emerged. "If this mother isn't in trouble—" A crest broke over him, dousing him in foam. He rose from the other side of the wave and finished his threat. ''—I am going to take it out of that Indian's hide.''

How Claude was going to accomplish this particular operation, Nanos didn't hear, for it was his turn to submerge, then rise spitting out water and curses against Mediterranean weather. And the forecast had been ''sunny and mild''!

The container rose with Nanos. It rose clear of the water, exposing the towing ring. At first glance it was intact. But Nanos hadn't come this far to turn back at first glance, so he waited for another cooperative wave.

This time he saw a toggle bolt that was cracked halfway through. It wouldn't set the tow loose by itself, but when it gave, more strain would be placed on the rest of the gear. That kind of failure had sunk more ships and drowned more sailors than all the naval battles of history.

''For want of a nail . . .''

At least they had the nail. Nanos had tools and spares slung on his belt; what he didn't have Claude did. The extra weight cut their buoyancy, but now they didn't have to swim back and get anything.

Tools and spares didn't calm the sea, though; the container continued its bucking-bronco act. For extra entertainment, *Claribel* sometimes played crack-the-whip with the towline.

The job kept Nanos and Hayes busy long enough for even the warm Aegean to begin to feel chilly. Too busy to notice that the clouds to the southwest were beginning to thin out and the wind was dropping.

They did notice that the swim in was easier than the swim out. By the time Nanos was back at the helm, bathrobe pulled on over bare skin that was getting itchy from the salt, the storm was definitely breaking up.

Nanos held a cup of coffee with one hand and the wheel with the other. Looking aft, he saw Lee Hatton and Billy Two wrestling the steadying sail down. The wind flattened Lee's spray-soaked shirt against her, outlining her trim figure as nicely as a man could wish.

Nanos was glad Lee had gotten rid of whatever ghosts were bugging her, besides Geoff Bishop's. Fine woman or battle buddy, he hated to see either ripping her up, and Lee was both.

Besides, more woman trouble was something Nile Barrabas needed like another Spetsnaz raid. He glanced at the colonel, standing in the corner of the pilothouse like part of the ship, his face unreadable in the twilight of the dying storm.

Claude Hayes climbed up from below. "I'll relieve you, if you want to take that shower. Better do it before the hot water system packs up."

"Again?"

"What's the matter, Mr. Nanos?" Barrabas asked. "Want to go to war in style?"

"Just getting old and creaky, sir," Nanos said, imitating an arthritic waddle as he headed below. "I do like my little comforts, I do, I do."

LIKE CAPTAIN LIEUTENANT Pokrovsky, Major Sinas didn't know the SOBs' timetable. He didn't know it was H minus thirty-nine hours when he pushed his inflatable into the surf on the coast opposite Haustim.

The swells left behind by the dead storm boomed and foamed on the rocks, but they looked worse than they felt, Sinas realized, once he was in them and had his boat under control. Still, he was glad he wore a wet suit under his fisherman's clothes. He would also surely have lost equipment, if he hadn't lashed everything in place.

Once he reached open water, he raised the bipod mast, strung the fore-and-aft brace and set sail. The inflatable was a clumsy sailor, but every kilometer it covered with the wind was one that needed his sweat.

He checked the lashings frequently. It would be the height of folly, to reach Haustim without a weapon due to carelessness. Of course, he could gamble on stealing something from the garrison or the Americans, and he was expert enough with knife and bare hands.

Alone on the sea, the major at last faced the truth. It would be better for him to die on the island, bare-handed against his own people, than to return and find that Rawson was in his place beside Heiss.

Then he would not only die, he would be disgraced. With his drug money gone, he would be unable to bribe anyone to hide his crimes. Some who had been his friends might indeed trumpet his crimes to all the world, particularly to the Americans, to show how clean their own hands were.

Sinas spit into the face of a wave. He hoped luck would send an American to him first when he reached Haustim.

H MINUS THIRTY-THREE HOURS.

Lee Hatton and Liam O'Toole pulled the camouflage cover tight over the SOBs' emergency dump, then scrambled, scuttled and occasionally fell downhill to the SOBs' main base. Perkostri was more rugged than Haustim. Lee was glad she was wearing field boots and camies, not her boat-bimbo outfit. The new garb didn't flatter her figure, but flattery didn't help a corpse or even a soldier laid up with a twisted ankle.

Lee and Liam didn't have to slow down to stay hidden. The rugged terrain of Perkostri took care of that. Lee mentally noted potential strong points for a defense around the high ground.

When they reached the camp, Billy Two was just hoisting one of the inflatables into its hiding place, while Nanos inflated the antenna balloon. Bluish white, it whipped about on the end of the wire even with Nanos and Barrabas holding it.

Then the two men heaved together, as if the balloon weighed a ton. It flew clear of the rocks and soared like a rocket toward the ragged clouds and the twilight sky.

Nanos watched the antenna wire unreel, then locked the reel and sat down at the radio. "Ready to transmit, Colonel."

"Go ahead, Mr. Nanos."

The scrambled, encrypted and compressed message took only seconds to transmit. It told Walker Jessup that they'd arrived safely and had left *Claribel*. The Greeks could be pushed into action now. Then the Turks and the sonar could follow as soon as possible.

"Are we still on schedule?" Lee asked after Nanos switched to a listening watch.

"Not quite," Barrabas said. "But everybody else should be slowed down, too. Sub X and the Type 88s need good sonar conditions for fancy navigating, and they won't have those for a while."

"Knock wood," Lee said. She looked around for some, couldn't find any and settled for tapping her fist gently on Nanos's forehead.

"Nobody home," he said in a deep voice.

"That, Mr. Nanos, I concluded some time ago."

SINCE THEY WERE AFTER a surface target, the helicopter's crew were all alert. The sonar operator was actually the first to spot the terrorists' yacht.

"There they are, the bastards!"

His gleeful shriek made Lieutenant Pappas drop his binoculars, but didn't bother the pilot at all. He was already losing altitude. The terrorists must have seen them, but if they flew in just above the waves until it was time to launch—

Pappas retrieved his binoculars and tried to retrieve his calm. It was fantastic luck, *Perikles* having been the closest ship to Perkostri when word came about the terrorists. Then his own personal luck in being already airborne at the time, with an SS-12 missile on one weapons rack.

He would have preferred another missile in the other rack, instead of a machine gun, in order to have a second long-range shot. He could only use the machine gun by coming within range of the terrorists' automatic weapons and risking *Perikles*'s one helicopter.

Pappas's calculations lasted until the pilot had the Lynx down to what the altimeter said was ten meters and the lieutenant's eyes said was even less.

"Take her up a bit and arm the missile."

The helicopter climbed and the weapons board lights turned from red to green. Pappas finished his calculations and arrived at a course and altitude for attacking.

"We could come in over the island itself, sir," the pilot replied. "It's rugged terrain, right up to an easy shot with the missile."

"It'll also be an easy shot for any terrorists who've landed with automatic weapons, all the way across the island."

"Next time let's let the army do this sort of thing."

"What, and miss a chance to add to *Perikles*'s name?"

"I don't give a shit about our ship's name. I just want to kill Turks."

Was the pilot trying to draw Pappas out, to compromise him? No, he probably just thought the same way as a good many people in the fleet. The lieutenant hoped that none of them were admirals—at least until the Turks really started shooting.

"These terrorists wouldn't be here if they weren't helping the Turks. Besides, there are too many terrorists in the world as it is. A few less won't do anybody any harm."

"Aye, aye, sir."

The pilot swung onto the course he'd been given and increased speed. Pappas felt the helicopter juddering in the low-altitude air currents and buckled himself in with one hand. His other hand never left the missile trigger.

NILE BARRABAS watched the Greek navy helicopter's attack with a professional eye. He noted the skilled low-altitude piloting, the precisely timed pop-up, the use of the missile's smoke cloud for cover and the missile's straight flight to its target.

The Greeks would have hit *Claribel* even if she'd been under way, maneuvering and shooting back.

Barrabas went on watching until *Claribel* lay on her beam ends. She sank in a cloud of spray, leaving a spreading patch of foam and wreckage as she drifted toward the bottom eighty feet down.

"Now, unless the Russians send divers to probe the wreckage, we should have everyone nicely confused," Barrabas said. "Mr. Nanos, prepare to transmit." He looked at the Greek sailor again. "Mr. Nanos!"

"Yes, sir."

"Something bothering you?"

"Not until—not really, Colonel. I just hate to see a good ship die like that."

"She'll have a lot of company if we don't get moving, and she didn't take ninety-four people to the bottom with her, either."

"That, Colonel, was a low blow."

"I am a low, sleazy, homicidal merc, Mr. Nanos. Any more comments? Good. Then start transmitting."

Barrabas kept watch with his binoculars as the helicopter circled the foam. Finally it flew once around the island, keeping a good klick offshore.

Barrabas was tempted to add a little color by letting off a few LMG bursts, but decided against it. The Greeks might have some airmobile troops ready to go if they had a hard target on Perkostri. Alerted by the navy, they might arrive before the Turkish helicopters flew in tonight. Then the SOBs would have some explaining to do, about why they were on the island.

Even worse, the Greeks might arrive at the same time as the Turks. Then the SOBs would have to explain why they'd started the Greek-Turkish war they were supposed to prevent!

WIND AND WAVES fought a battle against Major Sinas all the way to Haustim. He finally won, staggering ashore at the bottom of the south ravine just before dawn.

It was an expensive victory, though. He was exhausted, soaked, caked with salt and too late to move against the camp today. The ravines would certainly be guarded, and by paratroopers whose quality he knew. It would be stupid to do anything but find as much cover as the ravine provided and go to ground during daylight.

Quietly he unpacked his weapons and first-aid kit. Dabs of salve from the kit helped the worst of the saltwater sores.

He oiled and dried the weapons, placing them ready to hand.

Then he put his head on his pack and fell asleep.

LIEUTENANT HOARE'S F-14 was on the northern leg of its dawn patrol when Wally Simms spotted the splash.

"Somebody's gone in, bearing 260, about ten miles."

"Radar check?"

"Down in sea effect. Can't get—no, wait a minute. Looks like a couple of choppers in hover."

The TV camera in the nose confirmed Simms's evaluation. Hoare and his wingman turned as if they'd been wired together and headed southwest.

Before they reached the helicopters, their radio crackled with a message in accented English.

"Hello, American fighters. Can you call a rescue helicopter? We are Turkish Air Force Flight 54. All the men in the crashed helicopter are out, but we are too short of fuel to take them on board."

Now the Americans could see three Hueys, one sinking in the Aegean and two hovering. Three men were swimming in the sea churned by the rotor wash.

"This is F-14 206, Zulu Patrol from *Kitty Hawk*. We will relay your message."

"Thank you. We were returning from landing troops to fight terrorists on Perkostri. A turbine blade failed, but the pilot was able to autorotate into the sea."

"Good work."

Hoare kept his promise about relaying the message, then looked back at Simms.

"Perkostri? Wasn't that where the Greeks zapped a terrorist boat yesterday?"

"Yeah. Some of the SOBs must have swum ashore."

"I can believe that. But Perkostri is Greek. Either Greek troops are riding in Turkish helicopters, the Turks are cleaning out Greek territory—"

"Or something's fishy."

"I am friggin' well sure something's fishy. I also have a real strong feeling F-14 drivers aren't on the need-to-know list.

"Anyway, we'd better get those Turks fished out. Whoever's playing games, I'm damned sure they don't know, either!"

Simms repeated their Mayday as the two F-14s circled over the crash site. By the time *Kitty Hawk* replied, the two surviving Hueys were nearly out of sight to the east.

WALKER JESSUP cupped his hands and shouted up the hill to the nearest Turkish sentry. "All the men aboard the helicopter survived, and the American carrier is sending another helicopter to save them."

The sentry shook his head at Jessup, without taking his eyes off the sea or lowering his G-3.

"Alex," Jessup shouted, "can you translate?"

Nanos detached a pressure gauge from an air tank, nodded and shouted the message in Turkish.

Jessup mopped his forehead with a handkerchief that was already sodden. "Got a spare sweatband, Nile? Or maybe a sentry who speaks English?"

Barrabas grinned. "I think four out of our twelve Turks speak English."

"Just as long as they can tell English from Russian or Greek. Being shot at by my own side would be adding insult to starvation."

"Fixer, you could live on stored fat for a month."

Jessup waved an up-thrust finger at Barrabas and turned back to the radio. Barrabas looked out to sea, checking the F-14s through his binoculars, then settling down on a rock to watch Nanos, Billy Two and Hayes pull their gear together.

He was feeling good. Their Turkish reinforcements had flown in, twelve rock-hard paratroopers eager to fight the Russians who'd played Turks for fools. The sonar was up and operating, and had a better fix on the likely position of their target.

"If I thought the Russians were crazy in the head," Chief Mages put in, "I'd say they were running a friggin' taxi service with one of their Type 88s. She keeps shuttling back and forth over a three-klick course."

"Anything at either end?" Barrabas asked.

"Nothing, unless you count what sounds like air conditioning. Has to be a hell of a big set, though."

"An underwater shelter would need a big one." Barrabas knew he wanted the Russians to be there so badly he could taste it. And not just because the SOBs would look dumb if they weren't. Starting the search over would take time they didn't have.

Nanos hooked the second air tank to its harness and stood up, hands on hips. "Colonel, that's it. All we need from you is the order."

Barrabas surveyed the team's equipment. Three electric personal propulsion units—not as fancy as the Russians' manned torpedoes, but quieter. Repeating harpoon guns, with explosive warheads. Explosive charges, with every known kind of fuse and a few known only to Liam O'Toole. Scuba outfits, wet suits, knives—

"Where's the camera?"

Billy Two held up his belt pouch. Nestled inside was a waterproof miniature camera. "We can even make a videotape if you want it," he said.

"Don't take chances. Take pictures, blow it and get back out," Barrabas said. He realized there was one thing that would have made him feel better—going with them.

But he was a dry-land soldier, who'd only be a burden to the three amphibious SOBs. His going along would break one of the basic rules that had kept the SOBs alive for so long: don't jiggle an expert's elbow while he's on the job.

"Good luck," he told them. "Good luck, and good hunting."

"No," *Glubov*'s political instructor said. "I need no emergency gear. Within hours I will be returning to the valiant men of our submarine, who know how to endure hardship."

Pokrovsky and Isakov looked at each other. Pokrovsky had never thought of Seahome as luxurious. Perhaps the political instructor was hallucinating from breathing an oxygen-helium mixture. More likely, though, it was the vodka the man had been gulping since he'd arrived. It would be a waste of time to give him emergency equipment or training; chances were he wouldn't remember anything he was told. Better just to have spare equipment ready and put it on him if anything went wrong.

Not that anything should go wrong now, Pokrovsky told himself. *Glubov* was bottomed three kilometers to the south. The Team Hurricane divers were at Seahome, along with their own equipment and the supplies for Team Seahome. They were even behaving themselves!

But getting the Hurricanes to Seahome had used up too much fuel for one of the Type 88s. Then *Glubov*'s political instructor had added the crowning touch by insisting on another round trip, for "important files" he needed for a "vital conference" with Seahome's *zampolit*.

What the two *zampolits* might be hatching between them, Pokrovsky didn't care. He just hoped nothing would go wrong before *Glubov*'s man sobered up. Not only was he senior to the Seahome *zampolit*, he was also the son of a former chief political representative of the Soviet navy. Failing to keep him alive, no matter what the circumstances, would mean the end of Pokrovsky's career.

THE THREE SOBs were 150 feet down when they saw ahead the vast flattened greenish cylinder squatting at the bottom.

At first Alex Nanos thought it was a sunken ship, possibly from World War II. Both sides had lost several ships, of all kinds, in the Aegean.

Then he saw a conning tower rising above the hull. It was a submarine—and no World War II submarine had been a quarter this size.

He finned closer, but hardly needed to make out the Cyrillic lettering over the torpedo tubes.

They'd found Sub X. Now if Chief Mages was right, they were within three klicks of the Russian base. If there was a Russian Base, other than Sub X . . .

Nanos hand-signaled Billy Two to get some pictures. While the Osage worked the camera, Nanos pulled out an explosive charge, some monofilament wire and one of Liam O'Toole's fancy fuses.

They had to save most of their charges for the Soviet base, but they should be able to arrange it that Sub X didn't go anywhere soon.

Nanos swam aft, mentally measuring the submarine. From bow to stern, she was about the right size for a converted *Papa*-class. She had the *Papa*'s distinctive notched fin. And those housings forward—they were about the right size to have held cruise missiles.

On the high fin, Nanos read off the name *N. V. Glubov*, then plunged down to the twin propellers. On the port propeller, he wired the charge to the base of one blade, then shoved the fuse in and set it.

It was a fuse that reacted to hydrostatic pressure or vibration. If *Glubov* moved off at low speed, the charge would blow the minute she dived below two hundred feet. If she tried to go fast, it would blow the minute she hit fifteen knots.

Either way, she'd lose a propeller blade, maybe a propeller or the packing in the shaft. Her engine room might flood, and force her to the surface. Certainly she'd be slow, hard to maneuver and noisy as hell. That would give any competent antisubmarine skipper all the advantage he needed.

Nanos kicked twice, then floated up to the top of the fin. On the far side, Billy Two had taken his last picture. Claude Hayes was squatting on the seabed, hard to see but able to spot anyone approaching.

So Nanos was prepared for the worst when Hayes shot up from behind the submarine, hands dancing in the alarm signal. He was already unslinging his harpoon gun when the minisub came out of the undersea gloom.

It had a window in its stubby conning tower, and Nanos saw a blond-haired man staring through the window, eyes widening as he spotted Nanos.

The submarine was already starting to turn, when Billy Two signaled.

One of the hatches aboard the *Glubov* was opening, and a diver was swimming out toward them.

Nanos swung his harpoon gun and shot the diver twice. It was long range for the gun, but the explosive harpoon heads did their work. The diver sagged back into the hatch, dark threads of blood curling up from his ruined chest.

Claude Hayes was pointing back toward the hatch, then at the explosive charges. Nanos shook his head.

It was tempting to stay and put another charge in the sub's hatch. But the crew would be alert now; they would find and remove it. The SOBs' job now was to follow the minisub to its base and hit that base before *its* crew was alerted.

The sub might not be able to put enough divers in the water to fight off the SOBs. The base surely would.

CHAPTER TWENTY-TWO

Captain Abakumov heard the alarm from both the Type 88 and his own men within two minutes of his diver's death.

That was too long. He said so in plain Russian, then snapped orders. "Battle stations! Send out the divers to inspect the hull. Rig for collision and silent running. Warn Seahome that enemy assault divers are in the area."

The alarm shrilled and sailors shot back and forth on the way to their stations. "Start the engines?" the deputy captain asked.

"Fool!" Abakumov shouted, then added more quietly, "Sorry, but you're not thinking. The divers could have planted limpet mines, or be in contact with enemy antisubmarine forces. Our best chance is to clear our hull, warn Seahome and let them clean up the divers."

If they can, Abakumov did not say out loud. All the participants in Operation Claw had been taken by surprise, and things would be quite exciting for a while, even if Seahome reacted correctly and wiped out the threat. But Abakumov was well aware that Isakov hadn't commanded a submarine in five years, and the poor fellow would have the added disadvantage of *two* political instructors breathing down his neck every time he opened his mouth.

THE MINISUB WAS FASTER than the SOBs, even with the propulsion units wide open. Nanos hoped its skipper was too spooked to think of following an evasive route home. If they didn't find the Russian base by trailing his wake, they wouldn't get to it before it was alerted.

In five minutes, the minisub had disappeared into the dimness ahead. Nanos took a compass reading on the sub's course, then signaled the other two SOBs to move along the bottom as he was. They'd be less visible and less audible there.

One consolation: running wide open, that Type 88 must have told Chief Mages everything except the color of its skipper's girlfriend's panties!

Nanos looked back, half-expecting to see a gigantic green shape on their trail, like the great-granddaddy of all sharks. But *Glubov*'s skipper hadn't moved the sub. Maybe he had the sense to play it cool—

Nanos's torpedo scraped the top of a rock. He nearly lost control of it, and narrowly missed a head-on collision with an even bigger rock.

The biggest rock around, Nanos decided, was the one in his head. He should do the same as the Russian—play it cool. Or follow the old pidgin Chinese motto: Hurree, hurree, catchee no monkee.

Or in this case, no Russkee.

POKROVSKY PUSHED HIS MOUTH against the Rope's ear and shouted over the howl of Seahome's alarm.

"Get the first six Seahomers you find suited up and in the water. Don't wait for anyone or anything, don't listen to anyone, including the premier, and shoot anyone who gets in your way!"

"We've only got five underwater guns checked out, and a few snake-poison darts. What *Glubov* brought—"

"Son of a bitch! Well, give them to the five best shots. Move!"

The alarm died as Pokrovsky shouted the last word. His voice echoed through the passageways. Heads popped out of doors and hatches at the sound of the notoriously calm leader of Team Seahome shouting.

Pokrovsky took a deep breath, then another, as he thought about how to tell those idiots he was angry, not frightened. Angry, and also excited at the idea of the Americans who'd killed his people on Haustim swimming straight into a trap. No, he wasn't thinking clearly. These didn't have to be the same Americans. But they would be elite NATO combat divers, worthy opponents for Spetsnaz, and a loss to NATO.

Another deep breath, and he said, "The Thorn and I will suit up and follow the Rope and his group with as many more people as we can. If we have to—"

He broke off. No, they would not issue the underwater guns without checking them out. That was a rule Pokrovsky wasn't going to break even now. No piece of equipment ever went to a diver without being checked. He'd enforced that rule with an iron hand. Breaking it now would be as bad as hysterics for causing a panic in Seahome!

"If we have to, we can meet the NATO divers barehanded and still bring home their balls! We are the Spetsnaz Naval Brigade, and who are they?"

CLAUDE HAYES KNEW that Brother Alex had come pretty damned close to blowing his cool a few minutes ago. But he wasn't going to say a word if it didn't happen again. This mission was one hairy mother!

What was even worse, in Hayes's book, was that success was really hanging by a thread. If that minisub skipper had two spare brain cells to rub together and think of evasive tactics, the SOBs would lose the way to the Russian base, and miss their chance to find it before its divers were alerted. It wouldn't be just a hairy mission for the SOBs then. It would be suicide.

Which was better than going home without even trying, particularly against this bunch of Spetsnaz. The ones who'd banged Professor Biggle, the ones who'd blown up *Circe*— it had been to get rid of people like them that Claude Hayes had years ago signed on as an African freedom fighter. He'd soon learned that the scum didn't all wear the uniforms of colonial soldiers and policemen. They wore all sorts of uniforms or none at all, and there were too many of them for one man or even six SOBs to clear them all out before they went down themselves.

But you had to try. You couldn't hand them a victory on a silver platter.

Nanos hand-signaled for the team to spread out. Hayes looked at his watch. If they were on the right course and that three-klick estimate was anywhere near right—

The dimness ahead suddenly wasn't so dim. A shape sprawled across the sea bottom, a shape that looked like a batch of giant inner tubes covered with rocks and marine growth.

Hayes blinked. Could it be a wreck or a natural formation? Visibility wasn't the greatest, with all the bottom muck stirred up by the storm.

He got his answer. A "rock" on top of one of the "inner tubes" slid open. Bubbles floated out. So did a human shape. Five more followed him.

Hayes hit the brakes on his propulsion unit and unslung his gun. Billy Two unlimbered the camera. Then both saw Alex point at the nose of his propulsion unit and make a twisting motion.

Hayes understood. Each propulsion unit had an explosive charge in its nose, small but adequate for demolition. It could also be time fused, or even set to explode on contact.

Nanos wanted them to set the fuses for time detonation and ride the propulsion units straight in. Ram them into the Russian base, and there'd be three charges planted, ready to blow even if the SOBs didn't live to set any more.

The three SOBs soared up from the bottom and raced toward their opponents.

THE ROPE CURSED as he saw the enemy divers emerging from the murk, still hanging on to their torpedoes. Two of his men did more. They fired—at the torpedoes.

The Rope slapped their arms and shouted in their ears. "Fools! The cyanide's no good against machines. Kill the men and the machines can't harm us!"

He raised his gun and fired, but the range was long and he'd never fired at such a fast-moving target before. He noted a point in favor of the enemy: even if their torpedoes didn't carry warheads, they were using them wisely.

Then he had no more time for analysis. He leaped up as one torpedo broke free of its diver and plunged for the air lock hatch. Too late he thought of ordering it closed. The torpedo struck the lip of the hatch with a hollow *gunnnnngggg* and vanished into the lock.

The diver who'd lost his torpedo was the biggest of the three, but it was another who moved like a dolphin. The Rope turned toward him, firing as he turned.

He put an entire clip of darts into the man. Two of them were glancing hits, but he was sure the others must have gone through his enemy's wet suit.

Another man burst upward from the bottom. He'd dropped his torpedo, too. He came up between two of the Rope's men, one of them Thunderclap. Both of them were writhing and twitching and pouring out bubbles and— blood?

The man exploded out of the sea at the Rope, a gun in one hand and a knife in the other. The Spetsnaz fired at the only part he could aim at in time, the black-gloved hand that held the knife.

At the last moment he realized the hand wasn't wearing a glove. Its skin was black, and so was the skin of the face behind the mask. A face that was turning into a mask itself, with blackness flowing out of it like a river, flowing into the sea, surrounding the Rope, swallowing him up....

POKROVSKY REFUSED to let haste make him fumble fingered. With six Seahome divers in the water, he and the men beside him probably wouldn't be needed, but—

Krunkkkk! Something struck the inside door of the lock.

A moment later something else struck the outer hull, lower down and off to the right.

Pokrovsky and his men exchanged looks. "Check the lock," he ordered. There were TV cameras for inspecting each of the main locks, but none that gave a view of the exterior hull. Damn the bureaucrats for deciding there was no threat that required such an expensive measure. Especially since the political instructor had drunk a camera's worth of vodka since he'd arrived!

The TV screen flickered, started to form a picture, then went blank. Pokrovsky had a fleeting impression of a human figure carrying something.

His mouth was suddenly dry. The enemy was within reach, but in order to engage him he would first have to turn and waste time fighting Russians.

He punched through to Isakov. "Pokrovsky here. The tactical situation outside is unclear. Any signals from *Glubov*?"

"None since the initial warn—"

"Comrade Captain Abakumov of the glorious *N. V. Glubov* would not show fear by meaningless chattering," the submarine's *zampolit* roared.

Pokrovsky winced. Make that *two* cameras' worth of vodka. But oh, why did the fool have to be with Isakov now of all times? There went any chance of slipping the order to the crew quietly.

"Comrades, I recommend that all hands go to their emergency evacuation stations. Man all Iron Dolphins and Type 88s, issue survival equipment and prepare a message torpedo."

One emergency measure was a converted Iron Dolphin, stripped of everything except extra batteries and a powerful radio. Sent off, it would cover fifty kilometers, surface, signal on the 79B fleet frequency, dive, surface again kilometers away, repeat the signal and go on signaling until it ran out of power.

Within hours of receiving the signal, Soviet Mediterranean ships should be converging on a location they would receive from Moscow as soon as it knew the signal had been sent out. They wouldn't save Operation Claw now, but they might save its people and its secret.

No, that was defeatism. As long as the people lived, Operation Claw might yet be victorious.

"I refuse to accept that an emergency exists," Fokin added. "Comrade Captain, I urge—"

"Noooo!"

Even though Belyusev was screaming, Pokrovsky recognized his voice. He also recognized the sound of two gunshots, followed by another scream and a lot of gasping.

He didn't recognize the gasper. It might have been either of the two *zampolits*. It wasn't Isakov, because he came on the intercom with a not entirely steady voice, saying, "I am ordering all hands to emergency evacuation stations. I am also ordering Spetsnaz personnel to my office to place Captain Lieutenant Belyusev under arrest."

Pokrovsky hoped the reply to that wouldn't be another shot. Instead he heard the alarm again, and Isakov's voice shouting, "All hands to emergency evacuation stations! All hands to emergency evacuation stations! All hands—"

The captain was repeating the announcement for the fourth time, when the charge in the propulsion unit inside the lock went off.

NANOS HAD NEVER SWUM so fast in his life. It seemed that Claude, Billy and he were going as fast with their fins as they could have with the propulsion units.

That was impossible. But he hoped they were swimming too fast for pursuit. As far as he could tell, they'd killed or crippled the six divers who'd come out at them. If it *was* six; he'd been too busy to count. Anybody who hadn't got out wasn't going to get out in time to trail them. Even if—

The thump and pressure wave of an underwater explosion reached Nanos, squeezing his ears and belly. It felt like a low-order bang, even for the modest charge in the propulsion unit. Then he realized that the blast would have been kept inside the lock by the half-closed hatch.

Fine. Maybe it had ruptured the inner hatch door and drowned everybody. And maybe the Russians were on the ball with damage control, and the good guys hadn't disabled either their base *or* their sub enough to finish them off.

Nanos wasn't afraid of pursuit by *Glubov*. She was too big and too clumsy to chase divers in shallow water, even if her sonar could pick them up. If she cleaned the mine off her prop, though, she might be able to rescue the people from the base and carry out its mission on her own.

You had to hand it to the Russians. They hadn't gotten where they were by running from a fight after losing the first round.

Nanos spun and nearly coldcocked Billy Two as the Osage grabbed his arm. Then he saw where the other SOB was pointing. Both men flipped and backtracked.

Claude Hayes was falling behind, and his legs were flailing instead of kicking rhythmically. As Nanos swam up, he could see that Hayes was breathing heavily, too.

"Damn!" One look at the ragged tear in Hayes's hand told Nanos what was wrong.

"Billy," he shouted, "Claude's taken one of those poison darts they use. We've got to get him on dry land and help him breathe."

The two able-bodied men positioned themselves on either side of Hayes. He wasn't too far gone to notice, or even help them a bit. His kicking was irregular, but he still had some control over his muscles.

Nanos centered all his energy on keeping hold of Claude and keeping his legs moving. He knew he was using air much too fast and they'd never make it back to Perkostri on what was in their tanks.

He flashed up a mental map. "There's a little islet, not much more'n a reef, about a klick off that way," he said. "Hang in there, Claude, baby, and we've got it made."

"I—yeah—thanks—" Hayes had difficulty answering, but that he could get words out at all was a good sign.

On the other side of Hayes, Billy Two kept swimming on course as if he was a torpedo. But his eyes had gone blank.

Nanos couldn't spare the breath to ask questions, and he didn't like to bug his partner about Hawk Spirit at the best of times. He only hoped as he swam that Hawk Spirit not only worked out at sea but *under* the sea.

THE PROPULSION UNIT'S CHARGE had ruptured the seal of the inner hatch and popped seams to either side. Water poured through in a dozen places.

Pokrovsky started the flooding alarm with one hand, then checked the hatch to the passageway. It was properly sealed already.

"Gear up, everybody," he yelled. "We're going to wait for the pressure to equalize, then swim out."

He had to shout to be sure the orders got across because everyone's ears were ringing from the blast. Pokrovsky knew they'd all been lucky. If they'd been in the flooded lock when that charge had gone off under them, they'd all be dead and gutted.

He refused to think about what might have happened to the divers already outside. That way lay weakness, and weakness meant defeat.

It took a few minutes for the flooding to equalize the pressure. The hatch to the rest of Seahome seemed to be holding. If no other charges blew, they might not even have to abandon the base immediately.

"When we swim out, locate all our comrades." No need to say what to do with those too badly hurt to move without help. "Strip the bodies of all usable gear, then weight them down with rocks or scrap metal."

Blank looks put an edge in his voice. "Do you want your comrades laid out like dead fish for the capitalist press? Hide them in their mother the sea, and we may still win!"

Pokrovsky turned to the intercom without looking at his men. Let them think he was mad. If he filled them with his own desire to get his hands around an enemy's throat, their opinion of him personally didn't matter.

"Second team ready to move out," he reported. "We're going to salvage gear, hide the bodies, then move around to the Type 88 docks. After saving the men, our next priority has to be the Type 88s and Iron Dolphins."

"Yes, Comrade Admiral," Isakov said. He sounded as if he was smiling for the first time in weeks.

"Sorry, but—"

"Don't be. If we save the men and the weapons—we spineless uniformed navy bastards know what that means, too."

For the first time in his life, Pokrovsky blushed. He hadn't imagined that his dismissive remark had been overheard and would come back to embarrass him.

BILLY TWO'S HEAD broke the surface. The island was fifty yards away at most. It wasn't much more than a reef, and there'd be damned near no place to hide if the Russians came looking for them.

But Claude Hayes was still breathing. If they got him on the reef, he might make it. Billy pulled out his snorkel, popped it into his mask and started kicking again. He wasn't completely out of air, but he wanted to save a few minutes' reserve if he could.

It took both Billy Two and Nanos to pull Hayes out of the water. When they took off his mask, his lips were pale, his pulse thready, his breathing so shallow it was hard to believe it was there at all. And then it stopped.

Nanos began CPR while Billy stripped off his gear. Then Billy took over on Hayes while Nanos pulled out their radio.

"Colonel's not going to like having to run an inflatable across a couple klicks of Russkies to fish us off this reef," Nanos grumbled.

"He'll do it, though," Billy said. "Just like we'd do it if it was his ass on the reef."

"Amen."

They settled down to their jobs, Billy keeping Claude alive while Nanos tried to raise Nile Barrabas.

THE EVACUATION OF SEAHOME would have been praised in *Red Fleet*, the Soviet navy's official magazine, as "a triumph of Soviet discipline and organization." At least, it would have been praised that way if any of the survivors had been able to talk about it.

By the time Pokrovsky and his team were finished with their grisly scavenger work, the Type 88s were shuttling people to *Glubov*. With crews of two given barely enough room to work in, each minisub could carry nine or ten men.

Meanwhile, *Glubov*'s divers found the charge on her propeller. Its booby trap went off as they removed it, killing both of them, but not touching the submarine.

Pokrovsky heard about this when he led his divers around to the other side of Seahome.

"Only one mine?" he asked.

"They found only one."

"They ought to make a more thorough search. We're dealing with very determined people here."

"Yes, Comrade Admiral," Isakov said. "I will relay your orders. But remember that it will be your divers making the search. *Glubov* has lost hers, or weren't you listening? Also, you'd better not order around Captain Abakumov this way. He isn't as charitable as I am."

Pokrovsky began an apology that he never finished. As he opened his mouth, the charge in the second propulsion unit went off.

So did the charge Billy Two had slung through the hatch. The first explosion had disabled its main fuse, but Liam

O'Toole had installed a second, to be activated by the failure of the first. In Liam O'Toole's books, there was no such thing as a dud charge. There were only dud demolition men. The second fuse worked fine.

The two explosions together sent water roaring into Seahome at a rate the interior hatches weren't designed to handle. They began to give.

Isakov, standing with the last party in the Type 88 dock, knew he had to close the hatch on anyone still in Seahome. It was designed to resist full sea pressure; it would hold.

He pressed the button. Nothing happened.

He pressed it again. The same results.

"It will have to be closed from the inside," Belyusev said. He'd been disarmed but otherwise left free. Where could he go?

"Yes," Isakov said. He knew whose duty that had to be. He thought of his daughter Raissa, who was his joy and delight. He thought of setting out to drink Pokrovsky under the table, which he probably wouldn't be able to do, but—

"Excuse me, Comrade Captain," Belyusev said. Before anyone could move to stop him, he'd leaped through the hatch into the passageway.

"You—" Isakov shouted.

The scream of tearing metal and the boom of rushing water and air drowned him out. The hatch at the end of the passageway gave, letting a wall of water through.

The KGB man slammed his hatch so fast he nearly took off a couple of Isakov's fingers. Isakov was shaking his hand as the hatch light showed closed.

Not a trickle of water came through.

"We will record that Captain Lieutenant Belyusev died saving his comrades, in the highest tradition of the Soviet navy," Isakov told the others.

Outside Seahome, Pokrovsky's ears were ringing again, louder than before. Some of his divers looked confused and disoriented, as well. They'd been farther from these heavier explosions, but unprotected.

The last Type 88 lifted from the dock. Through the conning tower port, Pokrovsky saw Isakov signaling "All off."

The six divers fell into line behind the Type 88 as it headed for *Glubov*.

CHIEF MAGES SHOOK his head.

"Another underwater explosion, or maybe two of them real close together. I think I'm hearing flooding noises and maybe some Type 88s, but I can't be sure. Everything's interfering with everything else."

Barrabas raised his binoculars and looked out to sea. Was it just his imagination, or did he see some foam spreading on the surface? Foam, and what just might be bits of wreckage?

At this distance he couldn't be sure. "Chief, can you give me a position on those flooding noises?"

"If they are—aye, aye, sir."

Nate Beck's software delivered the goods again. In two minutes the sonarman gave Barrabas a thumbs-up.

"Close enough to that patch of foam."

"Good. I think our team got through."

"Want me to take a boat out and check for sure, Colonel?"

"Thanks, Mr. Mages, but I won't risk you with live Type 88s around. We'll wait to hear from Alex Nanos. Meanwhile, keep listening for Sub X. If you hear so much as one of her cooks dropping a spoon, yell!"

"Aye, aye, sir."

BILLY TWO RAISED HIS EYES without breaking the rhythm of Claude Hayes's CPR.

"Goddamn radio's as dead as those Russian divers," Nanos growled. "So much for solid-state electronics, rugged and reliable!" He put the radio down gently, though he looked ready to throw it down onto the rocks or into the sea.

"What about smoke flares?"

"They were on my propulsion unit. I didn't take them off before I crash-dived it into the lock. Sorry, Billy."

"So all we've got is that mirror?"

"Right."

"I remind you that it's getting hazy. By the time the wind comes up—"

"It'll be getting dark. Well, you go on pumping Claude's chest and I'll go flashing."

"What for, Alex? There's not a woman in miles."

Nanos said something impolite in Greek and scrambled up to the highest point on the reef, a whole three feet above Billy. The big Osage returned total concentration to saving his comrade.

He refused to ask Hawk Spirit to come and help. Hawk Spirit was not one to come when called, like a dog to heel. Also, Billy knew he might have lost some of Hawk Spirit's favor by forsaking his study of the sacred lands to join his comrades.

But loyalty to one's fellow warriors was also a sacred virtue. Hawk Spirit could not be too angry at Billy for showing that. Or if he was, then perhaps what Billy had been hearing was not Hawk Spirit at all but Coyote the Trickster.

A black thought, and one Billy forced out of his mind as quickly as possible. He continued his work on Claude Hayes, hoping only that his strength and his knowledge of how to use that strength would not desert him.

That knowledge was Hawk Spirit's gift. Even if it was the god's last gift it might be enough.

TWILIGHT SETTLED over the Aegean.

Aboard *Glubov*, one hundred meters down and thirty-five kilometers from Perkostri, Pokrovsky was trying to persuade the doctor that his eardrum wasn't ruptured.

"Even if it is, that doesn't mean I should go off duty. I can still pilot a Type 88 and launch a torpedo!"

"The risks—"

"Tell the devil's grandmother about the risks! Don't tell me, or I'll cut off your balls with your own scalpel!"

For making a joke like that, the doctor would have labeled Pokrovsky mentally as well as physically unfit for duty, except that he knew it wasn't a joke.

ON PERKOSTRI, Nile Barrabas looked at the deceptively bland Aegean. He wouldn't feel so helpless if he *knew* that it hid the bodies of three of his SOBs. Not knowing was worse.

Walker Jessup, sitting by the radio, stretched his massive legs, and dislodged a small rock. Its clatter on the beach hit Barrabas's taut nerves like an explosion. He spun around so fast that the Turkish sentry above jumped back and raised his G-3.

"Fixer—"

"Hey! No harm done. Look, Nile, all I know is what I got from the Navy. They have to haul offshore and get some sea room before the Russians show up. Every ship the Russians have in this half of the Mediterranean is headed our way. They're packing a *Kiev*-class flattop, among other heavy metal."

"So the Navy has problems. I'd be more sympathetic if they were trying to help us with ours. They ought to have at least a dust-off to spare!"

"Want me to get on the horn to the professor? Maybe his unofficial connections—"

"Can't hurt. But let me do the talking, Fixer. He's not too fond of the Company."

"Nile, I can't imagine how that fact escaped my notice."

ON HAUSTIM, a Turkish paratrooper at the head of the south ravine looked up at the clatter of falling stones.

He should have looked down. Major Sinas sprang up from the ground at the soldier's feet, knife seeking the heart and finding it. The soldier died with a gurgle and a choke, but the drumming of his feet on the ground brought the other sentry at a run.

Instead of standing back and giving the alarm, he closed with his bayoneted rifle. Against Sinas, that was a fatal mistake. The paratrooper found himself flying over the major's head and down the ravine. His scream ended abruptly as his head smashed against a rock and his neck snapped.

Echoes and falling stones chased one another down the ravine, as the major picked up the first man's rifle. It never hurt to confuse an enemy a little more by using his own weapons against him.

It hurt to be thinking of Turkish soldiers as "the enemy." But the major saw no other choice, and perhaps there would still be war with Greece to let him wash his hands clean in Greek blood....

The second soldier's body followed the first. The tumbled rocks hid them both from the casual glance, the way they'd hidden the major's approach.

There was still time to move, and fast, before anyone called the sentry post and was suspicious at their not answering. Sinas slung the G-3 over his own gear and broke into a ground-eating lope toward the archaeological camp.

IN THE FLAG QUARTERS of *Kitty Hawk*, a two-star admiral frowned at a captain.

"Our main job is the Russian fleet. We need sea room to deal with them. We also have to stay out of the Aegean. The most we can do is send in a helicopter, low, slow and sneaky."

"No problem with that, sir."

"What about fuel for a search?"

"The *Spruances* can land a chopper, even if they can't operate one. Put a fully fueled LAMPS on, say *Moosbrugger*, then have her run in at flank speed and keep station while the LAMPS makes the pickup. If things go fast, the bird can come straight back out. If not, he can land on *Moose* and transfer the passengers."

"You're figuring the people we're looking for won't want to go right back to their buddies?"

"If they want to, I'll be happy to oblige. We might even pack along some ammo and food in the bird. But my guess is they've got either casualties or hot intelligence or both. They'll want to be out here before either one cools."

"I'll bet the same way, Jake. Roust out a couple of Marines, too. They can load the supplies and make like door gunners. Just in case."

"Will do. Also, permission to position a couple of Tomcats, in case the chopper runs into trouble?"

"I don't think the Greeks or the Turks are up to spotting it."

"Maybe not, but that's near where they've both been zapping terrorists. They may be watching and trigger-happy. Anyway, sir, I'm more worried about the Russians. *Minsk*'s going to be in Forger range by the time our bird is over Perkostri."

The admiral looked at the plot. It confirmed the captain's opinion.

They were there to stop a war, not start one. But sometimes people who wanted to start a war were so determined, that being ready to shoot at them was the only way to stop it.

That wasn't what the admiral had learned in Sunday School, but his Sunday School teacher had never faced down a Russian fleet.

"HEY, PARTNER. Wake up. We got company."

Nanos couldn't believe Billy Two didn't hear the approaching helicopter. The Osage was seated in lotus position beside Claude Hayes, his eyes staring into nothing, his chest moving even less than the black man's.

Nanos didn't know if Billy was talking to Hawk Spirit, he was crazy, or he was just flat-ass exhausted. He'd kept up CPR longer than anybody should have been able to, and had managed to get Claude breathing on his own again. Still shallowly, but any breathing was better than none.

The helicopter was now directly overhead. A voice boomed out of the night, over the roar of the turbines and rotors.

Nanos wondered if he was hearing voices, too. Then he understood. A rescue chopper was trying for a positive ID before dropping into range.

"Sweat-colored. Never seen a clean one."

"Does Lee Hatton wear a bra?"

"Most of the time."

"What god does Billy Two worship?"

"None of your damned business, white man!" Billy roared, bouncing to his feet.

The speaker laughed into the microphone and someone else in the background shouted, "Bingo!" Then the speaker came back on. "Sorry about the questions. They told us to ask. We're off *Kitty Hawk*. Want a lift?"

"Yeah, but we got a casualty."

"So the brass figured."

A spotlight suddenly shone from the helicopter's door, revealing a cable unwinding, with a rescue collar at the end. It took Nanos and Billy twenty seconds to stuff Claude Hayes into it.

Claude disappeared into the chopper. The cable came back down, and Billy went up. When his turn came, Nanos made sure the camera with its precious pictures was firmly strapped to him.

Before Nanos's legs were fully inside, the helicopter was climbing away from the reef.

THREE HUNDRED YARDS from the archaeologists' camp, Major Sinas went to ground and studied the area. His lightweight binoculars weren't much good on a night like this.

Finally he decided that his best approach was to disguise himself as one of the soldiers. That meant killing another sentry, without getting blood on the uniform. It also meant hiding the M-16 and using the G-3. Sinas regretted this, as the American rifle was lighter and more effective on automatic fire, which he would need.

However, it was time to take his own advice. As he'd always told junior officers, a good plan in time was better than a perfect plan an hour late.

He stayed low to the ground, as he rounded the perimeter, chose his sentry and began stalking the man.

CHAPTER TWENTY-THREE

"What the—" the pilot of the LAMPS asked.

He turned to look aft at the two big men who were pounding each other on the back and cheering as if they'd just won a championship game. Then the pilot saw the black man trying to sit up and being gently pushed back down by his buddies.

"Okay, you guys, keep it down. Tell your friend to relax, 'cause we're on our way back to the best sick bay in the U.S. Navy, with hot and cold running nurses—"

"Hey, Red. What's that?"

The copilot was pointing off to port. The pilot banked to get a better view. "That" was something raising a tiny feather of foam and leaving a thin wake behind it.

"Looks like a submarine periscope—"

"What?"

The white man they'd rescued, who looked like a weight lifter, scrambled forward and stared. "Drop your sonar," he said. "Right now."

"Hey, what's with the orders? Only orders I've got are from an admiral and a captain to find you guys and haul you back to the *Hawk*. Nobody said anything about hunting subs."

For a moment it looked as if the weight lifter was going to try a roughhouse right there in the cockpit. But he was only angry, not crazy. After a bit he cooled down and went back to his friends, muttering something about "flyboys with golden balls."

The pilot ignored the muttering and kept on heading out to sea.

BARRABAS WATCHED THE LIGHTS of the helicopter slowly disappear.

He would have liked to have his SOBs back on the island, because all his instincts told him the Russians hadn't given up. He wouldn't have, if he'd been left with any assets at all. Not with so much at stake.

"I'm getting Type 88 noises again, Colonel," said the duty sonarman. "Not real loud. Sounds like they're either real slow or real far-off."

The sonarman was the least experienced of the three. Barrabas decided it wasn't worth waking Chief Mages for an expert opinion. The chief needed his sleep a lot more than Nile Barrabas needed reassurance.

Barrabas leaned back against a boulder and began the ritual, almost automatic check of his weapons he did whenever he had hands and time free. He'd just about finished it, when Walker Jessup loomed out of the night. He'd definitely lost weight since the mission had begun, but when he stood above you, "loomed" was the only word for it.

"Quiet night."

"So far."

"You're the most god-awful pessimist I've ever met, Nile."

"I'm still alive. A lot of the optimists are dead."

"Want to bet on our having a quiet night?"

"What are you betting?"

"A bottle of Jim Beam."

"Make that a case and you're on."

Barrabas could see the Fixer doing mental calculations about how much of his fee a case of prime bourbon would leave him.

"You're on."

MAJOR SINAS COULDN'T believe his luck when he saw that one of the men on the ridge was Moolay, his agent.

He had to take care of the other soldier first, though. He'd screwed the silencer into his Browning during a halt on the way to the ridge. Now he pulled it out, crept forward as low to the ground as a snake and sighted on the other soldier's head.

Pfffutt!

The silenced automatic made a noise like someone spitting. The soldier drilled through the head made a considerable clatter as he toppled off his rock. From behind the rock came an even louder clatter as Moolay chambered a round in his G-3.

"Lightning," the major called softly.

"Lightning?" came the bewildered reply.

Sinas turned from a crawling snake into a leaping tiger. He vaulted over the rock, landing with his revolver pressed against Moolay's forehead. "Look at me."

The soldier stared wide-eyed at the dark, sweating face inches from his own. The code word meant a good deal. The pistol that would kill the man if he didn't cooperate meant even more.

"Thunder," Moolay finally said.

"Good," the major said. "I've killed the sentries at the south ravine. If we reach the camp before they're missed, we'll have surprise on our side."

"How are we going to get off the island?"

"My boat's large enough for two."

The soldier nodded, seemingly reassured. Sinas hoped the man was as desperate or as trusting as he seemed. If he started thinking about the odds on the major leaving any witnesses alive—

"I stole a couple of grenades from the Americans," Moolay added eagerly. "I've been keeping them rolled up inside my spare socks."

Clearly the man's sergeant must have been lax with inspections if the grenades had not been discovered. The major prayed that the Greeks, cowards that they were, would still fight hard enough to drive such slackness out of the Turkish army.

"Do you have them with you?" The soldier nodded. "Good." Sinas looked at the man he'd shot. There was no blood on the uniform. It might even fit him.

"Let me change clothes with your dead friend, then we'll move on the camp. Use the grenades on the radio and the machine gun. I'll kill the archaeologists. We'll meet near the ruined wall halfway to the south ravine. You know where that is?"

"Yes." The man sounded more confident. All he'd needed, apparently, was firm leadership. If he passed his final test—

The major lowered the pistol and stepped back. "Hand me your rifle."

Moolay snapped the safety on his G-3 and handed it over. Relieved, the major began to strip the dead soldier. With three assault rifles and lots of ammunition, they should be able to do plenty of damage even if the alarm reached the camp.

ALEX NANOS SAT UP and stretched cramped arms and legs. He was beginning to think that *Kitty Hawk* was somewhere in the Indian Ocean.

In stretching, he jabbed a foot into Claude Hayes's ribs. Hayes was in good enough shape to use a little street language about muscle-bound Greeks with big feet.

"Sorry," Nanos said. "Hey, Lieutenant," he called to the pilot. "When does this bird get home?"

"Hey, we've only been on the way ten minutes. This here ain't the Concorde, know what I mean?"

Nanos looked at his Rolex. Damned if the pilot wasn't right. At least this time he was getting spooked *after* the mission, when it couldn't screw things up!

He stretched again, more carefully. As he finished the stretch, a faint whine sounded astern. It grew to a howl, the helicopter shuddered and something large and dark shot past the windshield.

The pilot and copilot both swore in chorus. "What the—" the copilot said.

"It's a damned Forger off a Russkie flattop," the pilot snapped. "He just buzzed us." He keyed in his radio. "Forger, Forger, you have just made a dangerously close pass to a humanitarian mission. Please keep a safe dis—"

Nanos saw the jet getting larger and louder again. "How the hell can he turn—" he began, before the noise and the shuddering of the helicopter made it impossible to speak. He tried to brace himself and Claude, and not think about midair collisions.

If the Russians suspected what this chopper was carrying, they might order their pilot to do a kamikaze act. He might even obey those orders.

The noise of the rotors changed and the floor tilted. The helicopter began to climb.

"With our fuel load," the pilot explained, "he's a lot more maneuverable than we are down on the deck. Specially if he uses VIF—"

"What?"

"Vectoring in flight—using his lift engines to tighten his turns. So I'm climbing, so we can dodge and maybe show up on friendly radar."

Nanos hoped all the radars they'd show up on were friendly.

RAFAEL MAGES COULDN'T have told anyone on Perkostri what had woken him up. It was a sixth sense for danger that it had taken twenty years on sonars to develop, and the other two operators didn't have that much time between them. They would be as good as he was when they had as much time in, but right now they weren't what was needed for trouble.

Mages pulled on dungarees, a T-shirt and his .45 and slogged down the hill to the sonar post. Barrabas rose to greet him.

"Can't sleep, Chief?"

"Not too good, Colonel." Barrabas didn't wear any insignia, and Mages knew some of the people with him, like that foxy dark lady, called him "Nile." Others called him "Colonel," and he sure as hell looked like field grade and then some. "At least not until the Russians have gone home," he added.

"Don't know if they're doing that or not," the sonarman said. "I got some Type 88 noises, but they sounded a long way off."

"Or slow and close," Barrabas reminded him. "You said that, too."

Score one for the colonel! Mages held out a hand for the earphones, put them on and listened briefly.

"Nothing now. But just in case—" He began punching in a combination.

Barrabas knew what Mages was doing. He was activating the dead-man timer on the demolition charges in the set and its computer. If a canceling signal wasn't sent every ten minutes, the charges would detonate, blowing all the top-secret electronics to bits, along with anyone around.

Just before the detonation, another signal would go out, this one to the miniature sonobuoys. It would set timers on their charges to go off in five minutes.

When the smoke cleared, the Russians wouldn't be able to learn much from the bits and pieces. Not unless they had magicians, not electronics experts, working for them.

Barrabas saw that Mages had things under control and turned away. It was time to crawl into his sleeping bag for a while. He might not sleep, but he'd be damned if he was going to show how concerned he was over the divers!

ALEX NANOS WAS on Adrienne Biggle's mind, too. This surprised her, under the circumstances. She was sitting in Professor Stewart's tent, where he was threatening her with budget cuts, loss of tenure and even blacklisting for her lack of cooperation with the SOBs.

As she listened to his low-voiced tirade, she began to understand why she wasn't afraid of his threats. Any damage Stewart could do to her career was minor by comparison with what she'd faced the night the Spetsnaz came, and she had survived that.

What the hell! Maybe she and Alex could set up as boat bums together somewhere—

"Adrienne, you're not listening."

"Are you saying anything worth hearing, Ian?" She watched rage choke him for a moment, then added, "The budget's not entirely in your hands, you know. The interdepartmental review board has to pass on my tenure, and blacklisting is illegal. So stop farting off and be quiet."

In the lamplight she could see his face, which had been flushed, turn pale. His cheeks had a mottled appearance, like a dead sponge.

When he finally spoke, the words came out slowly. "Have you picked up Alex Nanos's language? I hope to God you haven't picked up anything—"

He broke off, but not because Adrienne Biggle had slapped him. However, she was winding up to do just that when a Turkish corporal pushed his head inside the tent. "Pardon, Ian *Effendi*. No answer, south ravine post. We alert."

"Thank you," Stewart said. He pulled his old .45 from the holster hanging on the camp chair and laid it on the table between him and Adrienne.

He waited until the soldier's footsteps had faded away, then he turned back to Adrienne. "I'm sorry. That was uncalled for. But you've been a damned fool about this business from the beginning. And please don't interrupt me again."

Adrienne thought the apology deserved at least that much. After listening to him for two minutes, she decided to bargain with Stewart. She agreed they couldn't work together again, but if he could find her an equivalent position in another college—

That was as far as they got before they heard a sharp explosion on the other side of the camp. Shouts followed, at least one scream, and a couple of shots.

Stewart shoved Adrienne off her chair to the floor, then snatched the .45 off the table and whirled toward the door of the tent. As he snapped off the safety, he shouted, "Get down and stay down!"

Those were his last words. A black-faced, filthy figure burst into the tent, holding a Turkish assault rifle. A burst from the muzzle tore into Professor Stewart's chest. He flew backward, knocking over the table and dropping the Colt.

Adrienne didn't know much about guns, but she'd learned to keep cool facing death. As the assault rifle swung toward her, she snatched up the .45, rolled to the killer's feet and squeezed the trigger, putting three .45 bullets into Major Sinas's belly with the muzzle practically touching his skin. He flipped backward out of the tent, dropping his rifle. Adrienne clutched it with her free arm, then rolled out of his reach in case he came back. But she knew, somehow, that she'd killed him.

After a minute, she sat up and pulled herself together. She'd just noticed that she was covered with the blood of both men, when the corporal and another soldier burst in the door.

Adrienne and the soldiers nearly shot one another by sheer reflex. Then the corporal gaped, and cried, "Ian *Effendi!*"

"He's dead. I shot the man who killed him. That's him, outside the door. What happened?"

"But Adrienne *Hanim*—"

"This isn't my blood, but it'll be yours if you don't tell me what's going on." She switched to Turkish. "In the name of the dung-fed bitch your mother, what's happened?"

"We do not know who they are, but two men came to the camp. The other one tried to throw a grenade into our ammunition. It went off in his hand and killed him."

"Anyone else hurt?"

"Only a few soldiers with fragment wounds from the grenade. The captain has turned everyone out."

"Good."

Adrienne thanked God for the foresight of those who had sent the camp workers into "protective custody." It had seemed like gross injustice at the time, but who could tell what might have happened if they'd still been on the island?

"Adrienne *Hanim*..." The corporal put out a hand to help her to her feet.

"Thank you. I'm—all I need is some coffee. Or tea. Hot and strong. Fast. Then I'll change my clothes. I'll be all right."

The corporal looked dubious, but hurried away to find the archaeologist some strong coffee, to which he decided to add some brandy from the medical supplies. A devout Muslim, he would not have drunk it himself, but Adrienne *Hanim* was not a Muslim and had looked uncharacteristically pale and unsteady.

Adrienne watched the tent flap swing to and fro in the breeze as she fought down the urge to be sick. Then she spread the plastic tablecloth over Professor Stewart, sank into a chair and waited for the Turkish soldier to bring her coffee.

THE FORGER PILOT banked vertically and checked his weapons board. The internal 30-mm cannon was all he had, since this mission stretched the Forger's low-altitude endurance to the limit. Beyond the limit, if he had to play games with this eel-slick American helicopter much longer. He decided to push things a little closer on the next pass. If he had a chance, he'd rather clip their rotor with his wingtip. He could stand losing a wingtip better than they could losing a rotor blade.

It would also look more like an accident, which would help. He'd been promised the Red Banner if he took out the helicopter, but his superiors might not keep that promise if he caused an international incident by shooting it down. He and the helicopter were doubtless on some American radar by now, so even if he killed their radio at the first burst too much might be learned.

The Forger pilot was so busy congratulating himself on his tactical wisdom and setting up for the next pass that he forgot to check behind him. Since the Forger lacked a tail-warning radar, this was a serious mistake.

Suddenly he found his rear brightly lit. As his eyes adjusted to the illumination, he saw two American F-14s on his tail. They were flying in a stepped-up pair, the nearer one just below him and less than three hundred meters away.

He was still trying to recover from the shock, when his radio came to life.

"Forger pilot, you can see the F-14s on your tail. You've been told to stop buzzing a humanitarian flight. If you do it again, we'll have to regard this as a hostile act. You don't want us to do that, do you?"

The Russian was heavily accented but understandable. So was his situation. Against two F-14s, no Forger could be more than an easy kill. They had 20-mm cannon and short-range missiles to kill him if he stayed, long-range missiles and radar to kill him if he fled.

The only way to survive was to break off the engagement. He'd been told that it was worth major risks to destroy the helicopter. He hadn't been told to kill himself if necessary. The absence of such an order might not count for much at a court-martial, but at least he'd be alive to argue. If he continued to buzz the chopper he'd be dead and not even a hero!

He switched to transmit and said, "This is Forger. I understand and will cooperate." He waggled his wings and banked away into the night, mentally calculating his best altitude for making it home to *Minsk* with his present fuel load.

AS THE FORGER VANISHED to the west, Alex Nanos wiped the sweat off his face. Then he set down the waterproof bag he'd been tying around the camera. If the Russian had come in for the kill, he'd planned to toss it clear before the helicopter went down. Just maybe, the search-and-rescue people would have found the camera.

The pilot was talking to the F-14s. "Thanks, guys. You looked beautiful out there. Got a name for me?"

"Grits and Cannonball," said the pilot of the first F-14.

"Grits? You don't sound like a good ol' boy."

"I eat like one."

"Fair enough."

The second F-14 didn't give his running names. Instead there was a long silence. Then Grits came back on the circuit.

"Just got word from the *Hawk*. The friends of those guys you picked up are under attack. Don't say who or how many, but sure as God made little green apples they're up to their asses in alligators."

"I'd bet Spetsnaz," Billy Two said, his mouth against Alex's ear.

Nanos didn't say anything. Rage and frustration silenced him. Then he heard Billy again.

"Hey, Alex. These guys did save our asses! Don't pound a hole in their helicopter."

CHAPTER TWENTY-FOUR

The Spetsnaz of Team Hurricane and Team Seahome came to Perkostri aboard two of the last three Type 88s and the last Iron Dolphin. They carried waterproof AKRs and grenades. Some of them carried dart guns, short-ranged but silent.

All of them carried the long-standing Spetsnaz grudge against the Soldiers of Barrabas. Pokrovsky wasn't with them, but his words were enough of an incentive. "We may never have a better chance to avenge our comrades who fell to those bandits," he told the teams just before they set out. "Killing them will make Operation Claw a success, no matter what else happens."

The Thorn thought of criticizing that statement on political grounds. Then he took a good look at Pokrovsky, and decided that arguing with him might be more dangerous than the Soldiers of Barrabas.

MAYBE Sonarman First Class Dixon didn't have the best ears, but he had good night vision. He spotted the attack from the sea even before Nile Barrabas did.

Barrabas scanned the visitors through the Starlite, made a rough count and passed it on to the Turkish CP on the high ground. The Turkish lieutenant sounded positively delighted.

"We shall come down at once," he promised.

Barrabas frowned. He didn't have command authority over the Turks, but he could make suggestions. "Why not wait and see if this is all?" he asked. "If you come down now, a second squad could attack the high ground. We need to hold it, for the heavy weapons."

"We do not shrink from battle," the lieutenant snapped.

"I would not expect you or any Turk to do so," Barrabas said. Appealing to the man's pride, he added, "Right now there are hardly enough Russians on the island to be a fair match. They don't even outnumber you."

The appeal worked. "Very well," the lieutenant grumbled. "But inform us if any more come."

"I will," Barrabas said, and cut the connection, mentally damning all lieutenants of any nation with more *cojones* than sense.

The Turks didn't have to wait long for their piece of the action. The second Spetsnaz team arrived onstage literally with a bang, as two rockets soared from the sea and exploded on the hill. The orange flare hadn't faded before one of the Turks' M-60s opened up. In the middle of its rapid bursts, Lee Hatton came on the radio.

"Nile, we've got a second Spetsnaz squad coming up. From their location now, I'd say they're going for the hill, with your visitors providing covering fire. Keep your head—"

Before Lee could finish the suggestion, 5.45-mm bullets flailed the air over the sonar post. Barrabas studied the shore in both directions, knowing that the Russians must have a couple of men closer than he'd expected. Those AKRs didn't have much range, but if they were close enough to hit you they were dangerous.

Barrabas poked his G-3 between two boulders, detected movement beyond a limestone outcrop and put a burst into the area. The only result he saw was the Russians' return fire.

Dixon yelped as a bullet tore into his leg. Then he screamed as one ricocheted into his chest. The scream turned into the gasping of a sucking chest wound.

Rafael Mages dived under the sonar set and came out with a first-aid kit. He bent over the sonarman, furiously stripping open dressings and laying out morphine ampoules. He'd just dressed the chest wound and injected the mor-

phine, when the sonarman took a breath that rattled in his
throat, and died.

"Must've hit the heart on its way out of the lung," he
muttered. He shifted position, bringing his head up just as
a Spetsnaz lowered his aim and fired. Three bullets punched
into the back of Mages's head and neck, leaving him
thrashing briefly on the ground before he died.

Barrabas wondered briefly if one of the Spetsnaz out there
had a 5.45-mm slug with his name on it. Then he reviewed
his lines of retreat, and rejected them all.

As long as he was alive, the Spetsnaz squad had someone
in their rear. At best, they'd have to leave a couple of men
to pin him down while the rest either assaulted or gave covering fire to the other team. At worst, they might mistake
him for a target worth the whole squad. That would buy
Lee, Liam, Jessup and the Turks badly needed time.

Barrabas squirted five more rounds at the outcrop, then
rolled to the left, changing magazines as he rolled. From ten
yards closer to the water, he fired five more rounds. Then he
low-crawled twenty yards inland, stopping every five yards
to fire a random two or three rounds.

He might not be hitting any Russian flesh, but he was
damned sure he was giving them the notion that they faced
a bunch of live opponents. Just let that notion get firmly
fixed, and he'd have their number as thoroughly as they had
his.

ABOARD *KITTY HAWK*, the admiral turned to the captain.
"What have we got?"

"Two Tomcats in the area, but they're a bit skosh on
fuel."

"Launch the ready tanker. Rendezvous over *Moose*. Is
the second chopper on the way?"

"Negative. They've got fuel to come straight out."

"Good. Let's get off a second tanker and four F-18s.
Sidewinders, tanks and two 500-pound clusters apiece. We

don't need to apologize for supporting Turks against terrorists, even if they're on a Greek island.''

"We may need to apologize to the Turks for assuming they need support,'' the captain pointed out.

"Oh?''

"The Turks have never been wimps, and fighting Russians is one of their national sports.''

"Let's launch now and apologize later.''

"Aye, aye, sir.'' The captain put down his coffee cup and picked up the telephone. "This is the captain. I want to talk to CAG.''

HALFWAY UP THE HILL, Lee Hatton and Walker Jessup were beginning to wonder which side the Turks were on. The two rocket hits on their position had made them mad. So mad, in fact, that they couldn't seem to see straight.

"Damn!'' Jessup said as a burst came out of nowhere and sprayed rock chips all over them. "If those Turkish mothers get the radio, we are in deep kimchi.''

Lee thought this was a minor risk. Jessup was cradling the radio in his lap like a premature infant. The bullet hadn't been made that could get through his bulk and still smash the radio.

From up the hill, a back blast flared orange. Sand, spray and smoke leaped up from the beach. The Turks had their Carl Gustav recoilless rifle in action.

"Hope they haven't forgotten to move after each shot,'' Jessup said. "I don't know if those Spetsnaz have a machine gun, but—''

The Russians did have plenty of AKRs, and most of them seemed to let fly at once. Lee heard some of them farther up the hill than she liked. The rest were still down by the water. Between the AKR bursts, she thought she heard the lower-pitched, slower sound of a G-3. Liam or Nile? Probably Nile. From where Liam had been, he'd probably found it simplest to join the Turks.

Jessup was punching a frequency into the radio and holding the microphone. Lee counted her bandolier of magazines again. She told herself firmly that security for the radio was an important job, even if it didn't involve killing Russians, even if those Russians were trying to kill her friends—

Brump! Brump! Brump!

A noise Lee would have picked as the one she least wanted to hear—a Soviet AKG-17 grenade launcher, firing a burst of 30-mm grenades at the friendly on the beach. A friendly who almost had to be Nile Barrabas.

She knew that nobody would hear her except Jessup, but she still jammed her free hand into her mouth for a moment, until the urge to cry out passed.

When it passed, she was the cool warrior again, listening—and wanting to cheer when the G-3 fired a quick burst.

WHEN THE CARL GUSTAV TEAM fired a second round from the same position, Liam O'Toole knew he had to do something. The Russians must have the position blueprinted by now. If they didn't sweep it with bullets, that had to mean they were still out of AKR range. That wouldn't stop them for long, and meanwhile, they might have more rockets aboard one of those subs out there—

"Hey!" he shouted at the Turkish lieutenant. "We need to take out that grenade launcher on the beach." He pointed downhill.

"They may have another," the lieutenant replied. "We must meet the attack here before we move against the beach."

Before they moved against the beach, Nile Barrabas might be dead and the Carl Gustav smashed. O'Toole's Irish temper flared, then his training and experience at being sneaky and subtle came to his rescue.

"We can move across the slope, fire a couple of rounds into the beach party, then take the people here in the flank. At least, we can if your men here can hold without the—"

"My men could hold here with only knives and teeth!" the lieutenant snapped.

For a moment O'Toole thought the Turk was going to draw on him for insulting Turkish soldiers.

"Fine. Then let's go." O'Toole shouldered the Carl Gustav before its gunner could object. The loader fell in behind O'Toole, with the gunner bringing up the rear, G-3 at the ready.

They scrambled down the hill, bullets spanging off the rocks to either side.

"GRITS, this is Sorcerer. How much fuel you got?"

Lieutenant Hoare looked at his gauges, then answered his wingman. "Five thousand pounds."

"Can I tank up first? I'm down to forty-three hundred."

"Leak?"

"Naw, this bird just guzzles like a wino on handout day."

"No sweat."

Five minutes later they saw the lights of the KA-6B tanker riding the night ahead of them. Sorcerer raised his Tomcat's fueling probe and crept in toward the drogue trailing from the tanker.

"Bingo!" came over the radio. Sorcerer was plugged in and taking on fuel. Hoare concentrated on relaxing and started the breathing exercises he always did before an aerial refueling. He couldn't do much, not strapped into his ejection seat with all his equipment on, but it helped.

"Clean scope?" he asked Simms.

"Squeaky clean, 'cept for that chopper heading out for the *Hawk*. When they supposed to launch those 18s?"

"PDQ was all I heard."

Hoare would be perfectly happy if the F-18s never showed up. After that Forger had chickened out, he figured he and Sorcerer were entitled to a piece of somebody else, just by way of compensation!

NILE BARRABAS WONDERED how much longer he could go on dodging grenades.

So far he'd been fast, jumping to where the last grenades burst and hitting dirt while the next burst came over.

He'd also been lucky. Sooner or later, one of the Russians on the AGS was going to try putting two bursts into the same area. If they got the interval right, they would also get Nile Barrabas.

So far all they'd done was waste the radio, put a few fragments into Barrabas's skin and make him scrape off more skin diving over rocks and into gravel. That was no worse than annoying.

He had the feeling, though, that he hadn't even annoyed the Russians. Delayed them, maybe, and that could still be important if the Turks used the time he'd given them. But he hadn't heard the Carl Gustav in a while; if the Russians on the hill had knocked out the Turks' big punch—

An 84-mm rocket-assisted shell ripped overhead and exploded on the beach. It was wide of the grenade launcher, which promptly fired another burst. It hit somebody, though, judging from the scream.

The screams ended in a pistol shot. By then Barrabas was crouching halfway between his old spot and where the grenades burst. The Starlite scope had survived; he took a quick glance, snapped a magazine of tracer into his G-3 and started counting seconds.

When he reached seventy-five, he figured the Carl Gustav team should have had time to move and be ready to fire again. He aimed the G-3 and pumped half the magazine of tracer straight at the cluster of rocks concealing the grenade launcher.

CHAPTER TWENTY-FIVE

The Thorn knew the Seahomers were beginning to look daggers at him. Whether their beloved Pokrovsky could have done more, he didn't know, but certainly the situation was not under control. It was moderately satisfying that the wounded screamer he'd had to shoot was one of the Seahomers.

The satisfaction lasted about two seconds. First another Seahomer muttered what sounded like "The Frog Prince would not have done that." Then that cursed Carl Gustav fired again, following the mark given by the burst of tracer. Those fools with the AGS should have moved at once! Instead they'd let themselves be pinned down for a few seconds too long, even after the tracers had stopped coming.

That was long enough for the Carl Gustav to land a round squarely on the grenade launcher. It burst apart, its fragments joining the shell's to chip grenadier and loader to raw meat. One fragment touched off a magazine of grenades on the loader's back. The explosion blew him apart and sent fragments scything through the air all the way to the water's edge.

Most of the flying debris was harmless. The Thorn saw the men of both teams looking behind them, and wished that one of the fragments had drilled his brain. In another moment he would face the supreme disgrace for a Spetsnaz team leader, mass disobedience. There were too many men to shoot, which made it worse....

Inspiration came. "Back, everybody!" he called. "We'll withdraw around the beach and support the hill attack from a flanking position. We'll be less exposed there."

As long as the retreat could be presented as an ordered one, the Thorn could defend it himself. Just to avoid tempting anyone to further disobedience, he decided to take the rear guard himself.

That decision was the last one he made. His men got clear, thanks to the pattern of shadows on the beach throwing off Barrabas's aim. The SOB leader also was down to his last two magazines, and forty rounds in a firefight was like one Big Mac for a whole Boy Scout troop.

When the Thorn's turn came, though, Lee Hatton was up on the hill, with a better view, a clear shot and plenty of ammunition. Not that she needed more than two rounds to punch into the Thorn's heart and lungs and stretch him out on the beach.

BARRABAS COVERED Lee Hatton while she moved to where she could spot any Spetsnaz who had changed their minds about retreating. Then he covered Walker Jessup as he scrambled down the rest of the slope to join Barrabas.

The Fixer looked like something out of a horror movie or a hobo jungle, his safari jacket filthy, his pants ripped, the radio dangling from one strap and a three-day growth of beard on his jowls. The only clean things on him were his Uzi and his Colt Python. Jowls, flab and all, he still didn't look like someone you'd want to have mad at you.

"Fixer, we'll make a grunt of you yet," Barrabas said.

"I'd rather be in Philadelphia," Jessup got out between gasps for breath. "Even South Philly. How about we blow those sonars and get out of here?"

Barrabas looked at his watch and realized that the demolition charges in the main sonar should long since have gone off. He also remembered Liam O'Toole's advice on tinkering with dud charges: Don't.

"Let's drag the bodies clear and grenade the set."

"Nile, the word from the Navy is they're sending in a flight of F-18s loaded for air-to-ground. Anything on the beach in a few minutes is going to be cluster-bombed to a fare-thee-well."

"All the more reason for moving the bodies. What if Mrs. Mages doesn't want a closed-coffin funeral?"

"Nile—"

"Fixer, if you screw up Chief Mages's funeral, yours will be next."

Barrabas's tone got results. Both men were sweating by the time they'd hauled the two Navy men clear and blown up the set with hand grenades. But Jessup worked steadily, even though sweat carved channels in the dirt on his face. He even led the way off the beach.

The two men joined Lee Hatton, and together they began to work their way cautiously around the hill. Barrabas was a veteran of too many night actions to hurry in a situation like this. Everybody would be trigger-happy, and hurrying would be more likely to get him shot by the Turks than shooting at the Russians.

"LIAM, THIS IS Barrabas. Situation report."

"The Turks started off on the wrong foot, but they're a pair of fine lads. They've been doing some fair shooting, in case you hadn't noticed."

"I have. Tell them they saved my ass."

"When I find someone who can tell them that in Turkish, be sure that I will. Where are you?"

"Working around to stay between the crest and the beach party. I think we've taken out half of them, but you know Spetsnaz."

"Indeed I do, much as I wish I didn't." O'Toole made a 360-degree scan of his area. "The Turks on the crest are staying put. They've got good fields of fire for their M-60s, and I don't think the other Spetsnaz squad has an ASG. Nothing from the sub, either."

"Okay," Barrabas said. "Don't use the Carl Gustav again until you have a clear target. The Russians must know they're racing the clock. That means they'll make a combined assault as soon as the beach party's in position."

"We'll be waiting, won't we, boys?" Liam grinned at the Turks, who didn't understand English but did understand his tone. They grinned back.

"Lee and I will trail the beach party and signal when they start to climb. I'll send the Fixer up to you. Don't worry about him, but save the radio at all costs. We may need to call in air strikes from the *Kitty Hawk*."

In the background, Jessup could be heard saying sharply, "I heard that, Colonel Barrab—"

Then he was cut off abruptly. Before O'Toole could even wonder what was wrong, he heard a slithering, scraping noise, a thump, Lee Hatton's "Kiyaaah!" and the stuttering of automatic weapons.

He found himself not only shouting into the radio, but pounding it, as if that would extract information about what was happening.

"Colonel, come in. Come in. O'Toole here. Come in, damn it!"

BARRABAS AND HIS COMPANIONS didn't walk into the Spetsnaz because neither side was walking. Both were moving on hands and knees, one step short of a low crawl. In that position, Jessup looked like a blimp imitating a tank, and his wheezing was loud enough to be heard in Istanbul.

Barrabas decided to take the radio at the next halt. It would be rude to the Fixer to give him a heart attack or slow him down so that they had to abandon him.

On this mission, Walker Jessup had certainly earned the right not to be treated rudely by the SOBs. He might have even earned his fee.

Moving shapes appeared on the slope ahead. Barrabas signaled everybody down. Lee had just hit the dirt, when one of the moving shapes suddenly burst out of the darkness, visible now as a black-clad man with arms and legs flailing.

Trying to cross a steep slope with a heavy load on his back, one of the Spetsnaz had overbalanced and rolled downhill. He rolled straight onto the rock hiding Lee Hatton, then over it on top of her.

It was too close quarters for firearms, and Lee Hatton's knife was buried under tons of rocks in Ravine Blue. Her hands, however, were as deadly as ever, as the Spetsnaz diver found out in his next and last moment.

A second Spetsnaz came down to help his comrade. He arrived too late for that, but just in time to take one of Lee's *shoto* strikes on his kneecap and another in his groin. He jackknifed and toppled off the rock, gasping but still alive.

Barrabas shot the third Spetsnaz as he was pulling a grenade. He hadn't yanked the pin, so it rattled off down the slope as Jessup rose from cover, Uzi sweeping back and forth. He shot off a whole magazine, but he thoroughly massacred the remaining two Spetsnaz before they could get off a shot.

The little fight triggered a reply from up the slope as Turks let fly at real or imaginary targets. The other Spetsnaz team opened fire, and from the sea two more rockets flew up toward the crest.

One of them hit short; the other flew clear over and hit someone, judging from the scream. Whoever it was, it wasn't the Carl Gustav team, because they fired two rapid rounds out to sea. The first churned up foam; the second got a solid *whumppffff!* with black smoke, then a secondary explosion that sent fragments and spray flying.

"Score for the home team," Barrabas said. "I think that was one of the minisubs."

Lee looked up from the Spetsnaz prisoner she had subdued, disarmed and given first aid. "That should have the others looking over their shoulders."

Barrabas pointed at Jessup. "Fixer, the radio, please."

"Yes, sir."

Barrabas shifted frequencies to the one he'd been given for Navy air, and lifted the mike. He'd heard jets approaching, and he wanted to make sure they could tell the home team from the visitors!

LIEUTENANT HOARE SLOWED to 350 knots and banked. "That's Perkostri," he said.

"Or if it isn't, then there's two islands around here being fought over," Simms pointed out. "There's smoke offshore, and I see some inland, too."

Hoare shifted to the air-ground frequency. "This is Juniper Flight, Grits speaking. Any friendlies down there?"

A commanding voice came on immediately. Speaking English, too, and Hoare thanked higher authorities for that. He knew enough Turkish to find liquor, the bathroom and sometimes a good belly-dance bar. He seriously doubted that was enough for air-ground coordination.

"Houseman here," the voice said.

That was the code name Hoare had been given for whoever was in charge on Perkostri.

"What do you have?"

"Two Tomcats, with Sparrows and Sidewinders."

"Any 20-mm?"

"Full load, but—"

"Do they teach you strafing in that fancy flying school at Pensacola?"

"Any turkey can strafe. But I remind you, this is a thirty-million-dollar bird designed for air-to-air. If—"

"Fine. If any turkey can strafe, then you must be really good. Come down and make a pass along the west beach of the island."

Hoare didn't know what rank Houseman had, but he'd been ordered to obey the man's orders. He sure as hell *sounded* like somebody who dined on filet of lieutenant anytime he wanted it.

"Reference points?"

"Keep your fire two hundred yards west of the military crest and everybody will be happy except the bad guys. Oh, one more thing. The bad guys are operating from an armed minisub. So far they've only used ground-to-ground, but watch out for ground-to-air.''

"*They* had better watch out for *us*, Houseman." Hoare shifted frequencies. "Sorcerer, we're going to make four passes, alternating the lead. I'll take lead the first time around. Leader strafes, second stays five hundred yards offshore and two thousand yards back."

"Roger that, Grits."

Hoare checked the Tomcat's 20-mm Gatling, the afterburners and the decoy flares. If somebody down there did pop a missile, it would be IR-homing, and that meant popping flares and hauling ass.

It might also mean reaming ass—specifically, Lieutenant Eugene Hoare's—if the Tomcat did get bent. But Hoare figured that orders covered most of what could happen, and he'd chance the rest for an opportunity to score.

With one hand he switched on the radar gunsight, and with the other he advanced the throttles. The Tomcat went into its next bank at 450 knots.

LIAM O'TOOLE WATCHED the beach erupt in smoke, spray and flying gravel as the 20-mm slugs sprayed the Spetsnaz line of retreat. Then he turned and counted the remaining rounds for the Carl Gustav. Six would be more than enough if the Spetsnaz lads chose a patch of beach that was in range at all.

The Turkish loader said something, then pointed at O'Toole's Gerber fighting knife.

"You want that?"

The man nodded.

"All right, lad, although I'm not thinking we'll be getting to that close quarters." He shifted to unstrap the knife's sheath.

The loader probably would do well enough if the Spetsnaz came close enough. He'd seen his gunner taken out by the sub-launched rocket, loaded two more rounds for O'Toole, then given the gunner rough first aid. The gunner might even make it if he lasted until Lee Hatton could lay her hands on him.

The Tomcats were coming in again, clearly visible with all their lights on. The beach erupted again, and part of the hillside, too.

That was enough to make the Spetsnaz desperate. O'Toole had time to hear Turkish shouts and the rattle of M-60s and G-3s. Then he was shouting for a round, as black-clad figures seemed to explode up the slope toward the crest.

The Carl Gustav bucked and spewed flame at both ends. O'Toole watched the round arc toward the Spetsnaz. The bastards had to be trying to get so close the flyboys wouldn't dare hit them. That was a dicey thing to try against Turks with an Irish SOB on their side!

O'Toole was too busy aiming the second round to see where the first one hit. He did see the second round catch a running Spetsnaz squarely in the chest. The explosion not only blew the man to pieces, it knocked the man next to him out of hiding. The loader's G-3 made sure he didn't live to hide again.

Then both O'Toole and the loader had to go to work with their G-3s. It looked as if the Spetsnaz had decided that the Carl Gustav marked the main Turkish position.

O'Toole was suddenly too busy even to consider his chances of being alive a minute from now. He was far too busy with the fight at hand to see the conning tower of a Type 88 break the surface offshore.

"GRITS" HOARE WASN'T too busy to spot the sub. In fact, he was looking for exactly that, since on this pass he was flying second to Sorcerer. For all of two seconds, his TV camera gave him the best view of a Type 88 any Westerner had ever had.

Then 20-mm shells streamed from the Gatling, churning the sea to froth until they reached the submarine. They chopped effortlessly through titanium, plastic, fiberglass and copper. A few of them chopped all the way to the fuel cell; one hit a torpedo warhead.

The combined explosion threw up a fountain of spray and pieces of submarine. Hoare didn't breathe until he was past it with nothing worse than a shaking. If he'd sucked a good load of spray or a chunk of conning tower into an intake—

"Grits, Sorcerer. This is Houseman. Thanks for the good shooting."

"Want any more passes?"

"Negative. The rest is just grunt work. Oh, and tell your bosses on *Kitty Hawk*—when they fly our friends back here to bring some SEALS with them. I think they might want to dive offshore and pick up the pieces. We might even have an interesting prisoner for them if Lee doesn't have to hit him again."

"I won't hit him in a vital spot" came what Hoare could have sworn was a woman's voice. Cool, but the sexy kind of coolness.

"I'll pass the word," Hoare said. It made as much sense as anything these past few days did, which wasn't much. But it was still better than having the Greeks and Turks shooting at each other, which made no sense at all.

Besides, he was now the only Tomcat driver in the whole damned Navy who could paint a Russian sub under his cockpit!

THE LAST OF THE FIREFIGHT sputtered and died without Nile Barrabas or his companions joining in. The range was too long for safe shooting when both sides were mixing it up hand-to-hand or close to it. Moving nearer would just get them shot at by both sides.

Walker Jessup looked angrier and angrier as they waited out the firefight. Before Barrabas could ask what was bugging him, the Turkish lieutenant came on the air with a report of victory.

"They are all dead, and only two of my men. Others will do well if we can have the help of your Dr. Hatton."

Lee slung on her first-aid kit and picked up her rifle. "On the way."

Then the four Hornets arrived, and Barrabas went back to being Houseman, to tell them that the Tomcats had grabbed all the targets. The Hornet pilots didn't sound happy about this; Barrabas hoped they and the Tomcats didn't meet for a few days.

Finally he had a minute to drink some water, clean his G-3 and ask what was bugging Jessup.

"I just wish the Turks had thought of taking a couple of prisoners," he muttered. "If those pics Nanos got don't come out—"

"Why the hell do you think I requested some SEALS?" Barrabas asked. "Besides, we've got Sleeping Beauty here." He prodded the unconscious Spetsnaz man with a booted toe.

"If he lives through the Turks' interrogation."

"He will. Lee's going to tell them he's suffering from a head injury that makes it dangerous to disturb him."

"Really?"

"Let's put it this way, Fixer. If Sleeping Beauty starts waking up, she'll sedate him right back down. And if he gets too rough, he *will* be dangerously injured."

Barrabas stood, stretched and contemplated the dark Aegean. Maybe the Fixer was right to still be antsy. The SOBs had probably fought their last firefight on this mission. But the Fixer's job wasn't over until two very stubborn peoples, the Greeks and the Turks, were convinced they ought to shoot at the Russians and not at each other!

CHAPTER TWENTY-SIX

The Greek patrol boat *Helikon* was old, so the Greek navy considered her expendable. She was also fast, had a good radio set to report trouble and a reasonable number of weapons to handle it. So she was an ideal candidate for patrolling an area about twenty-five kilometers northwest of Perkostri.

Ideal, except for one thing. Her sonar was an old model, and not well maintained. Against a well-handled Type 88, she had little chance of warning.

POKROVSKY NUDGED the periscope a few centimeters higher. On this calm bright morning, too much periscope would be fatal even faster than usual.

"*La Combattante*-class patrol craft," he said as the image steadied. "Gun forward, missiles aft. No real antisubmarine capability. Speed fifteen knots, course 250 and steady." Then he added, "Make ready all torpedoes. She's a Greek."

Behind him he heard the Golden Giant obeying. He armed the torpedo releases, set the "fish" for acoustic homing and reported, "All torpedoes ready."

Pokrovsky lowered the periscope and turned to his last surviving Seahome comrade. "Did I see you writing any messages on the torpedoes?"

"I wanted to write 'For our comrades,' Semyon Ignatievich. But I thought that might compromise us, if the torpedoes were found."

"I know I saw you writing."

"You did. But I was writing 'Vengeance.'"

"Really?"

"I was writing it in Bulgarian."

Pokrovsky clapped the warrant officer on his shoulders. "Oh, I almost hope one of our torpedoes does go dud. More confusion for NATO!"

Pokrovsky knew he was talking mostly to keep up his own spirits and his comrade's. Their chances of carrying out Operation Claw were now small. They had one submarine that had sacrificed much of her combat power for silence and barely dared move, one Type 88 with a minimum crew of two men, and two Iron Dolphins, which couldn't be manned at the same time as the Type 88!

Still, that was two Spetsnaz men still alive with weapons in hand. Also, both Isakov and *Glubov*'s skipper, Abakumov, had the Spetsnaz spirit—the belief that the only excuse for giving up was death.

Pokrovsky listened to the patrol boat's high-pitched screws and nodded. "Fire one. Fire two!"

Galina nearly broached as two one-ton torpedoes rolled out of their racks, started their propellers and headed for the Greek boat. Pokrovsky caught her in time, sending her down to thirty meters, only ten above the bottom.

Meanwhile, the torpedoes had run far enough to arm themselves and activate their homing gear. The Greek patrol boat was an easy target, so noisy they could have tracked her through New York harbor.

The torpedoes themselves weren't as quiet as they should have been. Damage in the hasty evacuation of Seahome had been repaired even more hastily, or had gone completely undetected. Even on the patrol boat's creaky sonar, they screamed a warning.

But it came too late to save *Helikon*. The captain fed power to his diesels, manned battle stations and prayed. He also launched two American-made Mark 46 homing torpedoes, installed at *Helikon*'s last refit only a month ago.

Both of *Galina*'s torpedoes hit, blowing *Helikon* into three large pieces and a great many small ones. A few of her crew not only made it overboard, but weren't too badly wounded to swim. They inflated two rafts that floated clear, wondered what had hit them, cursed the Turks and hoped for rescue.

The explosion jammed the rudder of one of the Mark 46s. It ran in circles until its power died, then sank to the bottom.

The other plunged, picked up something that sounded like a submarine and started homing on it. The target's noise level promptly decreased as Pokrovsky cut all power. Then it increased as Pokrovsky flooded the Type 88's tanks for a quick dive to the bottom.

He and the Golden Giant clung to handrails, oozing sweat as the high-pitched *screeeee* of the homing torpedo grew louder. It climbed until Pokrovsky expected the torpedo to burst through the overhead in the next moment.

Then an explosion thundered through the water. It tossed *Galina* nearly over on her beam ends. Pokrovsky heard ominous crunchings and grindings both inside and outside. But he didn't hear the collision alarm or the dreadful boom and hiss of water pouring through a breached hull.

When *Galina*'s crew could stand instead of being tossed around like dice in a cup, Pokrovsky wiped blood from his nose and mouth. Then he listened for more torpedoes. All he heard was the last breaking-up of *Helikon* and more noise from *Galina* than before.

"It must have hit a rock pinnacle," the Golden Giant said.

"As long as it didn't hit us. Check the power."

The fuel cell had survived. So had both propellers and the rudder. Pokrovsky listened to *Galina*'s newly acquired collection of noises and patted the control panel. "You're like me now, *devushka*. A bit battered, but still in there fighting."

If a Type 88 was so badly damaged it couldn't make it back to base or mother ship, standing orders were to scuttle and escape. If the crew couldn't escape—well, they could go up with their ship or use their cyanide capsules.

Galina wasn't that badly off. As Pokrovsky opened the throttles, one question remained. Could he find a speed that would take them home quietly? He wasn't going to leave a trail of sound leading straight to *Glubov*.

Fifteen minutes later, Pokrovsky knew he could take *Galina* home. At seven knots she made only as much noise as she normally did at fifteen. It would be a long trip, but they could make it, and they hadn't heard any antisubmarine vessels in the area.

Unfortunately for Pokrovsky, among the helicopters that had arrived in the area was *Perikles*'s Lynx with its dipping sonar. Lieutenant Pappas ordered it lowered the moment he got word of *Helikon*'s sinking, so his bird reached the area ready to listen.

Listen he did, and everything he heard was carefully recorded. He'd also shanghaied *Perikles*'s most experienced sonarman for his crew.

Every so often, there were advantages to being an admiral's son.

NANOS WAS FOLDING UP the map, when *Kitty Hawk*'s admiral entered. The SEALS were on their feet and saluting at once.

"Hey, buddy, that's a real live two-star—" one of them began warningly.

"At ease, everybody," the admiral said. "That means particularly you, Mr. Nanos, Mr. Starfoot. You've earned more than relaxing around admirals. I don't know if you'll get it, but you've earned it."

"Thank you, sir," Nanos said. "What we'd really like is another crack at the Russians."

"You may get that. Word is that a Greek patrol craft was torpedoed and sunk about an hour ago here." One weathered forefinger stabbed the map.

"There are plenty of people around who will assume it's Turkish retaliation for a Greek attack on their troops last night," the admiral continued. "There might be enough of them to start a war. We wouldn't have much chance of stopping them if you two divers and your injured friend hadn't brought the pictures. You SEALS should provide additional confirmation, and also smack any bad guys who stick their heads up around Perkostri."

The admiral opened his briefcase and pulled out a bottle of Maker's Mark bourbon. He handed it to Nanos. "This is for the people on Perkostri. May you drink it in good health."

"Thank you, sir," Nanos said.

Billy put the bottle in his flight bag, and the two SOBs followed the SEALS out onto the flight deck. As they watched the Navy men board their Sea Stallion, Nanos looked around.

The carrier flight deck looked like an accident waiting to happen, and Nanos wouldn't have switched boats for planes on a bet. But if you studied the deck long enough, the whole pandemonium of shrieking engines, scurrying deck crew, steam blasting out of the catapults and odd bits of machinery leaping out at you began to make a weird sort of sense.

Off to port, the plane guard helicopter hovered, waiting to fish crash survivors out of the water. Beyond the helicopter, a missile cruiser and a missile destroyer scrawled creamy wakes on the blue-gray sea. Off on the horizon and looking big even at that distance cruised *Theodore Roosevelt*, the other carrier in the task force.

A pair of F-18s ran up their engines, then one after the other screamed down the catapults and into the air. Nanos watched them climb away, and turned to see Billy waiting by the helicopter door.

"Good hunting, brother," Nanos said. "Don't let those Navy bastards hog all the game."

One of the SEALS gave Nanos the finger as he pulled Billy inside. Nanos backed away as the Sea Stallion's huge rotors thrashed the air, blowing them toward the island.

Nanos took one last look at the task force before he went inside. Normally a task force this size would be spread over five times as much sea. But this was the Mediterranean, where normal cruising formation would take the escorts halfway to Crete. Under their umbrella of fighters and missiles, the big carriers would hold the ring. They could keep the Russians from fishing in troubled waters—as long as those waters didn't get *too* troubled.

Ten minutes after the Sea Stallion lifted off, an SH-3 did the same. Its course was slightly to the east of the Sea Stallion's, and its load much lighter.

It carried a U.S. Navy commander, Alex Nanos and the photographs of Seahome and the *N. V. Glubov*.

POKROVSKY and the Golden Giant nursed *Galina* almost all the way back to *Glubov*. It took even longer than he'd expected, because halfway along they had to reduce speed to four knots. The Type 88 was slowly coming apart around her crew, and at more than four knots made more noise than an Armenian wedding.

There had to be sonars listening somewhere in range, and Pokrovsky was still determined not to lead enemies to *Glubov*. *Galina* would never sail again; the big submarine was the last hope of Operation Claw.

Their luck ran out four kilometers from *Glubov*'s position. Warning lights flashed and the emergency alarm started its insane peeping, like a thousand baby chicks all crying at once.

"Fuel cell's over its pressure limit," the Giant said.

Pokrovsky didn't waste time cursing. If an inflammable oxygen-hydrogen mixture was going to start leaking, *Galina* was finished.

Moving faster than a Cossack dancer, Pokrovsky cut all power, turned on the emergency lighting system and set the timer on the demolition charges. As an afterthought he also set the two remaining torpedoes to arm themselves and detonate in an hour.

The much bigger bang this would produce wouldn't hurt *Glubov*'s reinforced hull. It would certainly register on every sonar in the Aegean. If luck was with the Soviets, anyone who inspected the site would take the crater in the sea bottom and the pieces of wreckage lying around as the last gasp of the Soviet navy in the Aegean.

If they were unlucky, someone tracking the explosion might stumble on *Glubov*. But snugged down on the bottom, with all systems at minimum power, *Glubov* would be hard to detect from a ship directly over her.

The last thing Pokrovsky did was to pull his harpoon gun out from under the control panel and tie it to his air tank. He'd hidden it, because otherwise the doctor would have fussed at the hint he planned to dive. He wasn't going to leave it, not when he'd carried it on every mission in the ten years since he'd left the naval brigade's training school.

Then he clamped his mouthpiece between his lips. When both he and the Giant had a good airflow, Pokrovsky pulled the lever to start flooding *Galina*.

BILLY TWO WALKED out of the sea like a Greek god in a wet suit. The minute he hit dry ground, he stripped off his fins and handed his scuba outfit to Liam O'Toole. Then both SOBs sprinted for cover and Nile Barrabas's CP.

"Where's Alex?" was Barrabas's first question.

"How's Claude?" Lee Hatton asked, almost interrupting him.

Barrabas started to frown, then decided to let the breach in merc conduct pass. When you got right down to it, Lee Hatton juggled the woman, the doctor and the warrior every day of her life. That was juggling live grenades; she'd be blown to pieces if she dropped even one. It was time to stop worrying about the few times she missed. Much better to remember all the times she got everything right, and saved herself and others, too.

Even better, Barrabas realized, would be remembering that with Erika. She performed the same juggling act, not as dangerously or as often as Lee, but she didn't need her man grabbing her elbow at a crucial moment.

Not her elbow, not any other part of her.

Barrabas nodded at Billy. "How *is* Claude?"

"Beginning to complain about the lack of nurses," Billy said. "So I don't think there's anything to worry about. Alex is on a chopper heading for the Greek flagship, the frigate *Perikles*. The Greeks have sent out a real live admiral named Pappas to take command. The Navy figured they should take the pics to him first. The Greeks have lost more than the Turks, so they have to be cooled down first."

"Hey, people," Walker Jessup called from the radio. "Just got word from Haustim. Seems somebody landed on the island last night and wasted Professor Stewart. Adrienne Biggle blew him away."

"Hot damn!" Billy shouted. "Alex is going to love that. Not about the professor, but about Adrienne turning into a pistol-packing mama! We can run her for Meanest Mother in the Valley next year."

"Anything else?" Barrabas asked the Fixer.

"Seems the guy was a Turkish army officer, and he had a friend in the garrison. The friend tried to grenade the ammo, but blew himself away with his own grenade. They said all his other grenades appeared to be defective, too."

Barrabas turned and looked hard at Billy Two and Liam O'Toole. They tried unsuccessfully to appear innocent.

"Defective grenades, huh?"

"Well, I don't remember if I put all the booby-trapped ones into those caches," Liam O'Toole said.

"I think you did," Billy said reassuringly. "But I remember telling some Turk that anybody suspicious ought to be told about those caches. I forget exactly who I told, though."

"You forgot," Barrabas said heavily. "You also forgot to tell me."

"Well, Colonel, we meant to, but we somehow . . ."

"Never got around to it, with everything else there was to do. Right. I'm only about the millionth CO in the history of war to hear that excuse." Barrabas shrugged. "I'd run your asses up the flagpole, except that we don't have a flagpole. I've also used that excuse myself a few times, and you did get the right man. But tell me the next time you risk wiping out a few friendlies, okay?''

Before either man could answer, they all heard the sound of approaching jets. Four Greek A-7 Corsair IIs swept past the island, three thousand feet up and a mile offshore. Barrabas saw that they carried drop tanks and bombs or rocket pods.

The Greeks' reaction to the latest sinking had begun. If those Corsairs had orders to sink on sight the first Turkish ship they saw, the SOBs would have bled and sweated and still failed in their mission.

THE EXPLOSION CAUGHT Pokrovsky completely by surprise. A giant hand clutched him, not only squeezing his chest and belly but digging ragged fingernails into his flesh. He flailed like a skewered frog. Sheer instinct was all that kept him gripping his mouthpiece.

Pain and dizziness blurred his vision. He saw the Golden Giant spinning head over heels, curled into the fetal position. He didn't think he saw the stream of bubbles that would sign his partner's death warrant.

He wished he could be sure. If the Giant was dead, then Pokrovsky could give himself to the sea with a clear conscience. Nobody left to help, nobody left to help him, no duties left at all—

But it was not to be yet, he thought, as a voice spoke into his ear. "Damned timer. Must have gone off prematurely. That pounding we took from the torp."

"Can you make it?"

"Yes, but I'm not going to leave you."

"That's an order!"

"With all due respect, Comrade Captain Lieutenant, you can shove that order up sideways. Come on."

Pokrovsky didn't know if the explosion's pressure wave had done more damage or simply aggravated his previous injuries. He didn't care. Dying still seemed much simpler than going on.

But with a witness, giving up would be cowardice. He would be breaking the Spetsnaz tradition, shaming the memories of the other Seahomers who'd died fighting—

He bit back a scream the first time he tried to kick. The second time, too, and the third, and the fourth. He'd never felt such pain. He'd never even believed such pain was possible.

After a while, either his muscles loosened up, or he became insensitive to pain. He could barely feel his feet moving, but he knew they were. He also felt the flow of water over his face and hands. He was not only moving his feet, they were moving him.

He tried to focus on a point on the bottom to estimate his speed. Either the bottom was too far away, or he couldn't see clearly. He seemed to be suspended in an endless haze, which had to be water, not air, because it felt like water. Otherwise he couldn't tell where he was.

A hand groped out of the haze and took him by the belt. He turned his head, neck muscles protesting fiercely, and saw the Golden Giant.

So he had to be somewhere that living men could go. Unless the Giant had died in…what was it, an explosion? Yes, there'd been an explosion. If he and the Giant were dead but still swam, what did this say about official Soviet atheism?

Or maybe the God the atheists fought didn't exist, but the primitive tribes who worshiped the sea were right. Maybe the sea could keep dead divers alive somewhere in its depth because they'd worshiped the *real* god....

Pokrovsky hadn't answered that question when the sea ahead grew dark. He was still wrestling with it when the Golden Giant struggled through the air lock with him into *Glubov*.

As the Giant and Captain Isakov stripped off his diving gear, Pokrovsky thought the deck plates under his feet were quivering. He dismissed the sensation as being the result of his injuries. Either that, or he was just imagining that he was aboard *Glubov*, safe for the moment.

Pokrovsky sagged unconscious in his comrades' arms before he could recognize the vibrations of a submarine getting underway.

THE SOUND of *Galina*'s explosion reached *Perikles* just as George Koustas was passing the sound room on his way off watch. The chief sonarman opened the door, and Koustas saw the operator on watch rubbing his ears and swearing.

"What the devil was that?" the man snarled.

"Something just blew up. Plot the bearing and get it upstairs. Koustas, can you run a message? Damned intercom's shorted again. What is this, the Turkish navy?"

Koustas hastily stubbed out his cigarette and nodded. The sound chief growled a lot, but he seldom bit.

The soundman scribbled data with one hand and rubbed an ear with the other. The chief read the sheet over the man's shoulder, then snatched it off the pad and handed it to Koustas.

"Run this up to the captain, and I mean run! Then try to find the chief electrician and have him do something about the intercom. Turkish navy! Even the Turks wouldn't let the wiring go like that. This is the Bulgarian navy, if it's a navy at all.

"And what are you waiting for, Koustas? The recovery of Constantinople? When I say *run*, I want to hear the deck shaking under your feet!"

ADMIRAL PAPPAS and *Perikles*'s captain, who was acting as his chief of staff, put the photographs down and looked across the table at the two Americans.

They didn't have to look far. *Perikles* was the flagship of the Second Antisubmarine Flotilla. This didn't mean she had proper quarters for an admiral. Not unless the admiral was willing to turn half the officers out of their cabins.

Pappas wasn't that kind of man, which was one reason he was a vice admiral. The only Greek ship he could remember with a decent admiral's cabin was an ex-Italian light cruiser he'd served on as a lieutenant. She finally ran down and was sold back to the Italians, who promptly scrapped her!

The Italians, Pappas thought, were worse than the Turks in some ways. The Turks might be more brutal if they decided to be, but they would make decisions. The Italians would simply let things go on until they had a complete mess on their hands—and then they would dump it on somebody else. Like the Greeks.

Which was one reason Pappas was looking at the photographs with an open mind. He'd never suspected that the Turkish government was behind all the incidents. Oh, Turks were involved in some of them, Ikyros for example. But Turkish politicians were like Greek politicians or any other kind. They would snarl and threaten and maybe send out a few pawns too stupid to know what they were, to make trouble for others. But they'd steer clear of anything that would make that kind of trouble for themselves. Since war with Greece would be major trouble for Turks, politicians and soldiers alike, Pappas doubted anyone in Turkey really wanted it.

He didn't have the same doubts about the Communists. In fact, accusations against the Turks, made by Athenian politicians who slept with the Communists, made Pappas even more skeptical.

But Pappas's own beliefs weren't the problem. The problem was what he could persuade his superiors to believe.

Or—and here he looked around the tiny cabin, as if the walls had eyes to read his thoughts—what he could get away with by not telling his superiors until he'd done it.

A knock sounded on the door.

"Message for the captain."

The door opened.

"George!"

"Alex! I— Excuse me. Captain, a message from the sound room. They report an underwater explosion." Machinist Koustas handed over a sheet of paper.

All four heads bent over it, until the American realized he couldn't read the Greek and pulled back. Admiral Pappas looked at Alex Nanos. He was the junior man in the room, but he was also the one who'd swum close enough to the Soviet nuclear submarine in these photographs to read the name on her fin.

Pappas switched to Greek. "Mr. Nanos. Do you know Machinist Koustas?"

"He's my cousin."

"Then you know he's from Ikyros."

"I do. It was his brother Spyros's death that got me into this business. I don't go chasing Russian subs around the Aegean Sea just for exercise."

"What do you do for exercise?"

"Lift weights. Chase women. Run a little security business with a partner."

"Where?"

"Southern California."

"Hmm. I'm attending a surface warfare seminar in San Diego next month. Are the women of California all they're said to be?"

"Admiral, you haven't heard the half of it." He handed Pappas a battered business card that read Nanostar Security Services, and gave an address and phone number.

Pappas slipped the card in his pocket. "Mr. Nanos, if you can convince your cousin that the Turks really aren't the ones who murdered his friends on Ikyros, I'll act on your intelligence." Then he switched back to English. "Gentlemen, I would like to leave Mr. Nanos and Machinist Koustas alone for a while."

POKROVSKY AWOKE to feel the same vibration he'd felt when he'd lost consciousness. It *still* felt like a submarine under way. Running slow and silent, but moving.

He tried to speak. All that came out was a croak. Someone handed him a glass of water. He drank thirstily. Then he tried again.

"Your mother's not here," someone else said. "She'll be back after you wake up."

Pokrovsky had the vague idea he was too old to be calling for his mother if he was aboard a submarine. But it was too much trouble to think the thought through. Much better to go back to sleep, the way they wanted him to.

ADMIRAL PAPPAS STOOD on the signal platform of *Perikles*, with a look on his face that discouraged anyone from approaching him.

Perikles and the other five ships of her flotilla were steaming in a wide circle at twenty knots. Their wakes scrawled white foam across the blue Aegean. Overhead the air cover, a pair of Phantom IIs, cruised back and forth.

In the depths below, the Russians waited.

It had to be the Russians. The evidence was overwhelming. The photographs were almost enough. There was also the sonar contact his son had made, the one that so nearly matched the Type 88.

The Russians had been behind the whole business from the first, and they were still determined to set Greek and Turk at each other's throats.

Pappas didn't know whether the evidence would convince enough of the politicians in Athens. Probably not. In any case, he wasn't planning on sending them copies of the pictures. All that would do was warn the Communists. Then they would launch a campaign to discredit the American intelligence, inflame passions and put Vice Admiral Theodore Pappas ashore or in jail.

Pappas knew his career would end if he went ahead without the politicians' permission. He would look out at the Aegean from a villa, if not from a prison window.

It would still be better than looking at it from *Perikles*'s bridge and seeing it littered with sinking ships, drowning men and wreckage as burning planes plunged from the sky to add to the horror—

"Admiral? Sir?"

It was Machinist Koustas, standing on the ladder to the signal platform. Pappas looked down at the man. Koustas flinched as if he'd gazed on the Medusa and was just about to start turning to stone, but went on with the speech he was determined to make. "Admiral, I think we'd...I can't...Admiral, Turkish money won't bring back my friends. Fighting Turkey won't do it, either. We—we have to go after the Russians. First. Then—"

Pappas gave a great whooping laugh and sprang down the ladder. Everyone on deck aboard *Perikles* was treated to the spectacle of a vice admiral embracing a reserve machinist.

Nobody saw the meeting in the admiral's cabin five minutes later, and they would have had to be very quick to hear it. Pappas wasted neither time nor words.

"The Turks have to be persuaded fast, and secretly."

"If the Turks aren't behind this—" the chief of staff began.

"They can tell their own government anything they please. Even the truth. Just as long as they don't say a word to *our* government."

Reluctantly the captain nodded. Then he smiled, a smile that turned into a grin. Pappas clapped him on the back so hard his cigarette flew out the porthole.

"I thought you'd see it my way. Now, Commander Singer, I need to visit my counterpart. I think that's Admiral Pezcoglu. Do you know where he is?"

Singer shook his head as if he'd been punched in the jaw, then said, "We'll find out."

"Good. While you're finding out, can you also arrange an American helicopter for a visit to Pezcoglu? It's less likely to be shot at by the Turks, and all ours may be needed for hunting Russians."

"Well—how many people?" Singer asked.

"You, Mr. Nanos, Machinist Koustas, my son and myself."

The chief of staff looked annoyed.

"Sorry, Philip, but you're needed aboard *Perikles*."

"I wasn't worried about that, Admiral. It's just that you're senior to Pezcoglu. He should come to you."

"A Turk, come at a Greek's bidding? Now, now, Philip. I know I'm senior. I'll command our joint forces. But a harmless concession like visiting him—that should sweeten him up like a baklava."

Koustas laughed. "A Greek admiral giving orders to Turks! I love that."

"I hope you won't be the only one," Pappas said. "I doubt that many of them will be Turks. But their sailors know honor and the laws of the sea. They will not like it, but they will do it.

"Now, Commander Singer. Can you promise that helicopter?"

From his expression, the American officer would rather have promised his first-born son. But he swallowed again, and said, "If we don't get it, I'll carry you to the Turks on my back, like Zeus carrying Europa."

"Ah, an American officer with a classical education," Pappas said. He pulled out a bottle and five glasses. "I think we should drink to such a miracle. Then, although it may be tempting fate, we should drink to peace."

NIGHT SWALLOWED the Aegean.

In *Perikles*'s petty officers' quarters, the Snake cursed the lack of evidence. He couldn't activate the Party network aboard *Perikles* without more evidence. The men wouldn't risk the sentence for mutiny. They would be more likely to mutiny against him.

He had nobody but himself to rely on. That thought made him stare wildly and mutter to himself, so that even men used to him walked by more quickly.

Aboard *N. V. Glubov*, Pokrovsky listened patiently for the fifth time to Isakov's explanation.

"We have no weapons left except *Glubov*'s. Abakumov is senior to me and refuses to risk his ship by an attack this far north. Once we're south of Crete—"

"Once we're south of Crete, the Greeks and the Turks won't be following us!"

"Maybe not. But our own Mediterranean Fleet and the Americans will both be present in force. The Greeks and the Turks won't dare attack us when they can't tell us from an American or another Russian submarine."

"I'm not worried about their attacking us!" Pokrovsky screamed. "I want to attack them! If they're not around to be attacked—"

"Then we can rendezvous with a Mediterranean Fleet ship and transfer you. You need better medical care than *Glubov* offers, Semyon Ignatievich. I don't want to lose you any more than Abakumov wants to lose *Glubov*."

"So you've betrayed—"

"Semyon Ignatievich, you're too battered to know what you're saying."

Pokrovsky certainly felt as if several large men with steel-shod boots and gloves had done sambo exercises all over him. Maybe he *had* reached his physical limits for now.

"Sorry."

"In your position I wouldn't apologize. I would be careful what I said. Do you want to be put under arrest?"

Pokrovsky winced. His head hurt too much to shake it.

CHAPTER TWENTY-SEVEN

Karl Heiss watched smoke billow from the windows of his Anatolian safe house. Flames would soon follow, fed by stacks of papers and the bodies of the family whose house it was.

He let his driver help him into the jeep, then settled in the back seat as the jeep rattled off downhill. By the time they were rolling past the vineyards a mile west, the smoke was streaming up in an oily cloud.

More smoke trailed across the sky as a flight of Turkish jets climbed out of the air base. Silhouetted against the sunset sky, they were too far off to identify.

Heiss was on his way out of Turkey, or at least out of Anatolia. He might manage a long stopover in Istanbul, where men from both the international drug rings and the intelligence agencies swarmed like cockroaches.

But that sort of twilight existence couldn't even hold what he had, let alone recover lost ground. He'd be shaking the dust of Turkey from his aching heels for good, and before the year was out. The messages he'd received after Major Sinas's death made that explicit: his Turkish friends would be turning into neutrals or even enemies by then.

At least he could guarantee he'd be left alone that long by avenging Sinas's death. That was the way the Turks could be made to see it—and of course American intelligence wouldn't press the Turks too hard over the death of Joel Rawson. The Company might want to, but Heiss would have that danger covered, too.

Not at the time of Rawson's death, unfortunately. That would be today, set up with two phone calls after Heiss had learned that Rawson was coming to see him. But within forty-eight hours of a third phone call, documents would be available to prove far more against Colonel Rawson than even the Company would want let out.

Rawson wasn't going to finance a harem of teenage girls by sucking off Heiss. That thought gave Heiss more pleasure than the sunset, almost enough to make him forget the pain from the bumpy road.

TOGETHER aboard the Turkish flagship, Vice Admiral Pappas and Rear Admiral Pezcoglu reminded Alex Nanos of Mutt and Jeff. Pappas was short, immaculate, a dapper lady-killer. Pezcoglu was tall, gangling, unkempt, with a large mustache and a dry wit.

He was also easier to convince than Pappas had been, never mind Cousin George—Nanos would rather have free-dived to two hundred feet than have to go through *that* again!—the Turks hadn't suffered as much as the Greeks in the whole affair, and Pezcoglu also had more evidence. The SEALS diving on the Seahome site had sent more photographs, plus a few selected items of Russian equipment.

"I'm not surprised the Russians were trying to trick us," the Turk said as he shoved the whole pile into one corner of his desk. "I'm not even surprised the Greeks took so long to realize it. They don't have the bear growling right on the other side of their border like—"

"They've also lost too many people," Koustas interrupted angrily. Then horror began to supplant anger, as he realized he had interrupted and talked back to an admiral.

"Very true," Pezcoglu said. "Mr. Koustas, money can't bring back your friends. But the Turkish navy's honor demands that it do something for those who have lost homes and kin."

"Fine," Pappas said briskly. "Let's start by placing your ships under my command."

Pezcoglu looked ready to yank his mustache off his face. His breath hissed out. But then he gave a quick nod. "You're senior. There are Turkish admirals senior to you, but they couldn't be at sea in less than twenty-four hours. By then *Glubov* could be well away."

"More like twelve hours," Nanos said. "That's a *Papa* power plant she's carrying. Give her open water, and she'll run straight under the skirts of the Russian Med Squadron before you can piss out a bottle of raki."

"Very likely," Pezcoglu said. "On two conditions. One, that Mr. Nanos stops insulting Turkish liquor. Two, that we don't subordinate my ships to yours as a unit. We'll break up into pairs or trios, anyway, so the senior captain can command."

"No problem, if your captains will go along with that."

"If they don't, they'll be commanding garbage scows on the Black Sea coast."

Both sides were short of helicopters. Most of those they had weren't equipped for antisubmarine warfare. They would help, starting tomorrow morning, but catching *Glubov* would stand or fall on the surface ships.

"We have three submarines at sea—" Pappas began.

"No, you have four. Which is one reason we have six," Pezcoglu put in. "I suggest we order them all out of the area. That way we won't have identification problems. Any submerged submarine will be Russian."

The Greek air force wasn't going to be informed. Pappas trusted most of its generals, but again, time was short.

"Besides, if anyone overheard me communicating outside my own fleet, they'd probably assume I was planning a coup. Then I could be assassinated on my own bridge, which would be embarrassing, to say the least."

Pezcoglu had more freedom and more contacts with his air force. He expected that Turkish aircraft would be mostly on ground alert by dawn. The few remaining airborne would stay comfortably to the east.

"One trigger-happy pilot on either side could still screw us all," Pappas said. "The Russians will make enough trouble without us helping them."

Nanos grinned. It was nice to see brass who didn't think the opponent was a pushover. If they'd been twenty years younger, the two admirals might even have been turned into good mercs.

AT MIDNIGHT, *N. V. Glubov* crept southwest, as deep as the Aegean would allow and as slowly as she could go and still maintain steerage way.

"Is this the fastest we can manage?" Captain Isakov grumbled.

Captain Abakumov barely heard him. The pitometer repeater on the bulkhead of his closet-size cabin maddened him as much as it did his passenger. Neither of them could change facts to suit the desire they shared, to get Pokrovsky to better medical care as soon as possible.

The hunt was on. The sonarmen had picked up too many warship propellers to allow any other explanation. The hunt wasn't coordinated yet, but that could happen at any hour.

Isakov knew that. But there was something he didn't know, something the instruments had told only Abakumov, his deputy and a few technical warrant officers.

The rubber tiles were beginning to peel of *Glubov*'s hull. Her long stays on the bottom had loosened many. The explosion of the Type 88 had loosened more. When she headed out, many of them had dropped off.

Instead of the ambiguous returning sound of the rubber tiles, large parts of *Glubov*'s hull would now give off the unmistakable echo of steel. In shallow water, unable to use her speed to maneuver vertically as well as horizontally, she had to avoid being detected in the first place.

"I can't endanger the whole ship for one man," Abakumov said. The words rang hollow, even if they were true.

Isakov nodded. But as he did, his hand tightened around the tumbler of vodka, until the glass shattered.

Abakumov watched the blood and vodka dripping on his rug and handed Isakov a handkerchief.

LEE HATTON WATCHED dawn break over the Aegean from a CH-53 Sea Stallion on its way to Haustim. The SEALS and the SOBs were going on their way, leaving Perkostri to the Turks.

"For the time being, anyway," Jessup said. "The Navy's supposed to be sending some heavy hardware and technical intelligence types."

"Doesn't the Company have the *Glomar Explorer*?" Lee asked. "The one that fished that Soviet missile submarine up from the bottom of the Pacific?"

"Officially, yes. Unofficially, she's in mothballs and likely to stay there. Putting her back in commission would bankrupt the Agency. I'd be coming to you people for work! Either that, or opening a taco stand."

"I suppose that's one way of getting your groceries wholesale," Billy Two said. "If—what the hell?"

Lee stared. All the way from Haustim, they'd been flying over warships, steaming in twos and threes. Once she could have sworn that a Greek and two Turkish destroyers were maneuvering together. She hoped that wasn't just a hallucination induced by fatigue, that Alex and the pictures had really done the job.

Now she saw a huge cloud of black smoke pouring out of an old Turkish frigate. It looked for a moment as if the ship was on fire. Then the vessel steamed out from under the smoke cloud, her bow wave noticeably higher and her wake wider.

Two miles to port, a modern Greek frigate was also picking up speed. Straining her eyes, Lee made out a helicopter hovering low over the sea, about five miles ahead of the two ships.

Barrabas leaned forward. "Get on the NATO tactical frequency," he said. "Let's see what's happening."

The pilot saw Barrabas's fatigues, heard his tone, ignored his lack of insignia and switched the radio. An uproar of static and excited voices filled the cabin, even louder than the roar of the turbines overhead.

A minute later the SOBs and the helicopter crew were cheering. The two ships were communicating in English, and the message was clear.

They were tracking a submarine contact.

Lee wanted to dance, but her happiness was too great for words or movement. Instead she grinned at everybody, last of all Nile Barrabas, sitting rocklike by the window.

"Well, we've passed the ball to the navies," he said. "Let's hope they don't drop it."

PERIKLES AND HER PARTNER, the Turkish frigate *Izmir*, were cruising at fifteen knots when the helicopter signaled.

"Contact, positively identified as submarine, bearing 126, range 14,000 meters. Estimated depth eighty meters, speed ten knots."

"Ten knots?" Pappas exclaimed. "Listen for the acoustic signature. That sounds like a conventional sub that wandered in when we weren't looking."

Doubt didn't keep him from ordering speed increased to twenty-four knots. Any faster, and *Izmir*'s antique sonar would be deaf. It was tempting to arrange things so that the kill would be *Perikles*'s, but Pappas resisted. Pezcoglu was right. The honor of both navies and of all the seamen of both countries was caught up in this affair.

"Target speed increasing" came his son's voice. "Now nineteen knots. Nuclear power plant noises."

"Type?"

"Guess, Father!" was the reply. Pappas could almost see his son gloating. A hunter's delight swept through the admiral, making him ignore the breach of discipline.

"Drop your fish where they'll herd him back toward us," Pappas ordered. "If they kill him, so much the better."

"Aye, aye, fa—sir."

ONE OF THE Mark 46s from the Lynx sank straight to the bottom. The other began its search. Abakumov launched decoys, increased speed and turned *Glubov* as fast as she could. Twin screws and high power made that a much faster turn than the torpedo could follow. The high-pitched whine of its screws drifted aft then faded away entirely.

Abakumov held back premature relief. The helicopter hadn't lost contact, the two frigates had closed while *Glubov* was evading, and their sonars were pinging hard. He could hear the rising din of their propellers as they closed the distance.

"A *Themistokles*-class Greek and an *Ankara*-class Turk," the soundman said. "But I thought the Greeks and the Turks were on the brink of war?"

Abakumov was once again grateful to the late Captain Lieutenant Fokin for freeing his ship of *zampolit*s. He merely shook his head. "The situation could have changed since our last intelligence."

He pulled out a reference volume and flipped through it to the Turkish navy. "*Ankara*-class. Ah, splendid. Old, slow, American designed, lightly armed, poor sonar. A sitting target."

Isakov smiled. "You're going to try sinking a Turk?"

"Why not? That's one less NATO ship for our comrades to worry about, and a lot of confusion for NATO to settle."

He doubted it would bring success to Operation Claw, not now. But it should sow enough confusion to let *Glubov* escape.

"Ready tubes three and four. Acoustic homing mode."

Forward, the torpedomen flipped switches and punched buttons. Lights turned from red to green.

Abakumov saw them change on his board. He gripped a stanchion and said, "Fire three. Fire four."

BOTH SHIPS HEARD the torpedoes running, and both took evasive action.

Izmir, like *Helikon*, had one piece of equipment not listed in Russian reference books. It was a brand-new acoustic decoy, already streamed over the side. Her captain listened to the torpedoes' whine and ordered the decoy turned all the way up, even if it blanked out everybody's sonar.

The two torpedoes heard *Izmir*'s screws, then heard the decoy. They changed course, to home on the louder decoy.

In changing course, they passed within range of *Perikles*'s roaring propellers. One torpedo's acoustic homer overloaded its guidance system. The fish gave up the fight and headed off in the general direction of the Peloponnisos. It finally ran up on an island beach, where it was found a month later by some skinny-dippers just before the Greek police arrested them for smoking hashish. Their discovery saved them a term in a Greek prison.

The other torpedo recognized a target in *Perikles*. It accelerated toward her, reaching fifty knots and deafening her soundmen just before it struck.

THE TORPEDO EXPLOSION made *Perikles* flex like a whip. Admiral Pappas forgot dignity and flung himself to the deck as a storm of fragments swept his flagship's deck. Fist-size holes appeared in the bulkheads of the combat information center. Electrical arcs flared and smoked, and heavy equipment danced around, crushing a few unlucky operators.

With smoke pouring from the dead machinery and more pouring in from outside, Pappas could barely breathe. He stumbled through the warped hatch and fetched up hard against the bulkhead outside.

As he fought for breath, he felt something punch him hard in the hip. He forced himself to turn, and saw a petty officer with mad eyes and a small pistol. Pappas wished he hadn't tempted fate, joking about being assassinated on his own bridge.

Before the man could fire again, something leaped on his back. It was Machinist Koustas, grappling with the petty officer. They were equally matched, and the petty officer seemed to have a madman's strength as well as eyes.

Pappas lurched toward the struggle, then felt his leg growing weak as warmth streamed down it. He braced himself against a fire extinguisher case, hoping that at least the madman would drop the pistol—

A dark hairy arm thicker than a firehose wrapped itself around the petty officer's neck. He rose into the air, then jerked all over and went limp. Alex Nanos put him down and helped his cousin to his feet, then came over to the admiral.

"George, get a dressing on that while I put out the fire," Nanos said. He unlatched the fire extinguisher's cover.

A shrill whistling made him turn. "Forget the fire," Pappas grunted. "It's out of control. That's the abandonship signal."

They staggered out onto the deck, the two cousins supporting the admiral. As they reached the side, Pappas saw the stern completely gone or else lost in smoke. Then he saw men running, and finally saw two of the antisubmarine torpedoes carried amidships slide over the side.

It was quick thinking to jettison weights like that, but it couldn't save *Perikles*. She was already well down by the stern, power was fading, and she had the sluggish feel of a dying ship.

ADMIRAL PAPPAS had underestimated his men. Most of *Perikles*'s communications went out when the combat information center was abandoned. An emergency radio amidships let Lieutenant Pappas give *Glubov*'s range and bearing to the torpedo crew.

They launched two torpedoes before the power died completely. They tried to launch the third manually, until the Aegean was rising about their ankles. Then they followed their admiral and their surviving shipmates overboard.

In her death throes, *Perikles* made too much noise to let them hear one of their torpedoes strike its quarry.

Abakumov was also reckoning on that noise confusing the surviving hunter. He ran in as close as he dared to the sinking Greek frigate, engines wide open, not worrying about noise.

He ran right into one of the torpedoes, at such close range that it had barely had time to arm. The warhead struck the top of *Glubov*'s notched fin, crippling the rudder but not piercing the hull. The shock wave fractured bearings in the port shaft, though, and Abakumov quickly shut it down to avoid rupturing the shaft seals and flooding the engine room.

As *Glubov*'s speed dropped to fifteen knots, Abakumov looked grim. They might still escape if they could reach deep water, but they would have to find some way of operating the damaged propeller. With no rudder and no steering by the engines, *Glubov* would be helpless. Steering by her engines, she might reach friendly ships, or even the Libyan coast. Doubling back to throw off pursuers, they could go east around Crete and make their landfall in Egypt, and the Egyptian navy was junk—

Abakumov was pulling out a chart of the eastern end of Crete when six 305-mm antisubmarine rockets plunged into the water above his ship. They came from *Izmir*, which had closed during the confusion until she could have picked up *Glubov* by lowering a sonarman headfirst over the side!

The Bofors rocket launcher was obsolete by most standards, but like a sawed-off shotgun, it was efficient enough at close range.

Two of the rockets struck. One hit the conning tower, which promptly flooded, drowning Abakumov. The other hit forward, rupturing the outer doors of three torpedo tubes.

The inner doors gave, sending water and torpedoes flying back into the torpedo room, drowning or crushing everyone there. Then the propellant of one of the torpedoes exploded, sending a shock wave through *Glubov* that strained bulkheads and popped most hatches.

It also flung men about, so that most of them were unconscious when the water covered them. One of these was Pokrovsky, who wasn't smashed against a bulkhead only because the Golden Giant absorbed the impact of his superior. The Giant's skull cracked against a valve, and he was dead before his commander.

Glubov's forward momentum carried her over the edge of the drop-off. She sank bow first, beginning slowly, then faster and faster as more explosion-weakened bulkheads gave way under the increasing pressure.

She finally came to rest twelve hundred feet down. A trail of bubbles and wreckage marked her resting place briefly, then faded.

JOEL RAWSON CLIMBED OUT of the Land Rover and looked around the street. Nothing out of the ordinary—women on their way to market, a boy tinkering with a motorcycle on one corner, an old man pruning an orange tree in a courtyard.

Rawson still kept close to the walls as he walked down the street toward the restaurant where he was to meet with Heiss. He also made sure his Browning and his hold-out Walther were ready for a quick draw.

He wasn't sure what this meeting would produce, which annoyed him more than it should have. Maybe it was time for him to come out of the cold—in his own way. Sell all his information to Heiss for a cash settlement, then take the money and run. Run fast and far, ending in some country where teenage girls were a few hundred dollars apiece.

He'd just decided that it should be a country where blondes were available, when he saw the old man reach into the basket hung on the branch before him. Trained reflexes had the Browning out, but not fast enough. The "old man" had a Hi-Power, too, and the silencer didn't spoil its accuracy enough to matter.

Rawson was dead before he hit the ground. The "old man," an ex-Ku Klux Klan member who'd fled the United States after a terrorist plot had failed, watched the flies settle in the blood around Rawson's head. Then he unscrewed the silencer, pocketed it and the Browning and climbed down the ladder.

He was heading for the gate when he heard a car roaring up. It stopped as he opened the gate, and the door opened.

Three bullets hit him in the throat as his hand touched the gate latch. He lived longer than Rawson, but not long enough to feel more than the beginning of surprise.

Karl Heiss took one last look, then shut the door. He hadn't lost his marksmanship. He also hadn't lost his gift for covering his tracks.

IZMIR'S HULL loomed up like a gray steel wall. Alex Nanos gripped the scrambling net with one hand and pushed Admiral Pappas toward the sling with the other. George Koustas joined him, treading water as he hooked the admiral's arms into the sling.

"Heave away," Nanos shouted. Then he translated it into Turkish. The Turkish deckhands seemed to fumble for a moment. Nanos added a couple of impolite remarks in Bulgarian. Then the admiral popped out of the water like a missile. The pressure bandage on his punctured thigh came off as he rose, and blood flowed again, but Nanos figured he needn't worry about a man swearing as loudly as Pappas was. He hoped not many of the Turks understood

Greek, or there might be at least a Greek-Turkish brawl, if not a Greek-Turkish war!

Waves kicked up by rotor wash slapped Nanos in the face. He turned to see a CH-53 settling toward the water. A sling dangled from the rear door, and a tall man with a young face and white hair stood in the door.

Nanos let go of the net and slapped George on the shoulder. "Take good care of the admiral."

"You—Alex, you aren't leaving me to face the Turks alone!"

"You won't be alone." Nanos pointed at the heads of all the survivors from *Perikles*, splashing their way toward *Izmir*. "In fact, you could damned near take this frigate by boarding, if you wanted to."

George shuddered. "Please. I don't want to hear even jokes about war. I want to go home to Ikyros and help rebuild."

"Better tell that to the admiral, then. He wants to give you a medal or maybe a commission for tackling the Snake, then keep you in the navy."

"Me! An officer! The gold-braided idiot! What does he think he is?"

"I don't know," Nanos said. "But just tell him what you think, and you'll be a civilian again real fast!"

He slapped his cousin again, then churned away toward the sling. The Sea Stallion rose as soon as Nanos was in the sling; it was a thousand feet up before Barrabas pulled him into the cabin.

A thousand feet higher, Nanos looked out the cockpit windows. The Aegean seemed to have sprouted a whole fleet, as Greeks and Turks rushed to rescue *Perikles*'s survivors. Far off to the southeast, Nanos saw the two nations' Cyprus squadrons coming up, steaming in formation. The Greek ships from Crete weren't in sight yet, but they wouldn't be needed, either.

Nanos slumped in a corner. He felt as drained as an empty balloon, ready to crawl into bed with Adrienne and *sleep* before he did anything else with her.

He'd started to snore before the other SOBs realized that he was asleep. Lee Hatton spread a blanket over him, and Barrabas pulled off his wet shoes.

CHAPTER TWENTY-EIGHT

Admiral Pezcoglu lowered the binoculars and handed them to his aide. A quick inspection of the squadrons anchored off Haustim showed him that both lines were as neat as ever. The Turks were just inside Turkish territorial waters, the Greeks just outside.

Some of the ships had turned on a few more lights since the last time he looked. He thought he heard the strains of music floating on the breeze, but that had to be his imagination.

He continued down the path to where Admiral Pappas was sitting in his wheelchair. As Pezcoglu approached, he saw that his counterpart was definitely mending. He looked fit to be out of bed, at least.

He also wasn't alone, as he'd been the past few times. Pezcoglu suspected the Greeks were staying clear of Pappas until Athens decided what to do with him. The Turks, Pezcoglu knew, were still a bit ashamed of themselves in the presence of any Greek, let alone one who'd probably sacrificed his career for peace.

Pezcoglu quickly recognized Pappas's companions. The young officer standing behind the wheelchair was Pappas's son. The elegant dark-haired woman in a blue jumpsuit was Dr. Lee Hatton, one of the warriors to whom both Greek and Turk owed so much.

"Good evening, my friend," Pappas said. "Is there still any caviar at the buffet?"

"Only lumpfish, I'm afraid. I ate the last of the beluga myself."

"Greedy Turk! Oh, well, I'm still hungry. Lumpfish will have to do." He nodded at his son, who took Dr. Hatton's arm and walked off.

"I wish him better luck with her than I had, but somehow I don't think he'll have it," Pappas said. "I've never seen a woman so like Kipling's cat. She walks by herself even in a crowd."

"So do her comrades. They are warriors such as I did not think the Americans still had."

"The Americans are full of surprises. But you are right. Perhaps that is why Greek and Turk understand each other even when we fight. We still produce warriors, not just men wearing a uniform and carrying a gun."

"It is about Greek and Turkish understanding that I came," Pezcoglu said. "The Navy Ministry favors my suggestion. Every man in the Turkish navy will give one day's pay for the widows and orphans of this war. The Red Cross will distribute it."

Pappas rose from the wheelchair, grimaced but gripped Pezcoglu's hand so hard the Turk winced. "Thank God! Of course, there are two Greek warships also to be replaced—"

"That's for the two governments and the Americans to settle up. I thought of the naval contribution because it would not take so long, and the widows and orphans need to eat and pay for shelter *now*."

"Amen," Pappas said. "If we can cooperate on that, what about doing something with *Glubov*? The Americans have all the equipment in the world, but ours is closer. Have the Swedes delivered your rescue sub yet?"

"How did you bastards learn that?" Pezcoglu snapped. Pappas merely looked smug, Pezcoglu started to turn and walk off, then stopped and laughed.

"Trust a snake before a Greek, but a Greek before a Russian," he quoted. "I don't know myself, not being on the engineering side of things. But I can find out. I'd also suggest we consider hiring some people as divers and security for a joint dive on *Glubov*."

"People as in Alex Nanos?"

"Let's start by approaching Colonel Barrabas. I don't think he owns his people, but he might have some other mission in mind."

"In that case," Pappas said, "shouldn't we consult that fat man from the CIA?"

"The one they call 'the Fixer'? He doesn't own Barrabas, any more than Barrabas owns his people."

"I thought so. I'll speak to Barrabas tonight, if he comes by."

Pezcoglu laughed. "You'll have a long wait. The last I saw, he was going uphill with a blond woman almost as big as he is. I heard she flew in from Amsterdam for the party."

BARRABAS SAT across from Erika Dykstra on a blanket spread on the ridge. The remains of a picnic supper surrounded a bucket where a bottle of champagne was cooling.

Erika fished the bottle out, checked its temperature, then expertly undid the wire and pointed the bottle downhill. The cork came out with a bang, but most of the champagne stayed in the bottle. Erika poured out two glasses and lifted hers.

"To peace."

"To peace," Barrabas repeated.

Many people might have thought it was an odd toast for him to drink, but they didn't know him. The men who really loved war for its own sake were usually his enemies.

"So what brings you to our party, other than KLM?" Barrabas asked. "You've been looking like there's more on your mind than wanting my company."

"I won't say it's on my mind, because it's been largely settled. It will stay settled, too, unless Mustafa's brother acts up."

"Erika, would you like me to tickle you behind the knees until you confess?"

"No, Nile! Anything but that!" She put on a look of horror. "I'll confess. We've all been afraid the Turkish government might not punish the men who attacked Ikyros. So I used those contacts with the Turkish police I had, through the West German officer.

"The Turks who raided Ikyros are going to think they're being let go free. But they'll actually be flown to the Persian Gulf and sold as slaves. For life."

Barrabas was impressed. It would take years to trace them, if anybody even tried. By then it was long odds against most of them even being alive. The Arabs had long memories and little love for Turks.

"I made an exception for Mustafa's brother Abdul. He's being released into the custody of his brother. They've both been warned that if Abdul so much as sneezes at a Greek again, he'll join his friends, with one difference."

"Oh?"

"I will personally see to it that he's qualified for a job as a harem eunuch."

"I didn't know they still had them."

"Maybe he'll be a unique eunuch," Erika said.

They both laughed. Barrabas held out his arms, and Erika came across the blanket into his embrace.

"Unique," he decided, was also a good description of Erika. Everything about her was her own and nobody else's, including her skills, her motives and her methods.

So maybe it made sense to look more carefully the next time she seemed to want on the team. Maybe that wasn't what she was asking. Even if she was, maybe their next argument on the subject wouldn't be as dumb as the last one!

The embrace lasted until Barrabas felt something cold and wet on his pants. He sat up, pulling Erika with him. She looked at the overturned champagne bottle and said something impolite in Dutch.

"Shall we go down and get another bottle?" he asked. "Duty to a lady says stay here. Thirst says get that bottle."

"This lady will go along with the thirst," Erika said. They rose and started downhill.

WALKER JESSUP SAW THEM pass the rock where he sat sipping from a canteen cup of bourbon. He thought of stopping them to pass on the word he'd just received about Rawson.

Then he decided not to spoil the reunion. He'd wind up doing that if he told Barrabas the whole truth, about how thoroughly the killer had covered his tracks. The Turks were going to charge a very high price for any cooperation in chasing...the man who was really Karl Heiss. It was one the higher-ups probably wouldn't pay.

As for plunging into the cesspool of Istanbul to track the man himself—Nile Barrabas was damned good, but ten average men could usually lick one good man on their home turf.

Nile and Erika passed into the shadows of the bluff and out of sight. That was where the man usually was, Jessup realized. Nile Barrabas and his soldiers walked in shadow so that others could walk in the light.

"What's that, Fixer? Poetry?"

Jessup dropped his cup as Alex Nanos spoke behind him. He turned ponderously and started to glare, then saw Adrienne Biggle with the Greek. Both of them looked sweaty and rumpled, and Jessup didn't doubt for a minute what they'd been doing. The professor's newly discovered passion for outdoor sex was an open secret, even if nobody dared mention it in front of Nanos.

Jessup repeated his phrase.

"I like that," Adrienne said. "It may even be true."

"I like it, too," Nanos said. "Only don't start repeating it around Liam. He'll think you're setting up as a poet, and that could be downright dangerous to your health, Fixer!"

The past blew out in 2001.
Welcome to the future.

JAMES AXLER

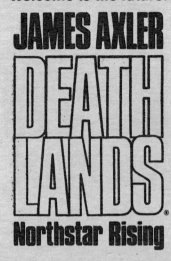

DEATH LANDS

Northstar Rising

A generation after a global nuclear war, Minnesota is a steamy tropical paradise of lush plants and horrifically mutated insects. In this jungle, Ryan Cawdor and his band of post-holocaust warriors uncover yet another freakish legacy of a world gone hideously wrong: Vikings.

U.S. Army Special Forces battle the Viet Cong in a bloody fight for stolen territory.

VIETNAM: GROUND ZERO.

EMPIRE

ERIC HELM

U.S. Army Special Forces Captain Mack Gerber and his team drive the NVA troops out of Binh Long Province and determine to push their advantage by taking the war to the enemy's doorstep. That's where they teach the VC the first lesson in how to win a war... move in, take ground and when you can, hit the enemy. Hit them hard.

ABLE TEAM

DICK STIVERS

Action writhes in the reader's own streets as Able Team's Carl "Ironman" Lyons, Pol Blancanales and Gadgets Schwarz make triple trouble in blazing war. Join Dick Stivers's Able Team—the country's finest tactical neutralization squad in an era of urban terror and unbridled crime.

"Able Team will go anywhere, do anything, in order to complete their mission. Plenty of action! Recommended!"
—*West Coast Review of Books*

by GAR WILSON

The battle-hardened five-man
commando unit known as Phoenix
Force continues its onslaught
against the hard realities of global
terrorism in an endless crusade for
freedom, justice and the rights of
the individual. Schooled in guerrilla
warfare, equipped with the latest in
lethal weapons, Phoenix Force's
adventures have made them a
legend in their own time. Phoenix
Force is the free world's foreign
legion!

"Gar Wilson is excellent! Raw action
attacks the reader on every page."
—Don Pendleton

Phoenix Force titles are available
wherever paperbacks are sold.

PF-1R

PHOENIX FORCE

GOLD
EAGLE

More than action adventure...
books written by the men who were there

VIETNAM: GROUND ZERO™

ERIC HELM

Told through the eyes of an American Special Forces squad, an elite jungle fighting group of strike-and-hide specialists fight a dirty war half a world away from home.

These books cut close to the bone, telling it the way it really was.

"Vietnam at Ground Zero is where this book is written. The author has been there, and he knows. I salute him and I recommend this book to my friends."

—Don Pendleton
creator of *The Executioner*

"Helm writes in an evocative style that gives us Nam as it most likely was, without prettying up or undue bitterness."

—*Cedar Rapids Gazette*

"Eric Helm's Vietnam series embodies a literary standard of excellence. These books linger in the mind long after their reading."

—*Midwest Book Review*

Available wherever paperbacks are sold.